The Uprising

Under
the North Star 2

Väinö Linna
(1920–1992)

ASPASIA CLASSICS IN FINNISH LITERATURE

Väinö Linna

The Uprising

Under the North Star 2

Translated by

Richard Impola

ASPASIA BOOKS

BEAVERTON, ONTARIO, CANADA

The Uprising: Under the North Star 2
ISBN 0-9685881-7-4 (Paperback)
ISBN 0-9689054-1-2 (Hardbound)
ISSN 1498-8348

Published in 2002 by
Aspasia Books
R.R.1, Beaverton, Ontario, L0K 1A0 Canada
aspasia@aspasiabooks.com
www.aspasiabooks.com

Translated from the Finnish *Täällä Pohjantähden alla*
First published in Finnish 1960 by WSOY (Helsinki, Finland)

Copyright © Väinö Linna & WSOY (Finnish original)
Copyright © Richard Impola (English translation)
Copyright © Aspasia Books (English language edition)

Cover design by Martin Best of My6productions

*Aspasia Books gratefully acknowledges the assistance of
the Finnish Literature Information Centre.*

Translator's Foreword by Richard Impola

Introduction by Börje Vähämäki

Aspasia Classics in Finnish Literature series editor: Börje Vähämäki

****
National Library of Canada Cataloguing in Publication Data

Linna, Väinö
        Under the North Star / Väinö Linna ; translated by Richard Impola

(Aspasia classics in Finnish literature, ISSN 1498-8348)
Translation of: Täällä pohjantähden alla.

ISBN 0-9689054-0-4 (bound : v. 1).—ISBN 0-9685881-6-6 (pbk. : v. 1).—
ISBN 0-9689054-1-2 (bound : v. 2).—ISBN 0-9685881-7-4 (pbk. : v. 2)

        1. Finland—History—1809-1917—Fiction. 2. Finland—History—
20th century—Fiction. I. Impola, Richard, 1923- II. Title.

PH355.L5T3313 2001   894'.54133   C2001-901901-7

TRANSLATOR'S FOREWORD

In this second volume of his "North Star" trilogy, Väinö Linna concentrates on the lives of the second generation of the Koskela family, a generation fated to appear on the stage of history at a time when Finland became involved in what is perhaps the most traumatic event in its history, one known either as the War of Independence or the Civil War.

It was an age of political ferment, when the theories of Karl Marx were provoking widespread discussion. They fell on receptive ears in the province of Häme in southern Finland, where the great majority of the rural population consisted of landless tenant farmers, who had contractual rights to the land and so were not serfs, but who could hardly be called free.

In his typical manner, Linna works out historical developments through the lives of his characters. After reading, we think of experiences endured rather than of great events or historical movements—of Akseli and others in the battlefield and in the prison camps, of the behavior of men and women facing a firing squad, of war as it affects the everyday lives of the people in the novel.

Of all these, Linna writes with a power seldom if ever equaled.

As a writer, Linna chooses a realistic approach. But his concern with realism is thematic in the novel as well. It is fascinating to judge the characters in this work with respect to their conceptions of reality as well as to their grasp of the actual realities facing them. Such consideration soon makes apparent the ironies they are involved in.

It is ironic that. Akseli, the central figure in Volume II, becomes a leader of the Socialists because he wants to own the land. Linna's consciousness of that irony is evident in Volume I, when the Socialist speaker Salin comments on the freeing of the tenant farmers: "In essence, we are working against socialism when we advocate their freedom."

Another ironic twist is that it is the free farmers of the North who save the day for the landowners of the South, whose tenants are anything but free.

v

Linna has little sympathy for the doctrinaire ideologists of either the extreme right or left who would impose their systems on the world. He sides with the characters whose acts of humanity stand out above the brutality and horror of the war and the prison camps. His comment that war is the ultimate stupidity of human beings is clearly relevant to this work.

I wish to thank all those who have helped me with knotty passages of translation, especially Tuula Tuisku at the University of Oulu and Päivi Pihlaja at the University of Helsinki. For any flaws in translation the responsibility is mine.

Richard Impola

INTRODUCTION

P art Two of the *Under the North Star* trilogy (*Täällä Pohjantähden alla*), *The Uprising*, was first published in Finnish in 1960. Part One, simply entitled *Under the North Star* (2001, Aspasia Books), introduced the reader to the Koskela family, Jussi and Alma, the pioneer tenant farmers who cleared a swamp for themselves on the edge of the parsonage's property, their three sons Akseli, Aleksi, and Aku (or Akusti) and their community called Pentti's Corners in Häme, northwest of the City of Tampere in Finland. Part One, called a testament to work by translator Richard Impola, covered a span of about 25 years, 1884 to 1907, setting the scene for the uprising which erupted in January 1918 in the immediate aftermath of the Russian Revolution in November 1917 and Finland's Declaration of Independence on December 6, 1917.

The Uprising deals with the escalation of the landless farmers' frustration with legislative impotence, with strikes and hardships. The powerful focus of the book lies in the emotional and often personalized attitudes to the uprising or the rebellion, and how these attitudes changed with the reports of the progression of the three-month long Civil War waged in Finland in 1918. The war was for decades known by many names: Civil War, War of Independence, War of Liberation, War of Citizens, Class War, and Internal War depending on the world view of the persons.

While Linna manages always to keep the larger historical picture in the background, staying close to his characters and reflecting nuances in their experiences, his organizing principle is still his commitment to historical accuracy. Those readers who are not familiar with the history of the Finnish Civil War of 1918 may find the abundant references in the novel to crucial events and battles in the war quite confusing. This book therefore includes two maps of Finland.

The war was fought as a socialist uprising, as an attempt at a Finnish revolution inspired by the successful October Russian Revolution in 1917. The Finnish uprising was led by social democrats, not communists. The socialists were called Reds, their military organization Red Guard, and the forces of the establishment were called Whites. Civil Guards were set up during 1917 on the White side to "uphold order." At the beginning of 1918 there were nearly 100,000 Red troops, of whom about 70,000 became involved in combat. The Civil Guards numbered about 70,000 as well.

At the end of January, 1918, the Reds seized control of Finland's capital Helsinki, of Tampere, and virtually the entire southern part of Finland. The Whites set up government, the so-called Vaasa Senate, in Vaasa, a city on the west coast and capital of Ostrobothnia, where the support for the Civil Guards was strongest. The fictitious Pentti's Corners was situated north west of Tampere. The course of the war effort, particularly on the western front, became ultimately a matter of pushing south from Vaasa to recapture Tampere and Helsinki and many other towns in Southern Finland.

This effort was successful for several reasons: the Whites were better trained, better disciplined, and those who had been trained in Germany to become Jaegers during World War I, returned to Finland with German forces landing in April 1918. Seppo Hentilä writes about the civil war

The civil war was short but bloody. The actual fighting lasted only two or three months, but the terror meted out by both sides and subsequent settling of scores resulted in more than 30,000 deaths.; of these 25,000 were of Reds. - -

At the close of hostilities the number of Red captives was some 80,000 and they were taken to concentration camps around the country. Because of the difficulties in the production and distribution of provisions, and defective health care, as many as 12,000 Reds died in the camps from hunger and disease. - -

In mid-May 1918 a special 'Tribunal of High Treason', consisting of 145 courts, was set up to deal with the Red prisoners These courts sentenced 67,788 Reds, and 555 received death sentences, of which half were carried out. More than 60,000 received various terms of imprisonment, two-thirds of which were for less than three years. In June 1918 a change in the criminal law came into force, allowing probationary sentences. On this basis 40,000 prisoners were placed on probation and in the autumn more were pardoned. However, at the end of 1918 there were still 6,100 Reds in captivity. (Osmo Jussila, Seppo Hentilä and Jukka Nevakivi: *From Grand Duchy to a Modern State – A Political History of Finland since 1809*, Hurst & Company: London, (1999), pp. 110-112).

Linna's *Under the North Star* trilogy, particularly its second part, *The Uprising* has been given credit for much of the national healing that occurred in the 1960s. The novel ignited a wide and lively debate that ultimately led to some kind of consensus in the nation: Monuments were finally erected also to the Reds; even the bourgeoisie admitted that the Red victims had fallen "for their convictions", "for workers' ideals." Mandy Hoogendorn writes:

> -- the emphasis has been on the redemption of common guilt, quite like the position taken by novelist Väinö Linna in his fictional trilogy, *Täällä Pohjantähden alla* --. And Linna is a good point to begin on. His view on the 'demon' of 1918 was to confront it head on, in hopes that it would fade once the truth was in the open where later generations could try to understand it. But it took time for society and politics to catch up to the freer world of literature. Perhaps it is only now at the fin-de-siècle that Finland is at last recovering from the shock of the Civil War, although the process is still incomplete. (Mandy Hoogendorn, "Remembering and Forgetting the Finnish Civil War," *Journal of Finnish Studies*, Volume 3, Number 1, May 1999, pp. 28-29).

The Uprising stands as the center piece of the *Under the North Star* trilogy. Its ending brings the novel to a natural conclusion, yet contains hints at possible vistas for Part Three of the trilogy, which is to appear under the title *Reconciliation – Under the North Star Part Three*.

Börje Vähämäki

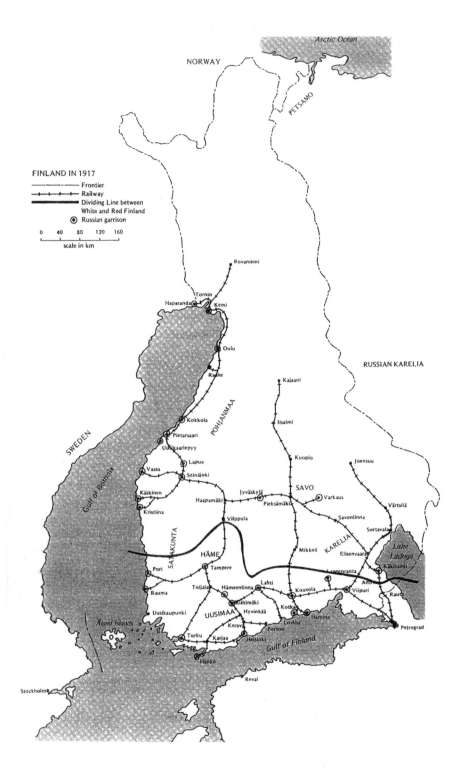

FINLAND IN 1917
———·——— Frontier
+—+—+—+ Railway
▬▬▬ Dividing Line between
White and Red Finland
⊙ Russian garrison

0   40   80   120   160
scale in km

NORWAY

Arctic Ocean

PETSAMO

SWEDEN

Gulf of Bothnia

RUSSIAN KARELIA

Rovaniemi

Tornio
Haparanda   Kemi

Oulu

Raahe

Kajaani

Iisalmi

POHJANMAA

Kokkola

Pietarsaari

Uusikaarlepyy

Kuopio

Joensuu

Vaasa   Lapua

Seinäjoki

Jyväskylä   SAVO

Varkaus

Käskinen   Haapamäki   Pieksämäki

Värtsilä

Kristiina

Vilppula   Savonlinna

SATAKUNTA   Mikkeli   Sortavala

HÄME   KARELIA   Lake
Ladoga

Pori   Tampere   Elisenvaara   Käkisalmi

Lahti   Lappeenranta

Rauma   Toijala   Hämeenlinna   Kouvola   Viipuri
Riihimäki   Kotka   Antrea
Rauha

Uusikaupunki   UUSIMAA   Hyvinkää   Hamina

Åland Islands   Kerava   Loviisa

Turku   Karjaa   Porvoo   Petrograd

Helsinki

Hanko   Gulf of Finland

Stockholm   Reval

X

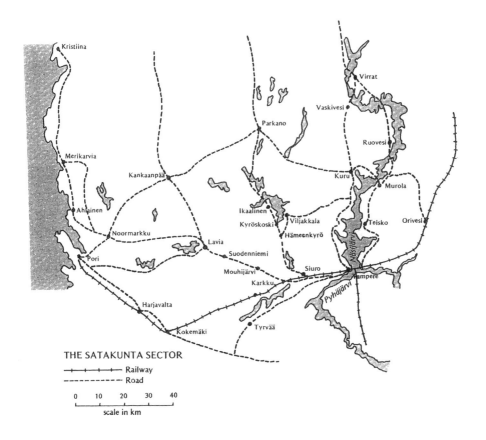

THE SATAKUNTA SECTOR
———+———+———+——— Railway
———————————— Road

0   10   20   30   40
scale in km

Maps from Antony F. Upton: *The Finnish Revolution 1917-1918*. Minneapolis. 1980.

The Uprising

Under
the North Star 2

CHAPTER ONE

I

After a bit of groping and fumbling, the new pattern of life at the Koskelas' settled by degrees into a daily routine, although Jussi, if he happened to be absorbed in thought, would walk up to the steps of the old main house before he noticed where he was going. If someone happened to see him, he made some excuse to cover up his error.

The terms "the old place" and "the new place" came into habitual use even among the villagers. The "new place" lay diagonally in back of the old. For a grandparents' cottage, it was large, with a kitchen, a small living room, and the "boys' bedroom." Deep down, Alma was sorely nostalgic on moving her housekeeping from the room where she had practiced it for over twenty years. Everything about the new place seemed a little raw and bare. In the old place, the homes, ceilings and floors were not just walls, ceilings and floors. They exuded innumerable small memories of thirty years of living, none of which existed in the new place. Even the yard was in a state of nature. There was none of the herbage there which grew without planting in a yard that was lived in.

But Alma settled in to keep house in the new place without a fuss. In a few weeks her dishes were properly placed so that she could lay her hands on whatever she needed with her eyes closed. Her things were never scattered at random; everything was always in its place.

If a faint nostalgia held sway in setting up the new place, the opposite mood prevailed in the old place. At first, Elina walked on tiptoe. Whatever she did, there was a shy and apologetic question in her eyes: is this the right thing to do, will they approve of me? When Otto came to move the stove into the baking room and make the other alterations the shift required, Elina said:

"It was fine the way it was, but now the living room will be less crowded. There won't be as much cleaning to do."

She wanted to be sure the move would not be taken as a criticism of the former arrangement.

Alma clearly sensed her daughter-in-law's delicate sensitivity and responded to it with the natural calm so characteristic of her. In a few weeks, the tension between the two had vanished.

"My, but those rugs of yours are pretty. And so well woven."

Elina blushed with pleasure, and then blushed again for having shown her pleasure. Alma had spoken to her as to an equal.

The boys made her acquaintance too. A little shyly at first, for a young woman seen close up was a strange phenomenon to them. Aleksi was the more reserved not only because of his shyness, but also because he was almost a man, which required of him a certain attitude toward his brother's wife. The livelier Aku, on the other hand, was more familiar with her. In private conversations, he might even ask questions that annoyed Elina.

Jussi was the most reticent of all. He very seldom went to the old place and never stayed there long. Once he happened to arrive just as Elina was spreading new rugs on the floor. He stopped and stood leaning against the door frame.

"Just come on in."

"No, I... With these muddy boots... into a person's house."

Elina coaxed and coaxed, but Jussi would not come in. Nevertheless his eyes took in every detail. Nothing escaped them, yet no one ever heard him express an opinion about what he had seen.

This exaggerated reticence was the hardest of all for Elina to deal with. It was a long time in thawing. But at length Jussi began to come inside and finally to drink coffee, although only after first having refused for a long time. Elina's keen intuition soon sensed where Jussi's weak spot lay. He was no glutton for tasty foods, but he could not resist a thirst for coffee. When Elina offered it to him, he finally took a first cup, and then a second, saying:

"I won't... no use to offer it. That isn't why I came here. You mustn't think so."

Then he would come in carrying the firewood basket with a slightly troubled and humble look on his face:

"I looked for some drier stuff back there."

An obvious buoyancy now ruled the once reclusive Akseli's spirit. It seemed strange to his parents to see him fussing about and helping Elina with the household chores. Earlier he had strictly refrained from meddling with "women's work," in exaggerated deference to the demands of manhood. At work and in town, his status as a newlywed even occasioned some annoyance. It was hard for him to endure the half-indecent joking that commonly surrounded newlyweds at home and at work. For one thing, double-entendres about private matters offended him on Elina's behalf, and besides, in the manner of young farmers, he was clearly ashamed of his love. If he had to speak of Elina in some connection, he hesitated between calling her "Elina" or "my wife." The choice of word changed with the listeners.

On the other hand, Elina adjusted naturally to her situation. She was

4

glad to take her place among the villagers as a wife and housekeeper. At first she visited her home often. It was nice to talk to her mother:

"... your flower... my flower... I'll leave a calf... I'll weave the fabric..."

Her father's smile embarrassed her a little, but it didn't mar her happiness for long. "Our Akseli" was such a conspicuous topic of the conversation that after she had left, Otto would say with a smile:

"Our Akseli knows everything and can do anything."

Oddly enough, Anna did not approve of Otto's good-natured mockery. Little by little, her son-in-law became better and better in her talk.

"Elina always has wood chopped for her. Elina has water brought into the barn for her. Elina has this and Elina has that."

When Otto rightly sensed that the emphasis on his son-in-law's extraordinary virtues was a blow aimed at him, he said:

"Ya-ah. Some people change overnight in this world. You wouldn't have believed it a year ago, when he was such an ogre."

Gradually the enchantment wore thin. By late autumn, some of Elina's work habits brought a frown to Akseli's brow. At first he restrained himself, but later on he would take over a task himself and do it properly. Elina turned a bright red, but offered no resistance. After a couple of such occasions, there were even words:

"Watch what you're doing. That's what comes of never having had to do anything at home. You never learned how."

Tears rose into Elina's eyes, and she finished the task with hurried, agitated movements. The tears annoyed Akseli even more, for they were hard for him to take. Elina was so sensitive that the slightest emotion brought on tears, not only when she was hurt, but also when for some reason she was especially happy. When she was unable to stir the blood during the fall butchering season, but was almost in tears for the calves' sake, Akseli stormed angrily:

"Damn it to hell. Life is going to be hard on you. You can't stand anything."

During the winter, the pig died. Akseli was hauling logs near the village of Salmi, and because of the distance, he had to put in long days. He was working with all his might; setting up housekeeping was a constant drain on their money and the debt he owed his brothers weighed on his mind. Weariness made him easily susceptible to gloom. His face grew thin, and he became grim and tight-lipped. When Elina, stumbling slightly, told him about the pig's death after he had gotten home, there was a brief silence. Then he said with a nasty grin:

"Well how the devil did you manage to kill it?"

"What could we do? Mother rubbed it down and we gave it alcohol. It was sick for only a little while."

"For only a little while? Of course then you should have known what it was. It ate a nail. A pig will eat anything at all, but it can't digest everything."

At first Elina just cried, but then she began to fight back. Finally they both resorted to all possible weapons:

"You should have married that Leppänen slut since you were carrying on with her. Your pigs would have been better cared for then."

"It couldn't have been worse. She would have done more than press her clothes and brush her hair in front of a mirror and pinch her cheeks to make them red."

"Why did you marry me then? I should have let you go when you threatened to kill yourself that time on the shore."

"It would have been better if I had, godammit. I wouldn't be struggling here with a helpless thing like you."

The old couple were aware of the quarrel and became involved in it, for they also shared in the responsibility for the barn. But Alma was silent. Her natural refinement, which prevented her from ever mouthing off, made her follow the fight from the sidelines without a word, but Jussi was offended by Akseli's accusations and opened up the pig's belly, checking it a centimeter at a time without finding a nail.

"Listen boy, you can't go around accusing innocent people."

To Alma he grumbled:

"He's strange, he is. Where does he get it from? He fumes to himself about something or other and when he's really worked up a temper, he starts to yell at others. I've had trouble enough in my life, but I haven't fussed at others about them."

Alma said nothing.

When all the bad words had been said, they were mute for a few days. Elina was hurt and it was difficult for Akseli to humble himself. In bed at night, they turned their backs to each other. Elina put out the lamp first and undressed in the dark. It was instinctive, a signal that the closeness between them was broken. Akseli was aware of Elina's silent weeping in bed, but not till the third day did he cautiously reach out and take her hand. It was jerked away angrily, but he took it again. That happened a couple of times. At last Akseli turned her toward him by force and tried to caress her.

"Keep your... hands off me... you've got no business here... go to Leppänen's and paw at her..."

For a long time, Akseli tried to resolve the matter by ignoring it, but he was finally forced to ask forgiveness. After that, they were able to talk, and Akseli said a little reluctantly:

"It was my fault, all right. But you mustn't mind. I'm having a hard time lately."

"Why?"

"Everything is getting me down. Debts and expenses... And when you don't know what will happen with this farm. They say that the law will be changed."

"But we can live somehow."

"Of course... somehow. But a laborer's life isn't all that easy. He has to travel around winters on jobs and work for day wages on farms in the summer, if there happens to be work. And there's more involved. We'd lose all the work that's already been done."

Elina relented, for now for the first time she realized the burden her husband was carrying. She understood that she had taken things for granted. After thinking over the question for a while, she asked:

"Would they really have the nerve to evict us no matter what the law is?"

A strange and bitter sound came from Akseli's throat. He whispered angrily into the dark room:

"Of course they would. They're such weird people they can always find a reason. They didn't demand to have the swamp back themselves. It was the church council. And the good of Finnish agriculture demands that tenants be evicted. There's one thing I've noticed about them. They always talk about their own affairs as Finland's affairs: *our* agriculture can't stand that, Finland's economy isn't on such firm footing. *Our* national prosperity cannot permit the reduction of hours. No matter what they want, it's always to the country's advantage, to the people's advantage, it's *our* society. Well, they're right about that. This is their society and this is their Finland. When a socialist representative can't speak book language, they squawk and mock him in their newspapers. Sometimes I can hardly breathe, I hate them so much. They're just like a beggar you feed and wash and dress in bed who snarls at his nurse and spits in her eye every time he's given anything. Sometimes I even think it would be easy to kill them."

"Don't say such things... If nothing else, father will give you work."

"He has only so much work. And I'm no builder... And then I'd have to travel all over the place with Osku."

Talking relieved the pressure. No quarrels arose for a long time after that, and when they did, Elina knew better how to deal with them. From then on, she began to show the first signs of maturity. Little by little, the spoiled child was changing. She tried to work as hard as her delicate body could stand. She tried to be sparing in her housekeeping, which was not her nature and which she had never been taught to do. She had learned that for them, life was not free.

7

When the first year of marriage had gone by and Elina was still not pregnant, it was noted even in the village. The families were concerned. Then when the advent of new life was apparent, their joy was mingled with the added pleasure of a released tension. Childlessness was a disgrace in these surroundings, and the fact ate at Akseli especially. His laugh was completely forced when Otto razzed him:

"Do we have to call in Rasputin to help? That boy can provide heirs for bigger houses than Koskela."

In 1913 a boy was born. He was of average size, weighing a "round three and a half kilos." Elina had feared the delivery very much, and rightly so, for it was a difficult one. For days she was unable to show any interest in the child. The midwife said it was because of weakness. Akseli felt pangs of conscience as he sat up all night by the bedside. He remembered how Elina had spread piles of manure that spring and almost fainted from weariness. He had told her to go home, but now he remembered that he had not said it definitely enough. He even recalled being quickly irritated at Elina's frailty, at her being unused to hard work.

When signs of awakening gradually appeared in Elina's lifeless eyes, Akseli's joy burst out in clumsy banter. He himself wanted to help Elina into her bed. Alma took care of the boy, declaring that he looked like her because of a cleft in his chin. Taking the swaddled child into his arms for the first time, Akseli said laughing:

"Hey, old man!"

Jussi looked at the boy for a long time, for he was somehow afraid of little children. When Elina, after she had recovered her strength, offered the boy to him and said with a smile:

"Take the boy into your lap, grandpa," Jussi refused in fear and panic:

"I wont touch him... I won't touch him."

The birth of the boy did something to relieve the bitter disappointment which the discussion of the land rental law in the assembly was causing. When an attempt was made to renew the law that was to expire in 1916, it failed. The landowners, you see, considered the law too advantageous to the tenants, and opposed its continuation. Whenever the boy was referred to as the "young master of Koskela," Akseli was bitterly silent. Or else he would burst out:

"In three years there won't be a master of Koskela, neither an old nor a young one."

The question brought to a boil his political fervor, which marriage had somewhat cooled. On the job, he spoke bitter words about the parsonage gentry, which came somehow to the ears of those concerned. Relationships stiffened into an ever-greater formality. Akseli had tremendous difficulty in adapting to the situation. It was impossible for him to act humble, and since the gentlefolk could clearly see his attitude, it increased their enmity.

"How different his father was."

Humble, timid Jussi had indeed been a dream tenant for the gentry, but his son came to seem more and more a nightmare. His formal, matter-of-fact demeanor could not mask the curt hostility that lay beneath it. There was no talk now of the land and its rental, since the law had frozen contract terms, and so there was nothing to discuss. The strained relations made the couple's views on the rental question more reactionary. Yet in discussing the topic, they were unaware that Akseli's harsh and unsmiling gaze was an unconscious influence on them.

Embittered, they dropped the small gifts and concessions they had been so pleased to offer. The twenty marks at Christmas no longer gave them the pleasure the recipient's humble gratitude would have afforded, and so they stopped giving it. As if to show their feelings, they increased their benevolence toward the old couple. If Alma or Jussi visited the parsonage, they were always invited in. They were offered coffee in the kitchen, and either the pastor or his wife, or both, would sit by the table and engage them in friendly chat. Seldom did Jussi or Alma return empty-handed from such a visit.

A completely official spirit prevailed during the child's baptism at the parsonage. Nor did the reputation of Janne, who served as godfather, help to lighten the atmosphere. Next to Hellberg, he was the man most hated by the powerful men of the parish, although he was known to be more moderate in his socialism. The antagonism of the gentry stemmed mainly from Janne's having defeated their attempt to take over the cooperative. The bourgeois minority of the cooperative tried to get control of it by using credit as an issue, but Janne collected the money needed to meet the payment. The emergency was so great that he worked day and night to round up the necessary sum, almost forcing his poor supporters to give him their last pennies as temporary loans. At the very moment when the savings bank was opening, he ostentatiously sold his bicycle and overcoat in the churchyard, a gesture that infuriated the gentlemen. He also acted as a lawyer in eviction cases and soon became so skilled at it that the landlords were usually unable to use the courts in getting rid of their tenants.

"There's not a worse bloodsucker on this earth."

Janne and Sanni were chosen as godparents specifically because of their reputation in the church village. Janne had in fact become quite estranged from his family; he had never been overly fond of his relatives. Sanni was partly the cause of the estrangement; with the exception of Anna, the Kivivuoris didn't care much for her. Even Elina's girlish idealization had changed, and she found it hard to conceal a dislike for her sister-in-law's petty self-importance.

The Kivivuoris were the only guests at the christening. Johannes Wilhelm's grandson became Vilho Johannes. The little one slept peacefully in his cradle in the corner of a room full of smoke and chattering voices. The mood was not fully harmonious. Elina was a little stiff after she had shown the child to Janne, who gave it a passing glance and said indifferently:

"He seems to have eyes and everything."

Elina was a little envious, for Sanni and her son monopolized everything. The little man in his sailor suit was nervous and stubborn, and no wonder. He could never get far before his mother would say:

"Come along now, mother will wipe your nose – But Allan, you mustn't do that..."

She would chatter on endlessly, her voice a grave, steady drone:

"My uncle, who is in the insurance business in Tampere, has promised to take Allan to live with him while he goes to school. He has plenty of room, and Allan will be well cared for. It will be hard to get used to his being away so long, but when you think of the future, it has to be done. We've been thinking he should become a judge. Since his father is a lawyer, the son has to go a step higher in the same field."

Now and then Janne made a joking comment on his wife's worst pronouncements. Otherwise he listened indifferently to her chatter. Sometimes tired, bitter lines appear around his mouth. When the boy managed to busy himself all alone at the coffee table, Osku said to Sanni:

"Look at that. The judge is mashing coffee bread into the sugar bowl."

Unmindful of the remark, Sanni began to scold the child. Janne looked at his brother, and a momentary smile gleamed in his eyes, but he quickly concealed it. Only when the talk turned to the land rental law was he roused from his silence. But his attitude was cool, that of a man who knew the whys and wherefores of the issue. He passed over Akseli's hotly moral views as self-evident. Swinging one long leg loosely crossed over the other, hands in his hip pockets, he held forth:

"The second section is the gist of the whole matter. A landowner has the right to evict a tenant if the lands are so located that their being returned to him is absolutely necessary for sound agricultural management. Those words open the way to so many evictions that it amounts to abolishing the law. The sections that deal with pasture and wood rights are not so impor-

10

tant, concessions would be possible there, but this is as clear as daylight. Who decides what is absolutely necessary to sound agricultural management? As long as the landlords have control of the rental boards, which will be the case as long as they have general control of the districts, it means that plot after plot will be absolutely essential to the main farm. It's better to let the whole law go than to leave the renters without protection under this semblance of legality."

The words Janne spoke in his clear voice fell like drops of poison into Akseli's mind. Anger made him breathe heavily. Stamping the sole of his shoe on the ground, he said:

"If I ever get my hands on their necks, I'll squeeze good and tight. Could there be worse goddammed people than that?"

"Oh yes there could. White-ribboned aunties who hunt out whores in the streets to serve as strikebreakers. If you don't go to the factory, you go to jail. That's what I consider the worst."

"Stop that now."

Anna scolded her son indignantly.

"Nobody does that. Those are lies."

"Well, I haven't been there to see it, but that's what they write."

"I don't know. You're always talking politics. Other people don't always go on like that. The child's just been christened, and he's been completely forgotten."

"He's the kind who doesn't call attention to himself," said Alma.It was true. Vilho had awakened, but stayed quiet in his crib. If the boy was fed regularly and had his diapers changed when necessary, he asked nothing more. The wail of a child was seldom heard in the house, and even then it sounded forced, as if the boy was crying from a sense of duty. Elina picked up the child to feed him, but was a little ashamed to bare her breast in the presence of people. Her black dress dated from her girlhood days, and was a bit small. When people noticed it, she started slightly in embarrassment. In an atmosphere where the tone was set by the relatives from the church village, she fully sensed her position as a tenant's wife, and could not relate to it.with ease. When the guests left, repeated invitations to visit were exchanged, but as mere formalities.

When the couple were alone, they characterized Sanni in a couple of words. Nothing was said of Janne, although her brother's distant coldness had hurt Elina deeply. Yet she felt a confused pity for her brother. She could not understand why, but she sensed that in spite of his facetious wit, he was somehow unhappy. This was not the first time she had noticed it, but today it had been clearer. His estrangement she had noticed earlier. Secretly happy and proud when people praised his success -- the gentry themselves called him a clearheaded man, one with whom even the learned would not find

11

easy to deal — she wondered why success meant nothing to him. Joy and preening were left to Sanni.

Gradually the mood caused by the visitors wore off. The room began to seem homey again. Having changed her clothes, Elina went back to her chores. Akseli was left to baby-sit. Janne's talk had increased his despair. The stiff behavior of the parsonage couple at the christening had taken on a new meaning. Thinking about it, he declared:

"They'll try to get rid of me the first chance they get."

In addition to these heavy thoughts was the fear that he would have to change the diapers before Elina came back.

III

In these years, the activities of the Workers' Association had greatly slackened, or rather, their nature had changed. Mainly there were dances, for which Halme indeed tried to arrange programs, but possibilities in the community were scant. The enthusiasm for political action which had followed the great strike had slowly died away. Great hopes had remained unfulfilled. In the legislature, one defeat followed another, and victories were fruitless, for the laws passed were not put into effect. The land rental law was the only one that had any significance , and now it looked as if that too would be lost.

"You can be sure of one thing: no day will dawn for the worker. There's no point in voting. It's all worthless babble."

Only Halme was not downhearted. True, one could almost see him growing older. His health was failing and he sometimes had dizzy spells. At night he had to wear thick woolen socks; his feet were cold because of poor circulation likely the result of his strange eating habits. With benevolent superciliousness, Halme steered people away from subjects that were beyond their comprehension, but they talked behind his back:

"Even the pine trees will be bare of needles — he strips them all."

Halme did in truth make all kinds of pine-needle and juniper-berry beverages, thinking up ever-new effects they were supposed to have on a person's organic and spiritual functions. Having stopped eating meat, he had begun to explain that even animals should not be slaughtered. In that way, his socialism acquired new characteristics and changed to a kind of life-preserving and spiritual-development doctrine, in which social change had no meaning except as the indispensable prerequisite to the spiritualization of man. This was the source of much friction with Hellberg. He warned Halme not to confuse matters, hinting that Halme wasn't a socialist at all. When their differences of opinion grew hotter, Hellberg thought of expelling

Halme, but that too was impossible. He lectured Halme in private on Marxism, lectures to which Halme listened with a bored expression, sometimes politely correcting Hellberg's mistakes.

Being a member of parliament had somewhat changed Hellberg too. He was still just as sure of himself, but not quite as bristly and arrogant. His behavior had taken on a kind of polish. When Preeti Leppänen yammered at him that "them there work-hours oughta be shortened," Hellberg would say in a serious, businesslike tone:

"Well, we'll do our best."

Earlier he would merely have looked and smirked. When he came to give a talk to the Association, the people gathered respectfully about him. They almost stood to attention when Hellberg looked at his watch and said:

"Well then, I have to go on up to headquarters."

He was going to Helsinki, where there were larger-than-life big shots, incomprehensible plots, slick operators, and above all, committees and deliberations.

"The boy is off to give those politicians what-for..." said Victor Kivioja.

Halme watched Hellberg leave, with a slight twinge of envy in his mind. Because of his unorthodox Marxist tendencies, his dreams of being a representative of the people were completely dead. He was merely the leader of the local alliance, a man with his own peculiar idiocies.

When Victor Mäkelä died, Akseli was chosen to replace him on the Board of Directors of the Workers Association. At first he found it hard to adjust to his position, but he settled purposefully into his duties. He brought home circulars, party decisions made at meetings, program statements, and other literature. There, in his few spare moments, he grounded himself thoroughly in such matters. His lips moved as he read, for his unfamiliarity with reading made him sound out the words as he grasped them. Elina had no connection of any sort with socialism, but she regarded her husband's travails with some pride.

"He went to a board meeting... He is reading the board's letters."

The new position meant increased respect in the eyes of the community. When on a Sunday he walked through the village on his way from Halme's with a large Manila envelope under his arm, people would say"

"There goes Koskela."

When they spoke of Jussi, they got in the habit of calling him "old Koskela." In spite of his twenty-seven years, Akseli began to be respected even among the older people. It was not only a result of his membership on the board, for it was well known that Halme would procure that for him at the first opportunity, but something in his character and habits awakened a small respect. When he was spoken of, one often heard the words that signified the highest recognition the community would give to one of its members:

"He's a good man. He means what he says."

But above all, he was a working man. Although the relations with his masters grew worse and worse, he never resorted to the renter's usual passive resistance, but did his full work-days. Actually, as relations deteriorated, he worked more efficiently as a kind of general protest. But his masters' anger was not alleviated; rather it was increased, for as much as they would have wanted to, they could not disdain him. When they went out to the harvest field, Akseli's shoulders swayed ahead of the others, the back of his shirt black with sweat. But when the others shyly spoke to the masters during a break, Akseli stood off to one side leaning on his scythe, looking off past them with a drawn mouth and a dark, fixed look in his eyes.

The cause of the breach some ten years back was no longer recalled, unless some special reason brought it to mind. Both sides were bitter with a clear conscience.

Everyday life settled into an established routine. The young couple rose early, but even as they dressed, they could hear Jussi's cough and his quiet monologue from the direction of the cow barn. Having drunk his weak morning coffee, Akseli went to work, either at the parsonage or in his own fields. On his return in the evening, he would see Elina at the window with the child in her lap. They had come to see the father and his horse.

Akseli took very little alcohol. Actually, it was limited to what others gave him, mostly the Kivivuoris. Even Anna did not hold it too much against him, for he was solemnly good-hearted when he had been drinking. She was pleased at the son-in-law's openness, when he spoke of things then.

"I know how much a woman is worth. No matter what you do, if the distaff side is weak, you're lost. I don't mean to be like my father, but I have to keep a tight rein on things until I'm out from under these debts... But like I said, I'm not talking about Elina... she didn't know how to work at first, but she tries hard."

He praised Elina without caring about Otto's and Oskari's mockery. They ridiculed his "praising the old woman," but Akseli said weightily:

"Say what you like, but it's the truth."

On his way home, he walked with firm steps to hide his intoxication, refusing to talk to those he met for the same reason. If anyone asked a question, he replied with a monosyllable and went on his way. At home, these rare spells of intoxication were among the best moments in their family life. Then he discussed affairs in a congenial and sober fashion. He would take

Vilho up into his lap or sit him on the toe of his boot and sing in his wretched voice:

"Doo, doo daddy's boy, rides his horse to town..."

In the midst of her chores, Elina would feel a hand on her shoulder and hear the words:

"What's mama up to?"

Although this tenderness reeked a bit of liquor, it was pleasing to Elina. She did push away the hand with a verbal rebuff, but afterwards her movements were lighter and her spirits clearly higher. As she washed the dishes, Akseli sat with the boy in his lap, talking:

"Next winter, Aleksi will be paid. Although he's not in any hurry — you can't even tell if he'll marry, since he's kind of a bachelor type. But he'll be paid off. All I ask for is to get this tenancy matter.settled. If we could get at least a fifty-year contract, then I would clear the part of the swamp father didn't get to. But it's no use doing anything. If I so much as replace a rotted board, right away I think it doesn't pay. And I don't know why they hate me. I can say that for my part I've been a fair man and done whatever I've signed my name to. I treat a man well if he treats me well, but I look every man right in the eye, no matter how high and mighty he is. I don't remember the poem, but it went something like this:

> Many a man did weep and sigh that they did mock the right,
> But Ilkka did not wet his eye as others wept his plight.
> ... .
>
> A farmer only was this lad, no kin to high-born folk
> But noblest of the Finns, he bowed to no man's yoke.

And then there was something like:

> He lived his life a trueborn Finn and died upon the gallows.

"That's what a man should be. If he crawls before another, that alone makes him good for nothing. You can see it in the men from the manor. They live their whole lives hat in hand. They don't do a thing in the association. They keep one eye on the crack in the door, their ears pricked up like a rabbit's. What the devil can you do with men like that. It isn't just that slavery is a disgrace, it turns men into foxes. That is so."

"Stop all that talk. And don't drop the boy."

"He won't fall. He holds on. He takes after me. I can tell from the way he holds onto his bottle. All my life I've been the kind to take hold of something and hang on. I'm not bragging. You know I don't like bragging

15

and boasting, not one little bit, but a man is allowed to tell the truth about himself."

"Stop now. Let's go to sleep."

"I'll take a look at the animals first. Even if I take a drop now and then, my work doesn't suffer."

Akseli was gone a long time. He spent much of it talking to Poku, the horse.

"It's fair to say we do all right, the two of us. Isn't that so, boy? We've both got a little bit of the old Nick under our hides when it's needed. If they drove us to the worst hell in this world, we wouldn't go hungry, nosirree. We'd wring out our food when others are praying for the Lord's mercy. I'll get yours and you'll get mine. We're two of a kind. If we fall, we fall straight off our feet. Rust or moths can't hurt us."

Then he went to praise his bull and to rail at a cow that had not calved the desired female. The cows were second rate. Poku, the bull, the ram, and the rooster were his kind of animals. Smiling with pride, he looked at the rooster on his perch, and his voice rang with the same pride as he said:

"Goddamn rooster."

He stood out in the yard for a long time before going in. It had become a habit with him in the winter when he came from the evening chores in the barn or in the summer when he went to move Poku's tether for the night. It was a kind of final check to see that everything was in place. At the very end, his eye sought the horizon to judge the next day's weather.

As the intoxication dissipated, his face became grimmer. He cleared his throat in the usual way, as if to cough himself into his former self and shake off the slight compunction caused by the thought of his being drunk.

He knew that Elina waited for him inside. Life was at its height. A few weeks, the talk of the village was that Elina Koskela was expecting again.

IV

Although the association was not very active, it brought much more work to Aleksi, whose days were already full enough. What he found most objectionable was to spend evenings and nights keeping order at the workers' hall. Everything that went on was alien to him; he could not take the slightest interest in it. Although many of his former comrades danced the night away like young men, he was no longer one of them. His dress alone gave evidence of that. He would stand in the doorway wearing a collarless shirt and work pants. Only his suit coat was better, the one that went with his "good brown suit."

It was annoying as well to get involved in disturbances of the peace when most often they involved his former comrades. But he was quick to steel his mind, and the words would come sternly, accompanied by a wide-eyed, threatening glare:

"Keep the noise down."

Mostly a word was enough. Sometimes the Laurila brothers caused a little more trouble. Arvi, the older one, was just an idiot, but there were clear indications that with Uuno, words would not suffice for long. Arvi was said to have in him a little of his older brother, who was in the asylum. He was foul but not violent. When a serving girl from the manor refused to dance with Elias Kankaanpää, he took Arvi out for a drink. Shortly afterward, Arvi bowed to the girl and asked for a dance. He was a poor dancer and she refused. Roaring with laughter, Arvi spewed out the obscenities Elias had taught him in a voice that carried throughout the room.

The girl began to cry, people giggled, and Akseli, red-faced, led Arvi out. Arvi did not resist. He staggered more than his drunkenness warranted and was happy that everyone saw him being led out by the officer. But the sight roused his younger brother's pugnacity. It was as if he envied the attention bestowed on Arvi, for he walked back and forth in the crowded hallway bumping his shoulders into people and gritting his teeth with self-induced rage. The ostentatious shoulder bumping produced a war of words with other drunks, quickly followed by invitations to "go outside." A familiar situation arose in the hallway of the dance place.

"I mean, don't push me. You wanna do that, then step outside."

"OK. Bring on a whole pastureful of calves if you come one at a time."

Akseli fixed his attention on the ruckus before the men went out. Actually he had nothing against their fighting outside the workers' hall, since he considered that none of his business, but one of the brawlers happened to have a girl with him, who was fearfully trying to stop him from going out. When there was no end to the wrangling, Akseli told them both to go out. In tears, the girl explained that it was all Uuno's fault, and the spectators supported her argument. So Akseli told Uuno to leave alone. The boy hesitated for a minute and then took his ticket from his pocket with an exaggerated gesture. Displaying it, he insisted:

"I'm not leaving till I get my money back."

"You'd better start listening."

Uuno flexed his knees and slammed his hands together:

"Maybe you should watch your mouth before I lose all my faith, hope, and charity."

Akseli stepped quickly toward Uuno, but a dim sense of a watchman's duty made him add:

"For the last time. Listen to me."

17

"Don't you put on airs, damn it. You're just a Koskela ditch digger."

In spite of his eighteen years, Uuno was already counted a man, and the violence of his bodily movement increased his strength. Now the door frame shook as the two of them went through it like a whirlwind. Akseli drove the boy before him, not slackening his fierce pace for a second, and Uuno had to give ground. He tried his best to resist. His shirt came into view as his pants slipped down and his hat fell off too, but Akseli snatched it up without pausing. Wordless and panting, Akseli forced him on, with Uuno cursing and screaming the whole time:

"Don't kick me, you goddammed bushwhacker. You're a nothing, you're just tight-fisted Jussi Koskela's boy. Go home and count slices of bread with your father."

Only when they reached the road did Akseli let up. Stamping angrily back and forth, he said hoarsely:

"Don't you glare at me... If you don't behave, I'll give you such a thrashing you won't walk for three days... Once I get started, I won't stop till you're trampled in the mud... Just keep that in mind."

Uuno was too tired to try anything more, and Akseli went back to the hall. For the remainder of the evening he stood silent on the threshold. No one tried to talk to him; they avoided him almost as if they were afraid of him. Those who were drunk tried to talk sense as they passed by him.

Uuno went lumbering down the road. Suddenly he snatched his knife from its sheath and shouted:

"I'll kill everyone I meet."

But no one met him on the road, and Uuno continued on his way. He did not go home, but headed for the center of the village. Catching sight of the store, he put his knife back in the sheath and said, as if something had just dawned on him:

"Agh... by... God."

He marched headlong to the side door of the store and banged on it with his fists.

"Hey, fatbelly. Get up and pay your goddamn rent. You've lived in my house but you haven't paid a penny of rent."

A mumbling could be heard inside and the entry curtains fluttered.

"Godamn old man, colts grow into horses and boys into men, you know. Rise young lads of Finland..."

There was a clatter and the sound of running feet inside. Then the store-keeper's words rang out:

"If... if... Go away now or I'll fire through the door."

"Fire away, goddamn..."

Uuno began to kick the door and to sing in rhythm with the thumping:

Lullaby my little lamb
keep on butting little ram
you may sleep the morning through
though heaven come to waken you...

"Hey, you goddammed Finnish capitalist. Now you'll hear some real noise."

On the edge of the porch was the storekeeper's green-painted water-bearer's yoke. Uuno seized it and began to smash the windows to pieces. He had managed to break the entry windows before the storekeeper fired.

"I'll aim the next one at you... I tell you... that was a warning shot... I, I..."

Uuno ran off, but as he went, he tossed the yoke in through the bedroom window, whereupon the storekeeper fired again. As the bullet whined over Uuno's head, he turned and shouted:

"Aim, goddammit... is your hand shaking... I tell you, I don't care much about life... But I'll burn down your store one of these days, and your miserly brother's house too. Shiver for a while longer and stay awake nights."

Back on the road, Uuno leaped up, slammed his hands together and whooped:

"Well, by squirrelly Christ... I'm the top dog of Pentti's Corners and bleary-eyed Koskela's gonna get a knife through his lungs."

He started off toward home, but stopped a while and stood there grinding his teeth. Wolf-Kustaa was returning from night-fishing, the heavy, dragging steps of his hobnailed boots sounding on the road. He was walking along the opposite side and Uuno stepped over to it, whereupon Kustaa stopped and looked tight-lipped at the boy. Uuno looked back at him, his head slightly cocked and still gritting his teeth. Then he hissed:

"Shake my hand, Kustaa."

"Hmmh... kiss my... hmmh."

"Shake my hand, like I said. This hand, Kustaa... Goddammit, you've got to, or else you're dead."

Kustaa took a couple of steps to one side to get by Uuno and went on, mumbling, without looking back. Uuno had already taken a step or two after him, but then another idea struck him and he began walking toward his home. Nevertheless, he stopped once on the way, looked back, and muttered:

"I should have killed that goddammed net-minder anyway."

Passing the Kankaanpää's he saw the head of a bull sticking out from the window of the stable, which was right beside the road. The Kankaanpääs kept the bull there during the summer, and it often stood and looked out the open window. In passing, Uuno struck the bull on the brow with his fist, and the animal drew back its head with a bellow.

"Stop staring, goddammit!"

Reaching home, Uuno kicked the door open so hard that it slammed into the wall. From the bed in the rear came Antto's threatening growl. Uuno threw off his coat and lay down. For awhile the room was still, until the cautious gnawing of a rat broke the silence. At first it chewed at intervals, as if pausing to listen for reactions, but when nothing happened, it gnawed more feverishly. Uuno pulled off one of his boots and threw it into the corner:

"Keep still, you devil, when people are sleeping."

"Lay off, boy."

Aliina's vague complaint came from the kitchen. After a period of silence, the rat, which had been frightened by the thump of the boot, began to gnaw again. Uuno shouted to his mother in the kitchen:

"Give it some soft bread so I can sleep."

"Shut your mouth, you bum."

Even fourteen-year-old Elma called out something which Uuno could not make out. He got up from the bed, went into the kitchen, and finding a loaf of soft rye bread, tossed it toward the sound of the rat's gnawing:

"Gnaw on that so you won't make so goddammed much noise."

Aliina appeared in the kitchen doorway, with Elma behind her in a white nightgown.

"But what are you doing? Since when have we had bread to throw away?"

"I won't listen to that kind of gnawing. We always have enough to stop a rat's snout. We don't count slices like they do at Koskela."

Now Antto too rose. He stood by the bed and said:

"Go and get that bread from the corner, boy."

"Shut up, old man."

"By God... Jesus... what I'm going to do..."

Antto darted back and forth for a time until he remembered the bunch of ropes hanging by the door. Snatching it up, he ran back to the bed. Uuno was just getting up when the ropes struck him in the face.

"Listen, old man. That's the last time you'll hit me."

The two kept jerking at the ropes until they were locked hand to hand. The floor rocked, curses hissed, and occasional screams could be heard from Aliina, who had rushed between the combatants.

"Jesus, Jesus..."

Father and son grunted and cursed as they wrestled face to face. When they fell, the father lay underneath, and Uuno hammered at him with his fists.

"Squirrelly Christ, father, it was a bad time to lay a hand on me."

Aliina tried to tear the boy loose. Elma darted back and forth with her white nightgown flapping. Finally she snatched up the baker's peel from the oven corner. Skillfully, being careful of her mother, she hacked at her brother's back. All the while a sound kept escaping through her teeth:

"... ee... ee... ee..."

It helped enough so that Antto got on top, and now the tables were turned. Having beaten Uuno for a time, Antto carried him to the bed, yelling for Aliina to bring him the rope. They tied Uuno to the bed with it. Quickly and nimbly, Elma carried the rope end under the bed, striking her brother's face with her small fist at every circuit.

"Goddamn... goddamn..."

The knot was tied underneath the bed so that Uuno could not reach to open it. Panting, Antto kept threatening him by the bedside:

"You know now that Antto Laurila is still top man in this house. That's the way it is."

His mother fetched water and a towel and began to wash Uuno's face while he mumbled through his cut and bleeding lips.

"Don't wash them, goddamn... Let the blood run... down to the last goddamn drop. We're not stingy here."

"Oh, my God... What have I come to! What kind of child did I bear?"

"There's nothing wrong with the child you bore... You won't see a drop of water in these eyes, you won't."

"Shut your trap."

Elma had already gone to bed and Aliina followed suit. She lay with her eyes open, tears rolling from their corners as she stared at the sooty ceiling.

V

At first the storekeeper threatened to have Uuno sent to jail, and there he would undoubtedly have landed if the matter had been tried in court, but it was finally agreed that Antto would have Otto Kivivuori fix the broken windows. Antto was not concerned about the store windows. To him, it was the one good thing about the night's ruckus, although he was of the opinion that the boy had carried on in the wrong place:

"That suckface deserved it. I wouldn't have said a thing if he'd lighted a fire under the corner of the house."

When he was drunk, Antto even bragged about his son a little.

"He's going to be a devil... But I don't hold a grudge against Akseli for taming him a little... You don't riot at the workers' hall. But you can break rich men's windows."

Soon the story was forgotten when something new came along to talk about. Lauri Kivioja got married, and Valenti Leppänen was seeking passage to America.

Valenti's situation had gradually become unbearable. Halme, who guarded his reputation zealously, did not dare let Valenti do anything on his own. A couple of times he had given Valenti the material and pattern for some kind of apprentice showpiece. He did not lay a finger on the work, having decided to let the boy manage all by himself. The result was that the master would press and turn over scraps of cloth and keep clearing his throat, while Valenti reeled off an endless and senseless explanation, which made the master cough more and more significantly.

Valenti's incompetence became a real problem as he grew up. Halme did not know what to do with the boy. He couldn't keep a grown man as an errand boy forever, and it was impossible even to think of his doing physical labor. Valenti applied himself ever more firmly to writing poems, which were sometimes printed in labor publications. That fact had no significance in a time when every person capable of writing had published a poem for some occasion or other. At bad moments, Valenti went to the lake, crossed his arms over his chest, cocked his head, and stared at the opposite shore. If there was a breeze, he took off his hat and turned his face toward it. Wolf-Kustaa might stare at him in wonderment, but that didn't bother Valenti. Otto Kivivuori saw him on one such occasion and asked:

"Are you thinking up a poem?"

Valenti lowered his arms, turned slowly toward Otto, and mimicking Jussi Jukola, said as if he had just returned from a distant world:

"The mind of man soars everywhere, and who can set nets to catch it."

The thought of going to America grew out of talk about the money that the son of Hollo's overseer had sent home from the States. At first the master opposed Valenti's imaginings, but finally consented. *The People's Press* had been censured for one of Valenti's poems, and the boy hinted to the villagers:

"I'm on the gendarmes' list. It's time I disappeared."

The idea appealed to the master so much that he half believed it. Therefore he told the villagers that it wouldn't be too much to remember their secretary with a small collection. The suggestion was put into effect, and with the master's gift and the sum from the sale of Leppänen's cow, the necessary travel money was collected. The farewell party was held in connection with Lauri Kivioja's wedding.

"Those itchy feet come from me," Vikki said of his boy. Lauri really was a bit restless. He didn't stay on a job for long, but might walk off in the middle of the day on some impulse. He worked with Janne Kivivuori for a short time, but they soon quarreled. Janne gave him some directions a little nastily, and Lauri said:

"Guess, Janne, who's leaving your job just about now!"

He worked at the station for a time, just long enough to buy an old wreck of a bicycle from another employee. He rode it back and forth, always pedaling with all his might. He found a bride too in the station village, and while other young men wisely hid such trips, he rode through the village very ostentatiously.

"In half an hour, boys, Lauri will be sighting down Finland's railroad." *

People came to Kivivuoris' to see the bicycle. Lauri walked around it looking important, jiggled the pedals with pursed lips, and said, apparently to himself, since the others understood nothing about the contraption:

"Son of a gun, it's loose. It needs to be fixed."

The bicycle was forever dismantled. Lauri would put it together and take it apart, cheeks smeared with blackened vaseline, jawing at the spectators:

"That was some ride I had last night, boys. The chain came off on Tammikallio Hill and I couldn't brake. I thought, goodbye country, Lauri Kivioja's brains will be spooned up into a paper bag from the roadside tomorrow."

The wedding was held at the Pentti's Corners Workers Hall, for Vikki wanted to show off to the villagers. Among the wedding dishes was a rarity, a macaroni casserole, and Vic himself fussed about, serving spoon in hand:

"Have some macarooni... good... we'll get used to it. Hulivili brought it..."

Hulivili was a fish peddler who had begun to sell macaroni on his rounds. During the ceremony, Vic could not be still. From time to time he repeated the words after the pastor, interspersing everything with comments to those nearest him:

"... for better or for worse... the boy didn't pick a girl from his own village... He likes to roam... Do you think she shows it already... There's one on the way, all right, but don't bother to talk about it..."

Vic served drinks while the dancing was going on. Akseli's face gradually reddened, and his talk became stiffer and more deliberate as he struggled to seem sober. Elina had gotten a holiday dress and her joy at it kept her from looking indignant. After a time, Vic came up, plucked at Akseli's sleeve, and kept babbling on:

"Come on for a little while... You're a true-blue man... But no horseman... I did business with your father once... They're killing those dukes and their women... Those foreigners are something.. Although you can't get rid of them otherwise... Don't you think so too!"

On the rear bench names were repeated at short intervals: Sarajevo, Serbia, Franz Ferdinand.

Then it was time for Valenti's farewell party. First he read a poem he had written:

> *With what wonder did the race of man see light*
> *rise from the west with glow of morning sun*
> *and backward then did course of daylight run*
> *and freedom's day sank not in gloomy night.*
>
> *For see, beyond the mighty ocean main,*
> *a brilliant torch does pierce Europa's night,*
> *showing a new world with its guiding light,*
> *to bless those fleeing raw oppression's reign.*
>
> *There once 'neath coats of hide of woodland beast,*
> *to freedom's morning men did ope their hearts,*
> *and Washington with men of valiant parts*
> *did crush the glutton rule of lord and priest.*
>
> *Farewell my native land whose people sag*
> *in tyrants' night 'neath slavery's foul sway.*
> *I watch, yet try to turn my eyes away,*
> *the last wave breaking on the rocky crag.*

Valenti sat beside his master, chatting more familiarly than usual because of the prestige accorded to one who was leaving. His master.was not exactly pleased and spoke in the broadest of generalities to demonstrate his complete mental mastery of America and its history.

"Give our regards to the free people of America. Tell them that here as well, the spirit of man has not abandoned the struggle against the powers of darkness. Although this old world of ours has degenerated to the clanking of swords and the threatening clashing of helmets, yet say to them that the spirit has not abandoned the fight. The few people of Finland stand at the front as well, surrounded and in chains, but neither despondent nor despairing. This I ask you to say to G. Washington's and A. Lincoln's people. And remind them of Lafayette, and that they, as did he, rushed to fan the fire of freedom there where the black ravens of reaction tried to dim its light with the wings of death's angel.

"But there, far away, on the opposite side of Tellus, keep deep in your heart the whole picture of our homeland, its benign motherly face, despite the fact that it places into your hands the walking staff of a refugee."

Henna wept and blubbered to the womenfolk:

"You only have to sell newspapers there for a short time and you get to be a rich man... so they say... I haven't been there..."

Preeti too explained ad infinitum:

"Well, still, your own country... although that freedom is really... At least he has something to start out with, I left so little for myself. Although the butcher said he couldn't pay the full price, it was sort of poorly fed, but still it was on summer pasture... But it was something anyway... I'll always get along somehow, tho' we'll have less money now that we have to work for milk... But if the boy just gets a little better life. That's the way things are for people like us."

Nevertheless they missed the boy, although he had become distant from them while at Halme's. On the other hand, the departure raised their self-esteem, which was already high for another reason: the Baron had spoken to Preeti. Henna had already repeated the story many times, but could not resist telling it again:

"He told Preeti in the way he has of talking that weather is goddamn hot, Leppänen. And Preeti said he said that there might be a thunderstorm. Is that so, said the Baron and Preeti said he said that it was."

Valenti paid no attention to his parents. He sat on the back bench in his new travel suit wearing fine chamois gloves that Halme had made for him as a farewell present. He answered his sister only under duress, although she was clearly trying to engage him in conversation.

Valenti managed to set out before the war began.

VI

The first measure taken by Jussi Koskela as a result of the war was to hide his money in the ceiling insulation. Akseli got him to take it out by frightening him with the possibility of a fire. He urged Jussi to take the money to a bank, but Jussi flared up"

"Just like that. Take it there. For them to shave off the gold."

On the third day after the war broke out, he went to buy a funeral plot for himself and Alma. The pastor wondered what had suddenly made Jussi start thinking about death.

"One never knows... when they've done this to the world... if one doesn't have anything when he needs it... at least one will have a grave ready."

"I hope that Koskela won't need one for a long time. Koskela may well drive me to the graveyard as he did my predecessor."

"That's one trip I won't take. I'm starting to feel so sick. No matter how hard I try, it does no good."

The pastor was somewhat partial and sold Jussi a valuable plot from the old section of the cemetery, although it was reserved for the better people of the parish.

"It's a pity I can't lower the price, although it wouldn't be wrong for you to get the best place free of charge. A man who has cleared some twenty acres of swamp shouldn't have to pay for those last few square meters."

Abruptly the pastor broke off, coughed, and hastily changed the subject. In spite of his miserliness, Jussi took the expensive lot just because he was afraid that the war might somehow rob him of his money.

When he had left, the pastor remained deep in thought for a long time and concluded at length:

"Yes indeed. He really doesn't ask anything of anyone. He would probably have diapered himself if it were somehow possible. To the very end, to the grave itself, he will go on taking care... How beautiful the life of man can be when it is at its best."

The war gave rise to lively discussion at the parsonage. The children were at home, and every conceivable possibility was weighed. Ilmari was highly enthusiastic about the war and argued with his father, who presented common humanistic opinions:

"We-ell, we-ell, But in any event, war is somehow against human nature."

"Is that so? If anything is according to human nature, then war is."

Ilmari was lying on the sofa. He would whistle the opening measures of "Summer Evening Waltz" and start over from the beginning again. Ani, who had some needlework in her hands, finally said in a weary tone of voice, with her usual careful enunciation:

"Please stop whistling."

Her words had no effect. The whistling continued as before. Ilmari was in shirtsleeves and without a collar. His mother often scolded him for his carelessness, and he was indeed a bit negligent. His mother felt that his speech habits were a little suspect. Sometimes they showed signs of being common. Where could he have caught that? What were his friends in Helsinki like? On the surface everything seemed perfect with him, but the parents sensed that their son had a life that was hidden from them.

Ilmari sat up on the sofa, shoved his hands deep into his trouser pockets and looked at the floor in silence. Ani, who was indignant at her brother's indifference to her request, repeated:

"I asked you just now to stop whistling."

"Was there something wrong with it?"

"First of all, it was unpleasant."

"Is there anything about me that you don't find unpleasant?"

"Well, at least your being purposely nasty is unpleasant."

Ani's tone of voice was cold and formal. There was something carefully precise in it, as there was in her entire being. The servants, who referred to her as the "young miss," thought her proud and arrogant. In actuality, that conception sprang from her formal demeanor, which made her seem rigid. She had adopted all the formal attitudes and mannerisms of the petit bourgeois, while her brother, some said, was a devilish, rough-and-ready hellion. There was a bit of admiration in the latter characterization.

Ilmari was very direct in his dealings with people. Any lack of spontaneity in his relationships with his inferiors did not stem from him, but from the timidity and suspicion of the latter. Sometimes he would work for an hour stacking hay in an effort to loosen up the workers and get them into a discussion. But he soon tired of it, stuck his pitchfork into the ground, and walked away.

He found summer vacations boring. There was no one to keep him company, hence his attempts to socialize with the employees. Young serving girls who had been hired to replace the aging Emma and Miina were ecstatic about him. The "Master" was a handsome boy; he was natural and had just the right amount of provocative arrogance. Ilmari was well aware of their blushing and instinctive fawning, but the atmosphere of his home quickly killed anything that the realizationπ might have led to.

He was not yet a "Master." He was way behind in his studies, and Ani continued the previous conversation in a low and troubled voice, as if she were ashamed of the unpleasant subject:

"And it's no fun to hear you lying to father and mother. It's awfully stupid too, because some day they'll find out the truth about your exams."

Ilmari gave a derisive snort, but a troubled expression crossed his face.

"'Lie' is too strong a word for the matter. Why should I bother them with a problem that I'll solve first chance I get? I'm thinking of them, not of myself. You have the very nasty habit of meddling in matters that can't be helped and are therefore none of your business."

Near the end of his statement, Ilmari's tone of voice became heated. Her words had touched a sore spot, and he was angry. Ani was silent to demonstrate how improper it was to quarrel. Having calmed down, Ilmari went on, as if repeating an idea he had often mulled over:

"Why does a person have to be born into such a limited existence? Everything crushes, everything smothers me. Others are living a great age in other parts of the world. Darn it, I'll go and sell myself to the Russians for a hundred crowns. They take volunteers into their army."

"Are you sure they'd pay that much for you?"

Ilmari walked to the window and looked dully out at the landscape. Nothing about it attracted his attention. He was completely bored, and that was the source of these often repeated quarrels.

He went out to take a walk, to wander aimlessly, which is what his excursions were. In the hallway he met his mother, whose face lighted up at once when she saw her son.

"Are you going out?"

"I am."

"But dress properly. You can't walk around so carelessly dressed."

Ilmari obeyed.

Without conscious thought, he turned toward the shore where people swam and washed clothing. The path led through a thick alder grove. It was wet for a long way because the shore was so low, and he stepped from stone to stone. In the shady grove, the mosquitoes buzzed angrily. His nose caught the scent of rotting straw. As he came closer, he heard splashing at the shore. Some laundry lay on the rocks, and a short distance from them on the grass was a woman's dress. Aune Leppänen was swimming in the lake, kicking vigorously with her feet. There was an enormous discrepancy between the amount of strength she expended and the results in the swimming.

At first Ilmari turned back, but recognizing Aune, he walked to the shore. He had heard people talk about her, and something told him that delicacy was not called for. Noticing him, Aune shrieked and crouched down in the water up to her neck.

"Good evening. Aino bathing."

"The Master will please leave so that I can get out."

"What if I turn my back? I promise not to look. If I went behind that bunch of alders, how could you be sure I wouldn't watch from there?"

"Ah, ah, you mustn't do that."

Ilmari walked some distance to one side and turned his back. For a moment, he had a vision of a nude woman in his mind as he heard Aune splashing up from the lake.

"Well, are you dressed?"

"Yes."

Ilmari found a suitable rock and sat down on it. Aune began to rinse the washing and wring it out. Ilmari glanced at her in passing, and Aune noticed it. The effect of the parsonage "Master's" proximity could be seen clearly in her behavior. She tugged at her dress to cover her knees and handled the laundry with stiff, somewhat affected movements. Ilmari remembered someone at work having said that Aune was good-natured. He asked how she showed it.

"She's so good natured that she can't say no."

The words were followed by a sly, meaningful laugh and Ilmari caught the drift. Now he noticed Aune carefully covering her knees. It brought a vague picture to his mind, which soon disappeared. Then he looked out at the lake, and his thoughts shifted onto a well-worn track. Last winter he had come to the remarkable realization that he existed, that there was such a person as Ilmari Salpakari. Some kind of breakthrough had occurred, he couldn't quite say what. All he knew was that gradually many things came to seem different from before. His friends, the events of university life, everything had begun to seem boring. The central theme of the young, Russification, its acceptance or rejection, seemed quite trivial. The Russian grip tightened, everything seemed hopeless, his studies lagged. A dull and melancholy depression surprised him at times. It was at such a moment that he became conscious of his existence.

The naive idealism of his schooling and upbringing did not last. And he was too honest to take refuge in the unconscious self-deceit of everyone around him. He scorned himself for his "Welschmerz," which he considered childish, but he could not shake it off.

But the war had awakened his imagination.

"If I were a German, I would be riding somewhere in Belgium. Or if an Englishman, I would be doing the same. What must it be like to be an Englishman? With the whole world at his fingertips. For us a trip abroad is remarkable, but for them it is an everyday occurrence. They go to India and live like kings. They barge into places where no white man has ever been. A hundred bowed backs surround them, and lovely dark women clasp their hands, bow to the earth, and say, 'Sahib.'"

He smiled a bit scornfully at his thoughts. Aune's splashing attracted his attention. She can't say no.

He rose from the rock, walked over to Aune, and sat down on the grass.

"Aino is doing the wash."

"My name isn't Aino... aah..."

"Then what is it?"

"You know it."

"Of course. It's Aino."

"That's not it at all."

Aune was a little ashamed of the wash and gathered it up into the basket. Ilmari asked her to sit down, and Aune did so, slightly hesitant and covering her chapped legs with her dress. Ilmari asked her about community matters and she told him about them. When she spoke of Valenti's departure for America, she became pretentious and put on airs.

"I can go too when my brother gets settled."

"Why?"

"This place is just so... I don't like it at all... farther away..."

"What happened to your finger?"

"I cut it with a sickle."

"Let me blow on it. Isn't it a custom to blow on places that hurt?"

"Ha, haa... you're so terrible..."

That was how it began for Ilmari. For a long time his advances were mere play, until all his troubling doubts vanished. But he had to employ all his brazenness and experience, for he first had to overcome Aune's fear of her masters. He ran his fingers up and down her leg and repeated:

"To the woods the mousy ran, and hippity hop he's back again."

"You mustn't... you don't like me anyway."

"If Aino is nice the master will like her."

"Get it through your head that I'm not Aino... Ha, ha, but you're impossible."

As he neared home, Ilmari's feeling of shame grew stronger. But he forced it away with the help of the indifference he had built up in his mind. When he reached home he was calm and expressionless. The matter was further overwhelmed by the situation that prevailed at home.

"Hurry up. We have clippings from a Swedish newspaper. They sent them from the church village."

His father stood in the living room with the clippings in his hand and said enthusiastically:

"The Germans have captured Liege and the Italians are advancing in Galicia."

VII

The war soon faded into the back of people's minds. Only extraordinary pieces of news revived their interest, but these were few and far between because of the censorship. The activities of the Workers' Associations became more and more difficult to continue. Every festival program had to be submitted for advance scrutiny. The sheriff often sent a policeman to programs where there was a speaker. Once upon a time Halme would have liked to be haled into court for lese majesty. Now old and ailing, he no longer sought it, but he managed to talk himself into jail anyway.

The talk was not really political, but he attacked war and armies from his own vegetarian point of view. That was considered to be criticism of the authorities.

Calmly and loftily, Halme accepted the sentence, which was in fact only four months in prison. The leadership of the Workers Association he left to Akseli for that period, and since others were present, he chose words of sweeping significance:

"I pass on the baton to you. Don't drop it along the way."

He suffered his punishment late in the fall. Emma and others near to him were worried about his health, for his diet would cause more problems. But Halme himself was not upset, considering it of minor importance. He was more concerned about the prison garb, which he detested.

The news of Aune Leppänen's pregnancy frightened the young men in the community. Aune blamed Oskari Kivivuori, with whom she was most in love, but there were several men to claim as the child's father: Elias Kankaanpää, Uuno and Arvi Laurila, and Ilmari from the parsonage, although the latter never entered her head because it was impossible to think of marrying him. Aune followed Oskari around for a long time before she got him alone. The result was an ugly encounter. Aune cried and Osku was brutal.

"Listen, I can bring four or five men into court and then all you'll have left is the costs and the shame. The wisest thing for you to do is to shut up."

"But you were with me then."

"So I was, but so were many other boys, and I'm not taking the blame when you can't know."

Preeti did not drop the matter but went to Kivivuori. Osku was adamant and finally appealed to the large number of possibilities. When he offered proof, Preeti was downcast and left. Anna wept for shame and annoyance and Otto read his son a sarcastic sermon:

"That was really stupid. The common sluts are the most dangerous. It's bound to happen with someone, and then what's to be done? Thank your lucky stars that the others were dumb enough to hang around her too."

"God have mercy, God have mercy... what disaster will strike us, God's forbearance won't last. Talking like that, thinking only about how to hide it, as of it weren't even a sin..."

The matter hurt Anna's pride so badly that she fell slightly ill. After a few days she got out of bed and sighed with a sorrowful expression on her face:

"God knows why we bear these heavy burdens."

The talk about the Aune's condition was not really malicious. The occurrence pacified the women whose expectations on that score had been disappointed for so many years. There was a kind of sympathy for Aune because her fate had now settled into the groove assigned it in the minds of the community. The mothers who had for years accused her of corrupting their sons were now appeased. A few gave Henna an extra loaf of freshly baked bread or a piece of meat.

Elina Koskela, who wept when she chose a calf or lamb to be slaughtered and scolded little Vilho if he crushed an ant in the yard looked grave, and said in a tone of voice inherited from her mother:

"Yes, she'll try to get Oskari in any way she can, even by using others. It's a pity about the child, but Aune got just what she was asking for."

Akseli asked hastily:

"Have those pigs broken their trough? I'll go and work on it."

Late one dark evening, Anna Kivivuori appeared at the Leppänens'. It was dark in the cabin, for the smoky lamp on the wall, whose tin reflector was rusty too, gave little light. The family stood up in greeting, and Henna scurried to get a chair.

"Sit down, it's a little dark. Your eyes will get used to it."

"I... this matter... It's God's bidding... Although I'm not involved. But my son, I don't want to interfere, but you understand..."

"I do. These children a problem. My son too... gone into the big world. And now this... My cow went for that too, but that's nothing... Yes, and they talk at the manor... sailed to America on a cow... It's envy... I won't talk... I had coffee at your house too when I came to borrow a flax comb... didn't bring it back... nothing to offer you."

"Thank you. Nothing for me. I just came to find out. It's hard to talk but I have to. I'll talk frankly and ask you to talk frankly. Has Oskari... has..."

Anna searched for a word until she found one, a roundabout expression the source of which was incomprehensible:

"... had a relation?"

Anna raised her head and since she represented something close to gentility sitting on the Leppänen's bench, the answer was extraordinarily formal:

"He has had a relation."

Even in the dark one could see how much the blow hurt Anna. The corners of her mouth twitched, and she was silent for a time. When she looked at Aune, there was a hint of hatred in her eyes.

"If he has, then before God I ask you... was Oskari the only one? Don't... I don't want to hurt... but I must know the truth."

"He was. It wasn't like that with others. Oskari was my sweetheart."

32

"But still there were others."

"Maybe a few sometimes. I didn't with everybody."

"But we must know the truth."

"Anyway I was with Osku the most."

Preeti shifted his feet and said:

"To the best of my knowledge it was Oskari. I'm not going to say there weren't others. It's like that with these kids. But he was one of them anyway."

"If there were others, then how can you blame Oskari? I'm not defending my son. But it's not right either for him to be held responsible... it would be impossible... to take on someone else's child..."

Aune's head sank trembling lower and lower. A kind of primal weeping came from her in a long howl, which finally ended in babbling.

"I'm... not the only one to blame. They're all good then. But they all deny that..."

Anna felt a tremendous surge of relief. Tears rose to her eyes, but an inner happiness lighted her cheeks. The relief turned into a deep sympathy for Aune, and she said weeping:

"Poor child, poor child. Don't cry. We're all in God's care. He gives us trouble out of love. One has to bow to him in whose hands everything lies."

"So it is. It's sort of like life goes by His direction. What's given from above has to be borne here on earth. Such is life. And with one child... somehow. I asked the overseer already could I hoe a corner of that lot. Get a little bit of land. There'd be some spuds anyway. Oh well, I had two kids, so a third's all the same. Tho' my boy went to learn from the master when he was small. And when he kind of gets to be high-class and then comes here... Others get it from there. The son of Hollo's overseer sent some money."

Anna was not ashamed of her tears, but wept freely in her relief. A kind of piety that radiated joy filled her mind as she said:

"I will try to help you, although my son can't be blamed. But the child who is coming is not guilty, so we're all answerable for him..."

Aune had finished crying and said suddenly:

"It's Osku all right."

"But my dear child. You just said there were others."

"Even then. It was mostly Osku."

A sullen look came over Anna's face.

"You must know when. Not every time counts, but just certain times."

"You don't have to test me. I'm sure it was Osku, but I won't run after any man. I have lots of sweethearts. Such sweethearts that this town would be bowled over if I told them. And some that I've left to others. Some fine ladies are keeping my cast-offs."

Anna looked at Aune in astonishment. She did not understand the hint, but she was amazed at the girl's attitude.

"Is that so? I came here at God's bidding to find out. But I can no longer demand that my son take responsibility for this."

"No need to. I don't care for a man who sends his mother on errands. I can even get gentlemen. I don't care to say who, but you'll soon see."

"Girl, don't jabber such nonsense. The lady doesn't care... this kind of thing will make her nervous too."

Anna rose.

"Well, I didn't... and since my son may be involved, I will help you. But before the Highest, I have to say that I can't consider him guilty. And although your misfortune is great, I tell you that it was wrong to blame one person for something that you can't even know about yourself."

There was a condemning coldness in Anna's voice, but then she sighed, stepped to the door, and said:

"Evening then. They say I trouble people with my God, but I leave you in His hands."

"Evening. The lady doesn't have a light... It's a little dark out there."

"One has to manage here. The poor men at the front, in the rain and darkness."

"Yes, that's what it's like. How can they even aim when it's so dark?"

After Anna left, there was silence for awhile at the Leppänens'. Each one sorted out the feelings caused by the visit. Then Preeti yawned and said:

"You could patch that blouse of mine."

Then he lay down on the bed. Yawning and stretching out his legs, he sank into his peaceful evening state. After a long silence, he said once more:

"At least there are those potatoes."

34

CHAPTER TWO

I

One late February evening in the year 1915, Ilmari arrived home unexpectedly.

"I'm going to Sweden. I just came to get some money and say good-bye."

"Why are you going to Sweden?"

"I'm going to check the archives there with a couple of my friends."

The trip was nothing unusual, but his parents wondered at its suddenness.

"I leave in the morning. Do you have any money?"

Their son's excitement and restlessness soon led his parents to suspect that he was hiding something. He explained the purpose of the trip in great detail, all the while smiling an absorbed inward smile. His father and mother had already eaten, and the left-overs were gathered up for Ilmari. They watched as he ate hurriedly. At length his mother said:

"You're hiding something. What is really on your mind? You'll make me ill."

"Nothing at all. Just calm down. I'm going to Sweden for four weeks, that's all."

"That isn't all. In God's name, what has happened?"

Ilmari stuck to his claim until his mother became so upset that the boy was forced to say, after a moment's thought:

"I see that I have to tell you. But you have to give your word of honor not to tell anyone what I say."

The words were so surprising that in spite of his agitation, the pastor started to laugh. A boy forcing his parents to give their word of honor. Then he said gravely:

"You know that you can depend on us in anything honorable."

"Actually I'm going to Germany. For four weeks of officers training. If you so much as hint at the fact, you'll endanger not only me but many others, and a great cause as well. It's plain that I will be a traitor to this government, but I hope you understand that I'm not a traitor to my country."

Their astonishment was short lived, for they had discussed such a possibility in connection with the war. His parents, however, began to have doubts, but the boy cut them short:

"There's no use talking. I've made my decision and I'm sticking to it. There's no backing out now. Everything is ready, including a passport and my orders, so I have to go through with it. And the fewer questions you ask, the better."

They withdrew from the kitchen to avoid the servants. His father was worried about the boy's decision, but his mother soon began to support it. The boy hotly attacked those who were willing to make concessions to the Russians, upon which his father took offense. He said almost indignantly:

"You're too young to judge such matters. It's wrong to question their motives. They are acting in the country's best interest as they see it."

"I see my country's interests differently. But don't worry. We're not planning to hang them when we get back."

The boy's laugh was happy and relieved. In place of last summer's bored and irritable young man stood an animated person, one who could not stand still for long, much less sit down. His mother's eyes filled with tears, but the boy's enthusiasm soon won her over. His father, on the contrary, resisted till the end.

"And then after the four weeks?"

The boy's expression showed his concern, but he said almost harshly:

"And then? I don't know. The only definite thing is the four weeks. The ultimate goal is rebellion, of course. But I'm not important enough to know how it will come about. I only know that it must come, and that those devils must be driven to the last corner of hell, as God is my witness."

Ilmari raised his hand as he spoke, smiling at the literal sense of his words, but not at their inner meaning. Even his worried father laughed and said:

"Well now. God won't help such angry people. I see that I can't stop you, but I tell you seriously that enthusiasm, however commendable, is never enough."

His mother had already agreed to his going. She took no real part in the discussion, but wept, trying to control her sobbing because she knew it upset her son. They stayed awake for a long time, and although Ilmari was not to leave until morning, their goodnights had the feel of a last farewell.

After a largely sleepless night, they behaved in a more ordinary fashion the next morning. The boy's parents found themselves hard pressed for money. Ilmari had not specified a sum, but they knew he could not start out on his journey with a pittance. And they had very little, for a shortage of money plagued this family as if it bore a personal grudge against them. Money did come in, but it flowed out again in such a steady stream that nothing ever stayed with them. The pastor had stopped agonizing about it. Since things had always gone on this way, why shouldn't they continue to do so? Sometimes he even consoled himself with Scripture:

"It's a sin to grieve over such things. Since God gives us the day, he will provide for our daily bread too."

Now they had to scrape up all they could, but the father was a trifle embarrassed when he offered the money to his son. The boy sensed their circumstances and refused at first to take it all, but soon his conscience compelled him to do so. He thanked them, explaining that there were travel funds for those leaving, but that he could not accept them when there were others in the group much poorer than he. The father kept clearing his throat when he spoke of the money, but that did not seem the sole cause of his embarrassment. He went over to a desk and took a New Testament from its drawer. Handing it to his son, he said with a smile:

"We've been too distant. Much too distant... I beg you to take this."

After a brief pause he said half-jokingly, to cover his embarrassment:

"It doesn't weigh much, it's so small."

The father had often tried to establish a closer relationship with his son, but some kind of constraint had always come between them. He sensed something in the boy's life which he could never analyze because it hurt him too much to do so. The book brought on the same feeling, causing him to react with awkward playfulness. The boy's face assumed a grave expression, actually too grave to be genuine. His words were only half articulated:

"Thanks... and for everything else."

His father straightened up and said in a thick and halting voice:

"We have to be cheerful... for your mother's sake... it hurts her so."

They left the office as if rushing to escape what had just occurred. The horse was already waiting in the yard, and Ilmari made his final preparations with an affected briskness. Walking, he thumped his feet heavily on the floor, as if he were already marching, and all his movements exuded a brisk decisiveness. His mother had withdrawn somewhere, and Ilmari knew that she was hiding her tears. When the moment of departure arrived, she came into the foyer. Her eyes were wet, but she was trying to smile. She struggled against breaking down by vaguely imagining a Greek mother. Her consciousness groped for the words: "Return bearing your shield or borne upon it." But she was an ordinary Finnish mistress of a parsonage, and everything tender in her involved the boy. Her smile was twisted, and all she could say was:

"Well then..."

She could only sob as she sank into the boy's arms. He patted her shoulder gently with one hand and said:

"There's no cause to cry... there's no cause... goodbye."

Ilmari bade his father a quick farewell and hurried out. Having sat down in the sleigh, he turned to wave a hand at his parents, who had followed him out to the steps. The horse started off, but Ilmari commanded it to stop once more and shouted back:

"Goodbye. Everyone has to take leave of his Corsica."

The words came with a joyful vivacity, but his parents did not understand them. At this point they were incapable of any thought. The sled runners screeched on the cold snow and the sled disappeared from the lane of birches onto the road. It was still not fully light. The sky was completely overcast, but in the east a fire-red strip between the clouds and the horizon showed the dawn of a February day.

II

"Come and see, quick. There are two cars on Manor Hill."

People who were not at work, mainly wives and children, gathered timidly around the automobile. None of them had seen such a thing before, although they did know what it was. Around the automobiles stood a group of Russian officers, who were spreading out their maps. Talking rapidly, they kept pointing every which way. When some gentleman's hand happened by chance to point toward the spectators, they instinctively drew back a couple of steps as if they felt they were in the way.

"Manu's coming."

The Baron walked up to the officers and shook hands with them. The people heard the strange broken language that he exchanged with one of the officers and took it for Russian. A sheriff accompanied the officers, not the same one who had evicted Laurila, but a new one. He spoke in Swedish for a long time to the Baron, who then bowed and left. The officers began walking through the fields toward Kettumäki.

The drivers remained near the automobiles, and gradually the people approached them.

"They have those kind of rubber tires. They run on gasoline. Lauri Kivioja knows about them 'cause he saw them at the station."

Smiling, the uniformed drivers watched the townspeople. Soon there were smiles on both sides. One of the drivers said:

"Hallo... jemenlina... jemenlina."

"Hello, heh, heh..."

"Pentti Corner, Pentti Corner... road many gate? Ahead many gate?"

"He asks if there are many gates ahead. No gate, no gate. Big road, no gate. No moo, no moo."

The driver put his hands up like horns and mooed laughingly. One of the little boys who was bolder did the same. Then they had enough courage to move closer to the cars. One of the drivers suddenly pressed down on the car horn, although softly, with a careful look toward Kettumäki. It scared the people, but they kept gesturing to the driver to do it over. The horn sounded again, and the boys repeated:

"Beep beep."

"Beep beep. Avtomobil avtomobil."

"Automopiili beep beep."

Group after group of people gathered around the car. Only the little boys stayed in place. Lauri Kivioja had been at work in a far-off field, but his wife told him about the car when she took him his lunch, and Lauri's dropped both lunch and work. He rode up puffing and sweating on his bicycle. When he arrived, he threw his bicycle to one side and stepped up to the car, tossing his work mittens to the ground at the same time.

"Is it a goddamn Poojoe?... Morning."

"Hallo jemenlina..."

"Is it a Poojoe? It sure is. I guessed it right off."

Lauri circled the automobiles and the drivers watched him, half smiling and half wary, for Lauri tried the door handles and peered into the cars' interiors.

"I knew it by the radiator... by God, boys, when you push that lever the kilometer markers whizz by along the road... Wait till I look... yup... it's on the side..."

Lauri opened the door and sat in the driver's seat. Before the driver could stop him, he had pressed on the horn.

"Nyet, nyet... nyet... Polkovnik colonel."

The driver shoved Lauri's hand aside, pointing to Kettumäki and shaking his head.

"Polkovnik... let's go... let's drive a little way..."

The driver finally got Lauri to understand that he mustn't touch anything, but he let him sit in the car. And Lauri sat there the whole day, leaning easily against the seat and even changing cars on occasion. The drivers soon made friends with him, and they chatted in pidgin language, neither side actually understanding the other.

The officers returned and then Lauri had to leave the auto. The people drew back a little. The center of the group was a big-bellied, mustachioed officer whom the others seemed especially to respect. Once he looked at the villagers, and a playful smile came into his eyes. He snapped his fingers at a little boy and said:

"Raggy pants... baggy pants... shirt in tatters... mouth all milky..."

The people didn't really dare to laugh, and soon the officer's eyes resumed their thoughtful, veiled expression.

The officers did not enter the automobiles, but went into the manor instead. Soon the news spread that they were taking their meals there. The servants had scurried around all day plucking capons and fetching this and that from the orchard. An hour later, the officers emerged from the manor and the autos went on. Lauri raced after them on his bicycle and was able to keep up with the slowly moving vehicles. In early evening, the automobiles returned, driving faster this time, but with Lauri pedaling along after them. The people were still standing on the manor hill, and the big-bellied officer waved to them. Lauri pedaled along puffing in the dust cloud behind the last automobile. His foot occasionally slipped off from the side where a pedal was missing. As he passed the people Lauri shouted between gasps:

"I'll follow them to Tammikallio Hill and then let them go..."

Awhile later came a another shout, as if in explanation:

"...uphill..."

The officers turned to look back, and laughing, they waved at Lauri.

The next day, little boys ran along the roads with gloves on their hands, making vroom-vroom noises with their lips and shouting "Beep, beep," in between.

"There'll be a lot of work. The Russians are going to dig fortifications into that hill," said their parents.

III

But the work did not begin at once. Groups of officers with their maps and field glasses kept coming and traversing the hill. When the rumor spread that the work here would not begin until the following spring, many went to places where work was already in progress. Among them were the Laurila brothers and Oskari Kivivuori. The Koskela boys would also have gone, but Alma would not let them, even though work was scarce near home because logging was almost at a standstill. Aleksi could have gotten day-work at the parsonage, but Akseli had forbidden the boy to do so. It would have meant poor wages, and besides Akseli felt the family was better off with the fewest possible ties to the parsonage.

"It's enough that I'm a slave. The more of us there, the more power they have over us."

The boys stayed at home helping Akseli, taking day-work here and there. In early winter, Elina gave birth to another child. It was a boy too, and he was named Eero. He was born at the same time as Halme was freed from jail, and the tailor was asked to be the boy's godfather. Halme said very little about his imprisonment. He answered questions about it with general comments:

"Well, it was what one could expect. And what does it amount to — a few months? My predecessors in the history of the human spirit, whom I revere, ascended the scaffold or were burned alive."

40

The quietly smoldering tension of waiting for a decision on the tenant question also broke. The assembly had not been summoned, and the protection afforded by the law was to end in a year's time. Then a proclamation was issued by the Czar, extending the law for a five-year period. It was in this context that Akseli made his first public speech. He had to talk briefly on the subject at the Association meeting, but finding the words was difficult for him. He spent many days planning what to say, but it seemed that nothing would do. Of course he understood what the extension of the law meant, but still the matter had to be taken up with the Association. First Akseli read the text of the proclamation, and then he said, after hemming and hawing for a while:

"This being so, tenants can rest easy for another five years. The secret hope of the masters has missed its mark. They may try a little bit of secret hunting in the courts, but the big public hunt with the tooting of horns won't come off. Five years at least they have to keep their dogs chained, tongues hanging out and panting, the same dogs they sicked on us eight years ago in Laurila's yard. But I won't tell you to shout "Long live the Czar" for this because I have this idea about good manners: we say thank you only for gifts, and not for our rights."

When the people applauded vigorously, he coughed sternly in back of the table to keep his mind on course. It wasn't really proper to show his pleasure. After the meeting, a bit of self-assertiveness, perhaps even arrogance, appeared in him.

"Ahem... On the other hand, it is the masters' position, but are we to trust anything like that. For ten years now they've all been pushing this business of ours. For how many years now have the bourgeois, the Suometar crowd, the Young Finns, and even the Farmer's League been freeing us in this way and that way. The bourgeois are sweating over the tenant question, Paasikivi and Haataja are running in circles with it, but tell me why we're still left to depend on an illegal proclamation of the Czar. What damned land-rent committee can explain that to me. When I listen to all that talk, all I can think is that only the tenants are fighting the matter tooth and nail and all the others are worn out when it comes to freeing them. A lot has to happen before I start believing in fairy tales. I've been around for awhile now. I used to believe that there was a heaven behind those clouds, but as far as I know now, there's only empty air."

At home, he still paced the floor in a slightly pompous mood. Elina could see that he had come through the speech satisfied with himself and she asked:

"What did you tell them?"

"I didn't say much. I thought about Halme's way, he sort of talks in a way people can't catch on to. You don't need a lot of words. You only have to fire so as to hit the bulls-eye... Vilho, bring your father that paper."

The boy got the paper, and his father sat in the rocker, spreading it out. At times he would set the rocker in motion by pushing with the toe of his boot. Occasionally he uttered a scornful laugh.

"That's right... that's just it. Kyllinki sees how it is. If I could only get to tell them a few precious words, I'd tell those equal-rights-for-Russians men... What would it be like if we got right down to cases and said, now old man let's talk straight. No lying or beating around the bush. Let's just hear a few of the facts of life."

The words were ground out slowly to the accompaniment of the chair's rocking. The family did not hear them, for Elina was getting the food ready and Vilho was fooling around in the chimney corner with his father's work boots. He tried to put them on and managed to do so, but when he stood up, his little feet could not touch bottom and he fell over, whispering to himself:

"Doddamn."

As touchy and troublesome as the subject was, the pastor still had to bring it up. Striving for a calm and friendly tone of voice, he said:

"Our contract has been frozen for five years now, so as far as I'm concerned, it can stay as it is."

"Yes. That's what one hears... They say the Czar got nervous."

"Why didn't he summon the Parliament to take care of the matter?"

"I don't know... what it might be... Maybe he thought it wasn't worthwhile when they hashed it over for years and always killed the measure... thought he should settle it himself to prevent a real mess. It's not easy to take help from there... it's kind of a disgrace, but since there's no other way..."

The pastor stiffened and said curtly:

"Yes, the proclamation was made under illegal conditions, but it has to be considered binding in these circumstances."

"Well, it almost has to be... Though I don't know if he'll send soldiers to stop evictions if they kind of think they're illegal... But he probably will try to stop them somehow..."

The pastor said no more, but went on his way. Left alone, Akseli continued working and tried to think nasty thoughts:

"Go and trade mutton for raisins and rice with the storekeeper. Go and do your goddamned black marketeering, the two of you."

That was one more thing Akseli was bitter about. The storekeeper didn't dare to barter goods with an ardent socialist like him because the socialist newspapers attacked people for evading price controls. Scarcities of many commodities were gradually developing. Kerosene, soap, imported goods, and other such items were disappearing from the markets. There were few opportunities for black marketing at Koskela, for there were now eight people in the family, but still an occasional kilo of butter or a calf hide could have been traded for kerosene. Through the agency of Otto they got a little and Janne was able to arrange something for the worst scarcities, but the storekeeper would just laugh at Akseli:

"I tell you, not this time..."

The storekeeper and Vic Kivioja held secret whispered confabs, the nature of which Akseli soon learned, for Vic could not refrain from bragging to him:

"Listen boy. The finest doors open now if you knock at them with pigs' feet. Will the master have a cognac, they ask you. Took me in and looked at me and wondered. Gave me just a little bit. I told him if a pig was whining somewhere in Finland, then Vic would get it. He laughed like the devil and poured some more. He didn't drink himself, just looked and laughed. He called his wife in and she asked me to sing a folk song. I sang the one that goes, they struck me five times, every wound was bleeding, it was awful, it was awful... They spoke Swedish to each other and laughed. They warned me when I was leaving, but I told them this wasn't Vic's first time at the fair. Don't talk about this, I'll get you bar soap from the storekeeper. Even the big bins in this town open up. Jesus, boy, they talk about their eternal souls, but I tell you, Vic will buy them for a thousand marks. I mean, the choice ones. I'll get the common ones for lamp wicks."

Soon a thousand marks would be a small price for a soul. Both money and spirit kept shrinking in value. Little by little, even the last pittances from Jussi Koskela's life work vanished, without his having any control over the process. Restless and oppressed, Jussi pondered the matter, and since there was no hope, he took refuge in the one thing that was left to him.

"At least we have the cemetery plots. Thank God I bought them when I did. It was expensive land, but I don't regret it. Soon I wouldn't even have had that."

IV

The following spring, the work on the fortifications began, disrupting the everyday life of the community. A detachment of Russian soldiers was lodged in the fire hall and their young officers in the manor. The first few days were filled with hubbub and wonder.

"They're supposed to be some kind of sappers. Many of them were on the German front."

"They're putting up some kind of board kitchen outside the fire hall."

"By evening, the women were all over the place. They kept walking back and forth along the road. I told my old lady to go and try her luck too, but she said she was no match for schoolgirls any more."

The soldiers had in fact set up a kitchen in the yard of the fire hall. Little boys, who were the first to make friends with the soldiers, circled the kitchen, and the cheerful cook distributed left-over food to them. The child of many a hired hand or of men who worked for their room and board carried the food home in containers, for it meant more to them than just interesting and different food. They had a continual, gnawing hunger, which a diet of potatoes and the salt water drained from herring stew could not satisfy, in spite of its abundance. A timid barefoot girl, her cheeks gray, belly swollen, bones malformed by rickets, would appear at the kitchen. A soldier would fill her container with a ladle and the girl would trip off homeward in joyful haste. There was a piece of meat in her dish, and she did not hear the soldier shouting:

"Hallo to big sister."

Soon the soldiers were a part of the community's everyday life. Their brownish-gray uniforms were a familiar sight on the road and in the cabins. With gestures and in a few broken words, the people tried to talk to some soldier or other sitting on a bench, who in turn tried to explain:

"Kaluga, Kaluga. Me Kaluga."

"He means his name is Kaluga. Me Victor. Me Kivioja."

The soldiers seldom came to Koskela, and they soon stopped those visits when one of them, imitating a chicken's cackling, tried to buy eggs. Akseli responded harshly:

"Nyet."

The soldier could tell from Akseli's expression that he was not a welcome guest, and left. When word of Akseli's coldness spread among the soldiers, they stopped coming completely. Akseli did not actually feel any nationalistic hatred toward them, since his feelings were no more than an instinctive aversion, but he would say to his brother:

"Why do you go there and gawk at them? Our masters rule us with their bayonets. They're an ignorant bunch."

Halme's attitude was somewhat the same, although he made a distinction between officers and enlisted men. He would sometimes condescend to nod to the men, but he never greeted the officers. One young officer was proud of being in command of a separate detachment. Every Sunday morning, he carried out a kind of exhibition ride through the community, dressed in his best uniform and sitting in the saddle — spiritually as well as physically. Often Halme happened to meet him, and he would always turn his head aside or look through the officer with a vacant and distant look in his eyes. The behavior of this nicely aging gentleman who was graying at the temples annoyed the officer, especially when he was forced to admit after each encounter that Halme's indifference was more genuine than his own.

When he heard from the baron that the man in question was the community tailor, he was confused. On their next meeting, a benevolent smile played about his lips; he had indeed misjudged the old man.

Now there was money to be had. It came from work and from payments for room and board, for outside workers came to the community in addition to the soldiers. Osku Kivivuori and the Laurila brothers also returned home.

Otto Kivivuori soon became a man of importance at the fortification site. He had a large group of contract workers and was able to get the best work for them. Some whispered that he had secret deals with the engineering officer who supervised the work, but Otto laughed at such talk and said:

"It's envy talking."

The Koskela brothers were in his crew, along with Elias Kankaanpää. Elias was a poor worker, but Otto mischievously set him to keeping the rhythm for men who were hammering a drill or pile-driver. And Elias sang, songs that all said the same thing with innumerable variations. He had a pleasant voice and a good ear for music, and his rhythmic song could be heard far off on the road, accompanied by the thump of sledges wielded by Osku and Akusti as Aleksi held the drill for them ..."and the boy asked for the price of the boots and the woman told him..."

Some of the women worked there too. Elma Laurila, a dark-browed girl just turned seventeen, worked at shoveling out a trench along with her brother, silencing the men's attempts at indecency with her blunt answers. The boys were much taken with her mainly because they saw something promising in her bluntness and shamelessness. Because of her behavior, they could think of her in only one way, even though she could be quite nice looking, especially when she smiled. She had a pretty mouth, but it often seemed tinged with bitterness. The carelessness of her dress spoiled her outward appearance, for she could not dress herself and Aliina was not much better at it. The boys, however, were mistaken in her. She often left a dance or a gathering place with an escort, but quarrels easily developed along the way, and she might very well tell her escort to go to hell.

Aku Koskela tried along with the rest, but the girl mocked him as she had the others, or loosed an obscenity with obvious intent. Sometimes, though, she would secretly eye Aku. If they happened to be near one anoth-

er, she would lean on her shovel and watch the boy when he wasn't looking. She was slightly cross-eyed, which always showed up when she was
looking at something and thinking. As she watched Aku, her dark eyes
would cross and peer searchingly from under her brows while her mouth
would purse itself as an indication of thoughtfulness.

Then she would spit on her hands manfully and start shoveling.

Aku noticed this attention and it awakened a slightly conceited pleasure
in him. Sometimes he thought he saw attractive things in the girl, but that
state of mind soon vanished when Elias shouted something between songs
to Elma, and she answered:

"Shut your shitty mouth, Kankaanpää."

High Kettumäki Hill had itself become a gathering place for the young.
They no longer went to the workers' hall, and Halme complained about the
members' no longer paying their dues and then surreptitiously leaving the
Association. Nevertheless they worked hard with Akseli during the summer
elections. Halme gave a speech and Akseli distributed campaign literature
to the people where they worked, on Kettumäki, and even to passers-by on
the road. On election day, he actually drove the indifferent to vote.

"What the devil good is it, when the legislature won't be called to meet
anyway? And what has the legislature ever done?"

"You have to go. We don't know what will come of it. Damn it, everybody just lets things ride. We have to try to do something."

As if in recompense, the legislature got a socialist majority, but many
laughed about the whole thing and went to play cards on Kettumäki.

Aku went there too, in spite of his mother's and father's prohibitions.
Aku was the liveliest of the brothers and the best at doing a ring dance. He
had his mother's brown eyes, and when he let them wander a little, girls
fluffed up their hair if he happened to look their way. Jussi grumbled angrily about the boy's running around and Alma asked him to stay at home in
her quiet way. But his mother melted at a wink or two and gazed with pleasure at the boy dressed in his Sunday clothing, who would some day be a
"good-looking man" as she put it.

Aleksi fulfilled his parents' hopes completely, perhaps a little too completely, in Alma's view. He never went anywhere in the evening. Quiet,
orderly, and industrious, he lived to himself, never giving anyone trouble or
causing them any offense. He was quite thrifty, and when Akseli paid his
debt, the boy said soberly:

"You could let it go now, if you're in a bind. There's no hurry about it."

But nevertheless he took the money with obvious pleasure, smoothing it
out and counting it when he was alone. Sometimes he gave Alma a little
extra along with the food money. It always happened in the same way.

Passing by, the boy would take his mother's hand in his own, press the notes into her hand, close her fingers around them, and then go his way without a word.

"Well, thanks, but it's not necessary."

Aleksi had a good and plentiful wardrobe. He enjoyed having clothing made but wore it carefully and sparingly. On Saturday evening he too dressed in his best suit and leather boots. But when his younger brother went to town, he stayed at home. Aku went to the old place through the yard, where Vilho might be standing somewhere near the steps like a little statue. Vilho would ask:

"Uncle Aku?"

"What is it?"

"Where are you going?"

"I'm going to Yllö's to chop potato stalks."

"With what?"

"I'm not saying."

If Elina happened to hear this dialogue, she snatched the boy up into her lap and took him inside. Nevertheless Vilho was very much attached to Aku, because out of all the men in the family, his own father included, his uncle devoted the most time to him. He made wooden horses for him, sometimes carried him on his back, and if there wasn't time for anything else, gave a tug at the boy's flaxen hair as he passed by.

After Aku had left, Aleksi too went out for a walk. But he never went beyond the perimeter of the yard. He would stand for a long time gazing toward the swamp, the woods, the roof of the threshing barn, the doorway, the steps, or whatever caught his interest. Shifting his position, he would look at the same things from a different point of view. Walking over to the shed of the threshing barn, he would stand there looking at the familiar working tools. It was a pleasure to look at them when dressed in his holiday clothes after coming from the sauna, as if the day of rest thereby gained a greater significance. Gently he touched the handle of the shovel with his fingertips, the same shovel he grasped with all his strength on weekdays, tossing thousands of heavy shovelfuls one after another.

When Akseli and Elina had come from the sauna, Aleksi sat there spending the Saturday evening. Legs spread open, he sat on the bench, occasionally tapping the toes of his shiny boots on the floor or brushing off an imaginary spot from their tops. There he would talk to Akseli, now back from the sauna, about work and sometimes about politics, agreeing in his quiet way with his older brother's assertions:

"Yes, if you think that nothing can be got for the right price, then it's good that wages have gone up by a half."

When the family got ready for bed, Aleksi left. In the yard, he repeated the procedure of standing and looking. On the steps, he listened for a time to the muddled shouts from the town. Then the door of the new place creaked.

The lonely man's evening had ended.

V

At the parsonage, life in the village was frowned upon. The "barracks" were suspect, as well as Kettumäki. After Ilmari's departure for Germany, the pastor's wife had stiffened in her attitude toward the Russians, especially inasmuch as her husband's tendency toward compliance had suffered a final defeat and there was no longer a conflict between them. He was that much more angry on seeing the girls of the village hanging on the arms of soldiers. Aune Leppänen had a "steady boyfriend" who openly visited the Leppänens'. The pastor's wife seethed with rage. Meeting Aune with her "Tiiham" on the road, she could not control her expression. Aune noticed it, and from behind her back, the pastor's wife heard:

"Aah, ha, ha, ha."

The wife urged her husband to reprimand Aune.

"You not only have the right to do it, it's your duty. Why do you ask questions about sin among sectarians on reading days when you let it happen before your very eyes?"

"Yes, yes... I have the right to reprimand anyone in the congregation. But I can't regard her as more sinful than the rest. It would be bad to single out one person."

"Well then, wait until she brings a child into the world. A child may well be involved, and the child of a Russian at that."

The pastor did not yield. It would have been too disagreeable. He did preach against depravity on Sunday, but on his way from church, he was often forced to drive through a group of men who worked on the fortifications standing on the road. The clatter of wheels prevented him from hearing what they said as he drove by, but he could easily guess the nature of the talk.

After having given birth to a boy, whom she named Valtu, Aune had been frightened for a while. The boy's appearance did not reveal his paternity, for he clearly took after the Leppänens. But with the arrival of the soldiers, Aune reverted to her old ways. At first she had several "handsome soldier boys" but before long a Corporal Tihon became her regular boy friend. "Tiiham," who was quite a rogue, half lived at the Leppänens'. Sometimes he would even drink with Preeti. Aune fed little Valtu with morsels she bit off from a Russian rye bread, while Preeti, mellowed by drink, talked with his "son-in-law":

"The girl is one good worker. Especially at outside jobs. Our boy is in America. He's a temperance man there, a craftsman. I've got nothing against it, we all live the same kind of life in every country, so if the girl is willing..."

Tihon knew only a few words of Finnish, so he understood very little of Preeti's talk. He wore a decoration, and when Henna wondered at it, he began to explain why he had gotten it. In his story, he showed with gestures how the Leppänens' bench was a bridge, Preeti's old boot an explosive charge, and a piece of hempen twine a fuse. Then he showed how the Germans had come, and he had lighted the fuse and fled. A bullet had hit his elbow, and Tiiham showed them a nearly fresh scar. Henna marveled at it, and Preeti jabbered away half dozing.

"Yeah, but when there are even five angry pigs in a pen, it's a bad place to go. My father was a hired hand at Korri, and he did."

Having fed the boy, Aune petted and hugged him hurriedly.

"Mummy's sleepyhead... little sleepyhead, looking at mummy so wisely."

Putting the boy down on the floor, she adjusted her blouse and otherwise spruced up her clothes, for she and Tiiham were going to the village. On leaving, Sapper Corporal Tihon Privalihin snapped to a thunderous attention and Preeti answered by laboriously raising two fingers to the temples of his sleepily nodding head. Sitting on the floor, the thin, pale-faced child, who was just learning to speak, said:

"Mama... soldier... went."

"Yes, mama and soldier went. Valtu sit there. Grandpa's boy. Grandpa will take care of Valtu."

Aune and Tihon went to Kettumäki. In the village others could be seen on the way there. Even Arvi Laurila was standing on a corner with a new bicycle between his legs. He did not usually go to Kettumäki or even to the village except sometimes on a Sunday at noon. At home he had been forbidden to keep company with the village boys, and once that was known, no one would say a word to him. He stood alone for awhile at the corner, rang his bicycle bell a couple of times, then went home again, where he wiped his bicycle clean of dust and carried it into the main entry, where its bright colors gleamed all week long.

Aune and Tihon caught up with Aku Koskela, who laughingly exchanged a few Russian words with Tihon. There was a crowd of people on the hill: villagers, fortification workers, and Russian soldiers. Most of the people on the open ridge felt they belonged to a better class. There they did ring dances. Farther off in the thickets were the card players and the drinking crowd, those considered to be of dubious reputation. Something out of the ordinary was going on this evening, for the boys whispered at once to Aku.

"There's a woman here who does it for money. She's making out well. Let's go and see her."

"She's with Uuno's crew. Vänni brought her from somewhere. She's a real whore. If you didn't know till now what that is, you'll soon see."

Akusti didn't think it right to show too much interest. The girls were proud, and answered the boys' advances by saying:

"Go there. We're nothing... there you'll find what suits you."

Rumor had it that the prostitute was drunk. Osku Kivivuori had gone to see her, and he was declaring loudly:

"The talk about money losing its value is no lie if they're telling the truth about what she charges."

First one and then another went to see, for although they had often heard talk about prostitutes, few of them had seen one. Finally Akusti went too, curious although a little embarrassed. The woman was sitting near a card-playing group, among them Uuno Laurila and a man called Vänni. No one knew whether the latter was a family name or the alteration of some first name. There were also a few strangers from the fortification crew in the group. Aku squatted down to follow the play, but began to look furtively at the prostitute. It was hard to tell her age. She was bareheaded, and the bun of her hair made from a thick braid was half undone. Her eyes were large and dark brown; their rims seemed almost bloody. The edges of her large eyeballs showed the marks from broken blood vessels. She wore her clothes carelessly, and the hem of her dress had risen so high it revealed the garter above her knee. She had trouble with her *r*'s when she spoke, laughed a noisy drunken laugh, and called the card-players com...*r*...ades."

"Lau...*r*...ila's boy lost."

Although Aku tried to study the prostitute on the sly, she noticed it, smiled, and winked at him:

"Take a good look, sonny."

Aku blushed in embarrassment, which made the prostitute burst into a broken laugh that shook her whole body. Aku tried to smile and the prostitute said:

"Nice brown-eyed sonny-boy. Innocent eyes. I like that kind of eyes."

Vänni, who had lost his wager, threw his card angrily onto the deck and said in passing:

"Lead him not into temptation, or you'll have to deliver the boy from evil."

Aku was getting more and more embarrassed, for Vänni's arrogant scorn of his shyness and inexperience were apparent in the man's words. But they made the prostitute angry and her face took on a serious look:

"Shut your mouth. I'm not talking to you, I'm talking to sonny-boy. I like this sonny-boy. Come on sonny, I'll pat you on the cheek. Just a little, don't be afraid. You have innocent eyes... I like innocent eyes. Come here sonny. I like you because you're so sweet that you blush. You have fine feelings. D'you know what I like? I like fine feelings, but these buddies of mine can go sniff shit."

Another spasm of laughter followed. Even Uuno looked at the prostitute and although he was angry at having lost so much at the game, he gave a transient laugh:

"Well, of all things!"

"What'd you say, Lau...r...ila's boy? Gimme a drink, Goddamn."

Uuno gave her the bottle and watched in delight as she tilted it back and drank. Vänni, who had also been losing, snapped irritably:

"Don't guzzle it all down. You're gulping half a bottle at a time."

"Those are nice words to say to a woman. Goddammed flunky."

The prostitute spoke in a highly indignant tone of voice. When Aku saw that she had forgotten about him, he left. It did not feel as if he were running away.

Nevertheless, the prostitute noticed his departure and said with still another wink:

"Sweet sonny boy."

Aku went back to the hill, where a few soldiers were singing a Russian folk song accompanied by one of them on a stringed instrument. Plaintive melodies sung by the deep and slightly coarse soldiers' voices echoed in the summer night. When they had finished, some of them began to urge the player:

"Nikolai, do a little bit of *jeekeli naakeli stoorje...*"

Nikolai played, and Arvi Laurila clapped his hands to the rhythm as he had seen the soldiers doing. At the end of the song, Nikolai began to make playful gestures to the girls, asking them to dance. When Arvi noticed, he grabbed one of the girls by the hand and led her to Nikolai.

"Nikolai, plituski plituski... You know how to play, it's the best way to get the girls."

The girl tried to tear herself loose, and Arvi let go of her. Making obscene gestures with his hands and pointing to the girl, he said to Nikolai:

"Nikolai, plituski... like this, zig, zig."

The girl slapped Arvi across the face and half-ran away from Kettumäki, her head hung in shame. Her friends began to scold Arvi, but the boys laughed. Arvi, angry at being slapped, ran after the girl, cursing roughly. Enraged, he at first intended to strike back, but hearing the laughter, he stopped doubtfully. He was not sure what the laughter was directed at, his gestures or the slap he had taken. Anger and a half-stupid joy alternated in his mind, depending upon what he judged to be the cause of the laughter. Finally deciding that it stemmed from his words, he had a fit of joy, let out a bellowing laugh himself, and looked around for something to vent his happiness on. Seeing a large stone nearby, he rushed over to it, grabbed its corners, and hoisted it up, bawling out at the same time:

"Work is a man's honor and a big ass is a woman's."

That brought another raucous burst of laughter. Elma, who was standing in the group, drew back quietly, looking away. Nikolai, who did not understand the cause of the merriment, got carried away too, and began to do a few Cossack dance steps to his own accompaniment. His comrades began to sing, keeping time by clapping hands. Arvi, seeing that Nikolai was drawing the group's interest away from him, began himself to do a few gawky dance steps. Clapping his hands, he sang:

On the bridge at Kymijoki, Tildy played penny poker too.
Yelled out to all the lumberjacks, ain't I one o' your crew?

Then they changed their way of having fun. The young men held a minor competition in chinning themselves and some even wrestled. Vänni, who had lost all his money and left the card game, was watching the wrestlers. He kept saying with a dry arrogance:

"Wrong hold."

Irritated by the tone of his voice, the boys began urging one of the bigger workman to wrestle with him. The man, who had been christened Little Kalle by someone with a simple-minded sense of humor, did not want to, but in his childish good will, he was easy to persuade.

Kalle would laugh into his hands in embarrassment, then look speculatively at Vänni, raise his rear end from the rock as if to get up, and then sit back down again. Finally he came forward.

Vänni stood in a crouch, moving his body in an exaggeratedly tigerish fashion, his hands ready crooked for a hold. He glared at Kalle from under his brows, waiting for him to make a move. Kalle stepped back and forth nervously. He was still laughing in embarrassment, but suddenly he sucked in his breath, and with fear giving him extra energy, he rushed forward and pushed Vänni in the chest with his huge palms. Vänni fell on his back. Kalle drew back as if in flight and kept repeating between tension and joy:

"I can't wrestle at all. I just push like that."

Vänni got up.

"We were supposed to wrestle, buddy. If we're going to start shoving, we might as well go a little further."

A helpless smile appeared on Kalle's face when the others too began to demand a proper wrestling match. Sober-faced, he let himself be grappled and the wrestling began. Vänni tried to apply holds he had learned somewhere, but Kalle understood nothing of that. The two fell to the ground. Kalle understood enough of wrestling to keep his shoulders off the ground, so he turned Vänni underneath him. The latter held out on his hands and knees for a time, but 110 kilos of muscle soon vanquished him and he lay pinned. Kalle broke away panting with joy and shock as if he had just gotten a bucket of cold water on his neck.

"You all saw it was right... I can't wrestle... but his shoulders got wet... you all saw it."

Vänni rose and took two angry steps toward Kalle. Black rage twisted his face, but he controlled himself.

"I don't admit losing. I mean, it wasn't fair. I was wrestling a pig's carcass and not a wrestler. I don't admit losing."

Kalle sat on his rock and said in his slightly shrill, childish voice:

"I can't wrestle... but his shoulders got wet. I didn't promise anything else."

Vänni looked at him with angry contempt and said as he went back to the card players:

"If I had your strength and my character, I wouldn't be sitting with a rock up my ass. I would be doing wonders."

"Heh, heh, I can't wrestle. I just turned him over like that... like I said, like that."

Brushing the dirt from his hands, Kalle shifted his rear end on the rock. He kept trying to shape his lips into a whistle, but stopped when he noticed a rock on the ground that weighed some ten kilos. He picked it up and started tossing it in one hand like some kind of ball.

"Like I said... like..."

Then a young man stepped to the smooth-packed ring-dance ground and began to sing, clapping his hands:

"Dark blue was the ship and yellow was its door..."

He had built up a head of steam for the purpose, but when the others did not join in, his solo exhibition began to wear on him. To cover it up, he stamped vigorously on the ground in time with the song and reached out for the others, urging them to join him.

"You are rich and I am poor and we don't go together..."

Gradually the ring dance developed. Akusti chose Elma Laurila and she in turn chose him. Arvi's recent performance had the effect of making Elma toss her head more scornfully than usual. Aku tried to talk about many things, but got only nasty comments in reply. Still the boy kept trying, for the prostitute, in spite of her grossness, had set his imagination to work. Her comments about his eyes also caused him to roll them noticeably.

"Could I go home by way of Laurilas' tonight?"

"Go ahead, if it's so early that Antto isn't asleep."

"No, just the opposite. We won't go until he is asleep."

"Go whenever you want, as far as I'm concerned."

But when Elma watched Aku circling in the dance during her pauses, her eyes crossed. Then she suddenly looked at her clothes, closed an open snap on her blouse, and brushed a spot on her dress. She stepped stiffly backward a couple of paces, as if fleeing the sight of her stained dress front. When Aku repeated his suggestions the next time, Elma said, looking away:

"I'm not going with Alma Koskela's precious boy. People might talk."

Aku ignored the remark, blushing and trying to think of something to say. Their courting tradition required a certain readiness of tongue, and they tried their best to uphold it, even though half forcedly. Elma's roundabout consent came at last.

"Go ahead to Laurila. I can't stop anyone from using the highway."

Aku became too enthusiastic. He gave Elma a meaningful squeeze, whereupon she said with a veiled look of anger in her eyes:

"You think you're some kind of masseur? I'm not for sale and I don't want Koskela's precious boy to think so."

In the middle of the ring dance, Elias Kankaanpää ran out of the woods, his face pale:

"A bicycle, quick, has anybody got a bicycle. A doctor... Uuno hit him badly."

When he realized that no one there had a bicycle, he ran on at full speed, shouting to let the others know the thought engraved in his own mind:

"To Kivioja... Lauri can go..."

The people understood from Elias's words that something unusual had happened and the whole gang rushed to see. Uuno Laurila stood in an opening among small trees, and a few steps away lay Vänni, with a man kneeling by his side. Those rushing up heard him say to Uuno:

"You hit him in a bad place."

"No, just where I should have."

After the wrestling, Vänni had gone back to the group playing cards. He had squatted down behind Uuno and said:

"You drew wrong, buddy."

Uuno had lost a lot, and hissed angrily:

"Keep your goddammed trap shut about another man's playing."

Vänni was still angry because of what had recently happened and hissed a reply, but the quarrel was interrupted when Uuno resumed playing. He laid down the last of his money, but when another still raised him, he took out his watch:

"Will this meet your bid?"

"What make is it?"

"It doesn't tell you its name, it only tells the time. I guess it's a Junghans."

The man accepted the watch as meeting his bid and showed his hand. Uuno paled slightly, but put his cards under the deck and said in an unnaturally calm voice:

"It's yours. Pick it up."

"Laurila's boy is cleaned out," said the prostitute.

"Stop babbling, you whore."

The prostitute spat out something, but Uuno paid no more attention to her. He turned toward Vänni:

"It's my game, you bum. I mean, a buddy wouldn't keep bugging me about it."

Vänni threw back his shoulders and muttered:

"Don't, don't... Don't you try it, you hear. Look, don't you try it, you hear. Look, you're not a big enough boy."

"Goddammed blackmouth. You need your head smoothed out a little. And what are you doing here anyway? You should have stayed where penniless bums belong. You damned warehouse rat..."

Uuno stood with his hands in his pockets, arms pressed tightly to his sides, his body weaving easily back and forth. Then he took his hands from his pockets and struck. His blows were fluid and controlled, one after another. There was no wasted motion; the blows were short but powerful. Vänni staggered back unable to resist. Then a knife flashed in his hand. He lashed out with it but missed, and Uuno dodged backward a couple of steps. Vänni followed and said:

"Listen, there's a few accounts been read on the walls of hell."

Uuno drew his own knife from its sheath. His words came through lips pressed into a thin line:

"Is that so now?"

He struck quickly and Vänni staggered a few steps before he fell. As he did, a few unclear words came from his mouth:

"...you hit... on the sly... man..."

One of the men leaned over Vänni and spoke the words that the first to reach the place heard. Elias, who had been with a nearby group, had seen what had happened, and left quickly to find a doctor. He sensed that Vänni's staying alive would mean much to Uuno's sentence.

The frightened prostitute rose and paced back and forth repeating:

"Tell them, com...*r*...ades, that I wasn't he...*r*...e... I wasn't he...*r*...e. When the cops come, tell them I wasn't he....*r*...e. Remember com...*r*... ades, tell them."

Then she started off swaying unsteadily. Her button shoe slipped on one foot so that she almost fell, but she was able to catch hold of an alder branch. As the group of people walked by, she said manfully:

"Tampe...*r*...e's playboy got killed, goddamn."

When Elma arrived and understood the situation, she pressed her face into her hands and, head bowed, set off running swiftly for home. Aku watched her go, and felt a sort of relief rise into his mind, which became crystallized into a few uncertain words:

"...good I didn't... get to go... the talk..."

Uuno sat on a stump looking away from the body. The circle of people approached him. A few women could be heard screaming faintly. Arvi looked at the nearest faces as if seeking guidance on what attitude to assume. When none was clearly evident, he said brashly but still a little uncertainly:

"One in the coffin and the other in chains, goddamn."

When no one laughed, he too became serious. Some of the men stepped nearer, and one of them asked, with a kind of expert authority in his voice:

"Is he done for or what?"

The man who had knelt by the body stood up, wiped his hands on the grass, and said:

"The boy is done for, all right. The stuff coming out below his heart is like berry pudding."

Now the mood was one of somber exaltation. People spoke in soft, muffled voices. Uuno sat there morosely, but now and then he looked at the people, staring them straight in the eye without flinching. The Russian soldiers spoke rapidly in their own language, pointing now at Uuno and now at the body.

The doctor was the first to arrive. People backed off, but as the doctor checked the body, they drew near again.

"Is he badly hurt?" asked a respectful voice.

Behind the doctor's gold-rimmed eyeglasses gleamed the coldly supercilious look of a professional man, but he said nothing. He handled Vänni's clothing cautiously with his fingertips, as if afraid of getting his hands dirty. He looked at Uuno a few times with interest and finally asked:

"Are you the one who stabbed him?"

"You take care of him and the police will take care of me. Don't meddle in things that are none of your business."

A look of irritated scorn appeared on the doctor's face. He laughed as he said:

"Ah-ha, ha... exactly."

Elma had reached home, and Father-Antto arrived on the scene. He looked at his son and at the body and said bitterly:

"Well then."

Turning toward the people, he said:

"Aren't you men enough to take knives away from boys?"

Someone tried to explain, but Antto left, grim and sullen, without so much as a glance at his son sitting on the stump. When a policeman arrived, Uuno stood up. The policeman asked him to give up his knife and Uuno loosed it from his belt, sheath and all. Then he slammed it violently into the policeman's open palm.

The men who were on the spot were ordered to appear in the village for questioning the next day, and the doctor and Lauri Kivioja were charged with removing the body.

"Lauri isn't afraid of the dead."

The policeman asked Uuno if he wanted to stop at home, but Uuno said shortly:

"I always have everything with me."

Hands in his pants pockets and shoulders thrown slightly back, he walked away before the policeman saying:

"We're off."

Aliina and Elma were waiting on the road by the manor. Aliina had a lunch wrapped in pages of the *People's Press* under her arm. She gave it to Uuno, and said with an attempt at harshness:

"So at last..."

The boy took the package, and seeing the tears in his mother's eyes, he growled bluntly:

"The less squalling the better."

Aliina handed Uuno a few twenty-mark notes.

"Here you are, since you lost your own at cards..."

The policeman stood to one side leaning on his bicycle.

"Those hills are some place..."

Aliina's lips tightened. She broke into a torrent of abuse at the police-man:

"You yourselves bring crowds like this to these hills... and you have the nerve to come and bawl us out. Better if you set traps for those bootleggers, but you're in on their schemes. You make wars and rob and collect crowds like this... and then you come and shoot off your mouth."

The policeman controlled himself and said stiffly:

"Jaaha, say what you have to say. We have to go now."

Uuno turned and left:

"Bye then. And I tell you once more, there's no point in crying over me."

Aliina was left standing in the road. Elma ran a few steps after the two but then stopped and returned to her mother's side, sobbing quietly. Together they set off for home. Mute, a fixed expression on her bony, angular face, Aliina walked along, crumpling in her fist the money the boy had refused to take.

Lauri Kivioja got a horse to take the body away. The people began to shake off their somber mood, and Lauri blustered as he lifted the body onto the wagon with the aid of some other men:

"I tell you nobody ever made it from Pentti's Corners to the church village as fast as I did... And goddamn, before Elkku even finished talking I was on my Olympia, out the gate, and on the road."

He handled the body callously, and when he drove off, he roared out:

"Well, well, my madcap. This is your last good ride. Lauri will drive you to lie under the cross so fast your head will bounce... Heyah, goddamn gelding, let 'er rip, let's go to town."

The hum of talk and chatter immediately became more animated. Arvi stood in the center of the group and showed how one struck with a knife.

"Like this —point into the lungs. Drive it home like Jukka Hanssi."

Little Kalle explained to everyone in his shrill voice:

"I didn't... I didn't, but I thought if they wanted... What do I know about wrestling, but I just turned him like this. I was waiting for him to draw a knife if he got mad. He came toward me like that... I was just fooling around and turned him. What do I know about wrestling, just a little boy, heh, heh, but I turned him under me like this, like I said, like..."

The soldiers asked as much as they could about the event, and they were told:

"The *puukko*, the Finn stabs with it... That's how it is, boys, Finnish kids are born with a *puukko* in their hands. We're the kind, by God, that won't take much ribbing before the blade bites... See here goddammit, Prohori — you might have been on the German front, but here every hill is a front."

"Finnski *puukko*... goddamn goddamn..."

"Finnski knife goddamn."

The talk became more and more expert in tone. One of the fortification workmen who was on the scene said:

"But he was a goddamned smooth boy. I haven't seen anyone stabbed that neatly for a long time. It was like a lightning flash. I've seen this and that, but you rarely see a stabbing that's such a treat to the eye."

That put an end to the meetings on Kettumäki. People came to view the scene over and over. For a time, the black stain of blood could be seen on the trampled grass until the magpies had pecked it clean. The older people in the village told each other with malicious glee:

"Those things will happen when you spend your time like that."

At Koskela, his mother and father warned Aku and passed judgment on the Laurila bunch. They did not know of Aku's attempt to keep company with Elma, and he himself thought it better to stay away from the girl. Although the young men of the group spoke half admiringly of Uuno, the reputation of a murderer cast such a light over the whole Laurila family that from then on Aku did not approach Elma even secretly. His older brother said curtly, with regard to his visits to the village:

"If you can't find better company than the world's bums and drudges, then it's best to be alone."

At thirty-three, Akseli had already adopted a rigidly moralistic view of such gadding about. It was due in part to the bitterness he felt because people, especially the young, were leaving the association, but the fact that such behavior had not suited him helped a good deal in setting his attitude. Aku tried to evade his brother's judgment with a few jokes, but they didn't help.

"You could look at a newspaper sometimes. And there are some of the party's fliers so that you could begin to understand the workers' cause like Aleksi."

"A sledge and a shovel will teach you to know the workers' cause better than those fliers of yours. And it's only ten years ago that you were going to the village yourself."

"Yah, but I wasn't going to any hills. And with a crowd like that. I guess you see that now."

"You just hung around the Kivivuori corners."

"I hung around where I hung around."

Uuno got a five-year sentence, which some thought was too stiff.

"The other one had his knife out too."

For a long time, little boys went around with knives at their belts. If they did not have a real one, they made one of wood. Standing face to face, one would say to another:

"A few accounts have been read on the walls of hell."

"Is that so now?"

Then they would strike with the blade forward, but just before the blow landed, they would turn the dagger so that the other end struck. At the same time they would pinch their pal's breast with the thumb and forefinger of the hand holding the dagger. Sometimes real fights arose.

"I'm Uuno."

"No, I am. You can be Vänni. I've already been him many times."

The knives were put away, and they battled in other ways. For all of them wanted to be the knifer and say cold and drily: "Is that so now?"

The people from Pentti's Corner were glad to go to the church village after the event. For a little while it was as though they were better people when they were explaining to the church villagers what had happened. Vic Kivioja stood up on his wagon in the middle of the churchyard holding his restless horse and shouting to the men standing around:

"Easy there... Did you hear? It's what he said... the man said that he never saw such a pretty stroke... he said it was just a treat to watch... he's quite a boy, all right. He's a smooth worker, but he's still better at stabbing."

On the way home, Victor himself was carried away in spite of his age. He whipped the horse into a run, spread the reins, and when he was near people's houses, he began to sing:

> *Five times they struck me, blood ran from every wound,*
> *how horrible it was, how horrible it was...*
> *And when father brought home a new mother, the start*
> *   of this boy's sorrow...*

"Heyah, goddamn, let 'er rip."

After all, a man had been killed at Pentti's Corner.

CHAPTER THREE

T he March sun shone through the window into the main room at Koskela. It fell upon the fire burning in the fireplace, making it look pale and colorless. The remains of one of Elina's twig brooms still burned on the coals, hissing because of their freshness. A few broom handles had been kept to make a collar-bow for Vilho's wooden horse.

The man of the house lay on his bed taking a mealtime nap. It had become a habit with him, as it had been with Jussi. Stretching out for a short time was part of a tenant's daily routine, a moment sacred to father, during which even the boys dared not ask anything. Even Eero knew it, although he was not yet two years old.

Elina, who was working on something at the window by the table, interrupted Akseli's rest:

"What brings Halme here now, in the middle of a weekday?"

Akseli awakened from his stupor. Halme could be heard wiping his feet in the entry, and then the door opened. The master wore his good overcoat with the velvet collar. On his head was his best hat, a peaked Crimean lambskin. He shook hands courteously with Elina, for he seldom saw her. As was his habit, he made a polite comment:

"And here you are, working away, just as beautiful as ever."

Elina laughed with pleasure, although she knew the master's words were purely conventional. Akseli sat up on the side of the bed. Standing in the center of the floor with his hat in hand, Halme turned toward him. There was a ceremonious look about him, and when he spoke, he seemed to be addressing the whole room:

"Get up and get dressed. You must go to the workers' hall at once. We have to hold a meeting to prepare ourselves. I came myself to bring the word, since I wanted to be the one to tell you that Nicholas II is no longer Czar of Russia and much less the Archduke of Finland. The steeds of revolution are trotting through the streets of St. Petersburg."

"No... hell no... that can't be."

"Do you think I come running over here just to make jokes?"

Akseli had spoken in astonishment and doubt. Just to be sure, he asked again, afraid that the master was joking after all:

"Are you sure it's true?"

"Hellberg has been in Helsinki for two days, and he phoned Silander. I've also talked to him personally. The fact that such talk is possible should verify the matter."

"That's it then. 'No other ruler or lord than the almighty people... '"

Akseli rose. Exuberantly he tossed each boy into the air in turn and went to get his Sunday clothes. He changed in the presence of the others, for he could not wait to ask the master more about affairs. Halme was, if possible, in an even more jubilant state of mind. He explained what he knew, and sketched out possible consequences.

"In any case, the saber senate will have to go. Deep down I was always sure of this. I am in great debt to those periods of silence that I have observed at night, when I hear a mysterious voice assuring me that the kingdom of the spirit is coming. I can't help talking about these things, although it may annoy you... I can assure you, however, that 'there are more things in heaven and earth than are dreamt of in your philosophy.' But whatever the case, we must, in any event, get the people together and let them know. If any countermeasures are taken, we will be ready. The more informed public opinion is, the harder it will be to put such measures into effect."

Vilho was sent to take the news to the new place, and it brought every-one over. Seldom was there such a buzz of talk in the main room at Koskela. At first Jussi couldn't really understand that there was a power in the world that could bring czars and archdukes to their knees. When he was finally forced to believe it, he said:

"Hmmh... Then the money will be good for nothing."

Both of the women in the family had always stayed clear of politics, but this was something else, and little Vilho had to tug energetically at his mother's skirts to get her attention:

"Mummy, mummy."

"What is it?"

"Close the damper. The fire will go out."

"That boy... he notices everything. We'll lose the heat in all this hub-bub."

Aku and Aleksi were sent to spread word of the meeting, and Halme left with Akseli to make ready a report and get further information if possible. The revolution was not a complete surprise, for all kinds of rumors had been heard recently. Because of them Hellberg had set off for Helsinki. But nevertheless, the fulfillment of their hopes had electrified their minds. When Halme and Akseli set out, the demeanor of the former was more solemn and dignified than usual. Developments in matters of state always affected his speech and gestures, for he felt them with his entire body and soul. He patted the boys lovingly, but they avoided his attentions. As chil-dren, they were quick to sense the slight insincerity in them. Halme was always exaggeratedly friendly, but something in his behavior smacked of formality and ulterior motives, and he could not deceive the children.

He said to Elina with a smile:

"I ask your pardon for taking your man again, but 'Base is the farmer now, who will not leave his plow....' I would hope to see you at a meeting some time, although to tell the truth, you are a pretty sight among your children."

The master often demonstrated a special courtesy to Elina, adopting an avuncular demeanor toward her. Then he hemmed and grew serious.

"Aha. 'Silent, our country awaits; time stands and holds the flag.' Till we meet again. Let's go."

The family watched from the window as they left, Halme swinging his cane in the lead, refined and dignified, and Aleksi following, wearing his best coat and boots.

Jussi was still muttering:

"But we have to get locks for the doors... we have to... What is the world coming to? What would the Czar of Pentti say to all this?"

Akseli got even Elina to come to the evening meeting. She finished her chores a little early and Alma offered to look after the boys. When Elina dressed, they noticed that her coat had gotten a little small, and Akseli said as he looked at it:

"If we have to get rid of the last calf to do it, I'm going to get you a coat on the next trip to Tampere. Even a tenant farmer's wife can get better looking clothes now."

Then he quickly made a joke of his words, but repeated his promise of the coat seriously. Going to the rear room off the porch, he brought out Elina's red ribbon and cut it in half, putting one piece in her lapel buttonhole and another in his own.

"They say they wear red ribbons on their breasts in Helsinki. Halme put a big red loop in his lapel. We're every bit as good here."

Walking abreast in the winter evening twilight, they talked in a playful, friendly way. Even love seemed to revive from its everyday stagnation. Elina took her husband's hand and said:

"Let me hold on to your hand because my foot keeps getting twisted in the sled tracks."

"Hold on then. Or does daddy have to carry the child on his back?"

They walked on, arm in arm. The man's coat smelled of the stable and of tobacco, which seemed very pleasant to Elina. When they passed the parsonage, she asked:

"What can they be talking about now?"

"They must be worried now that their support and safeguard has fallen."

"Is their Ilmari in Germany? Then they must be glad."

"Listen, the way things are, Finland's masters' sons may be in Jerusalem, but that makes no difference as far as the workers are concerned. It doesn't matter to them if one son is in Germany and another in the Russian army, as long as they can shut a poor man's mouth in one way or another."

Nearer the village they began to see others on their way to the hall. Many of them joined Akseli and Elina because it was nice to appear at the meeting in the company of a board member and vice-chairman. Humble questions were asked, to which Akseli replied briefly and a trifle officially:

"Halme will explain things. We do have closer knowledge."

Akseli went back to the chairman's table but Elina hesitated in choosing a place to sit. She was the target of significant looks, for she had not been seen at the hall before. Akseli told her to come forward, but she resisted. People sitting on the ends of benches began to whisper to her:

"Of course you'll go up front. Your husband is there... since he's a board member."

This whispered servility to Elina stemmed from a bad conscience. Dues had gone unpaid, and there had even been derogatory words spoken about the Association. When all hope had died, people had been bitter, and the few faithful had heard them say:

"We can't put our money into something that gets us nothing."

Memories of this sort caused people to say half aloud:

"Out of the way. Koskela is coming."

Elina sat in the first row trying to look unassuming. When the rattle and clatter of arrival had died down, Halme made his appearance through the kitchen door. Taking a place behind the table, he was silent in thought for a time, like a minister before a prayer. Then he said with exaggerated calmness and restraint:

"Comrades. Let us stand and acknowledge our common belief in liberty, equality, and fraternity by singing the song dedicated to those noble values."

Raising his hand, he began:

Now forward our native sons...

The song began forcefully from the first words without any fumbling. During Halme's speech, which followed, he was frequently interrupted by demonstrations of approval. The slightest sharpness in a turn of phrase evoked clapping and cheering. In addition to the enthusiasm aroused by new possibilities, there was in the response a subconscious compensation for the indifference of recent years. The feeling at the meeting was like that stirred by the great strike. It could be seen in Halme too. His speech was more enthusiastic than usual, and more uncompromising.

"From the bloody forge of this capitalist trade war, there has risen a lovely flower, freedom for the poor of Finland. Comrades, the power of the spirit prevails over the power of the cannon and the sword. In its kingdom will man's issues be decided from now on, in that noble and beautiful kingdom, which our carcass-bound spirit has long yearned for."

During the period of open discussion, questions were presented and answered by the board members. Otto Kivivuori was still one of them, but he had been a kind of slacker, his membership merely a formality. Nor did he now take part in the discussion. Akseli answered the tenants' questions, for in a sense he was their unofficial representative. No separate section had been officially established for them; everything functioned within the framework of the Association. When asked how the Czar's extension of the land rental law now stood, he rose, rested the knuckles of his clenched fists on the table top, and said:

"Of course I can't exactly say. But we won't be satisfied with that any longer. The masters wouldn't even have given us that much, but I think they'll soon see the day when they'll have to give us all they have to give. We'll drive stakes at the corners of our land and say don't touch it, it's mine. It has to happen and it will happen now that Bloody Nick's throne has fallen."

As Akseli spoke, Elina looked nervously at the floor. She was afraid that her husband would get confused, that he would forget the words or begin to stutter. When the applause began, she looked about, blushing with pleasure. But when her eyes met those of her father, who sat opposite her, she was embarrassed, for he had noticed her expression.

Then Preeti rose and asked for the floor:

"I sort of think that, that we should, although someone else would be better able, sort of thank the master. Now that the Czar is beaten, we should show the master some kind of approval or something. Maybe even a cheer. That's all I was... I mean, he's been coming and going for our sake... and sat in jail... so that some kind of approval."

There were loud shouts of support, and Henna whispered:

"Keep still now... they're backing our Preeti."

They shouted long live the master, and Halme swallowed very visibly:

"I thank you. Although cheers for one person sound odd at a moment like this, when we celebrate the defeat of one-man rule, I am grateful for your good will. I see by it that your faith in our cause has been restored. And I don't want to criticize those who lost faith. Ahem. The Apostle Peter was great only after a certain cock-crow sounded continually in his ears."

His last remark was spoken a little sharply, but the slight sarcasm in it went unnoticed by the audience. The *Internationale* which was sung at the close of the meeting rose to a peak of power it had never before achieved in the workers' hall at Pentti's Corner. As they sang, they looked their neighbors in the eye and smiled as if sensing their thoughts, while their shoulders reinforced the tempo:

"No other ruler or lord than the almighty people... "

People delayed their departure for home. Large groups of them stood about in the yard of the workers' hall. Their talk contained every imaginable opinion.

"Now we'll put into effect everything they've overturned with their plots... it has to happen now. How can the majority not rule? I mean, those three men sometimes did a lot... Goddamn, it's not good enough just to kick them out into the fields. A few of them should be at the end of a rope to scare the rest. It would be a helluva thing just to give them a pat on the shoulder as they leave."

Even Preeti's voice could be heard, soberly energetic:

"A trade war, yes... They try to grab raw materials from each other, as the master just said in his talk... "

Akseli stayed on in the hall after the meeting. Countermeasures were being planned, and those present agreed to go to the town meeting the next day. Family groups were already on their way home when Elina and Akseli left. It was a clear March evening and voices could be heard plainly. Near the manor, the *Internationale*, sung by men's voices, rang out strongly.

"By God, the boys are letting Manu know the winds have shifted. He'll sure know the weather vane has swung around."

"He must have thought it was rusted in place."

"You can say that again."

Later people thrust themselves upon Akseli.

"Listen, Koskela, how is it that... "

Akseli explained to them how things were. Elina did not take part in the discussion, but hearing Akseli's thoughtful, somewhat guarded words, she tightened her grip on her husband's arm. They were asking her man about matters of state.

When they were left alone, the lightheartedness that emanated from her husband increased her feeling of happiness. He spoke animatedly and spontaneously to her. It was something that seldom happened. For the most part, she was fearful of Akseli's quiet spells. There was always something heavy and gloomy in him then, and after the phase had lasted a few days, it came to a head in an fit of rage over some trifling matter. For the sake of the children, such displays had actually become more controlled over the years. The fact that Elina had stopped fighting back also alleviated them. When they occurred, she usually took the children into a bedroom and sat there with them. The boys stared at her gravely and she herself looked out the window, her eyes dim with unshed tears.

Akseli always made amends afterwards by means of some word or remark which could be taken as a very distant plea for forgiveness. A warmer period would ensue, during which she forgot what had occurred. It felt like one of those periods now. They were walking along the road to Koskela, which was darkened by the surrounding woods. Akseli opened up and spoke of his thoughts and plans:

"I'll gladly pay the price of undeveloped land for it. I won't ask anything for nothing. And if I could get the rest of the swamp, then clearing it would compensate for what was lost. We could begin a real life at last. We could try to think seriously about leaving something to the boys. So far we've never been able to trust in anything. There's always been the feeling that we've made it through today, but don't know about tomorrow."

The branches of mighty Matti's oak arched over the road, forming a roof. It was so dark underneath it that they instinctively looked up. The clear sky of March glimmered through the branches, foretelling the coming of spring.

II

Akseli sat on a piece of board affixed to the side of the manure wagon. Poku walked a little lazily, for they were on the way to do rent-work. It was a beautiful morning in early spring. The roadside was already greening vigorously. The woods were fragrant and the morning-spry birds competed in song. The cup of chicory he had just drunk was pleasantly warm in Akseli's midriff.

The rent-work ahead seemed disagreeable, as all his routine work had seemed of late. Every day he read something new in the newspapers. From time to time circular letters came to the board.

These concerns governed his consciousness, and daily activities seemed dull in comparison. He stared at Poku's flanks, which swayed more than usual with the horse's slack and reluctant stride. He did not urge the horse to go faster. A barely noticeable twitch at the reins to indicate his state of mind would have been enough to make Poku to pull more strongly, for the animal easily sensed his master's inclinations and responded accordingly.

Now he ambled along as if resisting slightly with every step, and the man sat with his elbows resting on his knees, staring thoughtfully ahead, his shoulders swaying loosely as the wagon bumped along the road. One of the reins had slid down almost to the horse's feet.

"If they start here, then the the manor tenants will be the most eager, now that there is nothing to fear. Although on the other hand, they have the worst conditions."

He was thinking of the agricultural strikes. They had spread like wildfire through the tenant and manorial regions of southern and southeastern Finland. And last evening he had heard of restlessness among the workers on church village lands. There had been stirrings among them, demands to join the strike. The workers' executive committee for the town was to have met late at night, but he had heard nothing of its actions. Halme had gone there in the evening. They were to have discussed forming an agricultural workers' branch, for if strikes developed, they would have to handle them.

He had nothing against a strike. The demands involved shortening the work day. He himself was forced to work an eleven-hour rent-work day, which meant that with travel and the lunch hour, the day stretched out to thirteen hours.

"Well... from sunup to sundown, they say. But take the whole year into account, not just midsummer, and the Finnish worker puts in a longer day than the sun. And the sun shines for the good and bad alike, so they say, but it's different with the worker. He has to toil for devils only... uhuh, Poku. Shake a hoof a little, so we'll get there on time... so they won't be grumbling."

Poku pricked up his ears, tossed his head once or twice, and switched to his usual sturdy pulling gait. He seemed to toss each hoof forward, and his head bobbed up and down with every stride.

They were spreading manure on the parsonage fields. The strikes were the topic of discussion there too, but the exchange of opinions was guarded, for the parsonage hands avoided taking a stand. There was little proletarian spirit among them, first because great care had been taken to screen out socialists, and secondly because those living in the home circle were under closer scrutiny. Akseli naturally enlightened the parsonage workers, and that increased the gentry's hatred of him.

To their astonishment, the workers saw the vicar arrive in the field that morning, rather oddly dressed and with a manure fork in his hand. He wore an old summer topcoat, and the rest of his garb was gleaned from worn-out, cast-off clothing.

By way of explanation, he said to the workers, who stood looking at one another:

68

"I thought maybe I could do this kind of work too, now that things are so tough... such a crying need for food and no planting in many places."

"Yeah... of course... like that... "

A silent rage emanated from the vicar. His going to work stemmed from the bitter anger which the strikes had roused in him. Reading in the newspapers that dairies were shut down and milk drivers turned back on the roads, he had repeated furiously:

"This is... this is... unheard of. I can somehow understand why men would go on strike, but to prevent others from working... That isn't... that is an out-and-out crime."

All winter the vicar's family had felt a fearful uneasiness. A socialist majority in the legislature seemed ominous to them. After the revolution they had indeed spoken about reforms that should be put into effect. Suffrage they were ready to approve, but not as broad a one as the socialists demanded. Even freedom for tenant farmers seemed at last to be inevitable; whatever doubts they still retained on that score resulted only from their antipathy toward Akseli.

"That break has to be made. It's just too bad that it will come as a reward for such evil and malice."

But when the strikes began, the uneasiness changed to rage. The vicar made long speeches to Ellen, wondering at the people's brutality:

"The country is short of food. Don't they even realize that the first people to suffer from strikes are the workers, who aren't able to buy anything on the black market? No, this is both stupid and criminal."

"No, this is *svaboda*."

The strikes gave rise to outbursts of rage in Ellen, which intensified till she almost wept with chagrin. She had become even more nervous. Her prominent eyes, which had enhanced her beauty when young, had begun to protrude even more, with the opposite result. Downward drooping lines had appeared at the corners of her mouth, which made her chin seem separate from the rest of her face. She often grieved at night for her son, whose fate she did not know. She had many dreams about him, dreams in which he was always in great danger. They had received only one personal message from him. On a dark, sleety night, an unknown man had knocked at the door, given them a letter and left without telling them his name or where he had come from or where he was going. Curious to hear more details, they had asked him to come in, but the young man had refused.

"Whatever I could tell you is sure to be in the letter."

For many days the vicar had intended to go out and work, but did so only after hearing of troubles in the church village. At first he stood and watched the work as if he were learning. Akseli had answered his greeting with a harsh growl, and all the vicar's anger and vexation were now directed at him. Akseli was driving the manure from the large manure pile to smaller piles on the field, from which it was spread. For awhile the vicar stood in doubt as to whether he should follow Akseli or someone else. On the one hand, their strained relations made him hesitate to follow Akseli, but on the other hand, goaded him into doing just that. And when he saw Akseli's forbidding countenance and heard him barking unnecessarily at Poku, he sensed what it conveyed. Akseli's entire outward appearance, even his clothing, was repugnant. His sweaty shirt was nauseating, and his tightly clenched jaws and small, glaring eyes aroused a silent, seething wrath in the vicar, wrath he tried not to show. Indignation for once seemed to give him the upper hand; he would not quail before his tenant. Resolutely he stepped into Akseli's row and began to spread the manure.

Every time Akseli came to dump a load, the vicar tried to see his expression. Sometimes he thought he saw a slight amusement in it, but he tried not to let it bother him.

"Let him have his childish fun. The only thing he can do is to despise a gentleman's clumsiness and ridiculousness."

At first the vicar went at the work too furiously. Bit by bit he had to slack off. In addition, he spread the manure too carefully, so that it took a long time. When he saw a spot behind him that in his opinion had too little manure, he took a little on his fork and carried it to the bare spot. After spreading the forkful, he might still go back again if he thought the manure had been spread unevenly.

This caused a mixture of amusement and anger in Akseli, and when he saw that the vicar tried not to fall behind, he speeded up the tempo of the work. Loading up at the manure pile, he glanced at the vicar and pressed down on the fork with his foot in order to get a larger load each time. In rhythm with his work, he grumbled silently to himself:

"One of these days, old man, you and those coattails of yours will eat shit in hell."

On the surface he tried to make his work seem slow and easy. He merely enlarged the forkfuls, and while emptying the loads, he would dump a pile on the fly without bringing Poku to a stop. The backlog began to mount, and the vicar could see that it was intentional. A small fit of anger led him to try closing the gap, but before long he had to give up the effort, a little ashamed at having been provoked into a childish competition. The work was beginning to tell on him otherwise. There were red, rubbed spots on his hands which foretold terrible water blisters the following day, and his body, unaccustomed to the work, was sweating heavily. His physical decline had already begun. He was nearer fifty than forty, and although he was slender of build, loose flesh had begun to appear on his loins and belly. In the morning there were traces of puffiness under his eyes.

But he would not give in. His back ached and his biceps hurt, but he kept up a lively tempo of work.

Later in the day, he had to take off his topcoat. Underneath he had on Ellen's old woolen house coat, and the workers recognized it. They were greatly amused, and one of them whispered to another:

"... his old lady's coat on... "

It was somehow funny to them that a man could put on an article of women's clothing. But on the other hand, they had noticed that the gentry had all kinds of ways. Once they had even seen his wife wearing the vicar's fur hat.

"Sometimes they're so fancy and sometimes they wear anything at all."

The vicar himself saw nothing unusual in the woolen housecoat, but thought it a quite comfortable piece of clothing. The wind came through the weave and pleasantly refreshed his body.

The men nearby were talking softly about the strike, and the vicar asked: "What did he say?"

"Just that Mellola will shorten the workday at the sawmill but not for farm work."

"That's right. It's impossible on a farm. Of course you can arrange things at a sawmill, but conditions on farms are such that everyone should work harder. If the imports of grain from Russia stop, one can't even imagine how awful it will be."

Akseli had just dumped his load and was setting the withe that held the manure box in place:

"For some it will be awful, for others it won't. For the black marketeers, it will be great. The workers, of course, will suffer and we might even see death from starvation in the cities. But who cares about the rabble. There's been enough of them in this country to kill along the highways before this."

"Does Akseli mean the famine years? We can't do anything against the disasters caused by nature, but now it's a question of people's good will. It's madness to bring hunger into this country on purpose."

"It's sort of a question of a farm strike's not being of any use in the winter. One soon gets cold under the quilt then. And like I was saying, if there is less grain, the price rises accordingly."

The vicar spoke calmly to keep from showing his anger, for he had vowed to maintain his spiritual ascendancy over his tenant. Continuing to work, he said:

"Black marketing is just a result of low price ceilings. Akseli is a farmer himself."

"I don't sell much grain, since I have eight mouths to feed. And only a

71

patch of land... What are you milling around for... Listen to me, or you'll get a taste of the reins... It would be a different story if I had land. But left-over patches like mine the lambs gnaw bare. Well what now?"

Poku got an entirely uncalled for jerk on the reins and they went off at quite a pace toward the manure pile. The vicar stopped talking and concentrated on his work.

That afternoon Osku Kivivuori came to the parsonage fields. He went over to Akseli and spoke softly to him. Akseli called out to the overseer so loudly that even the vicar overheard it:

"I have to go though it's the middle of the day. There's been some kind of ruckus in the manor fields. I'm supposed to go and straighten things out. I'll fill out the day some other time."

The overseer looked a little helplessly at the vicar:

"Well, I don't know. What do we do in a case like this?"

The vicar said in a dry, matter-of-fact voice:

"Akseli will go, of course, if the matter demands it."

Akseli put on his coat and climbed on the wagon with Osku. From a short distance away, he said loudly:

"Has the rabble started rioting there too?"

Osku answered in an equally loud voice:

"The hooligans are on the move there, all right."

III

People were gathered at the workers' hall, most of them men from the manor. Even Elias Kankaanpää was there, for he had been doing rent-work for his father. The fortification work had stopped for the winter, and there was talk that it would not be renewed at all. Elias came to meet Akseli, as he arrived with Osku, and shouted from a distance:

"That goddamn Manu started playing the bigshot and we walked off from work."

With confused enthusiasm, the group then explained what had happened. A few men from the church village had come to the manor fields and urged them to join the strike. Hearing of their presence in the field, the baron had come to drive them off. At a wisecrack from Elias, the baron had begun to rail at his own tenants too.

"He says he won't shorten the work day by so much as an hour. His beard waggled and he fumed that 'I not talk to outside ones, go away, go away.' When he said that he would only talk to his own workers, then I said, let's talk about an eight-hour day. Then the pidgin Finnish started to flow, and there was plenty of it. He promised to kill the cows in their stanchions if there was a strike."

The group surrounded Akseli. He hardly knew which one to listen to.

"Let's go on strike right now. An eight-hour day or we don't work one hour. The Association has to tell the bosses and order everyone to strike."

The mood of the group was boisterous and defiant. Their vehemence was increased by the fact that unless they all went on strike, they would be in trouble individually. Akseli calmed them down and told them to wait until the board had time to assemble.

Gradually its members arrived. Halme was the last to come. A call to the church village had delayed him. Janne was supposed to come in person to explain the situation, and Akseli went out to let the people waiting outside know about it. The crowd contented itself with the explanation, although a few shouts were heard:

"What does Kivivuori have to do with it? We're the ones going on strike, not Kivivuori."

A short time later, Janne arrived. Entering the yard, he tossed one leg over the bicycle seat and braked to a stop by standing on one pedal, skillfully guiding the bike to the wall, with just the right momentum.

"Where are these directors?"

"They're in the snack room. Don't start any revisionist talk in there, you hear?"

Janne looked at the man who had shouted, and laughed. There had been a trace of humor in the latter's voice as well.

Janne stepped into the snack room, tossed his hat onto a nail, and said:

"Now rule by force comes crashing down... good afternoon. You're all looking so serious."

"It's not that bad. But whatever we do, there's the devil to pay."

Moving in his usual lazy way, Janne took his customary place at the table.

"Most of them have likely stayed in the fields?"

"That's true. But a majority will go along if the Association makes an official decision."

"Well, that decision has to be made. It's the only way to deal with things here. The trouble is spreading quickly through the whole parish. The landowners have decided to meet force with force, and are pressuring and threatening those who might go along."

"What are they saying in the church village?"

"Everyone has his own line. They're not too willing now that they hold the trump card because of the scarcities, and their own men in the government would be caught in between. But it's useless to side with the landowners. And there's no reason to. They make enough on the black market to give us a little."

"The very goddamn devil... Are we going to side with those suckfaces. We won't even think of it."

Antto was fervently in favor of a strike. Whatever their personal opinion might be, the others considered it inevitable. The only one who hesitated was Halme. He got up to walk from time to time and repeated:

"We should wait for the Parliament's decision on the matter. We should have at least that much confidence in our representatives. This matter does not, so to speak, concern us alone. The situation can become bad. I can't accept resorting to such violent action against the scabs. What can you achieve by it? A bad name and worst of all, perhaps bloodshed."

"Well in any case, things won't calm down now. It depends a lot on the kind of resistance. And the only tactic is to see that the demonstrations and other measures are organized. Nothing wrong with pressure if the band plays while it's applied, they say. It's best for you to try negotiation, though I don't think that mop-beard will talk to you. But if it comes to a fight, then choose a strike committee to run things. And then establish a trade section. It's not good for the party organs as such to handle the matter. Call a meeting for this evening and take a vote on it."

Akseli had taken little part in the discussion. He had weighed the matter in his mind. Leaving rent-work undone was no simple matter, but in his circumstances, it was impossible to think of standing aloof, and he said decisively, not so much to convince the others as to convince himself:

"Well, that's it then. Let's get on with it. And what we start, we finish. Besides, it's good to give them a little reminder. In March they weren't in the fields much, and they were writing about workers' rights. They trusted a lot in the organized workers. And their trust is, you see, so great that now the old neck is beginning little by little to show from under their collars. They understand the workers' cause so very well, but not just at the moment. Not just yet, but soon. When we get through these hard times. Well, that means that when they are more firmly in the saddle, then they'll say, 'Shut up, you hooligans.' Finland's master won't fool me any more. He's eaten his word before my eyes."

"You're goddamned right. Those are great word, Koskela."

A long discussion of details followed. In a thick cloud of tobacco smoke, they deliberated on the proposals for the negotiators and the upper and lower limits of their demands. Gradually Halme's doubts vanished. It was nice to sit at the table and approve or reject the suggestions of the younger men. He himself went out to announce the board's decision. The others followed along, but remained in the entry as Halme stepped out onto the steps.

"Comrades. The Association will meet tonight at eight o'clock to discuss the question of striking. Spread the word as widely as possible."

"Good. Everything comes to a stop. We'll see if Manu kills his cows in their stanchions. We'll see how the old man does. Will he get up on the manure pile himself?"

The news was received with shouts of joy. Even the quietest ones shouted with enthusiasm. Janne leaned against the door jamb and looked at the crowd. A small and thoughtful gleam appeared in his eyes and he muttered to himself:

I'm only poor Kuntrat, and took fire into corners.
I took a Bible for my guide.

Then turning to the others, he said:

"Get in touch with me after the decision is made. If the masters organize, we'll have to handle the strike together."

He leaped onto his bike and went pedaling off up a slight rise. The bicycle wobbled from one side to the other each time his full weight bore down on a pedal. The crowd dispersed to carry the news to the fields and village.

Long before eight o'clock, people were stirring in the vicinity of the workers' hall. Rapid, heated discussions went on in various groups, and when they gradually gathered in the hall, the loud buzz of talk continued until Halme quieted it with his gavel.

First the demands were adjusted and crystallized. That took much work, for here opinions were badly divided:

"No more than an eight-hour workday. No overtime."

"Well for my part there could be some overtime if we were paid extra."

One of the women barn workers from the manor got the floor. She too had been overcome by the general sense of victory. Loudly and spiritedly she cried out:

"And the slavery of milkmaids has to end too. Say what you will, but a magpie is a bird and a milkmaid is a person and the cows have had things better in the barns than they have till now."

"Good, good... Your right, Tyyne, goddamn it."

Almost any speech brought shouts of approval, as long as its tone was heated enough. When the demands were put together after a fashion, Halme moved for a vote.

"What do we need a vote for? Up with the strike."

Halme cleared his throat loudly and sternly:

"We should at least listen to what is being said. The strike isn't a goal, but a means. If the matter is settled by negotiation, then the strike is off. The question is whether the demands are unconditional and if their rejection means a strike without a separate decision. We'll vote on that. The vote will be by paper ballot."

"No ballots. A voice vote. Surely every man dares to make known what he wants."

"Everyone who wants to strike on behalf of these demands, raise his hand."

A large number of hands rose quickly. Heads turned and glances crossed, causing more and more hands to rise, the last few delaying only until the stares of those around them were sufficiently concentrated. Finally every last hand was up, and Halme said:

"Those for the strike have a clear majority. Are there opposing opinions? Raise your hands."

Heads turned again; not a single hand rose.

"Is a secret ballot called for?"

"No need for it. The result is clear."

"I ask for silence. A man can't hear himself talk. Does anyone want a secret ballot?"

When the silence had lasted for some time with no one saying a word, Halme said in his official chairman's voice:

"The meeting has thus decided to authorize the Board of the Workers Association Endeavor to act as the workers' agent in negotiations concerning working hours with all the community's employers. A concomitant decision is to demand the establishment of an eight-hour workday, the rule to be nine hours during the summer and seven hours during the winter. Overtime totaling no more than 200 hours will be permitted during the summer with a pay increase of 50%. The decision also concerns those working in the dairy industry, where the internal arrangement of working hours will be in accord with circumstances. Are there any questions? The decision is approved."

The gavel fell and a mighty roar echoed in the room.

"Hurrah! And we'll stand by this. 'March on, you mighty multitudes, no lowly herd of slaves... '"

The workers' march began spontaneously. Attempts at the *Internationale* and the *Marseillaise* were mingled in the first verses they sang, but the *Workers' March* happened to have been begun most loudly and carried everything with it.

Early next morning the Board left on its rounds. At Kylä-Pentti, Halme presented the matter as sympathetically as possible, for the master there had rented them the lot for the workers' hall and was otherwise well-disposed toward them. But a strike was too much for him.

"What will the others say... I, I can't decide the matter by myself. What will it come to now? I'll go along with the rest. But what about the barn work? Do we have to kill our cows then... ?"

"Well, we've been instructed to present these demands."

The young master of Mäki-Pentti said a bit nastily that he didn't care how long the Kivioja men worked:

"It doesn't matter at all to me. But I won't make any separate agreements."

The master of Töyry was hitching up a team of horses in his yard. After Halme's presentation, he moved around to the front of the horses to hook up the reins to the bridles. From there they heard smothered, intermittent phrases:

"That's my men's business... I've always had the habit of dealing with my men. It's their business."

"In this case, it's not just their business alone. We should reach a general agreement."

Antto stepped forward from behind the others, and although Halme had warned him about renewing the old quarrel, he said:

"Listen Kalle. You seem to stick to the old ways no matter how much the world changes. It's about time you started watching the signs in the sky."

"Heh, heh... you don't seem to have changed either, heh, heh, heh..."

The landlord spoke with a forced playfulness. After a brief silence, his forced control failed him, and from behind the horses' heads, he said stiffly:

"I recall driving you off my land once for rioting. And stay off it from now on. Aren't there other men to send on these errands?"

Halme calmed the two of them down. Nonetheless, Töyry refused to negotiate, merely repeating that the matter depended on his men. The board members knew, however, that the Töyry hired hands who were on house food would make no demands on their own, and Halme ended the discussion, his annoyance clearly visible:

"I consider the master sufficiently enlightened to make further explanations and arguments pointless. But there is good reason to take the matter seriously."

"I've always taken practical matters seriously. Right now I have to try to get my crops planted, as I've tried my best to do every year."

The master took up the reins, stepped up onto the wagon, and commanded the horses a bit harshly to start moving.

The board members left. Antto ranted and threatened, but Halme finally said, to put a stop to his fuming:

"One should avoid useless wrangling. It will never make them more compliant."

"No, it won't. But if you once screamed at them good and goddamned loud... "

The vicar came to meet them on the steps. Both of his hands were bandaged and he asked their pardon for not being able to greet them properly. His hands were obviously stiff, and he said with an attempt at casualness:

"In my ignorance I didn't wear gloves. It seems that one has to learn everything by experience."

His wife also came into the office. She greeted everyone amicably, but she could not conceal her coldness toward Akseli. The pair chose to work on Halme. They spoke of the general situation, of the shortage of necessities, and of the state of the nation. It was a long time since Halme had discussed affairs with the gentry, and he spoke with special enthusiasm. He tuned his pitch to theirs, and the strike at Pentti's Corners was discussed only in passing. Instead, Halme uttered statesmanlike pronouncements:

"Certainly, we do not willingly take on the government's responsibility. If the gentry knows a little about social democratic principles, then they should know that we aren't eager to take on partial responsibility. But it is exactly the country's changed circumstances that have caused this change in our position. I beg you, however, to take note that something must be gotten into the workers' hands, and quickly. Perhaps you don't know how bitter and suspicious the people are. The position of our senators will soon be difficult. We have been forced to offer the people one disappointment after another in this ten years time. The working people are like a child that has been deceived too many times. They no longer believe in anything.

The vicar tried to maintain his friendly demeanor. He spoke as if he hadn't been ill-tempered for days because of the strikes and disturbances:

"We fully understand. We're ready to go a long way in offering concessions. That's the conclusion I've come to in following the course of affairs. And who wouldn't follow them at a time like this. But the law puts a time limit on negotiations."

His wife had been listening to the discussion for some time. Now she said with an exaggerated congeniality:

"But surely Halme, with his prestige, can get the workers to understand the matter. I've heard there were shouts of 'Hurrah' because the Czar was overthrown."

Halme laughed in pretended scorn at the notion of his favor among the people, to prevent their noticing how pleased he was.

"Heh, heh. They are well-intentioned people and courteous too. But it is a matter of life and death. Mr. Halme's prestige, and that of many others too, will end very quickly if he keeps showing them an empty hand. Ahem.

As much as I would like to do this or that, I can't really start to play God."

At last they returned to the negotiations. The gentry spoke at length of the demands of agriculture. The vicar said he could adjust somehow, but that it was difficult for him to make advance decisions that would bind the others.

"Shouldn't they really go on longer? We can't reduce the amount of work."

"We're not trying to do away with work. Taking overtime into account, the workday during the summer months can stretch out to almost the same length as it is now. Only the pay will have to be higher. Basically the question is one of money. And according to research, shorter hours increase productivity, so the loss is insignificant."

When the gentry realized that Halme was not to be swayed, their annoyance was progressively more evident in their discourse. The other members of the board had taken no part in the discussion because it was moving on such a high plane. While Halme continued the debate with the vicar, his wife said casually to Otto Kivivuori:

"But why is Kivivuori on strike? I had the notion that Kivivuori worked only as an independent contractor. You are self-employed, aren't you? Don't you even pay your rent in money?"

"Well, that is true. It is sort of that way. I've agreed to shorten my own work day and I'm just waiting for the other employers to join me."

The vicar's wife smiled deprecatingly at Otto's irony. Then she turned her attention to Akseli. She looked at him a number of times and then turned her head away as if in doubt whether to speak or not. Fingering the watch chain around her neck, she finally blurted out:

"Does Akseli intend to join the strike?"

Akseli sat with his elbows resting on his knees, swinging his cap between his legs.

"If things aren't settled otherwise."

"Is that so? We can probably get the planting done somehow. That is, if Akseli doesn't force the other men to strike."

"I... I don't force anyone... "

Both of them stiffened, and the woman stopped talking. When at length the discussion proved to be fruitless, the board members got up to leave. The vicar was clearly troubled. When the men had reached the entry, he rushed after them.

"Mr. Halme."

Halme stopped to wait while the others went out.

"I just wanted to let you know that my position is not a personal one. For my own part, I would agree... I'm not thinking of my own advantage...

that means little to me. But I can't go making advance agreements, which would be a kind of pressure on the others. I've often thought about these benefices; they're not a suitable way to pay people. I hope Halme won't misunderstand my position. I was only thinking about the general situation."

His anger had been quickly followed by the fear that he might be considered greedy, hence his uneasy explanation. Halme listened to him with a polite expression, his cane on his arm and said with a short nod:

"Mr. Vicar, I've made no such insinuations. And these matters are just as little to my personal advantage."

The vicar's tone became confidential again:

"Shouldn't we, just for that reason, do our part to try to settle this matter? I promise to try to get concessions if you can get at least some reduction of the demands."

"These are minimum demands based on a vote. If the negotiations fail, they can of course be taken up again, but I doubt the result. I very much doubt it."

"But is it proper to make clearly threatening demands right at the start?"

"Mr. Vicar, these people have never been given alternatives when they were given commands and decrees. It would in my opinion be too much to expect a fine sensitivity of them when for the first time in their entire lives they see that they have a tiny bit of power. But I give the vicar my word of honor that I will do my best to achieve a good and honorable solution. But you know that the baron's position will decide the whole question."

Halme shifted his cane to the crook of his other arm, bowed slightly, and left.

The vicar returned to the office.

"What arrogant condescension... What is going to happen? He's gotten more and more unbearable in his calculated impudence. Better... better those hired hands and tenants. I'd a thousand times rather battle them. What will come of this? How have we angered God?"

"That God's name is Edvard Valpas-Hänninen. This is straight from the basement of *The Worker*. But they'll have me in the fields yet if they start striking. I can do it, and it's the perfect answer to their naive ideas about the gentry. I'll go get your boots from the attic right now; I'll show them."

"You're not really serious... it's not proper. I, of course, can go."

"Now is no time to be concerned with propriety. Or would you bow down to a gang of hooligans who will shut down the dairy... A person has duties that can't be dodged. I'll get the boots. The overseer can hitch up my horse."

80

On the way to the manor, Antto grumbled to Halme:

"You went and told them that workers are childish. Goddamn. They know how to put us down themselves. You don't need to help them."

Halme glanced sideways at Antto and said indifferently:

"It was only a figure of speech. I really meant to say that when a child has been deceived often enough, he becomes so suspicious that he will say there is no Santa Claus even when he sees the real one."

"Huh, the real one. There's no such thing."

Halme swung his cane briskly and walked straight ahead, watching Antto walking beside him from the corner of his eye:

"How can we be sure of that?"

Dumfounded, Antto looked around to see the expressions on the others' faces. They had not heard the words, however, and after staring at them for a time, Antto withdrew from Halme a few paces, muttering angrily to himself.

Akseli walked along in silence for a long time. The others too were quiet. The only sound was the crunching of footsteps on the road, and then Aleksi declared:

"It's as if there had been no revolution."

The Baron did not let them in, but came out himself to meet them. A few times he asked Halme to repeat a word he had not understood. Calmly and courteously, he too informed them that he would not agree to the demands. Let the legislature establish the law. He would make no individual agreements.

"They're not my men. They sent by the village. They bring the riots."

When Halme pursued his claims, a rising anger began to show through the Baron's self-control. His utterances became brief and sullen assertions. Halme's attitude stiffened as well:

"I leave the matter in the Baron's hands. Your influence and position give you the power to decide the issue. I beg you at least to discuss the matter with the other employers. You can telephone me about any possible decisions. I ask you to take the changed situation into account."

They left, and Antto muttered half aloud:

"It gives me an earache to listen to them... Finnish society is now... goddamn... "

IV

The strike began on the following day. There had been discussions at the manor. The vicar had sought to mediate, but without effect. The masters from the church village urged them to join with them and not to yield.

The young slept late in the morning. It was nice to lie in bed, then get up lazily to dress and go to the village, where there was always fresh news and pleasing talk.

For once, the tenants did their own planting on the landowners' time. The old hired hands and the men who worked for their keep rattled and clattered away at their few chores in the yards or woodsheds. Many of them, however, were on strike although their consciences were opposed to it. It was hard to bypass inherited ways, and not all of them had joined the strike. Töyry's day workers were known to be on the job, as well as those at the parsonage, with the exception of Akseli. Even at the manor a few "yard-men" remained.

The Koskela boys went to town in the morning, where they often stayed until late at night. They dressed half in Sunday and half in everyday clothing. "Everyday" was the dominant note, accompanied by some better article of clothing, a hat or a coat.

Men stood around in the yard of the workers' hall. Some played cards. Even boyhood games came into use. They played ball or pitched pennies. Coins were tossed at a stick set in the ground, and the tosser got to keep all those he could reach with his index finger when touching the stick with his thumb. Long-fingered and skillful Osku Kivivuori collected all the others' coins, so that one side of his coat actually hung down from the weight in his pocket.

In the afternoon, small groups of girls would appear. There might be four or five together, walking arm in arm. They often stood in such chains, trying to answer the shouts of the boys with their united strength.

The boys liked to shout at Elma Laurila, for they wanted to hear her often totally obscene answers. Then they would say to one another, shaking their heads:

"She's a tough one, by God. A man doesn't dare try it with her. She'll put any man to shame if he can't keep it up all night long."

Aku stood with his hands in his pockets and spoke knowingly in the group's terms:

"She's quite a gypsy, all right."

Elma had begun speaking to him very tauntingly, calling him "Master Koskela" and "Sweetie Pie" and swinging her hips when she walked by him.

Afternoons they went to harass the strikebreakers. Little by little, their chatter took on a more heated and threatening tone. On the third day of the strike, they were once more walking along the road in a large group, talking and laughing. Some of them were throwing stones like little boys.

"Hey, look! The vicar's wife's in the fields."

The woman was actually driving a harrow. She was just heading toward the road from the opposite end of a strip, and the group slowed its pace to reach the spot at the same time. Elias Kankaanpää was slightly drunk, as he was every day during the strike, and he stationed himself at the head of the group. Further off in the field, the vicar was at work with some of the other parsonage men. His wife was driving a team of horses. Her skirts were turned up and fastened with safety pins so as not to hinder her walking, already clumsy and laborious because of the overly large men's boots she wore. The group stopped. Some of them drew back behind the others. Goggle-eyed, holding back smiles, they nudged one another. The vicar's wife began to turn the team around. Elias took off his hat and made a deep, exaggerated bow, which he repeated two or three times.

"The lady is mixing earth and seed, and the work, it flows like water."

There were giggles from behind him. The woman pretended not to hear him, and Elias bowed anew:

"It's nice weather for planting. It's a pleasure to put God's grain into the earth's bosom. Our country's earth is nice in this way, that if you put in one grain in the spring, with good luck you can get back seven or eight in the fall."

The vicar's wife had gotten the horses turned around and begun jerking at a marking stick caught in the spikes of the harrow. Having freed it, she answered Elias:

"I hope we can get some seeds this fall, when the entire nation will be suffering hunger."

Elias made another courteous bow:

"Not everyone will see hunger. The honorable lady isn't taking Mrs. Hollo into account. That old lady won't be able to see hunger because she's blind."

From the group came the voice of Aune Leppänen:

"Ah-ha, ha, ha!"

The vicar's wife set off, her head high and her lips tightly compressed. Although she tried to summon up all her contempt, it was hard for her to see the harrow tracks of the last strip because her eyes were dimmed by tears of rage and chagrin. The vicar had watched the entire confrontation and heard some unintelligible words. Although he could not make them out, he sensed their tone and started walking hastily toward the group. Rage and anger had for once provoked an unambiguous response to these people, and the strike disturbances had finally smothered his timid uncertainty about "the people." Having reached the roadside, he measured the group with a stern gaze:

"Was there something you wanted?"

"Not with the parson. But those men of yours don't seem to have heard that they should be on strike."

"If you don't consider yourselves able to work, then leave those who want to work alone."

"The vicar can sweat as much as he wants. So that he'll learn a little about what it's like. But we'll send the scabs away."

The parson saw the Koskela brothers in the group.

"The Koskela bothers here too. You might at least think of your honorable parents. Shame on you!"

Aleksi blushed and shrank back behind the others, nervously fingering his coattails. Aku saw many people watching him as if they were waiting. He thought of his father and mother and the family's relationship to the parsonage, but the stare of those around him was heavy and demanding.

"Koskela's boys have nothing to be ashamed of. Koskela's boys haven't stolen land from anyone."

The vicar's jaw dropped. He tried to shame the boy with a look, but the latter stood the test. He walked back to his work, repeating over and over:

"So that's how it is... there too... so that's how it is... there too."

The group departed. Aku felt cocky when they praised him, but the incident stayed in the back of his mind, troubling him. The encounter had so roused the group that it stopped at Wolf-Kustaa's shack. Kustaa was planting potatoes with a hoe, since he had no other agricultural machinery. Elias leaned into the run-down fence and yelled:

"It's too early to plant potatoes, Kustaa."

Kustaa concentrated on his hoeing but finally condescended to answer:

"It is a little. But I have to find time to work at the manor. I'm planning to go to work there tomorrow."

"Has Manu asked you to?"

"Yeah. He sent word. The strike is going to be put down a little. The Cossacks are coming tomorrow to jab the socialists a little with their bayonet points."

Angry yells rained on him from the group, but Kustaa began to gaze around as if he had forgotten them. Pursing his mouth thoughtfully, he raised his eyebrows, then took a few paces as if he were measuring something. A rod for measuring ditches hung on the wall of his shack, which he had found somewhere and brought home, although he never needed anything of the sort. With it, he began to measure up and down his yard. The group fell silent and watched his efforts. Once he went and measured with the rod from the window frame to the corner of his shanty, then holding a finger to mark the spot, he began to mark off the distance between two fence poles. Having done so for a time, he said to himself:

"The goddamned thing is fifteen centimeters short."

"Are you planning to build something, Kustaa?"

Picking up his rod again, Kustaa made a couple of measurements with it. Looking important, he stuck the rod upright at the spot where he had ended his measurement. Then he began to sight with one eye the alignment from the rod to the corner of his shanty.

As they left, the strikers shouted whatever each one could devise, but Kustaa did not answer. When the group disappeared from sight, he picked up his hoe and, totally calm, began to plant his potatoes.

In a riotous mood, the strikers continued on their way.

"Let's go and see Töyry's day workers."

"Right. That's where we were headed."

The road to Töyry's turned at the store, but since the storekeeper happened to be in his yard, they stopped there.

"Hey there, gouger. We heard you were planting at Töyry's yesterday evening. Helping out a little, so you'll have enough to peddle in the fall... so you can sell grain to the bigshots."

The storekeeper roared with laughter and went inside. During the strike he had carried a pistol in his pocket, for he feared the villagers, many of whom hated him. Some had gotten kerosene from him and others hadn't.

Elma Laurila stepped into the yard, hips swinging, and shouted to the storekeeper, who had ascended the steps:

"You could give me a little muslim too. The kind that Hollola hussy got. Like a little rent for our home... ."

"Ha, ha, you seem to be wearing muslim... and you don't pay rent with fabric, ha, ha."

"Give me some too, haah... I'll let you pat me a little."

Yeah, yeah, ha, ha. But what would the Russians say to that? They might even come back."

The storekeeper shouted the last remark from the doorway as if emboldened by being close to a safe refuge.

"Hang the gougers."

"Now let's go and see that other devil for a while."

Lauri Kivioja had hung back while they shouted at the storekeeper, but now in order to make up for it, he became more boisterous than the rest when they started toward Töyrys'. The crowd's enthusiasm and defiance increased on the way. Everyone tried to outdo the next person in thinking up something better to say. Without their being aware of it, their pace quickened. Those in the front ranks kept shoving ahead of one another, since everyone wanted to demonstrate the greatest fervor.

"Let's ask the devil where he's going to get the Cossacks now to whip the workers."

"There'll be no more whipping of Finnish workers these days. The men in power are of a different sort nowadays. I think the new generation is a little better."

"I was there then."

"We've seen a little bit of the world... "

They went through a small patch of woods, beyond which the Töyry fields began.

"There the devil is. And Arvo and Aaro too."

"But none of the day workers are there."

Töyry had sent the day laborers to faraway fields with his youngest son Ensio precisely because he suspected that the strikers would come brawling here. His older sons Arvo and Aaro had remained at the home fields with the master. The pace of the crowd slowed down somewhat. The enthusiasm kindled along the way declined in the face of reality. Nevertheless they moved closer, shoving one another forward at the end. The master went on harrowing as if the group did not exist, his gray hair pasted to his forehead with sweat. He was bareheaded and stripped to his vest, for walking in the soft earth was hard and tiring. Here too, Elias was the first to speak:

"Where are the day workers?"

The master did not respond, and Elias whispered something to Arvi Laurila, whereupon Arvi shouted:

"Hey, old man. When are you going to measure out new tenant lands for us?"

Elias's whisper and Arvi's shout were repeated a number of times.

"Did you send for the Cossacks yet? Did you vote against County unemployment money? Go to Communion now and then so you can swindle milk from the County with an easy mind."

While they were shouting, the crowd had drawn nearer to the master. He had just reached the spot where they stood, his horses sweaty and panting. Lauri Kivioja stepped forth from the crowd.

"Where are the day workers?"

"To the best of my knowledge, I don't have to give you an accounting of my men."

Lauri strutted up to the front of the horses and took hold of the reins, bringing the horses to a halt. Others stepped closer, and Arvi Laurila repeated:

"Is that the truth now?"

A sound escaped the master. Lauri Kivioja held onto the horses and said:

"Lauri is of the opinion that it's best to stop working now. Since you won't send the men off, you won't harrow yourself either. Not one bit."

"Let go of my horses."

The master's shout was hoarse and smothered. In spite of his age, he charged at Lauri, but at that instant he was seized by as many hands as there was room for. There was a rending sound and a shout. Arvo had torn loose a fence stake and was attacking the group. Half-blind with rage, he struck out at random. A blow fell on Aku Koskela's back, and with a grunt the boy crouched down low. Arvo was unable to strike again, for too many men were upon him. Aaro, who had followed his brother's example, attacked with his stake raised high, but did not have time to strike a blow, for Aleksi Koskela caught hold of his weapon. Aleksi, who had stayed in the rear, paled on seeing the blow land on his brother's back, and when Aaro approached, he rushed to the attack, mouthing quavering, sporadic sounds no one could understand. For a while he and Aaro struggled for the stake and then the two began to trade blows. Aleksi struck Aaro's face, causing his nose to bleed, but the fight had to stop when Aaro was crushed to the ground by a mass of men. Aleksi's face was completely white. His body shook, and his eyes were wide and madly staring. Confused words could be heard amidst his panting:

"No... not anyone... He didn't touch... Aku... he was just standing... you. don't hit with stakes...."

Slowly he returned to normal. While the others struggled, he drew further back. The wild look in his eyes faded, and he began to look helplessly around as if his mind were filled with a boundless astonishment. He seemed to be desperately seeking an answer to the question:

"Was that me?"

Aku stood up, trying to hold a hand to his back, his face twisted in pain. Elma Laurila glanced at him, and rushed toward the group scuffling with the master and his sons.

"Kill them... kill them... "

She tried to spit in Arvo's face but didn't get the chance because someone was always in the way. Spit ready at her lips, she thrashed about in the group, trying to thrust her head through the ring at any possible opening. Failing in her attempt, she spat at the ground, somewhat milder now, and hissed:

"Goddamn shitheads."

Arvo's smothered shout could be heard in the midst of the din:

"Come on... one at a time... or two at a time... you miserable things."

They began to carry men off the field, not beating them but shoving and bumping them roughly.

"Whoops-a-daisy, and over the fence."

"Hey, food boss... You haven't run out of kerosene... Goddamned scab..."

The master did not answer. He lay limp in the arms of the men, looking up at the sky. His rage had subsided into a calm and cold indifference.

In three groups, they went back to the road. Arvi Laurila was with the group carrying the master. Suddenly seizing him by the neck, he said:

"Say uncle, old man."

Then, breaking out into a roar of laughter, he let go of the master's neck, his rage dying as quickly as it had been kindled. Yelling and caterwauling, the group reached the road, where they released the men, who started back toward the farm. But after a few steps the master turned back toward the group:

"The day will come... "

He did not complete his sentence, but continued on his way. A few shouts were still heard from the group:

"Workers don't have horses to ride, but you can see, goddamn, that we can get the job done without them. Go and count your possessions... You have something to count... "

Threatening, still puffing with rage, the group started off for home. Akusti, who had been sitting on the roadside, joined them. He was still pale with pain, and walked very gingerly so as not to move his back muscles. He was the only one to have been struck with a pole, and the others consoled him.

"It'll cost so goddamn much if you go to the doctor. But you don't beat a worker just like that in Finland today... There'll be law for the bosses and landlords too."

When they reached the store, they struck up a song.

V

At Koskela, Alma rubbed tallow on Aku's back. Jussi had been thrown into absolute despair. He spent most of his time around the woodpile, and after his first lecture, he would only sigh now and then in passing:

"If death would just take me... I can't show my face to people any more."

"Töyry has just as much reason to hide his face," Akseli said to Jussi, but conversely he snapped at the boy:

"Weren't you told not to go raising a ruckus on your own?"

Aleksi was thoughtful. From time to time he would repeat, as if to himself:

88

"He would have hit him anyway, even if I didn't grab him... "

Alma too had scolded the boy, but when she saw the bluish-black swelling on his back, she changed her mind:

"It's strange that they go and hit people with poles."

Aku himself lay face down on the bed, gritting his teeth but not making a sound as his mother's hand rubbed tallow on the sore area.

"I can lick my own wounds. I don't need the sheriff."

They had learned that Töyry had gone to talk to the sheriff.

After the disturbance, Halme called a meeting of the strikers. There a farm worker's local was formed, of which Akseli was chosen chairman. In fact, its board was the same as that of the Association itself. Only Halme was omitted, because he was not a farm worker. Nevertheless, even with the new organization, he was chosen chairman of the strike committee, for he could not be sidelined.

In his speech, Halme touched on the disturbance. He appealed to the workers' honor of the strikers, even said something rigidly condemnatory, which occasioned shouting at him:

"But we're going to drive the scabs out of the fields by force. We won't put up with it."

Halme said that he understood the strikers' anger, but:

"We must control ourselves. The eyes of the entire country are on the working class. No matter how much oppression we have suffered, we must be on a higher moral plane than our oppressors. The final victory can be achieved only by the one whose morality is higher.. "

"Old man Töyry... Manu is a really honorable man, yeah... A real Jesus Christ... Always on the side of the poor... "

"I beg for your silence. I believe I know these people as well as I know the young men who now see fit to interrupt my speech. But we are rising to end oppression, not to practice it. We can make our position clear by orga- nized demonstrations... Random rioting is for others, not for organized workers. That is for drunken hooligans. I hope that no one who bears the name of social democrat will stoop to that level."

"Manu is civilized... gawdamn, gawdamn... Go 'way, Go 'way... Shit man."

The shouting died down at threatening commands to shut up from older men sitting near the ones who were shouting. Halme was able to finish his speech, although the muttering which followed showed that it had had no effect.

Tension increased the next day when rumors circulated in the village that strikebreakers from the church village were coming to do the spring planting at the manor.

"There have been university students in Yllö's fields. At least the doctor's son was there."

"Goddamn, if those party boys come here, there'll be a real blow-up. Those pantywaists have no business doing farm work. Not before and not now either."

Halme phoned the church village and asked Janne and Silander to stop the strikebreakers from coming. But the news from the church village literally frightened him:

"How can we stop them? There's open war going on here. The Yllö boy was beaten with a bicycle chain yesterday evening. Organize a demonstration and try to keep it under control. If they go off on their own, there's bound to be a fight. The landowners here are so heated up that they're carrying pistols in their pockets."

Halme called a meeting of the strike committee and it was decided to hold a demonstration.

Again that evening he called the church village. Couldn't Janne at least go and talk those who belonged to the gentry out of coming? The farmers and their sons would not arouse as great a fury. But Janne replied that the gentry had singled him out for attack, accusing him of having organized the whole thing.

Pale and sleepless, Halme arrived early at the workers' hall, fearing that the people gathering there might have set off on their own.

The procession with its flag advanced toward the manor. It was known that the strikebreakers had arrived early in the morning, accompanied by the sheriff. A short distance from the work site they struck up a song and continued singing after stopping at the edge of the field. Those in the field continued working, stealing side glances at the band of strikers. The baron was closest to the latter, with the sheriff at his side. Uolevi Yllö wore a bandage on his head, for he had actually been hit with a bicycle chain on his way home from work. Arvo Töyry was also in the field, for the landowners had agreed that they would help one another whenever they could spare the time from their own work. The strikers did not know everyone in the field. They did recognize the son of the county doctor and there were apparently other sons of the church village gentry in the field, along with the landowners and their sons.

When the song ended, Halme ordered the group to stay together and not to shout to the men in the field. Summoning up all his mental and physical aplomb, he walked toward the baron and the sheriff. They came to meet him. They greeted one another courteously, the sheriff seeming downright friendly. In addition to the trouble caused by the strike, he had other difficulties to contend with, for the workers' organizations and even some of the landowners were demanding his resignation for having been unnecessarily enthusiastic in the service of the oppressing power. For the time being, he had held on to his position with the aid of influential backers, and with the outbreak of the strikes the landowners had begun to consider him quite necessary. After the greetings, he asked the purpose of the demonstration and then said:

"I have nothing against the demonstration, as long as those working are not harassed."

"The demonstration will be peaceful, but I must state my position to the baron. It is a great wrong to use men who have never done any work as strikebreakers. It is the greatest cause of anger among the workers."

"I not use any but my workers if they do work. When they don't, I do with those I get."

"Master Baron's agreement to exceptionally easy demands would have ended the strike. Everything would be well, and the losses suffered insignificant."

The Baron was ready with his answer, which he had thought through many times, for it contained the entire basis for his position, but the words with which he expressed it came in an angry staccato:

"How care for cattle with hour limits? How do all the hurry work? City man. He work in factory, he can be short day, and he need short day. He no sun, no good weather. Farmer always out in nature. Don't need short day... I always out of my room. I strong. Lazy and without work get sick. Poor men come... Not good."

The argument continued. Meanwhile the demonstrators stood at the edge of the field, and little by little, their comments grew louder and louder:

"Look at that one. You can see he's never had a pitchfork in his hands before. What's that Yllö boy digging at. Is it chemical fertilizer? Is he coming this way? Let's tell him a thing or two."

Uolevi approached the group, strewing chemical fertilizer from a box hanging at his breast. The group struck up the *Internationale*. After a couple of verses, a song began to sound from the field as well, which one of the gentlemen's sons had begun:

For Finland's good we sacrifice, join we all in labor's battle!
Where our land's good fortune lies, therein lies our happiness.
No room now for factious minds, work is honor to a folk!
Hear, o hear the echoes ringing: work, to work, our country all!

When the strikers heard the strikebreakers' song during lulls in their own, they raised their voices. The power of their song was greater, since there were more of them, and the strikebreakers were scattered and worked as they sang. Some of the men in the strikers' group were actually shouting, their eyes bulging, so that the song lost its normal nature and began to sound more like bellowing:

Workers, you plowmen and all,
you hungry crew of laboring folk.
The land belongs to us, it must,
and not to idle loafers.

Uolevi was approaching the end of a strip with his box. He had joined in the song, and was tossing out fertilizer to its rhythm. His head wrapped in a bandage, eyes red from lack of sleep, and face drawn with weariness, he sang loudly, as if in defiance. He had been working day and night, first at home and then all over the parish, for he was in charge of a whole group of strikebreakers. The group was made up of church village farmers' sons and sons of the gentry, and while in some cases the older landowners were afraid of rioting and did not dare to work themselves, Uolevi took his crew to the fields, unconcerned about the tumult. Over a week of continual work interrupted by only a few hours' rest each morning, the painful blow to his head, and the daily threats and insults shouted at him had brought his mind to a feverish pitch, and he approached the strikers with a sullen gleam in his eyes.

The night's frost may lay the grain, or other ruin come.
Now everyone must toil, it is work which gives us strength.
No room now for factious minds, work is honor to a folk!
Hear, o hear the echoes ringing: work, to work, our country all!

The strikers' song grew fainter, and someone from their group shouted:
"Stop singing, you goddamned scab... Shame on you. Do you know what a scab is made of, Uolevi? When a little bit of slime was left on God's hands after Creation, he made a frog of it, and when there was still a little bit left, he made a strikebreaker out of that."

When the shouts began to be heard over the singing, Halme, the baron, and the sheriff started toward the road, but before they reached the group, they heard Uolevi shout:
"Who threw that? Who threw a rock... Throw one more and I'll shoot!"

Then everything was lost in a confused medley of heated shouts. Those who were working in the field began running toward the strikers and Uolevi.

Arvo Laurila had thrown the stone. It had only hit Uolevi's box, which had been the target. The box had tilted on its rope, and the fertilizer had spilled to the ground. Uolevi had pulled out a pistol, and another stone flew from the angry group of strikers. Then Uolevi fired into the air.

Halme ran into the group with his cane raised. Breathless from running he tried to shout, but his voice was drowned out by the din and clamor:

"My God, they're shooting at us... "

Do something. Calm them down... Order them... "

Akseli turned toward the one who was shouting the loudest:

"Quiet! Put the stones away... and the guns too."

His shout had no effect. As if in answer came Antto Laurila's yell:

"Goddamn puppy... with guns... You should be put down so you'll never get up again..."

The strikebreakers had come to Uolevi's aid, and now both sides were shouting at each other. When another stone flew, the confusion became total. Fortunately there were few stones on the road, and even fewer in the field, so that men had to search for them. When someone found a stone, another might snatch it from him in the heat of passion. And since there weren't enough stones, they rushed to fight hand-to-hand. Amidst the wrestling and punching, a medley of confused shouts filled the air:

"Is that so, goddamn... I'll shoot if I'm hit again... Disperse in the name of the law! Disperse in the name of the law... Away, away... Go away... Not good... Comrades, calm down... remember the honor of workers... remember that you are Social Democrats... Akseli, stop them. Otto, do something... Punch that snooty shit in the nose, he threw a rock at me... Goddamn no-good bigshot, go and screw your mother's housemaids, you haven't even done that yet... What are you doing here... Hit 'em so hard it'll knock their nose down to their neck. Comrades, listen... Sing... 'Arise ye slaves to work's oppression...' Jesus Christ, who threw a rock at me... I'll kill the son of a bitch... Remember the honor of workers... Be Social Democrats."

Halme rushed panting from one to another, his cane held high before him and his hands clasped prayerfully. A rock hit him in the back, and he crouched and gasped in pain, but only for a moment, then stood up again, to strive and shout, his voice cracking. Akseli too tried to control the group, but he realized that shouting would do no good in this melee, and began grabbing men to stop them. He shoved Elias's shoulder just as he was throwing a stone and barked:

"Don't, goddamnit... Didn't you hear me?"

Just then a stone struck him in the ribs. It knocked the wind out of him, and his eyes fogged with pain. When he regained his voice, he roared out:

"Who in God's name...!"

Plunging blindly into the group of strikebreakers, he seized the first man he could get his hands on. It was the son of the town doctor. Although blinded by rage, he was still somehow conscious that he should be calming the others down, so he did not strike out, but began tossing strikebreakers to the ground by their coat lapels. Arvo Töyry fell into his hands, and he too hit the turf like the others. The sheriff fired his pistol into the air and ordered the strikebreakers to withdraw farther back into the field. When they obeyed, the strife ended at last, for the strikers did not follow them. A cloud of dust hovered over the site of the battle. Panting, cursing, and moans of pain could be heard on all sides. Some had blood running from noses and cut lips; others were limping. One man sat on the roadside with tears in his eyes, rocking in pain and cursing. The last outbursts of rage spent themselves in shouting on both sides.

At first the baron had bellowed out pacifying shouts, but had soon stepped aside and watched the whole hubbub in silence with a calmly contemptuous look on his face. Halme, panting heavily, demanded of the strikers:

"Which one of you threw the first stone? Step forward... Who started it... This is... This is..."

The sheriff too had lost patience. No longer friendly, he said:

"This is a serious matter. You disobeyed my specific order. You started it. The men working were strictly forbidden. You'll answer for this."

"Gawddamn... No brain... all crazy... sick in the head..."

Halme turned to the sheriff and the baron. Shaking with excitement and shifting his cane from one arm to the other, he said:

"Please be so good as to stop provoking further fighting. Hasn't there been enough?"

There was another angry shout from the group of strikers.

"Shut your mouth, Big Manu. You need a goddamned good licking."

The baron fell silent, raised head erect, and started walking toward the field, looking haughty and disdainful. Halme ordered the group to start moving, and it did walk some distance away, shouting some final threats. Halme walked in gloomy silence, and then said to Akseli:

"You were supposed to keep order, but you were rioting with the best of them."

Akseli was holding his side as he walked. He answered Halme with a stiff-necked growl:

"Goddamn, I won't take blows like that lying down. No matter who it is."

Halme did not pursue the matter. Head high and looking straight ahead,

94

he marched behind the flag, ignoring the curses and threats being shouted behind him.

"We should really have let them have it... though I did smash that one in the mouth so hard I skinned my knuckles."

The group did not scatter, but stayed at the workers hall. Their excitement was slowly building anew. Halme had gone home to telephone, and when he returned he informed them that members of Parliament would come the next day to negotiate about ending the strike. Still rigid with indignation, he said:

"And I would like to say to all rioters that if you want me to be present at these negotiations, rioting must cease at once. I would hope that even the most feeble-minded would realize that such behavior greatly reduces our possibilities, for how can brawlers and rioters appeal to justice. I beg you to think, since an appeal to your honor seems fruitless."

The master's word fell into the silence, seemingly calm and controlled, but he was still plainly angry as he walked stiffly from the porch of the workers' hall, where he had spoken.

The announcement of negotiations gave rise to a new state of mind in the group. Threats about going to the fields again had already been voiced.

"And this time we'll leave behind those who side with the scabs. The boys who go will be the kind to empty the fields."

The information Halme had given them made even the most hot-headed cease their threats, but there was grumbling about his talk in small, private groups.

"Goddamn, do we have to stand nicely cap in hand while they stone us and shoot at us... He's been buddy-buddy with the bosses so long that he isn't altogether against them."

"And if they point a gun at me again, I think I can find something a little harder than a rock somewhere. I mean, I know where. And then you'll hear some shots from our side. And I tell you it won't be air alone the bullets go through."

Some of them, however, felt they had won the fight, and regarded even bloody lips and black eyes as badges of honor. A young day worker from the manor spoke proudly and boastfully through split and swollen lips:

"I got it so neatly in the face that for a while I saw three Great Bears and two belts on Orion."

The sound of raucous singing could be heard from the village that evening.

The Senate sent two members of parliament to arbitrate the dispute. One was Hellberg and the other a representative from the Suometar party, for the landowners of this old parish of large estates were mainly "Old Finns." Arrangements were made to hold the negotiations in the church village town hall, to which each side would send its representative. Both Senate representatives would then negotiate with their own group.

The leaders of the workers met at the church village workers' hall. Leaders of the strike committee from the various villages spoke in turn and presented their demands. Then they were coordinated, for individual villages and even individual farms had had different demands.

Then they discussed the degree to which the demands could be modified. Most of them were unconditional, although some concessions were promised, chiefly with regard to hours of overtime. Hellberg was silent throughout most of the discussion, but when it was over, he presented a synthesis of the demands and the terms of the negotiations. After the discussion, he spoke to a smaller circle of the more important men.

"Ending the strike is favorable from our point of view too. There are more important things going on. But it seems to me that the time is ripe for us to stick to our demands. I'll make a compromise proposition, but you don't have to approve it."

Someone proposed a demonstration during the negotiations at the church village, and there was a long dispute over its organization. Those opposed to it feared a riot and Halme, already frightened by what had happened, demanded that they give up the idea completely. Hellberg, however, was in favor of it, and Janne joined him, although they rarely agreed on anything.

They decided to organize the demonstration with the aid of a brass band and the male choir of the church-village organization.

"It's a good idea to keep reminding them of the situation while the negotiations are going on."

At the same time as the negotiators gathered at the town hall, the first parades of demonstrators appeared. Some of them even carried signs:

"Long live the eight-hour day! Down with barn slavery. The land belongs to its tillers."

When the demonstrators reached the church village, they were met by the brass band. Feet fumbled for the tempo, and postures straightened up.

"We've got a big gang here, boys. There's power backing us."

At the town hall the landlords looked at the group gathering. The master of Yllö asked Janne, with restrained sarcasm:

"Has a song festival been organized for the same time, or what is going on here?"

"They are curious, of course, to hear how things are going."

"And they'll riot too, of course."

"What is there to riot about, as long as we come to an agreement. It's a slightly different matter if we don't. But still it's better that they are here to follow the negotiations themselves. We'll find out immediately how far we can go. If we start to make an agreement they're not satisfied with, I at least don't want to go and face them. They'll stone us the way they did Stephen of old."

Janne looked thoughtful and sober, as if he himself had worried about possible consequences. Then they all gathered around a long table in the room, the two sides greeting one another stiffly and formally before sitting down on opposite sides of the table. It had been agreed that Silander would act as chairman, and he was just opening the negotiations when the sound of the demonstrators' singing was heard through the open window. The master of Yllö went to close it.

"They're holding a song rehearsal. A very musical people."

"They're crying out in hunger," said Janne.

First Janne presented the strikers' demands, and then the master of Yllö the landlords' position. The worst dispute arose over the hours for the dairy workers, for the landowners had not agreed to any regulation of them. The debate became heated, and the bitterness smoldering under the surface could be felt in the verbal exchanges. Janne described the workers' position and their working conditions and concluded by saying:

"You try getting up at four in the morning and going out to the barn, then rushing to do your day-work between your other morning and evening chores. No Sundays or holidays, but a muddy week of vacation in dark autumn. You can't go on treating people like animals forever. I knew one dairy worker who was always so tired that out of pity her mistress let her sleep in the calf pen without her master's knowing. She was only able to sleep two hours at night. I know a little bit about that life, and you must know something about it too."

Yllö's dry throat wattles wobbled as he cleared his throat:

"No one here is questioning Kivivuori's knowledge of the joys and sorrows of a maid servant's life. But does Kivivuori know about barn work too? What would the cows say if they were only cared for eight hours of the day?"

"Well, I haven't heard them talk, and I'm here representing the maids and not the cows, as the master seems to be. And the care of cows can be fitted into eight hours if other drudgery is left out."

"What about on small farms. They can't afford to have a servant free for a single day."

"There are very few small farms in this parish. You've swallowed them up over time, and there aren't many servants on them. And it's the very devil if the security of a small farm has to depend on the most unfortunate."

The fruitless argument continued. The representative of the Suometar party then offered a few concessions on the part of the landowners, and Hellberg made his own suggestions. Then an attempt was made to reconcile the two positions. All this was interspersed with talk of workers' conditions and the requirements for running a farm. Mellola, the owner of an estate and the sawmill, sat and watched the others with small, expressionless eyes. He was an enormously fat man, and his breathing was loud and labored. His whole body moved back and forth with each breath, for its governing part was his belly, which would not yield as he breathed, so that his back was forced to make room for his lungs. His massive head broadened oddly toward the bottom. There was something lazily imperturbable about his entire being.

When the talk turned to the quality of agricultural work, he too requested the floor:

"At home, we used to put this big an eye of butter into the stone dish. There was porridge in it, and we all ate from the same dish. We didn't ask for anything more."

Showing the size of the chunk of butter, he showed his fist, with the other hand gripping its wrist. After a short pause, he drew in a breath and expelled it with these hoarse words:

"And we worked hard... Ye-e-s!"

The others waited to see if Mellola would continue, but when he merely concentrated on his breathing again, Yllö again asked for the floor. He said that Hellberg's suggestion could be considered, but Janne demanded that it be presented to the strikers first, that at any rate he did not dare approve it on is own.

"Well, aren't you agreed on the matter? What is the point of this negotiation then?"

Hellberg looked at Yllö from behind his glasses. He looked somewhat tamer with his glasses on, but his snort had its former tartness when he said:

"Of course I can't give orders on my own. I've only been trying to think of something we might possibly get through. One can ask."

From outside could be heard now a song, now a speaker's voice. Hellberg promised to go and present his recommendation. He did go to the door and read it, but he had not properly reached the end when his voice was drowned in the uproar.

"Have you sold us out too? Do you mean to be a senator, or why are you on the side of the masters? We will retract nothing. We're not asking much as it is."

When Hellberg tried to go on speaking, the chairman of the Station Village Workers' Organization gestured to the band leader to strike up the *Marseillaise*, in which the crowd joined:

"Don't come here with your Senate business... not an hour more... 'and against the oppressor'..."

Hellberg returned to the room and sat down:

"It's hopeless even to try to get this through."

Yllö laughed with restrained mockery:

"If it had been presented to the Association, it would have gone through... If that had been the intention... maybe there was another reason for it."

"Here's the paper. You go and try to get it through yourself. First you torment people to death and then you demand that we keep them under control. It would be only right if we told you to stew in your own juices."

Halme asked for the floor. Although the others had remained seated while they spoke, he rose to his feet and began:

"Let me say a few serious words about a serious subject on a serious occasion. When chains long borne finally fall from the hands of the people, they do not at first know what to do with their freed hands. They may make the mistake of using them without due thought, in a manner that can hardly be approved of, so to say, as we have seen them do, unfortunately. Social tranquility among our people has suffered a severe jolt. And all this has happened at a moment when the possibilities for a happier settlement of our country's fate seem to have opened up. Understand the drift of my words. This disturbance — perhaps I should speak to you of a river. The waters in this river of our society have not been permitted to flow freely. Dams have been built along its course, and now when they are being demolished, the result is a seething and spattering. Your task now is to direct its flow into a peaceful channel. It can be done with very little: all it takes is money. My good gentlemen: I would give that money if I had it. But you have it, and so you have to give it. Let's not try to rebuild the dams, which have already collapsed. My good gentlemen, you must acknowledge certain facts and adjust to them. Do not believe that it is possible to return to the past. You must understand that you can no longer trample on the rights of the workers. The question is only whether they will be yielded voluntarily or taken by force. The train of history is advancing. You can hear the roaring of its wheels. The whole surface of our planet Tellus rumbles under their heavy weight. My good gentlemen. Elevate your vision. Look, and see! You hear

99

that song from outside. You don't like it, but it is dear to the singers. It is, so to speak, the song of their heart, to use the words of the great Aleksi Kivi, our immortal bard from Nurmijärvi. Perhaps I can trouble you gentlemen to take a little look into our past, although that may not necessarily advance the matter in question. The honorable judge has just presented to us the huge disparity between the increase in the prices of horseshoe nails and agricultural products. I concede the validity of his figures, but they are not in any way the fault of those who are outside. They have not raised the prices of horseshoe nails or of any agricultural products. It is the irresponsible industrial swindlers, who, using all the means provided by a state of war, have practiced such merciless robbery that the tales of misery from the early days of capitalism pale in comparison. Go and demand justice from them, not from those who have never received it themselves.

"But in addition, as I said, I would like to paint a picture of our past. The Highest Lord of our fate has given us a barren land, barren and beautiful, as the great Topelius says. The gifts of life here are few, and they are unevenly distributed, as the great Runeberg, for his part, has said in his line. 'Unequal are the gifts of fate.' Our state is compared to kingdoms, but our population is scarcely that of a large European city. My good gentlemen: Could I possibly have your permission to say: Why? Perhaps there have not been enough births? My good gentlemen. With your permission, I may reply to that question. It is not that there have been few births, but that children have been too industrious in dying. After perhaps a few months of life, when the milk from the exhausted mother's breast runs out, when chaffy bread is not yet digestible in a tender stomach. Or perhaps after a few years, weakened by a lack of nourishment. Perhaps one reaches adulthood and has lived for a time at the edge of a field or the side of a big hill, when the initially weak thread of life is snapped. My good gentlemen, there are few of us because our people's growth has wasted away in a sea of pain and suffering. The bosom of the earth has yielded life to too few, too many have succumbed beside it, with no share or rights in it. The increase and decrease in our population has corresponded with the size of the year's crop. Just as the number of squirrels increases in good years for pine cones and decreases in bad years, so have those sons of Turja, whose destiny it has been to die out of the way of those who have the prerogative of ruling those gifts of life which our land affords. I see a long, staggering procession on its hopeless pilgrimage, a scene from my childhood. My good gentlemen. The rise in price of horseshoe nails is a very troublesome thing to those who have to shoe their horses. But yet, if I place on the scales, let us say, all the nails needed for the entire parish, and place opposite them one wretched life, filled with pain and suffering, endured without even knowing the reasons for them, then, good gentlemen, those nails will rise as noticeably lighter. My good gentlemen, you hear that song outside. The ghosts of yesterday are singing there. To my sorrow, I have heard threats that the unrest be silenced with force. My good gentlemen, let me assure you that that road leads nowhere. For, as I have said, the ghosts of the past surround us and demand their right with sorrowful eyes. Let us give it to them, for you cannot shoot ghosts. I fear them, those shades of the staggering processions, and thus I beg you, my good gentlemen, to agree to these demands. They are a very low price for the right of these ghosts. Once more, my good gentlemen, accept them."

Having finished, he sat down and stared at the wall facing him with a look of imperturbable calm on his face. While he spoke the others had looked off in different directions, embarrassed by his solemnity. It seemed out of place in the mundane atmosphere of the half-empty room, in which his word echoed more loudly than usual. Hellberg sat turned to one side with an obviously dissatisfied look on his face. Janne's face wore an expression of affected sobriety, as he stared at the table top the whole time. Even those on Halme's side looked concerned. The master of Yllö gave a small, dry cough and said:

"No one has been shot here, either ghosts or living beings, but we've been under a shower of sticks and stones for a couple of weeks... You should have gone and given a speech like that out on the steps. Yeah... We seem to be getting nowhere. We've been jawing here for an hour now. If those on our side would go into the committee room..."

He rose and left, a kind of dry practicality clearly apparent in his bearing. This descendant of an old estate-owning stock, which had dried up in its juridical dignity, had run his large farm, as well as the entire parish, from the time he had been a young man. There was something patronizing even in his attitude toward strikes. He concealed the cold rage they had aroused with a kind of reassuring matter-of-factness, and it was with such demeanor that he now marched at the head of his troops into the committee room. Mellola was the last to rise from the table, puffing and straining, as he grunted out:

"I've always said that Halme is good with words. He should have been a schoolteacher like I told him once. He knows all those things. Poems and stuff... A schoolteacher, that's what..."

Having managed to rise, he crossed the room laboriously after the others, with little, short steps, preceded by his large belly, his hands rowing short strokes to either side, only half of his palms visible under his slightly too long coat sleeves.

There was a brief silence after they left the room, and then Janne half-whispered.

"I think Yllö is going to soften them up."

"You probably touched their conscience a little, Aatu," said Silander, but Halme did not reply, remaining silent as if still listening to the echo of his words. Hellberg snorted and said:

"You can only appeal to their conscience if they have one."

Then he rose and went to look out of the window at the crowd, which was being addressed by one of the organizers of the strike at the moment. In a sudden fit of rage, he turned from the window and said:

"If something comes of this, it will be the fault of that ragtag bunch. Really... sometimes I really feel like shouting: Lord, give us Barabbas."

Sitting down again, he went on in the same angry voice, as if he were talking to himself:

"And Santeri Alkio, with his gang of landowners, is demanding a higher price for bread, and obligatory work so they can get cheap slave labor for their lands. There are days when the Helsinki poor go without bread, and they have the nerve to be angry about the food laws that require rationing so they can't deal freely on the black market... But the rich have whole rivers of butter..."

He was so angry that the words came hissing through his lips, distorting the vowels in Alkio's name.

A small smile appeared in Janne's eyes as he observed Hellberg's rage.

The landowners returned and resumed their seats. The master of Yllö began in an official tone a statement that had obviously been shaped in advance:

"We have decided to accept the demands presented, in spite of the fact that agriculture, which is already in difficulties, will be subjected to such a strain that its effects cannot be judged in advance. We have reached a decision only so that work will go on in peace, since the leaders of the strike seem unable to maintain order in their ranks, either because they cannot or will not."

After a short pause, he continued in a more prosaic voice:

"This is of course our decision. I have to go and ask a few people for their opinions before we go and sign an agreement. I'll go and call from central."

He left the room, but returned from the steps, where he had been greeted by a storm of shouts:

"Does the old man mean to escape? Don't let him go... He goes nowhere until the matter is settled."

Yllö said as he returned:

"Well, it looks as if nothing will come of it.But what can I do?"

Janne went out to the steps, told the crowd to stop the racket, and explained the reason for Yllö's leaving. The latter started out again, and this time a lane opened through the crowd, through which he walked without looking to either side. One of the better known church villagers ducked behind another man as the master went by. His stance was still not firmly rooted.

The crowd had remained there throughout the negotiations. There had indeed been a small traffic to and from the group. Many people from outlying communities traversed the streets of the church village out of curiosity. The church and the hill on which it stood seemed extraordinarily strange on a weekday. The church was empty and ordinary. Some even took care of their business at the apothecary at the same time. The young people went to buy doughnuts, which the storekeeper had had the foresight to stock up, for the weight of the demonstration and the hope of success lured them into extravagance. One young hired man had bought a whole dozen of doughnuts. Taking the bag with him, he withdrew behind a corner of the cooperative store. The crowd was singing the Marseillaise at the time, and the boy looked around with the instinctive caution of one who feels as if he has done something bold and suspicious. Then he began. Concentrated, unconscious of his surroundings, eyes half-crossed, he embarked on chewing. His teeth snapped viciously at the side of a doughnut and his jaws worked ceaselessly. Doughnut after doughnut disappeared into his mouth. When one was gone, another was already in his hand awaiting its turn. Toward the end he began to feel a slight ache in his temples from his overtaxed chewing muscles and his jaws were stiff so that he could only half chew the last pieces. Then he licked his fingers, crumpled the bag, and hid it in the stone footing of the building. With one last careful look around, he went back to the crowd, his mind languid with satiation, but with a slight and vague sense of guilt, a little like what he had felt when he looked fearfully at his mistress's face as he filched a bit of butter from the dish or took one last herring, which custom and usage told him was over the limit.

Only when he was back in the group did he calm down and join in the song:

> ...you freedom, which leads us on
> where only soldiers march.
> To arms against the oppressor...

Among the men from Pentti's Corner, some were also eating doughnuts. There was happy chatter, and forced witticisms were attempted if none came naturally. Aku Koskela was there too, although his shoulders were still so sore that he could hardly bear to move. Seeing that others had doughnuts, he too began to want them, and went to get some, asking his brother if he would like some too. After a long hesitation, Aleksi said:

"Well, maybe you can bring me one."

Akseli bought none for himself, but ordered one apiece for his sons.

Aku, who was more free and easy by nature, bought several. Elma Laurila watched him eating and said:

"Koskela's baby is eating coffee bread. I could afford to buy a doughnut too, if I wanted to."

"Buy one them if you feel like it."

"Pooh, I've got more self-control than a baby."

Akseli had been asked to speak, but had refused. He was not among the more experienced leaders who mounted the steps of the cooperative store one after another and began in a resounding voice:

"Comrades, we will not retreat, we will not surrender, we will endure in this battle no matter how long it takes, but we will not yield. We are no strangers to suffering, we can stand it for a little longer..."

His own cohorts whispered to Akseli:

"Hey, Koskela, you go too so that one of us... Since Halme is in there negotiating... someone should speak for us..."

But Akseli did not go:

"There's been enough talk."

When Yllö went to call, the mood grew brighter. They watched curiously as he returned, but the landowner's face revealed nothing. When he entered the building, the crowd fell silent, in tense anticipation.

Inside, Yllö announced that he had gotten the consent of the most important employers. He did not mention how difficult it had been on the part of the baron. The baron had interrupted the call occasionally, but the baroness had come to answer a new call, and so Yllö had finally gotten the baron's consent.

"Well then, it's best to start writing up the text of the contract."

Janne took out some papers from a folder:

"I have it already written up here. All it needs is a signature. It has the conditions agreed upon already enumerated."

The master of Yllö read the pages and said with a snort:

"Kivivuori was very sure of everything."

"I have always believed in the triumph of justice. From childhood on, some such belief has stuck in my mind."

"Ha, ha..."

Janne went out to the steps with the text of the agreement in his hand. First he announced its acceptance by the masters, and then read the detailed clauses of the contract. He was the only one who could hear them, for the crowd broke out into a noisy demonstration of approval.

The last clause involved an agreement involving the riots during the strike. There would be no charges brought, except for those occurrences which were under official jurisdiction. The landowners also bound themselves not to bring charges, for strikers had also been attacked.

Processions left by turn for their homes. The male choir and the band took their places on the steps of the cooperative store, and the journey began in march tempo. Halme took his place alongside Akseli in front of the group from Pentti's Corner, still in a solemn and silent state of mind. There was enthusiastic discussion in the group.

"Nothing can beat seeing the gang start marching off... They could ring the church bells in honor of this day..." The music of the band, the rumble of the drums, and the song of male choir rang out over the church village. The echo rebounded from the walls of the cooperative store and reached the ears of those already farther off:

> *Forward, you mighty band,*
> *no sorry lot of slaves.*

Someone humbly offered a doughnut to Halme:
"Will the master have one... If it's good enough..."
"Thanks... but not on the road like this."
The master's knees rose in march tempo and his cane swung on his arm.

The choir and the band continued the march until the tail end of the very last procession disappeared from sight. The landowners had left the town hall by the back door to avoid seeing this show of triumphant rejoicing. With bitter contempt, the church village gentry watched the departing crowds from their windows. Were they the same people who had formerly come to the church village timid and shy, bowing humbly to the store and apothecary missies. People who, in the middle of their purchases, would duck to one side in panic if a landowner or a member of the gentry happened along. Were they the same thin-faced women, who looked in turn from the shelves of the store to the coins wrapped up in a rag, and then said, somewhat shamefaced:
"Could I have just a quarter..."
Tenant farmers, hired hands, and workers paid in food, most of them in coarse homespun clothes, day laborers in store-bought clothing, got with an abundance of money from work on the fortifications, maidser-

vants with white kerchiefs knotted under their chins, and in their hands the visible result of folk education, a handkerchief, into which they did not blow their nose, but which they clutched in their hand on the journey to the church village, their knuckles showing white.

But now a garish red flag was waving over the gray homespun and the white handkerchiefs of the maidservants. Over the church village echoed the strains of the orchestra and the male choir's song.

Throw down all barriers with your might,
and break the locks that bind you.

CHAPTER FOUR

I

They went back to work sullen and withdrawn. On job sites, groups of men were seen to gather, and from their midst came a soft, animated murmur of talk. When the landowner or overseer arrived, the talk ceased and the group scattered. There were smiles, looks, and vague remarks, understood only by members of the group.

The baron fired all of his temporary work force. Only the regular employees remained, and even the women were permitted to do only the mandated "gift days" for land, pasture, and wood rental. Employment for the young men ceased. Work on fortifications ended in other locations as well, so that it no longer paid to go there in search of jobs.

The Koskela boys worked around the house for Akseli in return for their food. There wasn't much to do for so many men, but they could not endure being idle. Akseli looked at the uncleared portion of the swamp, and said:

"Wait, boys, until the surveyor drives in markers at the corners of the fields, then I'll have work for you too. You can start opening a ditch. I'll get at least a four-hectare plot from it when I go a little way into those woods. Just wait for the rap of the gavel in Parliament. I'll make over that barn and put siding on the house. And then at last I'll take that stone out of the potato field there."

He was in a state of enthusiasm, which is why he spoke so freely to his brothers of his plans. Aku said with a sly gleam in his eye:

"And what will you buy rye with?"

"I'll show you boys what I'll buy rye with. In the winter I'll haul logs to the shore with Poku and in the summer I'll have you digging ditches. And even if I say so myself, I'll get a little of it done too."

Akseli worked in an exalted and energetic state of mind. When he went out to the hayfield with scythe on shoulder, the people at home could hear him busily humming. The children got a surplus of chucks under the chin and kind words. On such occasions they literally fought for their father's favor. Each in turn got to stand on his father's boot toes as he sat down or was allowed to drink from his coffee cup.

"Me from father's cup."

"No, me. Me fum fada cup."

The coffee was, in fact, mostly chicory water, but when had it ever been very good at the Koskelas'? It had improved slightly after Elina came, and they drank it more regularly, but now coffee was scarcely to be had, except on the black market.

Akseli spoke of a new barn to Elina. The old one was a low and dark manure barn, cleaned only occasionally. Elina had complained about it during the winter, and now she got a promise:

"You won't have to grow old with it. When freedom comes, things will start to happen around here. We might even build one of brick, like the Korris'."

"Will it be as large too?"

"Well, not quite."

He even went around to houses with the Association envelope and folder under his arm. There were constant meetings, and there were shouts of "Hurrah" at most of them.

"Hurrah for the eight-hour-day law!"

"Hurrah for the districts' right to vote!"

But the most overpowering shouts rang out when they cried:

"Hurrah for the Power Act! We're all Czars!"

The Power Act had been followed tensely and excitedly, for Halme had carefully explained its significance.

"Only through this law will democracy be realized in Finland. It will achieve the independence of the Finnish people on two fronts, both internal and external. That famous "Petersburg way" will no longer exist, and when the people, themselves the highest sovereign, exercise the Czar's power through their parliament, the laws which have been approved will be enforced. Where will the shadow men then find refuge? Kerenski can't offer it to them, even though some of our blackest Czar's secret-police bourgeoisie hope he can. Comrades, can I pose a couple of questions to you? When the people of Russia hurled their worthless Czar from the throne, to whom did his power shift? May I hear your opinion?"

"To the Russian people."

"Correctly answered. But when in the person of this Czar they also tossed out our equally worthless Archduke, to whom did his power shift?"

"To the people of Finland, of course."

"Correct. And Kerenski's government has exactly as much power in this land as we give him, or as he is able to uphold by force, therefore illegally. And if our bourgeoisie would for once join in a firm front on behalf of the country and its people without plotting and scheming, then Kerenski would have only so much power as we give him. Comrades, we are facing a severe trial, which will decide the issue. Gird up your loins to endure it. Comrades, forgive me if my voice fails me. I cannot help it, for I now see before me the end of the long red thread of my life in being able to say six words at this high moment, which fully express the sum of our society's strivings:

"Long live free and democratic Finland!"

His voice was far from failing him, and he beat time to the shout with his cane more gaily and enthusiastically than usual.

The trial predicted by Halme came quickly. Spurred by rumor and conjecture, people gathered at the workers' hall on many evenings without being called.

"Stay at your stations. No leaving. Remain united."

There was rabid support for the parliament, which was threatened with dissolution. During the day they had heard everything under the sun, news which came from Helsinki by phone, was spread by word of mouth, and gave rise to assumptions of various kinds. People could not abide waiting for newspapers but demanded that Halme phone.

"Go and call Manner himself if you have to, but we have to know what is happening."

Manner was indeed too great a man for even Master Halme to reach, but he did call the church village, where events in the capital were being followed. Those in the church village were in constant touch with Hellberg, on behalf of the county executive committee. Generally Hellberg notified Silander immediately of the most important happenings, although such information was completely unofficial.

Late in the evening, on his return from calling for the third time, a gloomy and silent Halme walked through the crowd in the yard to the steps, from which he had given a number of speeches that summer.

Turning toward the crowd, he looked at them for a while, thinking over the words he would say. This time his voice actually did shake as he spoke, not from weeping, but from total indignation and dejection.

"Comrades. Again I must inform you that we have been betrayed once more. The bourgeois senators, along with the governor-general, have again promulgated a declaration to dissolve the parliament. Once more the people of Turja have seen their provincial governors sell their country for the right to keep slaves. Well, perhaps you recall the verse about the lake in Turja the depth of which a man wanted to know. But his line broke and a voice was heard saying: 'It's as deep as it is long/Lake Inari's depth is still unplumbed.' Is your sufferance the same: Is it as deep as it is long, and still unmeasured? They have resorted to the excuse that it would otherwise be dissolved by force. But a firm, united front would not have been thus dissolved. Yes, they are accustomed to promulgations. They already issued a certain manifesto in the year ninety-nine. Shame on those already in their graves and those who will lie there in the future. And shame on those traitors, and on their memory too, tenfold shame on these promulgators. Shame on those hirelings of Kerenski, if in some corner of their dark souls there is still a fiber which can be stirred by such a feeling. Let them rejoice at being able to overturn our law once more, but the thunder of history can be heard behind and above their shouts of triumph, and what the Supreme Lord of Fate has decreed, neither these promulgators nor Kerenski can nullify. Of this my belief assures me. Only the demands of poisoned bodies can lead people to believe that treason and falsehood can lead to success. They are wrong to believe so, for those souls which peer toward the future from purified bodies know otherwise. Such souls may still be far, very far from the truth, but they are near enough to see its light through the darkness of the carcass-eaters."

Seldom had the people of Pentti's Corner seen Halme so agitated. He kept pressing a hand to his breast as he spoke, for the tumult in his mind was causing a pain near his heart. He had noticed it already at the fight during the strike, but had not been able to attend to it in his perturbation. The crowd listened to him in silence, and only when he was through did Akseli rise and ask:

"Is it really true?"

"It is true... Where... is there a rope for Judas?"

"Goddamn, we'll always find rope enough... I think there are still enough men in this country to string them up... Down with the promulgators... Socialists, don't dissolve... Stay in your seats. If they go, we'll find a rope for them too. Goddamn, those men were sent there to represent the people... The constitutionalists are making common cause with the Russians..."

The outbursts of rage and the shouting were still going on when the crowd scattered late in the evening. When they were near the manor, someone shouted:

"Peace to the cottages and war on the palaces, goddamn."

Akseli returned from the workers' hall alone, for the boys had remained there. His feet struck the road more angrily and forcefully than usual. His walk was generally vigorous: he did not drag his feet and his left hand swung little farther than his right, which he carried a little forward of the left. This time the hand swung more heatedly than usual, and the tail of his unbuttoned coat flapped with each stride. On his arrival home, his feet stamped so angrily on the steps that Elina came to the bedroom door to see.

"I wondered why you've come stomping in like that."

"What stamping? Am I supposed to creep up in my socks?"

"What... what are you mad about now?"

"Nothing. What are you looking at? Go to sleep."

Elina withdrew into the bedroom and Akseli went into the main room.

There was the sound of angry grunting as he pulled off his boots and a thump as he threw them into the corner. In the bedroom, he took off his pants in silence. From the bed, Elina asked timidly:

"What really is the matter now?"

Akseli set his pants on the back of a chair. Holding his underwear up with one hand, and jerking angrily at their waistband, he snapped:

"It's... it's something that... they'll soon be able to howl out that song they always bellow at their festivals... cruel war has been ignited... Oh Jesus... The way it is, you can't fill up those bosses' bellies no matter how much you shovel into them, so you have to rip them right open... Why the hell keep filling up this bottomless sack forever..."

Trying to avoid the anger directed at her, Elina asked in a sympathetic voice:

"Well, what have they done now?"

"They've dissolved the parliament... Since the parliament would have gotten the Czar's power, and the workers had the majority, it was the same as if the workers had the Czar's power. They've been plotting with the Russians... with that devil Kerenski. Good God, if a man could once get face to face with things like that. They would be no match for a man. I thought that when the Czar fell there would be no one for Finland's masters to lean on, but there seem to be enough Tahovitches and Kerenskis. And if that goddamn preacher says a crosswise word to me, I'll smash him right in the belly, no matter how spiritual he is."

As he spoke he turned from side to side, first pulling the tow cloth summer cover over him and then shoving it down.

"But won't there be new elections as always before?"

"Of course there will. But our majority comes only from the way the election was organized, and we may lose it. And do you think they would be plotting with them if we were to get a majority. No, I'm not even going to vote. When you're dealing with people like that, who always play crooked, it doesn't pay to vote. The best and only way is to let them have it."

They lay awake till morning, for Akseli's rage was slow in abating. Elina spoke soothingly, seeking hopeful possibilities, but her lack of expertise made them untenable, so that her suggestions frequently evoked an angry snort from Akseli. Gradually he was content to stay longer on one side, and when the rising sun began to light up the back room, he fell asleep at last.

After the strike, the vicar continued to work in the fields. He had observed a beneficial effect on his physical and mental condition from the work, and therefore he often busied himself with some of the lighter chores. Preferably he went to places where Akseli was not working. The stiff and oppressive atmosphere there was discomfiting and spoiled the pleasure wrought by the work.

Sometimes he worked so hard that sweat ran down his body. After such a session, he felt a great increase in energy. Along with an added bodily strength came a rise in spiritual self-confidence. His uncertainty vanished along with the excess flesh, and he felt himself to be firm in all respects.

After coming from work and washing up, he was likely to swell his chest and stretch out his arms as he had seen athletes do in pictures. There were heavy, old, leather-covered chairs in the dining room, and he liked to move them nearer the table, lifting them by the backrest with one hand. Reading the newspapers he was apt to say with unusual interest:

"Ah-hah. Hannes Kolehmainen..."

That helped somewhat against the perpetual gnawing uneasiness at the back of his mind. Although there was peace in their vicinity after the strike, the strikes went on elsewhere in the land. And in addition, the threat of a strike still hovered over them as well. It was difficult to concentrate on the daily routine, for the country, down to the most out-of-the-way community, was living fervently through the governmental change. Newspapers, rumors, and visitors brought fresh news constantly, which inflamed the mind and forced one to take a stand. Sometimes the vicar tired of it, and then the work seemed especially pleasant. He had developed the habit of going to work at the same time as the crew, and of staying in the fields until they left. If his official duties kept him from going to work with the crew, he usually stayed away the whole day. And after every news account of disturbances, he went to work.

"We all have to try. This country cannot afford either masters or workers. If only the concept of citizen would take root in place of those divisive terms."

He did not learn to work with horses, but steered clear of them, afraid that he could not control the animals. But he willingly pitched hay onto the stacks or from the stacks onto the loads.

Over the years, the parsonage family had grown distant from their relatives and acquaintances in Helsinki, but lately the latters' family affection had increased surprisingly. They came to visit frequently. Sometimes they came out to the hayfields and made a mess of something or other, for they had the idea that making hay was fun. The work appealed to them for a while, but soon they began to lean on their pitchforks with an annoyed and indifferent look on their faces.

"Exactly what are those flowers? I'm going to take a look... Oh my, strawberries. As children we always strung them on a straw."

Then they went to eat the strawberries.

But when Ellen and the servants had the table ready for the noon meal, their annoyed indifference vanished.

"Oh, real country food. I remember how glad I was to eat it as a child when we were in the country during the summer. I often felt like going to some farm just to eat."

The relatives were mostly well-to-do people who had never had to think about food except for what they would have at any given meal. For the first time in their lives they had to find out that it might be a problem to get food. They had plenty of money, but not all of them had yet learned to deal with black marketers, since that involved a degrading secrecy and the bold familiarity of those shameless swindlers.

It was nicer to bring Ellen coffee and sugar obtained from merchants they knew and get pork and butter from her. It was on that account that they remembered the old days of their youth.

"Do you remember how as girls we..."

They also told of the happenings in the uneasy capital, of the strike among the reserves, of the demonstrations around the parliamentary building, and of their own feeling of being unprotected.

"But the worst was to hear Jean Boldt speak on the steps of Nicholas's Church. The hairy throats of the hooligans were gulping down the saliva as he promised millions to them."

The uneasiness of the visitors was contagious. The people of the parsonage contracted it, even though the days went on as usual. The vicar worked in the fields and attended to his official duties as before. But his Sunday sermons had acquired much content from the new happenings. Hearing about some melee or verbal confrontation, he was angered, and its traces could be heard in the text of his sermons. In the history of Israel he found endless analogies to the situation.

"...for corruption rules the people. Everyone seeks not God, but his own advantage. The voices of prophets are drowned in the din and shrieking of the world."

"...is Baal then only a false god from Biblical history? No, he is still alive today. We see him everywhere around us. And innumerable are his prophets."

Vehemence made his sermons sharper and more forceful than before, and Ellen, sitting on a bench, was proud of him. The services were mainly boring and tiresome to her, but her position demanded that she go to church, although she was not inclined to religion by nature.

Sometimes an old woman would sit on the back seat of their carriage on the way home. It had become a habit during the summer to give such churchgoers a ride, for they admitted that they themselves were indeed guilty of indifference toward their fellow man. When such a stooped old woman withdrew to the side of the road, looking with twisted neck at the pair driving by, the vicar would tell the driver to stop:

"Since we're going a long distance in the same direction, Mrs. Lempinen can ride with us."

"Oh no... It'll be crowded... I can walk well enough."

"Mrs. Lempinen has had enough of walking during her lifetime. I'll help her... that's it. It's much nicer to ride in this heat than to walk."

With crafty humility, Mrs. Lempinen agreed, belittling herself as she sat on the narrow rear seat, at the same time examining the details of the gentry's beings with burning curiosity, for she had never before seen them from so close up. The vicar kept up a friendly conversation, trying to put himself on the level of such an old farm wife, and the woman struggled to intuit what kind of talk would please the vicar.

"Yes, yes, such godlessness has never been seen before."

When Mrs. Lempinen got off at her cottage, she thanked them over and over, and the vicar cheerfully brushed off her thanks. He felt lighter in mind, and said to his wife after some time:

"When you talk to people like that, you sometimes envy them. They believe with a naive innocence, like children. And when you think that you sometimes have to struggle with doubt yourself..."

"They are still unspoiled. And there are many like them. And they are silent, for only the slag froths."

"That's certainly true... but it's sad to think about."

Nor did the frothing cease. After the day's work the couple often sat together in the parlor and sifted over matters. What will come of this — it was a question they could not escape. The quiet voices of the summer evening carried in through the open window. The servants returned from the evening milking and made a clatter with the milk pans. The calm lake mirrored the evening sunshine. The curtain swayed in the evening breeze.

The calm about them was a nostalgic image of the past. A restful, sheltered life, whose griefs and troubles seemed trifling compared to those of today. Sometimes at such moments, the vicar felt depressed:

"Sometimes I wish I had been born a Laplander. They do not have such problems."

Ellen took it as a joke and said with a laugh:

"Would you be able to tend reindeer?"

But the vicar did not laugh and seemed offended by Ellen's playful tone.

"I said, if I had been born a Laplander. Then of course I would."

"But perhaps things will be more peaceful now, when we have the new election."

"If they lose, they'll raise a row over the dissolution of the parliament... They should not have issued the promulgation."

It was a sore spot with them. Ellen put her fingertips into her mouth and bit her nails:

"But they weren't aiming at any sort of independence with the Power Act. Military affairs would have been left to the Russians. What would they have done with that kind of independence?"

"Nothing, most likely. But it would at least have been a long stride toward independence."

"They're willing to accept the Russian soldiers in their rioting."

The vicar ended the discussion by saying:

"Why don't we have Socialists like those in England and Sweden. This is pure anarchy."

Later in the autumn the situation only grew worse. The vicar read about the butter riots in the New Suometar and he rose to pace about heatedly:

"They've simply gone and distributed the butter from the warehouses. No... we can't stand for this... Something has to be done."

But he himself did nothing, although he did donate money for the purchase of weapons when Uolevi Yllö came to ask for it.

"It's been decided to organize a civil guard. Father says the Russians will no longer obey their officers. We have to get rid of them, otherwise conditions won't improve. I won't shoot into the air the next time they throw stones."

"Perhaps nothing else will do. That's all I have to give now. I can give more later."

The vicar's reanimated activity also brought him a post on the board of elections. There he encountered both Halme and Akseli, and under the circumstances, discussions of a political nature were unavoidable. The Socialists had at first threatened to boycott the election entirely, but then they had nevertheless begun to prepare for it. The matter was discussed with completely open animosity prevailing. The meetings of the board of elections were held at the fire hall. Halme and Akseli explained that the elections were illegal, and the vicar and the schoolteacher asked why they were taking part then.

"To prevent at least a little of the reactionary scheming with the Russians."

"The provisional Russian government had the legal right to dissolve the parliament, and at any rate, we are now appealing to the will of the people, so there should be no reason for opposition."

"Ahem. Finland's parliament expressed the will of the people in the Power Act, but the reactionary bourgeoisie sought the aid of Kerenski's dragoons to nullify the will of the people. Well, the elections are good insofar as they make it possible to punish the betrayers of the people."

"Procurator Svinhufvud has said that the dissolution was completely legal and the only fault was in the basis for its declaration."

"What is illegal in its basis is illegal per se. And since the parliament of Finland had once declared itself the supreme authority, there is only one legal power which could dissolve it, and that is itself. I do understand a little too. Permit me to request that in spite of my insignificance, I be considered an adult individual. If I ask too much, then be so good, but it is my conception, and that of all Socialists, that you are afraid of democracy and not of Kerenski. For the sake of reaction you betrayed the people at the moment when for the first time it challenged the oppressor."

"Well, the Socialists themselves could see what the members of parliament were able to accomplish. They couldn't even get into the parliamentary building."

"Exactly. While the bourgeoisie applauded in secret and sometimes even openly. And one day when the unfortunate people of Turja looks at its history, should the Supreme Lord of Fate grant it that opportunity, then it will see one lone pure spot in our shame — those members of parliament who knew what they owed to the people. But what should I say of this country's upper class, those gentlemen for whom the people have given their all. The people have paid the price for all the civilization possible.to us. They have provided the upper class a sheltered and carefree life, kept their masters in a bed of roses — only to see their masters betray them at the decisive moment so that they could preserve their reactionary rule. Ahem. Let them pray for the ocean's floods to wash their hands."

Halme had been so stricken by the dissolution of the parliament that he could not speak of it without becoming heated. Reference to it shattered even his controlled formality, and then red spots burned on the peaks of his narrow, wrinkled cheeks. In the first days he was so worked up that he developed a fever. So great was his mental turmoil that Emma begged him not to read the paper, since his agitation always increased after he did. But never had his thinking been so sharp. Ideas poured out incessantly, but when his excitement abated, he felt completely exhausted. A cold sweat oozed from his brow, and sometimes a fit of vertigo forced him to grope for support.

But the vicar was also aroused. Groping for words and turning over the folder on the table before him, he stammered:

"I... I... I haven't dissolved any parliament... You must know that my son... that I have sent my son to Germany just for the sake of my country..."

Akseli sat opposite the vicar with his arms crossed, looking past him out the window. When the vicar stopped speaking, he said in a bitter, nasty voice:

"Then it's all the more ugly to make deals with the Russians here... But the gentlemen ought to think a little bit. A workingman's cup may run over some day, even if it is large. Senator Serlakius said, when he promulgated the declaration, that the result would be an anarchy never seen before. And I guarantee you that Serlakius will get his anarchy. The gentlemen have set out on such a road, that before we see the end of it, the women in this country will need many black dresses."

The vicar looked at him condescendingly and took out his papers, stating calmly:

"Whoever cannot accept the people's decision made in a free election can of course raise a rebellion."

Halme too spread out his papers and said:

"We do not fear the judgment of the people. So, with regard to making Hollo's Corner a separate voting district, I think the idea comes a little too late..."

Business was then conducted with very few words, and the two sides left separately. The vicar and the schoolteacher stayed on at the school, discussing Akseli. The teacher remembered his school days:

"As a child he was already quite difficult. I do remember him well. Very stubborn and covertly defiant. A very difficult disposition... an extraordinarily difficult disposition."

On the way home, the vicar stopped thinking about the matter, but the feelings it had engendered still lingered in his mind. As he grew older he had adopted the habit of walking with his hands behind his back if he were not in a hurry. Often he stopped to look at his surroundings if his eye happened to light upon something interesting.

A flock of birds was swarming about an autumn field. They would land on a strip of field, then burst into flight again. Most of them would start at the same time, but a few were late. The vicar observed to himself

"Look at that. Even they don't react at the same time."

Then he continued lazily on his way with his hands behind his back, causing the manor work force cutting the autumn grain along the road to whisper to one another:

"Look at the preacher ambling along with his hands over his butt."

The flock of birds turned the vicar's thoughts back to governmental matters.

"But still they have a much stronger sense of unity than human beings. It isn't rebelliousness on their part; it is a slowness to react. But among people, it is deliberate anarchy. Are our people unusually prone to it? Is civilization still only skin deep? Are we still so close to the forest? We've eyed the highway doubtfully from in back of a tree, and now when we've finally dared to step out onto it, we suspect everyone approaching us of evil intentions. I don't believe that their hatred of the elite is only the result of agitation. A suspicious nature has a part in it."

A group of young men from the community were standing at the parsonage crossroad. Since there was no work, they passed their time idling on the roads. The sons of tenant farmers sometimes got a kilo of butter into their packs, and took it to town to peddle on the black market, but that, for the most part, was the extent of their activity. When they saw the vicar coming, they fell silent and began to look vacantly in different directions. The vicar straightened up and took his hands from behind his back. When he reached the group, he raised his hat, but they merely gazed at the ground. After he passed the group, the vicar felt as if they were looking at his back and laughing nastily. The troublesome thought kept growing stronger, and involuntarily he increased his pace, drawing himself more erect and stiffening. In the end, he was marching along, his body rigid and his face red, thinking angrily:

"That sly, glowering malice..."

The boys looked after him, and when they were sure he was out of earshot, they went on with their prattle:

"The old woman haggled and said they were so small too... I said our chickens weren't about to rip their asses for the old women of Tampere. If they weren't good enough, I would leave. She sure changed her tune."

III

In spite of stipulations in the agreement, the strike riots led to court cases. Among others, Töyry refused to honor those stipulations, and so the Koskela boys received a summons. The melee at the manor brought a charge of resisting the authorities.

After the case of Antto's eviction, it was easier to get legal aid. Lawyers were obtained for the accused, although Janne directed their defense. During the summer he had been chosen as the workers' representative on the communal rationing board, and his first action on behalf of the defense was to conduct a large number of surprise inspections on the farms owned by the plaintiffs. The landowners who were caught hoarding food were summoned to the same session of the court on charges of violating the provisions of the food laws. He even snared Mellola on a tip from one of his laborers. Mellola had left a portion of his grain unthreshed and mixed it with a heap of chaff. He explained to Janne that he could not report it to the board because he could not weigh it or estimate the amount unthreshed, but Janne had said seriously:

"I wouldn't otherwise... But the matter is a little nasty... Since the rationing law is a law too."

In handling the workers' cases, Janne called these men as witnesses for the prosecution. The landowners did not really consider the concealment of grain a crime, since they felt the rationing law to be clearly an injustice, which had been drawn up only to "shut the mouth of the socialists."

But Janne made a great issue of it.

"I've heard that breaches of the law are being defended on the grounds of the strike riots last spring, but if the commission of a crime can ever be defended in court by the commission of another, then it is exactly the strikers who have much to adduce in their defense. Left completely to the whim of their masters, they have been forced to watch how many of them, using exceptional circumstances to their advantage, have avoided price restrictions and secured large farms for themselves, in which their workers have gotten no share. It's no wonder that they went on strike. And if in connection with it, there arose unpremeditated clashes with the strikebreakers, it cannot be considered at all astonishing. Unblinking circumvention of the law in those quarters which appeal to the law promptly when their own privileges are threatened has perforce confounded respect for the law, especially among the young and less thoughtful group. For this reason I, on behalf of the rationing board, having shown sufficient evidence, demand the severest punishment of the law, since at issue is not only an offense against the rationing laws, but a bad example deeply shocking to civil morality set by influential circles and people of respect and authority."

Carefully presenting deliciously nasty individual cases, he described the landowners' caches and his own actions.

"Having heard, although actually as an uncertain rumor, that the accused had turned over grain to a certain clandestine distiller, I saw it as my duty to investigate, for grain granted for one's own use certainly would not yield enough to use for bootleg liquor. I did find unreported grain, although I did not get proof of the rumor I mentioned so on that point there is no basis for a charge."

The story had some substance, for someone had told Janne that a certain landowner, when drunk on bootleg liquor, had said there was plenty of grain to use in distilling. But through skillful turns of phrase, Janne tried to convey the idea that the only question in the case was a lack of evidence.

During breaks he appeared among the landowners, sternly grave, shaking his head and expressing his wonder at one thing or another:

"I can understand this in vagrants, hooligans, and all sorts of riff-raff, but that we should find such things among the owners of large farms... Even those in positions of trust, even those in positions of trust..."

And the landowners, who were in court for the first time, and for concealing their own grain to boot, of which they had never before had to give an accounting to anyone, said to one another in their controlled but angry landlords' voices:

"One could put up with the others somehow, but that one is a snake. Just like an adder..."

In spite of Janne's efforts, the landowners' penalties were limited to small fines. The judge was lenient, for he knew that everyone who had the slightest possibility of doing so broke the rationing laws. He also knew that he himself would be taking half a pig with him when he left the village.

The case of the strike riots was taken up on the next day, and a large crowd had gathered around the community hall. When the accused arrived in a group from the workers' hall, where Janne had first coached and advised them, cheers and some threats were shouted. The accused reached the hallway of the building looking cheerful and anything but guilty.

"This is one boy who isn't afraid of the Kakola jail. I mean, I'm a bit of a wild one."

"I'll ask the judge if it's true."

Janne had indeed stressed the importance of good behavior, but the cheers made it easy to forget such coaching. Akseli stood in the group silent and withdrawn. His case was among the first to be handled, and he stepped into the room self-consciously stiff-necked in order to get rid of the troubling discomposure which appearing in public always brought on.

The charges against him included assault and the refusal to obey an official order. He admitted everything quite openly, but said, raising his head:

"I did not hit anyone. I pushed a few men over after they threw stones at me from the gang of strikebreakers."

"You were one of the leaders of the demonstration, and thus your example meant a lot. Your responsibility in the matter is greater than that of the others."

"If I had hit anyone, it would be a different story. I did push them over. And I repeat, I won't take such blows willingly. A dozen people here can testify that I held back the demonstrators, but they still hit me with a big stone."

Such speech made the judge especially ill-disposed towards him. That night they talked about him at the Yllös' for a long time. Aleksi, on the other hand, was humble and honest. When the judge asked if Aaro Töyry had threatened him with a pole, he thought for a little while and then said uncertainly:

"Well... I can't say that he threatened me in particular. But he did have his pole raised..."

"Then why did you punch him in the face?"

"Well... I don't know... how I got so mad."

When the first sentences were announced, an angry hubbub arose in the crowd waiting outside. Akseli's sentence was the heaviest: four months' imprisonment. Aleksi received only two, and Akusti escaped with a fine. When Akseli descended the steps of the community hall, he was greeted with shouts of "Hurrah!" and "Long live...!"

There was anger among the gentry in the hallway as well:

"Now really, there's never been a criminal cheered until this day. This is going too far."

But when after the session, the judge left for the Yllös', where he was staying, overt threats rained in his wake: "What gifts did you get from the bigshots since you gave them only small fines? What would you have demanded from the strikers to let them off the same way?"

"Hey old man, they earn the money for their fines from a kilo of eggs... We ought to show that son-of-a-bitch that even if we don't know the law, we can administer justice... We'll empty this hall tomorrow."

On the following day, a row of men stood on either side of the community hall steps. The hallway was also filled with men. More and more demonstrators gathered, for the word was spreading through the church village:

"Their civil guard is on watch there. Yllö's boy is walking around with his hand in his pocket."

"Is that so? Don't we have any men on our side?"

Then they went to stand on the step of the community hall with their hands in their pockets, glowering from under their cap brims at the members of the civil guard.

"Go and tell Janne to phone the Guard in Tampere. We have men there too."

"Why is your hand in your pocket, Sonny? What have you got there? Do you know what that bigshot Mellola paid the judge?"

The members of the civil guard did not reply. They tried to avoid even looking at the crowd, although its presence made them obviously uneasy. When the shouting continued and the crowd approached the building step by step, the sheriff came out. He spoke soothingly and courteously, explaining that the members of the civil guard were not there on their own, but with his consent.

"Are you their commander? Keeping order hasn't belonged to that sort before this. Everyone could just as well put a pistol in his pocket and tell the next man 'I'll shoot you.'"

When the members of the civil guard did not respond to the shouts of their harassers, the latter tired little by little. They sang a few revolutionary songs, and someone gave a speech, since there was an occasion for it.

The man was "learned" and, as a kind of freethinker, he went often to debate at the meetings of sectarian preachers. For lack of a better, his speech would do.

"Is there any significance in putting your hand on the Bible? Scientists have said that there is no god, but here we swear in his name. I will not believe until scientists say that there is a god."

The speaker was often interrupted by shouts:

"That Mellola thug's conscience lets him swear to anything with his hand on the Bible. Ask those firemen if they've read that he who takes up the sword will drown in its scabbard..."

When the speaker ended, a little boy climbed up to stand on the hitching rail. Some of the young men had urged him on, murmuring and whispering. The boy had resisted at first, but a fiver placed in his hand had won his consent. From under the broken brim of his too large cap, looking back and forth from his own group to the members of the civil guard, he shouted:

"Now by public request, the Triumphal March of the Constitutionalists."

Flapping his knees in tempo, he began to sing:

Old law is in effect, it has stood since Adam's time,
a constitutionalist am I tho' rabble pipes are playing.
But oh me, oh my, the law from Adam's time
is hampered now by progress and advancement.

The law's our whipping horse, upon it we do ride,
and lead the Finnish masses by the nose.
And my, we cheat and wring a living from their hide,
and ride roughshod over the necks of the poor.

We're born with boots and spurs, and estates on our back,
with open money bags beside our stills.
Oh my, beside our stills, with estates on our back,
betrayal in our butts, and fear no evil.

Our offices are mighty and our paychecks fat
with hoodlums and machine guns there to guard them.
Oh me, oh my, with hoodlums and with vicious cossacks,
machine guns, cannons, and black squads of cossacks.

Although the cost is counted in the hundred millions
when we are senators the people work to pay the price.
Alack and welladay, those plaguey Socialists
they dare to ask such tiny little taxes.

We'll form a butcher-guard and kill the lot of them
while sons of preachers say their last amen.
Oh me, oh my, oh joy, we'll sing out in our triumph
and rush like hell to meetings of the Diet.

We steal the best returns from all the people's work,
console the poor with promises of heaven.
Oh me, oh my, we cheat with promises of heaven,
but if you don't bow down you'll go to hell.

At the end of the song, there was hand clapping and other affectedly boisterous tokens of approval:

"That was a good song. Wasn't it a nice song, Yllö's boy?"

A quiet muttering arose among members of the civil guard. Some of them had difficulty controlling themselves, and Uolevi shook his head angrily at the most restless ones. Nevertheless one of them shouted:

"It's the red Cossack squads that have been helping you... to steal grain."

"Shut your snout, butcher. We're not afraid of guns."

The group began moving toward the members of the civil guard, and the latter drew closer to one another. There was hasty movement in the hallway, and the sheriff came out to the steps again. His exhortations to remain calm were drowned out by the shouts of the crowd.

"Order them to shoot... Start the slaughter... Godamned catspaw police... Have you checked out the program in advance? Why not demand the butcher guard's minutes for examination the way you demanded our Association's..."

The apothecary, who was standing among members of the civil guard, stepped out alongside the sheriff and sputtered angrily:

"Does... does... does an official have to listen to something like that... There has to be a limit somewhere..."

Janne came out to the steps. He could see that some of the men in the crowd were already searching for stones, and that those in the civil guard stood with their hands in their pockets. They had been forbidden to draw their weapons without the sheriff's command, but Janne could see that there was an uneasy fear mixed with their anger. One stone or a failure of nerve on the part of one of the men on the steps meant bloodshed. He took a couple of uncertain steps forward, and had already opened his mouth to address the crowd, but said to the sheriff instead:

"Get the accused out to the steps. Hurry!"

The sheriff hesitated, but when Janne repeated the command, he rushed inside, even though he did not understand the reason for doing so. Janne shouted in a loud and audible voice:

"Comrades, form a lane of honor on both sides of the road. We'll escort the accused to the workers' hall and hold a demonstration in their honor."

There was a small stir in the crowd. Some were already beginning to form the lane of honor, but it was not easy to change the mood of the crowd, and Janne shouted again:

"Bare your heads when they come out... Form up quickly... We'll show them what we think of these class-based judgments."

The accused arrived, and Janne urged everyone to go as a group to the workers' hall. Then he ordered the crowd to raise their caps to the accused, and the caps rose in the air. Tense and uneasy, he watched what was happening, meanwhile gesturing to the sheriff who had come to the porch to get out of sight. Shouts of approval for the accused rang out from the slowly forming lanes, and when they had passed through it, its tail end fell in behind them, although those who were nearest the steps kept on venting their rage at the members of the civil guard. A small smile of pleasure at having succeeded appeared on Janne's face. As he walked off after the group, he said to the members of the civil guard:

"I had guns too when I was a kid, but there's a time for everything."

The departure of the crowd freed the landowners from their promise of silence, and now they directed all their rage at Janne. They did not, however, shout at him, but to one another:

"Hats off! Here come the bums! When are the Russian soldiers coming to the workers' hall to help you?"

Janne was going, but he stopped when he heard the shout, took one more step before devising an answer, and then turned around:

"Who brought them into the legislative building? The promulgators. Keep your mouths shut about the Russians, you pups. Ask your fathers what right you have to say such things."

Without listening to the shouted answers, he went on to the workers' hall. As he walked through the crowd standing in the yard, he was the target of angry demands:

"Call Tampere, maybe even get the police from there... We have to get guns too... We're not going to stand with our arms crossed and be butchered..."

At the hall Janne was able to calm the crowd's anger somewhat by exalting the martyrdom of the accused and promising to seek amnesty for all those sentenced. But watching the men leave after the crowd broke up, he said to Silander:

"If we lose the election, there will be bloodshed."

He left the workers' hall whistling, with his hands in his pockets. Thoughtful, he kicked at an occasional pebble that happened to be at the right distance from the toe of his shoe. Lately he had been dejected at times. The course of events did not seem to be following the course he had anticipated. He did not like agitated people, wrangling and anger. He himself was very rarely angry, and such behavior most often evoked only a nasty laugh from him. And any enthusiasm stemming from emotion was not in accord with his cold nature.

Little boys were just on their way home from school in the church village. They had dallied on the way, for autumn had created mud puddles on the road, at which they had to dig and poke. Seeing Janne, they hurried to walk with him, shouting a comradely greeting while still far off:

"Hello, Kivivuori. Where you going?"

Janne's thoughtful melancholy vanished. A slyly sour look on his face, he coined a quick lie, which the boys denied, laughing joyfully. They accompanied him home, while he told them he had been in the church tower looking for a moose nest.

"I lifted the cover a little bit, and a whole herd of moose flew up at once."

"Don't lie... Liar, liar..."

The boys kept on chanting the words in chorus for a while, then asked Janne to give them candy from the co-op store. Stopping there, he bought it without other customers knowing, for candy was really no longer available. The boys did not thank him, but took the candy as if it were their prerogative. In parting they still kept shouting well-meaning insults, and Janne responded with the best he could muster. As a final leave-taking, they made faces at one another, and from the boys' group came a scornful shout:

"Ha, ha... You can't even make a face..."

IV

More people than usual were around the store getting their mail. Some vague information about the election had arrived, but nothing was certain. When the postman from Hollo's Corner left a mailbag at the store, the storekeeper distributed the newspapers, which were opened up and read on the spot.

"Ninety-two, if there are no changes."

"Falsifications, of course... The bourgeoisie couldn't get a majority otherwise."

"Illegal elections. Convene the old parliament, since it at least is a legal one."

The storekeeper was wiping off the counter:

"There really can't be a more legal parliament than one chosen by the people, heh, heh... But what do I know? I'm not up on politics. But don't you think the people should decide the matter?"

"They will decide it yet. And they will shut the mouths of the bourgeoisie."

"Yeah, yeah... Heh, heh... That's a different matter... I don't know... Yeah, yeah... I can't say. It doesn't say so... You can't find out anywhere..."

Those who had come for the mail went to take the news of the defeat to the cottages and tenant farms. Aku brought the paper to Koskela. The evening was already dark, and Akseli set a lighted splint in the door of the stove. Its flickering light cast a shapeless shadow of his head and the paper at the edge of the ceiling. Having read it, he rose and folded up the paper. Aku was seated on the bench, and asked a question his brother did not hear. Akseli set the paper on the corner of the table and went out. Meeting Elina in the entry, he went by without looking at her. Elina came in and asked Aku doubtfully:

"What's going on here. He looked so strange."

"The bourgeoisie won the vote and it gripes him."

"Where did he go? He's not going to do anything to himself..."

There was a gleam of humor in Aku's eyes:

"No way... but it'll be tough on us for a while."

The family walked on tiptoe that evening. Elina ordered the boys to be still if they raised the slightest ruckus. The flickering light from the splint, which barely revealed the room and the shape of its furnishings, increased the gloom of the atmosphere. The kerosene had to be saved for the barn and stable, for there one hardly dared move about with an open flame for a light.

Nothing happened that evening yet. The night went by peacefully, as did

126

the following morning, but at midday, visitors arrived. Looking timid and hesitant, a thin, exhausted-looking woman with two equally wretched-looking children, stepped into the house. Its master's glance and his begrudged greeting seemed to make them even more timid. Elina was not inside, and Akseli's irritation increased when he was forced to start speaking to the visitors, who were sitting on the bench near the door. One of the children was a boy, and he sat farther away from his mother. The woman looked at the floor, then in panic at Akseli, and began a somewhat halting explanation:

"We've come from Tampere... It's so bad there now. Would the master have a little bit of bread. It's so hard... Just a little."

"We don't have enough bread to sell."

The woman's entire body trembled. The harsh words frightened the children too, and the girl looked at Akseli in fright. Her eyes had an odd feverish gleam, which troubled Akseli, making him even more annoyed. Recovering from her fright, the woman looked offended, but asked if they could sit for a while.

"Well, we're not in the habit of driving people away."

Akseli went out, and seeing Elina in the barn, he said:

"We have visitors. Go and take a look."

"What visitors?"

"Beggars. Go and take a look."

Elina went. Guessing that Akseli had been rude to them, and in order to dispel their shyness, she greeted them cheerfully. The woman explained the matter with difficulty, and Elina said:

"We don't really have any. There are eight of us here. But I'm sure I can give you a little bit if your need is great."

She too noticed the wretched state the visitors were in and asked uncertainly, a bit shy at prying into the affairs of strangers:

"Is that child sick?"

The woman's lips shaped themselves into an oddly trembling smile, but then her face twisted into weeping and with it came a liberating admission from a mind at the breaking point:

"She isn't sick... She's starving."

Distressed, Elina began to calm and console the woman. She promised to give them food, and was going to get it, but returned, for the mother's tears had caused the child to weep too.

"Don't... I'll give it to you... I have milk in the storeroom."

Tears came to her eyes as well, and she was about to pat the woman consolingly on the back, but changed her mind since the woman was a stranger. Another person's pain always distressed and made her helpless, and only after a few panicky moments did she remember that she had to get the milk.

During that time the woman had ceased weeping and seemed ashamed of her recent behavior. She made a gesture of refusal when Elina offered milk to her:

"If the children could... I don't need..."

But there was no vigor in her denial, and she drank, trying to conceal her greediness. The children could not contain themselves, but drank like little animals, and only after emptying half-liter tin mugs did either of them draw a breath.

The encounter had made the atmosphere a little stiff, and Elina set about preparing food in order to escape the troubling situation. She had already begun, but a growing fear made her go and ask Akseli. He was in the stable, and Elina spoke from the doorway;

"It's terrible... when people are starving... I have to give them food..."

As if anticipating Akseli, she continued in an impatient voice:

"We have enough to do to feed our own... but you can't let a half-fainting person go without...."

There was a vague sound of bustling in the stable. A pitchfork slammed into a wall and a chaff basket flew from one place to another:

"Just give it away... let it all go... some goddamned support system this is... First we have to support our own parish bigwigs and then the city bosses send us their poor after they've plucked them bare..."

Elina did not stay to listen but hurried indoors. She prepared a beef soup. The visitor struggled a long time, a package wrapped in newspapers in her hand, but seemed unable to get any words out. First she explained that she had no money, and when Elina brushed off her explanation, she opened the package:

"I have a kind of girl's dress... it's not sewn... the material is good too..."

There was a soiled children's picture book inside the cut-out pieces of dress, and the woman said in a hurried and anguished voice:

"It isn't... anything... but if you have children... since ours are big now..."

At first Elina meant to refuse the pieces of cloth, but the visitor's troubled confusion was catching, and she was afraid that the woman would be offended by a refusal.

"They really look good... we have only boys... but something perhaps..."

Both were equally panicky, one fearing that the pieces of fabric were worthless, and the other that she would reveal their lack of worth in her expression.

The visitors ate the beef soup and prepared to leave, but shortly after eating, the children began to vomit and the mother to feel ill. The boys were at the "new place," but arrived just as the visitor's children began to vomit. Soberly, and with a questioning look in their eyes, they stood leaning against bench, staring, unblinking, at the visitors.

Elina went out. She could hear Akseli chopping in back of the threshing barn, splitting blocks of birch firewood. Avoiding his angry glare of inquiry, she stood near him with her hands underneath her apron, waiting for him to stop working.

"Those people are in no shape to go anywhere... If we could let them maybe sleep on the floor even..."

The ax began to strike furiously at the side of a knotty block:

"Is that.. so... Now... we're running... a hospital..."

"Well... I don't... But children in that condition..."

"Take them... to the... parsonage... goddamn... If they're... so happy... about the voting... they'll give them... a place... for the night..."

"They might say that we didn't."

"Let 'em stay... let 'em come... all the poor..."

Elina took his word as a promise. The visitors stayed, since the children were actually in no condition to leave. Elina gave them more milk to drink, and it stayed in their stomachs, which could not stand the strong meat soup. She was fearful of the evening and Akseli's return, but he had already calmed down somewhat. In the early evening the visitors did avoid him, and Elina was unusually talkative, in order to cover up her husband's grim silence. As if to explain the nature of their trek, the woman began to tell them about their circumstances. The man was on emergency relief work for the city, but it was not steady.

"And you can get nothing for the legal price even if you get in line... and we don't have the money for black-market goods. You have to get i n line at four in the morning so that you might get something by noon... The other day I fainted... I couldn't do it any more..."

Her voice began to crack. Her speech, matter-of-fact at first, broke down into a tirade in which anger and rage were mingled:

"I don't care about myself... But the children are starving... and they write in the papers that the city's money is being wasted... There's nothing left... I've taken the last of the sheets from the bed... Everything is gone, even the alarm clock... the wedding rings... I traded my old underskirt for three eggs... eaten weak watery gruel for months..."

The woman's anger developed into an insane rage. The blood vessels in her throat swelled and her voice rose to a shrill whine as she expended the last of the strength in her trembling body.

"And they pick and choose among creams... They have everything... At four o'clock in the morning, I've seen a pig in a hospital train... But if we have to die, they can't go on living either... We'll all have to die together... I'll tear them with my bare nails... The only thing they offer is courses in housekeeping. 'Workers are in need because their wives don't know how to run a household.' Death is too good a punishment for them."

The woman's strength failed, and she collapsed in a fit of exhausted weeping. Vilho and Eero drew back, astonished at the strange woman's behavior. When she had calmed down slightly, Akseli asked, with a constrained friendliness in his voice:

"Did you come on foot from Tampere then?"

"No, we started out on the train. The last of our money went for the tickets. But I thought maybe the children could get to eat somewhere."

When they went to bed, Elina whispered to Aleksi her pity for the visitor's situation, but he muttered in reply:

"Pity won't make things any better. Even the bourgeoisie are ready to dish it out. Pity doesn't cost anything."

In the morning, Elina fed the visitors again. She had gotten permission from Akseli to give them a little barley flour. She devised many possible uses for the dress pieces, but she spoiled things by exaggerating, for Aleksi said:

"What can you do with such things. Listening to you, it sounds as if the farm will crash if we don't get them."

Elina's lips quivered as she said:

"I was just thinking... if our own children... should come to this. You can see their teeth through their cheeks... plainly... Haven't you noticed?"

Putting the barley flour into a bag, she stopped a couple of times, but then went on scooping. Taking the bag back into the house, she picked up the dress pieces and returned to the storehouse, where she sliced off a piece of cured leg of lamb and wrapped it in the cloth. Peeking out fearfully, she returned and put a cheese into the bundle. She hid the bundle in the entry closet, or "cuddy," as it was called at Koskela. Akseli was inside, and as the visitors left, Elina escorted them out.

Distressed and blushing in confusion, she thrust the bundle upon the woman:

"I don't... these... no... since we have only boys... There's a little bit of... Go..."

Her heart in her throat, she stood in the entry, afraid of hearing Akseli's footsteps. When the visitors had left, she drew a breath of relief, saying with a sigh as she entered the main room:

"Feeding a few visitors here won't help much."

Later, inside with the boys, she said with tears in her eyes:

"If only God will spare you... If only you never have to take to the road."

"We haven't gone past Matti's Spruce."

There was a bit of panic in Vilho's words, for the same limit had been set on his mobility as on his father's. His protestation stemmed from the fact that the brothers had sometimes exceeded it.

The picture book had been left to them. After the evening chores, Elina read it to them by the light of a splint. There were lovely fairy tales in it, among them the story of the poor, sick seamstress who had one boy and no food. The mother lay weeping in bed, but the lively boy went out searching for flowers to earn money for food. At first he could not find them, but then the crows began cawing to him, "Caw, caw, here are buttercups, caw, caw."

There was an abundance of the flowers, and the boy picked a handsome bouquet. A fine, friendly lady bought them from him, and the boy rushed happily to the store to buy a little cereal. They ate the warm porridge, his mother got well, hugged her boy, and thanked God. The boy ran out happily, and seeing the crows flying in the air, he shouted to them, "Thanks, you nice crows." And the crows, equally happy, responded, "Caw, caw."

The boys listened to the story soberly, but when their mother read, "Caw, caw," from the book, they laughed their children's laughter and mimicked her: "Caw, caw."

V

Akseli was driving Halme home from the church village. The bright light of the November day was already beginning to darken, and with evening the chill increased noticeably. In the morning the puddles were already covered with thick ice. Akseli rearranged the horse blanket over Halme's knees and asked:

"You're not cold, are you?"

"Thank you, no, not really."

Master Halme had been silent during the entire trip. There was something absent-minded and vague in his responses. When Akseli had waxed enthusiastic over the Bolshevik revolution, Halme had been unusually withdrawn and merely said:

"Well, it is still difficult to judge what the course of events will be."

When the church village came into view, Akseli asked:

"Who all will be there?"

"It's hard to say. At least the labor union men. That's the reason you were called. But there will surely be others."

The inhabitants of the church village watched as the best-known Socialists of the parish kept arriving at the workers' hall. They did not wonder at it, for that had been quite common this fall. In the group gathering at the hall, an unusual intensity prevailed. Men meeting in the yard or hallway greeted one another but said nothing else. Usually they asked one another something about the reason for the meeting, but now they avoided the subject. Even while sitting on the benches waiting for the meeting to begin, they spoke only of unimportant matters. Silander took the chairman's place in back of the table:

"Esteemed comrades. As you surely know, the purpose of this meeting is to consider matters of organization. First we need to choose a chairman and a secretary."

"I nominate the man opening the meeting... I second..."

The secretary of the church village association was chosen as secretary. Silander rapped on the table with his gavel and said:

"Comrade Hellberg will present the issue... The floor is yours."

Hellberg walked behind the table with his peculiarly heavy, distinctive steps. First he set some sheets of paper on the table and then adjusted his spectacles. Raising his head, he stared through his glasses for a moment at those sitting on the benches:

"Comrades. We have called men in positions of trust in this parish to this extra meeting to discuss matters of organization. The purpose of this meeting is to make an initial decision on the matter at hand, after which we can choose a committee to expedite the decision."

Explaining the political situation at length, he continued:

"We will not accept these bourgeois schemes. We will support the Power Act with the striking of certain clauses regarding military and foreign policy. In practical terms, the exclusion of those clauses means a declaration of the country's independence. But the highest authority must remain in the hands of the parliament. If the bourgeoisie does not understand the age we are living in, we will call a general strike to force adoption of our demands. The caretaker government is an emergency measure of theirs, which they themselves do not really trust. But in it their fundamental intentions can be plainly seen.

"You understand what a strike in these troubled times means. Rioting is entirely possible. The bourgeois guard is likely to use that as an excuse for taking up arms, which is why I believe the proposal I am presenting is mandatory. The guard we are to establish will maintain public order during the strike and protect the working people against the highly probable violence of the bourgeoisie. With weapons, the bourgeoisie have also become more stiff-necked. You know that five-sixths of the parliament can kill every reform until after the elections, when a third can do so. That is also true of the future form of government. If their strength in weapons grows greater than that of the workers, the five-sixths and the one-third will soon be found. The rest can in good conscience vote for our side. The only thing that will make the smartest among them persuade the stiff-necked ones to yield is fear. This is the situation. When you make your decision, keep that in mind."

There were loud shouts of approval, but no hand-clapping, since they were all leaders of some sort, and slapping their hands together was not quite fitting for them. When the shouting quieted, Janne stood up with his index finger raised.

"The floor."

He rose from his bench and turned his body slightly, searching for his hat, which he had set near him on the bench. It had fallen to the floor, and as he picked it up, Janne said half-aloud to the chairman of the Salmenkylä Association, who was sitting beside him:

"Why the hell are you kicking my hat, Tuomenoksa?"

Then he cleared his throat, turned to look to either side, and began in a familiar and unofficial tone of voice:

"Well. First I have a few words to say about the nature of this meeting. The presenter has said that this is an extra meeting of the men of trust among the workers. I am of the same opinion. I think this is very much an extra meeting. I am really inclined to call it an unnecessary meeting. It is true that we all are, some less, some more, trusted by the workers, but nevertheless this meeting is not a lawful body to decide the issue under discussion. It may make recommendations, but those recommendations are subject to the official approval of the organizations. We cannot bypass them and decide anything here. In my opinion, svaboda has no place in workers' organizations, although it seems to be much in evidence. I've heard that gangs have quieted opposition with shouting and threats. And I've even heard that the organization's seal has not appeared on the minutes of meetings. That is just as it should be. The seals are used to confirm the official decisions of the organs of an association, not the decisions of some chance meeting. So much for that.

"As to the matter itself, the gun business. I guess you'll get all kinds of stabbers and shooters for this guard that's going to be formed. I believe the presenter spoke wisely of the reasons this guard would be formed. It is clear that the decision of one parish won't mean much of anything with regard to the entire question, but I would not favor the establishment of such a guard. That way lies war. You've seen it happen all over the world. The victory of the Bolsheviks in St. Petersburg may give rise to all kinds of ideas, but you can't build on that yet. Order can be maintained in other ways during the strike. I recommend having a crew of men to maintain order in every association, but without swords or firearms. In my opinion, that would suffice.

133

And as far as the bourgeoisie's opposition to the constitution and other matters go, I don't think they can withstand the pressure of the workers' organization and their numbers. That is why I consider this arming to be dangerous as well as unnecessary. On these grounds I ask that the presenter's proposal be rejected outright."

Janne's speech was followed by a vague muttering, with only one voice ringing out loud and clear:

"Right. I second it and ask for the floor."

It was Halme's voice. Silander nodded to him and said:

"One moment. Hellberg has the floor first."

This time Hellberg spoke from where he was sitting. He was not able to conceal his rage completely as he spoke.

"Of course we know in advance the opinions of our county committee's executive vice-chairman, so I don't wonder at what he just said. But I have to refute his distortion of a clear case. With regard to the power of decision, in that respect the decision is, of course, only on a matter of principle. Certainly every association and trade union will decide the matter for itself, but a start has to be made somewhere. The proper place would of course have been the county association meeting, which is what Kivivuori was driving at, but we know that such a meeting would be too large for these walls. It would have to be held out in the yard, with all the bourgeoisie of the church village listening to the discussion. And I guess that's what Kivivuori had in mind, in order to get their applause while he sneers at a serious concern of the workers. Furthermore, membership in the guard will be voluntary, so that no one will be forced into it. I give Kivivuori credit for his lawyers' tricks when he harasses the black-market landlords, but he had better lay them aside when dealing with our own affairs. For I would like to regard the workers' cause as Kivivuori's cause, at least for the time being. (Correct.) What? (I said correct. But it's the only point in your speech that isn't a misconception.) Humph. A misconception. You clearly said that this was an illegal meeting. (I said its decisions were not binding without the approval of official organs. Don't confuse matters.) I'm not confusing them. I believe I'm as clear on the matter as you are. (Why are you mixing them up then? An organization is bound by the organization's decisions. A decision in principal here does not require confirmation by the organizations.) I have said that the final decisions will be made in the organizations. If you don't have any better arguments, then stop harping on that one. (Don't get all heated up.) I'm not, but stick to the subject. For my part, the county association can take up the matter, but I wouldn't want it to be so public yet, especially since the bourgeoisie would get to know that there are those among us who lean toward them and that would make them bolder. (An old crack. Valpas's crack.) True, in any case. And once and for all, that kind of blather is fruitless. The guard will be voluntary. Kivivuori can stay out of it. (I will. Since I'm not a warmonger.) Am I one? (It really looks that way.)

Hellberg turned toward Silander a couple of times and said, his head shaking with rage:

"Shouldn't the chairman restrain this badmouth a little?"

Looking troubled, Silander rapped on the tabletop. Hellberg repeated his basic arguments, and Janne shouted less frequent interruptions out of deference to his father-in-law. Having spoken, Hellberg sat down, adjusting his position with a few spasmodic movements. Silander having granted the floor to Halme, the latter rose. His cane hung from the crook of his elbow, and his hand grasped his hat in a prayerful position.

"First, as to the power of the meeting to decide — in my opinion that is a secondary matter. As to the guard's becoming an organic part of the associations and the county organization, they of course must reserve the right to decide their position. But there is nothing to prevent us from making a decision of a preliminary nature here. Approval and rejection are of course an organization's affair. Ahem. But there is nothing to prevent us from pondering the idea here, and as our esteemed comrades can attest, after the recent statement of position by the esteemed vice-chairman of the county executive committee, that is my highest hope. The esteemed presenter and legislator, Comrade Hellberg, has given us a picture of the general political situation. Surely he, as one who has his finger on the pulse of the time, so to speak, is better apprised of it than we insignificant individuals here in our remote corner. But our isolation does not, however, prevent us from stating our position in a, so-to-speak, metaphysical context. I, in my insignificance, have had the high prerogative and honor to sit in jail for raising my weak voice against the inhuman mass murder to which the European nations have been subjected by their irresponsible governments and their thoroughly barbaric upper classes. Today a difficult question has been posed to my heart. That movement, to which I have dedicated my slight strength, is now threatened with the loss of its moral prerogative through fear of armed violence by the bourgeoisie. That is how I understand the esteemed presenter's statement. I am asked to approve the workers' arming themselves against this intent. In spite of the difficulty of the question, my decision is an easy one. Only the deeds of the spirit are creative. Deeds of violence are only seeming accomplishments. Power in the hands of the workers, raw, soulless violence, is of no more worth than the violence of the bourgeoisie. Esteemed comrades. Let me further point to certain individual motives. Respect for every created being has imposed upon me an unconditional prohibition against inflicting destructive violence upon the most elementary

135

manifestation of life." (What about lice and flees?)

Halme's cheeks twitched and he continued:

"With regard to the vermin mentioned, which have now been dragged so prominently into this business of arming the workers — I didn't notice who did it — well, with regard to these vermin, the case is such that you don't have to kill them if you guard against their being born,. The esteemed comrade, to whom the question seems so crucial — for what practical reason I don't know — can get directions from me on how to avoid them after the meeting. But to return to the real issue. I, who have believed that the workers would do away with weapons in the world, cannot favor placing them in their hands. I join the county committee's executive vice-chairman Kivivuori in his stand."

"Are there representatives of the bourgeoisie here too... a nice poem, but it doesn't help the workers... Hey, Aatu... You're in the wrong place... Sunday school teachers always gather at the parsonage to consult..."

Halme sat down stiffly, trying to control his expression. There was actually a note of familiarity in the barb, for everyone knew Halme intimately, but Janne rose quickly to his feet:

"Mr. Chairman, I object. Is this kind of shouting appropriate here, in what is called a meeting of the responsible men in the workers' organizations? You act like a crew coming back from harvesting. Here the parish's oldest association chairman is being reviled as a bourgeois, whom many of the hecklers can thank that they know anything at all about socialism."

Silander rapped on the table, but there was a mutter from the benches:

"Oh, so he doesn't yell himself... That big schemer..."

Hellberg asked for the floor, since in spite of everything, he was afraid of Halme's influence.

"Comrade Halme has set out here to decide so-called eternal questions. But as much as we respect Halme's ideas, we cannot take them into account when we are faced with an issue which may become a matter of life and death for the workers' movement. Once upon a time, people battled the devil with charms and conjurations, but we have to deal with a bunch of devils on whom such measures have no effect. When the Finnish capitalist feels that his money bag is touched even lightly, you must know that then neither eternal peace nor respect for life mean anything to him. He will strike, and strike without mercy, if he has an easy chance to do so. Kivivuori and Halme have conjured up a war here. A guard to maintain order does not mean war, unless the bourgeoisie resort to violence. There won't be a war even then, if the workers don't arm themselves, for they will be crushed without further ado. There will be a few disturbances here and there and a strident outcry in the papers that the country is in a state of anarchy and that order must be restored. And it will be restored in this way: the most prominent men will be placed against a wall and the rest clubbed into submission. The workers have chosen me for a position of trust, and I will not take the responsibility for their being struck down unarmed."

Janne spoke one more time. But the expressions of opinion following each talk foretold his defeat. The little bosses would cast their lot with Hellberg, and the next person to take the floor made it apparent.

"We've all been opposed to taking up arms. But in my opinion we should at least listen to someone who has followed the matter in the big city. And the workers' opinion is another thing. I'm very much afraid we'll have a lot of explaining to do when they understand that they have to look on while the others are having fire-department training exercises, such weird exercises that they have to put quilts over the windows of the fire hall. The hungry workers are first offered lichen to eat, and if that won't do, then it's lead. They're very much against the Russians now, so they've changed their minds since the dissolution of the parliament, but I know what the Russians are. So I support the one who best knows the matter. I mean Comrade Hellberg."

Halme and Janne did get a few supporters, but they were cautious and expressed their position in a roundabout way. When Silander announced that everyone should express his view, Akseli had to speak too:

"I start from this: that the bourgeoisie have no special right to bear arms in this country. So I'm of a mind to support Hellberg's proposal. I've seen that a worker will get nothing if he isn't strong. As soon as they get their guard in shape, all talk of reform will end. It's childish nonsense that the guard is there for independence. Since there is a workers' government in Russia now, we can get independence without the guard. And since their betrayal in July, it's no use for the bourgeoisie to come and talk to me about independence. It's all so that those three bourgeois kings will get a police force to put the workers down. Us tenants haven't declared our independence yet, and we need a guard for that too. Since independence doesn't seem to come without it. So that's what I think."

When he had finished, they could hear Halme's words:

"You too, my Brutus."

People laughed, but Halme had been rigidly sober the entire time. He no longer asked for the floor, since it seemed pointless. Janne did fight to the end, getting timid support from a few. When someone, hemming and hawing, pointed out that "this arming wipes out social democratic theory," it took only a couple of hints at support for the bourgeoisie to muddle the man's explanation to the point that in the end no one knew what he meant. But Janne was not of that ilk. During his turns to speak and in his shouts

137

from the floor, he became increasingly bitter and sarcastic as he saw the inevitable defeat. When the result of the vote, 14 - 9 in favor of establishing the guard was announced, he dictated a long objection for the record.

1.) The meeting was called arbitrarily and by private parties. 2.) Taking up arms turns the party into an army. 3.) It may mean war, in which a possible loss means the end of everything. And 4.) It was engineered by warmongering windbags..."

"That doesn't go into the minutes.... that's too much... The secretary can't write that..."

Janne waited until the tumult had died down and then went on:

"Then write that it was engineered by militarist-anarchist elements that have intruded into the party."

5.) It is against the principles of the Social Democrats. On these bases I present my objections and announce that I will in no way take part in the organization of the guard. Let the gentlemen war colonels, who are so sure they can command their army if need be, bear that responsibility.

When Janne had finished, Halme rose:

"I join the esteemed county committee's executive vice-chairman Kivivuori in his stand and ask the secretary to add these words on my behalf:

Believing in the future of pure social democracy, I declare myself opposed to arming, trusting that the ideal is stronger than its shadow."

During the final debate, offended, he had thought through the form his objection should take, and the image of the ideal and its shadow had struck him as extraordinarily good. But no one paid any attention to his words, which were lost in a grumble of objections.

Finally a committee was chosen to expedite the matter, and Akseli became the representative from Pentti's Corner. As they departed, a lively buzz of talk arose. Everyone said what he had left unsaid when he had the floor. The small-time operators thrust themselves upon the bigger ones to explain: "I meant to say... but it didn't come to mind..." Hellberg, the power broker and the people's representative, was surrounded by the largest group.

"You really hit the nail on the head."

Men also gathered around Halme and Janne, who spoke in concerned and quiet voices:

"This will come to no good... I'm not at all of their mind. I've always been for pure social democracy... At times like this, they should collect all the remaining guns from people... from the butchers as well as from the workers."

At the exit, Janne and Akseli happened to be side by side.

"Well, how are things with War Lieutenant Koskela..."

138

Akseli tried to laugh, but his rage flared up perforce:

"I don't see what there is to sneer at in this."

The men stepped gingerly out as their eyes adjusted to the darkness. Going to the edge of the yard, they stood there, still proclaiming their opinions to those around them. Janne's voice could be heard clearly when he said:

"Some get to be warmongers even in their old age. For example, that War Colonel walking with War Major Ylöstalo there."

When Akseli and Halme mounted the carriage at the hitching rail, Janne came to escort them, still hammering away at the decision. Akseli tried to control himself in Halme's presence, and he was also restrained by his childhood friendship and his family relationship, in contrast to the cold-natured Janne.

After Janne's departure Akseli was troubled at being alone with Halme. Carefully he again adjusted the cover over the master's legs:

"Do your legs still freeze that way?"

"Now and then. But what does it matter. An old carrion carcass. It seems to be going to the place it came from."

Akseli was silent for a moment, then said, as if he had not understood the true meaning of the remark:

"Surely not. You aren't that old yet. As long as you don't rush around with that heart of yours."

"Well, that's just an organ. Necessary in this life, of course, but not at all necessary in that true life of ours beyond the senses."

Akseli had no answer for that, and the silence endured for a long time, broken only by the clatter of the wagon wheels and the brisk and rhythmical clopping of Poku's hoofs. There was a pleasant nip of frost in the air. The tops of trees stood out clearly against the cold, translucent sky which arched over them, without a moon, but dotted with countless stars.

"Is it true that you are expecting a little one again?"

"Yeah, it seems to be that way."

"Is that so. Congratulations. That's very nice. Children... a child is a possibility. Age, on the other hand, is a lost possibility... Yes... That's the way it is with many. They have been given a spark of life... What is that racket?"

From up ahead they could hear the sound of voices over the rattle of a wagon and when they drew nearer they recognized the voice of the manor's overseer. Then in a softer tone, they heard the annoyed words of Arvo Töyry:

"Marttila... Try to be..."

Akseli whispered softly to Halme:

"They're coming from their Civil Guard training."

The two men were in fact coming from a Civil Guard training session in the church village. But the overseer had strayed into a familiar cottage, where there happened to be home brew, and now the Töyry brothers, angry and chagrined, had to drag him home. Marttila was crawling on all fours in the ditch beside the road, babbling:

"Go easy, brothers... Stop it, Töyry... I'll make it yet... by myself... I know you're our squad leader... but I'm older than you are."

Noticing the wagon, the overseer began to yodel cheerfully:

"Who's coming... Evening... Don't think badly... Look, boys, let's just sing:

The police army is our Power Guild
And coats we need our backs to shield...

Arvo recognized the oncomers and went into the ditch with Marttila. From it there came first his angry mutter and then Marttila's words:

"Don't, now don't do that boy. I'll get mad if you shove me..."

When they had passed the group, Akseli said:

"Marttila was really drunk this time. There he is with them, although he's a worker like the others."

"Well, it goes with his job."

The rest of the way, they spoke of everyday matters with no bearing on politics. Nevertheless there was still a slight stiffness in their relationship, and both of them sensed it. They did, however, say a friendly goodbye in parting, exploring in a few pointless phrases the numbing of limbs during a long ride. Continuing the journey alone, Akseli felt relieved at having escaped the master's condemning silence and reticence.

VI

The strike broke out before there was time to establish the Guard. And it had hardly begun when it ended. There had, however, been action in the church village. Guards had been posted at the post office and the telephone exchange, but they were unarmed. A couple of days after the strike, Jussi Koskela was on his way from the shoemaker's, where his old boots had been half-soled. The vicar saw him on the road and called to him to stop.

"Stop in, Koskela. I have a little business to discuss with you."

Jussi entered and was directed to the chancellery. "Business" in the chancellery was, in Jussi's memory from of old, a somewhat unnerving experience, and he peered at the vicar suspiciously, his face taking on a more ill and pained expression than usual. If something bad was about to happen, it was better to be pained in advance. The vicar's wife came into the chancellery as well, and soon it was clear to Jussi that the business involved his sons.

"I mean your younger sons. Akseli, now, is blinded by socialism. But the boys will surely listen to you. They are basically decent lads, so don't let them join such a group. News is coming from everywhere of brutal pillage and murder. One cannot believe the horrible things that are happening..."

Jussi mumbled and muttered something to himself. When the vicar described the murders and home searches that had taken place, Jussi finally said, a little tautly:

"Well, I don't know. Our boys haven't attacked anybody."

"Of course not. That's just why they should stay clear of such a bloody guard."

The vicar spoke in a friendly way, but his wife sensed the tense umbrage in Jussi's voice, and it made her feel a slight disaffection even for him. She spoke to him on the matter of independence as well, how when they were now preparing to declare independence, some were seeking their own advantage through gross violence. Jussi blinked his eyes and scowled at the earth, confused because he knew so little about the matter.

"Well... They have been talking about that independence. Isn't there something like that now... Didn't they take up the whole thing there in the parliament?"

"That doesn't mean any kind of independence... That was just a senseless law. Can Koskela imagine having two hundred Czars?"

"Well... I don't... But didn't they take the power away from the Czar early in the fall?"

The woman changed the subject. As Jussi left, they kept on urging him to stop the boys from joining the Red Guard. As he left the parsonage, Jussi felt resentment toward its residents on behalf of his sons, but as he got farther from it and approached his home, his anger was directed toward his sons, and especially toward Akseli. When he reached home, the words were ready on his lips, but the boys were in the old house. When they did not appear, Jussi did not have the patience to wait, but went to them. Still in the doorway, he said:

"Now you know that you're not going to go into that kind of killer-guard. People have turned into wolves... They go into people's homes with guns and kill them there... You still haven't served your old sentence. Do you have to get another before you serve this one?"

The boys let Jussi rant in peace until his aggressiveness was exhausted and he began to sigh:

"It's God's grace that I bought those burial plots in time... At least there's a place to go. It's really... what would the Czar of Pentti say if he were still alive... Oh, it's something, it is..."

Finally Akseli answered Jussi's sighs with troubled annoyance:

"I've never even been in Mommila... I don't even know where it is. But without a strike, the parliament would not have gotten any power, and the labor and local government laws would not have been passed. And as for the old sentence, if they don't send me off to jail, then let them forget it... That's the way things are..."

For a few days, there was tension in the family over the matter. Elina was frightened at Akseli's being in the Guard, for the whole matter had been repugnant to her from the start. But listening to her mother run Akseli down because of the killer-guard, she spoke out quickly and indignantly:

"Akseli hasn't killed anyone... Why do you blame him for those deeds?"

Alone, however, she grieved over the matter. Her pregnancy also made her tired and uneasy, and she sighed:

"And bringing a child into this kind of world. Who knows what will come of it."

But Akseli was able to console her:

"Only now does it pay to bring children into the world. We'll see if he is born a landowner."

But he became more and more convinced that freedom would not come without a war. The papers had much to say about the matter, yet Akseli had grown so suspicious that everything seemed to him a cover for secret plots. In tenant meetings held in various locations, there were threats of strikes against paying taxes, especially since the parliament had not taken up the Socialist proposal to free the tenants.

"But when I get my own land-rent committee ready, we'll see if they don't start taking it up."

A meeting to establish the Guard was held. There was not even a discussion, for Halme was absent from the meeting. Otto too remained aloof from the Guard, but Oskar joined; he was the only member who even owned a weapon. For he had bought a rifle to hunt with when he was out of work.

One dark night Valenti Leppänen arrived home by surprise. There was much ado in the cabin, which lasted until the morning hours. At midnight, Henna was about to go and tell Halme about it, but Valenti stopped her. Aune and Henna were frying pancakes from barley flour.

"Since we even have a little bit of butter."

Pancakes were the very pinnacle of the Leppänen cuisine, and they were proffered to Valenti with humble to-do. Preeti donned the least patched of his two coats and said in a respectful voice:

"Is it sort of the plan to stay, or is this just a visit?"

At first his father avoided all personal pronouns in speaking to the boy because he found it difficult to use the familiar form.

"Well, that depends entirely on the course of events."

Valenti was wearing relatively good clothing, but in his suitcase there were only one pair of underwear and some irregular bundles. For little Valtu, there were some glossy pictures. Valenti kept his distance from his sister's child, but once he stroked the boy's cheek lightly.

"He's the son of the Kivivuori boy, all right. But it doesn't pay to take them to court. They're such a powerful bunch because of that Janne," Preeti explained.

"Well, harder things have been arranged in this world."

Valenti said it briefly in order to put an end to the matter and to hint at some secret power backing him. When they went to sleep toward morning, a shortage of beds developed. Henna and Preeti surrendered their bed to their son, and when he protested, Henna said:

"You just can't sleep on the floor. We'll do that... Why should we... where we are..."

Preeti and Henna lay down on the floor with some rags wrapped up for pillows. Before they fell asleep, Henna's concerned voice spoke from the floor:

"There may be some bugs there... Bed bugs anyway... They may be a little harder on a visitor at first..."

"Well... I guess maybe here..."

The next day Valenti went to Halme's and remained living there. The people of the community were eager to see him and to hear news of the "West." In the end no one could make anything of Valenti's talk. There were plenty of questions, and there were answers, but they were quite vague. On the third day he asked Halme to lend him some money, since he had been forced to leave so quickly that he could not get his money "loose." The master lent it to him, although money was tight with him as well, for his income had shrunk because of the hard times. To repay him, Valenti told the master tales of America and even of its politics. It did much to revive Halme from his melancholy, for he was easily aroused to enthusiasm by new matters, and before long he had milked Valenti of all his information and, as usual, he began to correct Valenti's own ideas.

"Pershing... Wilson... Entente..."

The Association went so far as to hold a kind of welcoming celebration for Valenti. Halme handed him his old membership booklet and said a few words. Valenti replied, using a large number of English expressions so fluently that the crowd marveled. To explain his reason for coming, he said:

"...hearing of the revolution, I decided to come at once, but only now was I able to make arrangements for the journey. I bring greetings from the free people of America to the small population of Finland..."

As he spoke he played with a pen on the table, turning it in his fingers and continually tapping its head on the table top. One hand was in his pocket, with the tail of his open coat behind his arm. His speech was rapid and fluent, and frequently he repeated such words as "union" and "syndicalism."

Preeti listened with a devout expression and said when he had finished:

"That's an altogether new ideal."

Then Preeti looked at his watch. Two pocket watches had been found among the bundles in Valenti's suitcase. Preeti got one of them and Halme the other.

"That's how it sort of tells time... there's a kind of train picture on the back..."

There was talk of the declaration of independence at the same meeting, but the association did not arrange any kind of celebration. To the contrary, the matter was discussed in a demonstratively prosaic manner, and Halme, as he spoke, made the reason clear:

"The Finnish bourgeoisie, to the joy of all of us, has at last become conscious of its duty. As recently as July, we had the experience of seeing the right wing of our front betray us shamefully, for their retreat was coupled to a betrayal. As recently as last fall, they were still negotiating with Nekrasov, but the Bolshevik revolution developed in them a sense of their historical duty within a week. We are doubly happy to see independence declared now, with backs straight and heads erect, so to speak. Last summer they still did not dare to strive for their country's independence even by negotiation, but now they do not consider even that to be necessary.

"But the sick heart of a true patriot bleeds. They have taken my bright star from the sky and hung it as a decoration on their dishonest breasts. Unhappy ship of state, with my mind's eye I see before me a black crag, blacker even than our night. One by one, the strings of Väinö's kantele have snapped. Let us open the *Kalevala* to the "Kullervo" runo. With a heavy heart, a true patriot can offer only one last hope: good night."

Having ended, he went home. In the hallway, he exchanged a few playful words with Preeti, comparing their watches, but otherwise his whole being exuded a restrained and alienated superiority. In recent days, speaking to people about the situation, he had often used the expression, "my lowly corner." When someone asked why he had left in the middle of the meeting, he said with mundane brevity:

"One of the men from the manor sent his pants to be patched, and he has to have them by morning since they were his only pair."

Akseli was on his way to the church village. It was a wet and humid evening in December. The horse walked cautiously, feeling his way along the road. From ahead and behind came the clatter of wagon wheels. There were even a few carbide lamps to be seen.

"The gentlefolk are on their way to the independence celebration."

There were many people in the yard of the community hall and in the glow of the yard lamps horses could be seen farther off at the hitching rail, tethered side by side. The cigarettes of drivers glowed around them.

But Akseli drove on by. He was going to the workers' hall.

The community hall was hung with evergreen garlands. The lion flag hung on the rear wall and there were blue-and-white banners on both side walls. It was a compromise, since a fight had already developed over the national colors and the coat of arms.

The parsonage couple were the guests of honor. Girls in folk costume had greeted the couple at the door and presented the lady with a bouquet of flowers. They were escorted to the front bench. The show of honor was because of Ilmari, for the jaeger movement had suddenly become popular with everyone. Those who had formerly opposed it had always supported it "in principle." Nor did the vicar himself recall having opposed the boy's going. When the national anthem had been sung, there followed a long series of festive speeches:

"...there is a consoling assertion to be made. The complete unanimity of all patriotic Finns gives us assurance of triumph over difficulties. We are no longer Old Finns or Young Finns. On the most important questions we have achieved unanimity. Here as our guests of honor sit two parents, a father and a mother. We understand the care and sorrow that must have dwelt in their hearts during these dark years. Today we want to join them in their joy, and honor their sacrifice for their fatherland. Party faction must disappear from our midst, for we have seen how great is the issue which has brought us together. This is testimony to the ability of the Finnish people to found a nation, and it cannot be destroyed by the manifestations of Russian anarchy which have spread to our poorer element."

There were also speeches dedicated to the Civil Guard, to Svinhufvud, and to the Germans, who "in receiving the Jaegers had extended a sincere hand of friendship to our people."

The vicar spoke, the apothecary spoke, the master of Yllö spoke, and the vicar's wife spoke.

"Our past quarrels must be forgotten. Let us not ask what each person thought best for the country, for success attended the efforts of the compliants, the constitutionalists, and the activists as well. Disputes arose over the means, but never over the end. Our country is now free, but it is still threatened by one enemy: anarchy. Many homes have been desecrated and there is an effort to usurp the last vestige of peace from the hearth. As a woman, I cannot refrain from addressing this question. Under the pretext of shortages, there is agitation, and all kinds of boards are demanding the right to search homes. But to us women, home is a sacred place, it is our castle, as the English say. We will not permit an outsider's hand to come pawing through what is most sacred to us. We have declared our fatherland to be untouchable, but at the same time, savage bands break into our peaceful homes, looting and murdering. Finland's law-abiding people must rise to defend the peace of their homes. Isn't even the smallest, most humble hearth inviolable? Let not brutal hands ever destroy its sanctity."

She was accorded a strong show of approval, although there were many among the women who envied and resented her for always striving to be the leader in all women's endeavors, an effort which succeeded as a rule.

When the audience at the celebration thronged across the road to their horses, they had to avoid Akseli as he drove through the crowd. Voices of displeasure could be heard in the darkness:

"Did he have to drive through when it was most crowded... He could have waited that long."

"The highway is still free... and will remain free."

The voice came through the darkness, clear and threatening.

"Who was that... some drunk, apparently. You can't be secure these days, even on the highway..." Akseli twitched Poku's reins, and the horse's spirited steps echoed on the roadway, sounding as if it had no intention of stopping.

"You'll give me that independence some day too. Yeah, go a little faster, Poku, so we won't have to travel along with this bullshit crowd."

Aleksi and Akusti were waiting near the threshing barn.

"Is Father inside?" Akseli asked softly.

"Yes he is. Did you get them?"

"I did. But only three. The men from the station village took more than they were supposed to."

"Show them to us."

"We're not going to start playing with them. We're going to hide them."

Akseli took three rifles from the bottom of the wagon, and they carried the weapons into the threshing barn.

"Let's take a little look," begged the boys. "Strike a match by the fireplace."

Akseli agreed, and they inspected the weapons by the light of a match.

"It looks good. Look at the kind of firing pin it has. This is the magazine... Put the bayonet on."

"No, we'll hide them under the straw now. I only hope he doesn't start digging around here."

"Why would he do that?"

"You never know when or where he might be looking for something. He's always poking around everywhere and hunting for things."

"Are there bullets too?"

"Forty-five of them. So we can practice."

Aleksi scratched more matches as they inspected the cartridges. It was fun to hold them. They had seldom seen such nice, gleaming objects.

"You're dead if one of these hits you."

"But it doesn't hurt much. A guy working on the fortifications got wounded on the German front. He said it was like taking a whack with a club."

They thrust the rifles and bayonets under a pile of straw.

"But we have to move them before so much of the straw is used that they might be found."

"The straw won't be used so soon that we have to worry about that. I think we'll take them out long before that. I might still get a Mauser if I'm lucky. The boys are going to get them from the Russians."

"The Töyry boys have muzzle-loaders. They were molding lead bullets for them."

"Muzzle-loaders won't help much when these babies start to sing. They have a bit more in the magazine than a muzzle-loader."

When on the following day Jussi went into the threshing barn as usual with his basket for chopped straw, the boys lurked tensely at the window frame. But Jussi returned calmly with his burden. There was nothing out of the ordinary in his tired, harassed expression as he walked toward the barn tilting to one side.

In the background of everyday life, a silent sense of waiting prevailed. Jussi chopped wood and straw. Alma took care of the household as usual. Sometimes there was a melancholy, thoughtful expression on her face. The boys made dubious journeys on Sundays and even weekday evenings.

One Sunday afternoon as he was standing in the yard, Jussi heard the sound of rifle shots from the woods beyond the swamp. Alma too came out, as did Elina, with the boys following her. The shots rang out in series of three, with a pause in between. The sound carried over the swamp, crashed into the barn wall, and rebounded into the yard. No one said a word. The boys watched their elders in silence, their curious questions dying on their lips, for the grave expression and the worried looks of the

latter restrained them. After listening for a while, Alma started toward the new house, saying to Elina:

"At least take the boys inside."

Elina took the boys by the hand and drew them inside, pulling the front door shut behind her. Jussi was the last to remain in the yard, and then he too started off toward the sauna. Soon there arose a little clatter and a grunt or two as Jussi turned pails and tubs upside down.

From time to time the echo rang out in the yard, until a silence which lingered on and on indicated that the shooting was over.

Sparse snowflakes floated down onto the frozen yard.

CHAPTER FIVE

I

In the dark winter night a solitary man advanced along the road with a kick sled. It was tough sledding, for there had not been enough traffic to pack the road hard after the last snowfall. In addition, the temperature was a little below freezing.

Going uphill, the man pushed the sled, but when he reached a level or downhill stretch, he ran to pick up a little speed, hopped onto the runner, and began to kick strongly, switching legs now and then.

He was Yllö's day-worker, Ugly Santeri, the kick-sled messenger for the church-village Workers' Association staff. Haste and tough sledding had caused him to sweat. On one foot he wore an ice creeper, but it was actually a hindrance, since it dug so deeply into the overly soft road.

The young man wore a knitted woolen hat, with a tassel that swung back and forth with every kick. He had on a jacket, since he did not own an over-coat. Around his neck was a thick woolen scarf, over which the collar of his jacket was turned up, its ends fastened below his throat with a safety pin.

In his pocket was a folded paper, which had him in a state of tense solemnity, for on his departure, Hellberg had said to him:

"You'll answer with your life if this gets into anyone else's hands but Koskela's."

For that reason, he studied the road far ahead of him and looked back from time to time. In wooded places, he strove to see into the darkness of the fir trees, dimly lighted by the gleam of the snow. From time to time he patted his back pocket with one hand. On one hill he stopped to rest for a while, and, scanning his surroundings, took off his mittens and set them on the sled. First he checked to be sure that the paper was still safe, and then he drew a weapon from his back pocket. It felt cold in his sweaty hand. For the first time in his life, he was handling a Browning pistol, which was his own. Not permanently, but it had been entrusted to his care. It actually was a Browning, although to Santeri any handgun was a "Browning."

Checking to see that the safety was on, he raised it and aimed at the woods.

"When I let fly a full chamber from this..."

He raised the pistol in the air, then thrust it straight out again, repeating the motions a sufficient number of times to empty the chamber if the pistol had fired each time.

Looking at the weapon and stroking it one last time, he put it back in his pocket and continued on his way, panting softly as he pushed the sled uphill. Thoughts whirled through his mind: That road turns almost from the yard of the parsonage... if the butchers are lying in wait, they may be at the manor corner. Would they arrest old Yllö or only Uolevi?

He saw in his mind how the men would enter Uolevi's bedroom and say: "Hands up!"

Reaching a downhill he again concentrated on his pace. Kicking strongly, he mentally repeated a revolutionary song, emphasizing its beat with his kicks:

> *Finland's poor*
> *are cutting their chains.*
> *Their cup of suffering*
> *has overflowed.*
> *Against oppression*
> *an army rises,*
> *a noble people's finest*
> *forward into battle.*

Forward went the kick-sled messenger, his tassel swinging with every kick.

Akseli awakened at the sound of the first cautious knock. On recent nights he had slept very lightly. When the knocking continued, Elina too woke up.

"What is that?"

"I don't know. You stay here. I'll go and see."

In the inner entry, a suspicion assailed him.

"What if the butchers have started it and are coming now."

At first he thought of getting the Mauser from the main room cupboard, but then he realized that he could not resist in any case. Barefoot and in his underwear, he went into the cold outer entry. In his time, the old open porch at Koskela had been closed in and windows installed there. He peered cautiously out through a frozen pane. Seeing only one man outside, he asked softly:

"Who are you?"

"Only me. The staff messenger."

Akseli opened the door.

"Come in."

"I can't. I have ice creepers on. I would gouge your porch floor. Here is an order from the staff. It's starting now."

Akseli took the paper from the messenger.

"What's going on in the church village"

150

"They've just begun to gather. The messengers were sent out in the evening. They didn't dare phone because there might have been listeners."

"Are the butchers on the move?"

"They're said to have disappeared yesterday. But our Uolevi at least wasn't gone at seven. He went somewhere during the day, but came home in the evening. But his skis were up on the front steps, and they've never been kept there. They know everything, all right. But they don't know when."

"Well, be careful on your way back. Tell them I'll call at once if anything unusual happens. And remember to tell them to let me know at once if things go wrong in the church village. If they don't let us know, we'll be in trouble here."

Santeri left and Akseli went back inside. Elina had followed him as far as the inner hallway.

"What was it?"

"It was only a messenger. We've been ordered to gather at the workers' hall just in case. Go to sleep."

Elina knew by his evasive tone of voice that her husband was lying. Her first reaction was one of anger:

"Go to sleep! I haven't slept for a week."

Then she began to sob quietly and returned to the bedroom, where she began to dress. Akseli followed her and said softly from the doorway:

"There's no need to cry. Just go to sleep, and in the morning you might go with the boys to Grandpa's place and stay there with them. Nothing will happen here."

Elina was not too sure of it. Without answering, she dressed, and Akseli went into the main room, after first picking up his clothes from a chair. There he lit a lamp and read the order on the paper he had received:

To A. Koskela, leader of the Second Platoon

Mobilize the platoon immediately, without the slightest delay. Headquarters has ordered mobilization of the Guard. The revolution has begun. The second platoon is to carry out its mission without delay according to agreed-upon directives. We refer to earlier orders regarding the confiscation of weapons, the treatment of prisoners, etc. Possible resistance to be crushed immediately and without mercy. In the name of Finland's working class: Forward comrades!

K. A. Ylöstalo
Confirmed: E. Hellberg

(Burn order upon reading)

Akseli crumpled the paper and burned it in the stove. Although he had often anticipated this moment in his imagination, he now felt uneasy and nervous. While dressing, he kept glancing out of the window. What if they were ahead of the game? If he could at least get away from home. There mustn't be any shooting here.

He had, indeed, been assured that the Civil Guard would not be able to resist, but during the time the Guard had existed, he had witnessed so many mistaken assumptions that he no longer implicitly trusted the information put out by its leadership. He had tried to spy on the Civil Guard in his own community, but there was no certain information to be had.

Elina entered the room. She had stopped weeping, but there was a melancholy despair in her voice when she spoke:

"When are you coming back then? Shall I put up a lunch for you?"

"Put one up just in case, but quickly. I'll go and wake up the boys while you do. And fix some for them too so they won't have to ask Mother. Don't fuss about it. Just put in some bread and that cured meat."

Elina went into the baking room, and when she had left, Akseli took a large Mauser pistol from a cupboard. He had received it a couple of days ago when news arrived that the Senate had declared the Civil Guard to be government troops. It was then that he had also received the first orders from the staff to make ready.

Shoving the pistol into his pocket he made sure that it was not noticeable from outside. He did not want Elina to see the weapon. He himself had been reluctant to bring it into the house.

The cold made him cough as he crossed the yard to the new place. He did not knock on the door, but rather on the window of the small bedroom, where he knew the boys were sleeping. When he saw the white curtains move in the darkness, he said in a low voice:

"Come out to the steps."

Circling the house, he found the boys waiting at the open door.

"Get your clothes on. We're leaving. You can get lunches at our place, so you don't have to wake up Mother. And hurry."

"Did you think we could leave without being noticed?"

The answer was obvious. Jussi's growl could already be heard through the open door:

"What's all this banging and creeping around?"

"It's nothing. I have to go to the workers' hall with the boys."

Their mother came to the door as well. She merely sighed and said as if she were speaking to herself:

"I knew it... Because of you, I've been up nights... And I didn't even finish Aleksi's new socks."

Their father went angrily back into the main room. Akseli returned to the old place. Elina moved around, mute and melancholy, preparing the lunches. It bothered Akseli, but when he noticed that she was exaggerating her sighs and the difficulty of moving around, a slight anger mingled with his distress. "She's purposely making a show of her pregnancy."

But the situation prevented him from giving vent to his anger. As he threw his pack on his back, Akseli said in a calming and concerned tone of voice:

"There's no point in all this. We'll come home in the morning, but since these are orders..."

"What will I do if you don't come?"

"Where would I be going... 'Bye now. Grandma and Grandpa can help you in the barn. And maybe all of you can go to their place and wait there."

Elina did not answer, but when her husband reached the entry, she came after him and said:

"If only nothing bad... to people... Because of the children..."

"I've already told you that I won't raise a hand against anyone who doesn't do it to me first... There's no reason to worry and talk like that. Go back to bed now."

The boys were waiting for him in the yard, shivering from the cold of the night and their tension. Together they went to the threshing barn and took the rifles from under the pile of straw. There were only two, for the third had been given to Oskari, who in turn had given his hunting rifle to Lauri Kivioja.

Avoiding the main road to the village, they took a shortcut through the woods along the winter road. The road was open, for the manor crew had recently driven firewood along it. They said very little, for all their actions had been arranged in advance, and each one had enough to think about.

The boys separated, each going his own way to spread the alarm. Akseli went only to the Laurilas' and the Kankaanpääs'. He hesitated for a moment near the Halmes', but continued without going in.

"Let him stay out of it if he wants to. There's no time to explain things now."

He was the first to arrive at the workers' hall. Finding the keys in their hiding place, he went in and lighted a lamp, but turned the wick down low. The room echoed in its cold emptiness as he walked back and forth listening for the arrival of the others.

Although his mind was concentrated on the tasks at hand, it felt as if the whole weight of the enterprise were falling on his shoulders. The deserted, half-dark hall increased his sense of isolation.

"If they delay in the church village... then the others will come here in force... What can I do with three rifles and one Mauser...? Did the Hyrskymurro group get to the railroad... to keep them there..."

When the pressure of worry became too great, he tore himself free of it and went to the woodshed to get wood for the stove.

Oskari was the first to arrive. He was the leader of the first squad in the platoon, and he had a rifle, so he had rushed to get here.

"Morning. Have you started heating the place?"

"Just passing the time away. What did they say at home?"

"Well, you know what the old lady would say. The old man was a little sober too, and called me a cabinet minister. That's all because of Janne's urging. He went to Halme's yesterday too, and I'll bet it was to mull over Halme's ideal of peace."

"Yeah, let him do what he wants. As long as he doesn't go mouthing off too much. They're a little angry with him in the church village."

The men began arriving, singly or in small groups. Some were sober and tense, while others exuded an affectedly devil-may-care lack of concern. Among the last to arrive was Elias Kankaanpää, bustling around mysteriously, asking in a half-whisper:

"Do you have the sacks with you?"

"What sacks?"

"Well, the sacks, the sacks. To put the stuff in. Don't people usually go out to steal at this time of the night?"

Men laughed more readily at Elias than usual. Others cracked jokes compulsively, until Akseli took his place at one end of the room and began to speak:

"I don't need to say much. Everyone knows in advance what he has to do. I've gotten word from the staff that the revolution has begun. There's no point in making long speeches. We have to do our share. I myself will go and confiscate weapons with the men assigned to do it. Oskari's squad will stay to guard the workers' hall, and from there, men will be assigned to guard the roads later. The Hollo's Corner unit already knows its task. When you deal with people, you are to behave decently but do your job well. And now get busy."

Soberly the men left, speaking in low voices.

Akseli, Aleksi, Akusti, and Lauri Kivioja were approaching the Töyry farm. Akseli had decided to carry out the confiscation of weapons himself, repugnant though the task was to him. In spite of all his revolutionary zeal, he was still Akseli Koskela, and it was not easy for him to barge into people's houses, no matter how hateful those people were.

When the house loomed up out of the darkness, he stopped the group.

"If the boys are home, they may resist."

"Hah... damn it. We can always lay three men low."

"None of that... I'll go ahead quietly. Follow me at a little distance."

A light shone from the barn. The barn help was already doing the milking, and Akseli decided to go there first. Someone came out of the barn kitchen, and by the light that flashed through the open door, Akseli recognized one of the dairymaids.

"Tyyne."

"What... Is it Koskela there?"

"It is. Come this way a little."

The girl looked around and then came over to Akseli.

"Are the boys at home?"

"No, they left late in the evening with packs on their backs. And with rifles."

"Which way did they go?"

"They disappeared around that corner. That's all I know."

"Damn it to hell."

But there was relief in the curse. All things considered, this was the better result. He had been most afraid of the Töyry brothers. And the thought of war in his home community really gave him pause.

The dairymaid disappeared when it sounded as if the barn door was opening, but she came back again and whispered:

"You mustn't tell them I said anything."

"Why should I — Boys, come here."

At the entrance to the house, he told Aku and Lauri to stay outside and Aleksi to come in, but as they climbed the steps, he said:

"You stay out here too. I'll go in alone."

The master of the house was standing near the wall of the main room with his fur cap on as if he were on his way somewhere. His wife was in the kitchen, but through the open door she saw Akseli enter. As he opened the door, Akseli felt as if there were too much air in his diaphragm, and it was an actual relief when he breathed out heavily as he said good morning. The master of the house gave him a quick, searching look and answered in a barely audible voice:

"Good morning."

"Where are your boys?"

"Well, I just don't know."

"Have they gone somewhere?"

"Yes. They left in the evening already. Or during the day already."

Akseli noted that the last remark was a lie intended to lead him astray, but he said nothing.

155

"Did they take any weapons with them?"

"Yes, they did. Whatever weapons we have. Since we're not used to running around with guns."

Akseli's voice tightened just perceptibly.

"You can probably guess what this is about. But just as a precaution I will inform you that the working people have taken power today. So that from now on the orders which the working class gives are to be obeyed."

The woman of the house entered the room and said angrily:

"So Koskela is out hunting people now? Is there no longer any law in the world... when you hunt down people like wild animals..."

The woman sat down and burst into tears. Her husband ran one hand along the wall and said:

"Yeah, I've always lived by the law, and I'll stray from it only when forced to... And... and... I will say that I never expected to see you on this kind of mission. And as far as my boys are concerned, here is a letter."

He took a paper from his pocket and handed it to Akseli, who moved closer to the lamp and read:

To the Red Guard.

We testify that we have said nothing about our plans to our father and mother, so that they will not be forced to give any information. We swear that this is true, so that nothing will be done to our innocent parents. They know nothing about us except that we have left.

Arvo, Ensio, and Aaro Töyry

Having read the paper, Akseli returned it.

"Let them go wherever they've gone. This matter won't hinge on three men. But as a precaution I must warn you not to house any kind of guards in your corners. And if they come back, you can tell them that they can stay at home if they give their word of honor or bind themselves in writing to stay out of things. But there are to be no undercover doings then."

After closing the door, he breathed a sigh of relief.

That morning they were up early at the parsonage. Actually the couple had been sleepless the entire night. As late as last evening, they had been getting news of strange happenings. Red guard trains had been moving along the railroads. Helsinki could not be reached by phone, so all news was based on rumor. Late at night a man's voice had announced from the exchange that service would be temporarily cut off.

The maidservant had just risen and was starting a fire in the kitchen stove when she heard a rap at the door. Having gone to the entry, she ran into the parlor where the vicar and his wife sat, fully dressed:

"Koskela and some men are outside."

The vicar looked at the floor, drew a breath, and said soberly:

"Let him into the kitchen. I'll come there."

His wife rose too. For a moment she searched for a handkerchief. She was blinking rapidly and her breathing was on the way to becoming sobs, but then the symptoms of weeping disappeared and she said decisively:

"I'm coming too."

"It's better if you don't."

"I'm coming. I won't leave you alone. No matter what happens."

The vicar fingered the buttons of his coat and said, without looking his wife in the eye:

"Don't be afraid... I don't really believe that Koskela will do anything of that sort..."

Nevertheless his wife came with him. Akseli stood alone in the kitchen, fur cap with his mittens inside it in his hands. The vicar coughed slightly as he said good morning. Akseli shifted his feet slightly as he answered, but he seemed otherwise calm.

"What is Koskela's business?"

"It has been decided to take all weapons away from people temporarily. To my knowledge, you have at least Ilmari's hunting rifle. But if you have other weapons, they are also to be turned over."

"Are they being taken from Koskela too?"

The vicar's wife said it briefly, looking Akseli from head to foot unflinchingly.

"They will be well cared for. And if you have cartridges, they are to be turned over too."

The vicar noted his wife's implacability, and it sharpened his stance as well:

"I beg to ask by what right Koskela issues these orders. That fact has a bearing on our obeying them."

A slight tremor ran through Akseli's whole body.

"I issue them by the same right as you have issued your orders up until this time."

The vicar left the kitchen and returned immediately, carrying a hunting rifle in one hand. He carried it off to one side as if he were leery of it. In fact, he was; he had never handled weapons, was totally unfamiliar them.

"Here it is. I know nothing about the cartridges, for these were all left by my son, and I have never fired a shot. So I'm not familiar enough with these instruments of power."

Akseli took the weapon and slung it over his shoulder by its strap. He was about to leave when the vicaress said:

"For my part, I wish to inform Koskela that I will obey only the mandates and orders of the lawful government. And I believe that Koskela will also obey them some day."

"Ha, ha. If such time ever comes, that government will have only one single decree for me. But you are too late. You were supposed to kill the workers at once, but your butcher guard doesn't seem to be in any condition to do it."

"Does Koskela believe those gross lies? I pity you. Your worthless leaders and newspapers deceive you. They have always done so, but now they have outdone themselves."

The vicar's tone of voice caused Akseli to turn around angrily. As he spoke, his rage increased with each word:

"Leaders have always betrayed us, leaders of all kinds. And I tell you straight that you are the last man to speak of betrayal by others. Your whole life has been a betrayal from start to finish. Your word has never been good, not even your signature on a paper. You would be ashamed, goddamn, if you could feel shame. But this is the end of your living on the necks of others, and this time you'd better bow down nicely. This time the only neck that won't bow is the one that stands by its own right. All your other props are gone. Remember that."

Raising the rifle angrily, Akseli started out, but before he reached the door, the vicar said in a quiet voice:

"If Koskela thinks I'm afraid of his ranting, he's mistaken."

Akseli disappeared through the door without answering. The couple returned to the parlor. The vicar was silent, but his wife walked back and forth until her indignation had frozen into a solid, immovable rage:

"We'll see what comes next. Perhaps the very worst. Oh, my poor country. The unfortunate, defenseless people. What will their attitude be toward religious services? Will they allow them to be held... Well I will go to the church in any case and speak, if only to the bare walls."

Underneath his concern and worry, the vicar was pleased with the statement he had made to Akseli. It was a kind of foundation for the coming trials.

The lane of trees leading to the manor was silent and deserted. A light shone in one of the windows of the main house. There was no answer when Akseli knocked at a door. He hammered more strongly on the door, but was soon forced to conclude that they did not want to open it. The result was the same at every door.

It created a disturbing situation.

"Goddamn. Let Lauri stick a bayonet through it."

"Wait a little longer. I wouldn't want to break in."

They heard what sounded like a door opening somewhere inside the manor house, and a woman's voice from the hallway:

"Who's there?"

"Koskela. Open the door."

The door opened, and a frightened housemaid appeared.

"Is the baron at home?"

"Yes, he is."

The girl turned away and opened the door to a study. The baron stood in the lighted room, watching Akseli as he entered. He did not respond to the latter's greeting. When Akseli stated his errand, the baron said:

"They gone away."

"Is that true now? And who took them?"

The baron turned his head slightly to one side as if to hear better and asked:

"What say? Not understand."

"I asked where they were taken."

"I don't know where. Other men take them."

"I have to search the house. And it's the baron's fault."

"You want you do. I no way to stop it. Be so good."

The baron opened a door leading to the inner rooms and stepped aside. Akseli told the boys who were waiting in the hallway to come in. They did so, squinting in the light. A trifle uncertain, the boys shrank back behind Akseli, studying the baron curiously from that position. There he stood, gripping the back of a chair, his hair and beard gray, withdrawn behind a round, expressionless gaze. "He's wearing bedroom slippers, and he doesn't have on the tie he always wears. He lives here. The housemaids have to put out clean underwear for him every morning, and he puts perfume on his toes because his feet sweat."

Lauri stepped to the center of the floor, unconcerned with the baron.

"We're checking things out here."

Akseli went into the inner rooms, telling the others to follow. In the first room sat the baroness, small and gray, with a shawl over her shoulders. She rose from her chair, uncertain because of her tension, and also because of her poor Finnish:

"Why you men come.... You have home too... You go away from old people..."

"We're looking for the manor's weapons. We have to search the rooms."

The baroness's dove-like being and her pleading voice forced Akseli to summon up all his harshness. But the search they conducted was nevertheless completely superficial, for he found it difficult to paw through others' property. Lauri looked around, making loud comments:

"Look at that bearded guy on the wall. The frames are gold. There's gold on the furniture too. Smell this, boys. That's how high muckamucks smell."

Akseli snorted something angrily to Lauri, for the unpleasant situation made him tense and irritable. There was a bearskin rug on the hearth, and it awakened even Akseli's interest.

"They say it can kill a man with one blow of its paw. A paw like that must really leave a mark."

"What would people say if I pulled that over my head and went walking down the road?" said Aku, and Aleksi laughed softly, thinking about it. Aku had the only rifle in the group, and he aimed it at the head on the rug.

"One shot from this would put an end to him."

"Now then. Let's leave it alone."

In the end, they merely walked through the rooms, glancing into the corners. Akseli did know that there had been plenty of weapons at the manor, although the baron was an exceptional estate owner in that he did not hunt. But it was plain that he had given the guns to the Civil Guard, so they left the attic totally unchecked. They left by the same route they had followed into the house, and as they passed the baroness, Lauri said:

"We put everything into its place. No need to clean up after us. We are, I mean, that much gentlemen ourselves."

The baron was awaiting them in the study.

"You didn't find them."

"Not this time. But I tell you that if there are any, they are to be brought in by six o'clock this evening. And if any are found after that, the baron will have to answer for it."

The baron looked over Akseli's head. There was a slight trace of superciliousness in his studied calm. Angry words whirled through Akseli's mind. He was inclined to hammer his fist on the table and explode, since he imagined the baron's boldness to depend on his knowledge that they would not resort to violence against someone they knew. But he controlled himself, for he knew that an outburst would be an acknowledgement of the baron's attitude. Instead he tried to make his voice as businesslike as possible when he said, already at the door:

"I would advise the baron to pay attention to the orders that the workers issue from now on. They are not jokes."

On their way to the next house, the storekeeper's, Akseli was silent, but Lauri and the boys carried on a lively discussion of what they had seen.

"The old boy lives a high life... Do they heat all those rooms? Would you even get to go into them all in one year? Did you see the goblets in that cupboard? They look as if they were made by a country smith."

The village was quiet, although on other occasions it was beginning to stir at this hour. All remained in their dwellings, watching through slits in their curtains at the group of men traveling along the road, one with a rifle and the other with a fowling piece on his back.

It was already dawning on the first day of the revolution when men began leaving the workers' hall in pairs and stationing themselves at road junctures. Gradually people dared to come out of their cottages to speak to the guards.

"What are you watching for now?"

"We're on the lookout for the butchers. The workers have taken the power from the bosses."

"Well done, boys. That's the way."

II

When the searches were completed and the guards posted, Akseli took a short breather. The tension that had gnawed at the back of his mind the whole time eased. He had done his share.

Then he went to Halme's house. After returning from the searches, he had hung the Mauser from a strap around his neck, but before reaching Halme's yard, he put it into his breast pocket.

Halme was sitting at a table in the main room. When Akseli stepped inside, Halme greeted him briefly, straightening his posture to dispel the slightly mundane atmosphere created by the unlaced indoor boots and the sweater of Emma's he was wearing. Akseli knew Halme had phoned the church village, for Valenti had told him so on his arrival at the workers' hall, but he did not question Halme, merely asked if he himself might call.

Replacing the receiver, he said simply, in order to keep his joy from being too apparent:

"They've all run away from there too, but they won't get far. Could we move your phone to the workers' hall for the time being? Since it's close by."

"Of course. What would I do with it. Apparently there will be very few calls about work."

Akseli sat down and said in a humble voice:

"You could join us too. We have to set up some kind of staff, and Otto has left us. There is Valenti, but you know what Kankaanpää and Antto are like. I can't be everywhere myself... and you'll be better at it if new laws and stuff come."

The master drank some brown liquid from a glass on the table and said:

"Thank you very much, but I will be content in my insignificant corner here."

"Just come in with us. We haven't had to shed a single drop of blood, so there shouldn't be any reasons of conscience... And you understand everything better. There isn't a single thing you don't know. You could even go and be a senator. You have to join with us now that we can do what we've always talked about."

The master drank from his glass, tasting the beverage in order to conceal any change of expression which might result from Akseli's sincere praise. He lowered his glass quietly and deliberately to the table and said:

"One has to pose the question for serious consideration: is there any point in fruitless opposition? But violence is in all respects repugnant to me."

"Should we have waited until their well-organized power was in control? You know what would have happened to reform then. If the tenants had been freed, the price would have been high, and there would have been so many added clauses that many a man's rights would have been gone. You saw as late as last fall that they meant to put in three kings to rule, and that legislative rule horrifies them. If they would give us anything at all without being forced to, we would have had it many times over."

Akseli's humble tone diminished from word to word, and his last phrases were clearly heated. The master listened as calmly as one does to explanations he has thought through many times himself.

"Well then. Perhaps my thinking may seem wrong, but nonetheless there is a basis for it. In no way do I consider our bourgeoisie good masters who deal out gifts to their children with lavish hands. But they would not have been able to hold out long against the rising strength of the workers. I believe in your integrity. I always have, and since things are as they are, I wish you success in your work. But as I have said, it is impossible for me to take part in it."

The master spoke in a controlled voice, as from behind a distant cloud, from a world that only he knew. He seemed tired, as if he wanted to have as little as possible to do with the matter. Akseli prepared to leave, and said:

"Well, then I can send the men to move the telephone. It will be paid for and returned when it is no longer needed, or when we get our own."

"Please do."

When Akseli had left, the master's solemnity collapsed. After a time, he called the church village, trying to conceal his burning curiosity under a deprecatory tone of voice. For the remainder of the day he was restless and nervous. At times he tried to work, at others he picked up a book, but nothing appealed to him. Still later he called a number of times, but to different people, for he did not want to reveal his interest. In the evening he was sunk in thought for a long time, not talking to Emma, until he said to her:

"They seem to have succeeded. Well, they did... they did... well anyway... my speeches did matter to them."

It was late at night before Akseli was able to stop in at home. Elina was calmer now that everything seemed to be over, but his mother and father were downcast. "They go poking into people's houses with guns." Jussi had been in the woodshed as long as he could see even slightly, as if he had wanted to flee the revolution altogether. Alma, however, did try to understand the boy. When the two were alone and Jussi accused Akseli, she said:

"It isn't just one person's fault when two are fighting. The wrong that was done us should not have happened... But I don't mean... They shouldn't have started anything like this because of it."

When the news of the revolution's success spread during the next few days, people began to stream in to the workers' hall. They spoke to Akseli fawningly when they sensed where the weight of authority was shifting. Many who had hesitated earlier now joined the guard. Valenti wrote travel permits for people, permits which were confirmed by Akseli's signature. Sitting behind a table with Halme's telephone within reach, signing his name in his slightly clumsy handwriting, Akseli sensed a bit of power exhibiting itself in his posture and movements. Success had also made him enthusiastically energetic. He came and went, gave advice and guidance:

"Uhuh, boys... Put it there..."

The workers' hall was converted into a barrack. In the yard, a cook shack was built of boards, and in it a fireplace for a large iron pot was constructed, for the stove and buffet room inside were too small to serve as a field kitchen. Many women offered to serve as cooks. At Antto's request, Akseli took on Elma Laurila, but he was reluctant to hire Aune Leppänen. It was difficult to refuse her, however, and because of the Leppänens' need for money, he finally agreed to accept her. His reluctance stemmed merely from the fact that, because of her job as cook, he would often have to come in contact with her, and that he had always avoided. The past came to mind in annoyingly nasty way when Aune, in hopes of getting the job, said:

"Oh my, you sure make a handsome officer... aah..."

The first confiscation order Akseli wrote was directed to the manor:

"Since you gave no guns, then give a pig."

They went for the pig. When the matter was presented to the manager, he showed his passport and refused to do anything. He was a Swedish citizen, and demanded appropriate treatment. When the order was presented to the overseer, he took it with him to speak to the baron. The overseer was a little bit afraid because of his membership in the White Guard. Because he was a family man, he had not gone with the others, but had stayed at home, like many of the men with families. On his return from speaking to the baron, he said:

"He says he won't take a receipt... but he can't do anything if you take it."

They took the pig, and Victor Kivioja slaughtered it.

"And we'll get potatoes from the parsonage. But demand them from the bin on the right. They are for eating; the ones on the left are fed to the pigs. Those are the ones they would be sure to give us."

Straw for bedding was fetched from the Töyrys'. The couple had been spending restless days and nights. The woman of the house wept often, grieving over the unknown fate of her sons, and if her mind knew a momentary freedom from those thoughts, it was possessed by a concern for their "proppity." Nevertheless, the two did their everyday chores as usual. In actuality that was the only consolation they had. Doing the chores helped pass the hours of torment and diverted their thoughts from the repetitive path of fear and concern. They hid whatever money and valuables were at home, as well as any surplus food. Although the Töyry servants had stayed clear of the rebellion, the woman was suspicious even of them. She was even more tight-fisted than usual:

"Who spilled pig feed on the barn kitchen floor... Is the Red spirit showing up here too..."

In the evening, she sang, weeping, hymnal in hand, and having wept her weeping and sung her hymns, she voiced her sullen complaints:

"Won't God at least intervene... Since it is He who put a lawful government in power... And if they divide everything equally, will they leave anything for the farm owners themselves... Since they said they would divide everything, even up to the plates... But no one has command of his property any more... Boards give orders and mandate prices... Has anything like this ever been seen before?"

The master of the house wandered restlessly around the grounds. In his solitude, he summed up the situation to himself, for he took the worst possibilities into account. Outwardly, however, he remained calm and controlled, even before the men who came to fetch the straw. In a few words he directed them to the straw, taking Oskari's receipt, although he did not plan to collect the money. He said nothing about the revolution, but his wife could not refrain from comment:

"What do they mean to do? What kind of society will this be?"

Osku spoke seriously:

"I don't know exactly, but there should be some kind of equal distribution."

"So that's it. Will they leave us the clothes on our backs?"

"Well, ye-es, the clothes that you're wearing. Of course they'll take away what you don't need... We're going to start living according to Jesus's teachings now. If someone has two pairs of underwear, one will be given to someone who has none."

The woman was silent, in doubt whether Oskari was serious or not. You couldn't tell about that Kivivuori gang. They had lived all their lives just by shooting off their mouths. Although that one shyster and grain checker had gotten into a quarrel there... That must have cost him a top job..."

The couple did understand that the case of Antto Laurila's eviction would somehow come up. In the first few days, Antto began to demand that the staff look into the matter:

"I won't let the matter drop, goddamnit I won't. I've thought about it so many times these last ten years. If the staff won't take care of it, Antto is the kind of boy who knows what to do. I've suffered so goddamned much in this life because of that old man, and for no reason, that something has to be done... either measure out new land or pay me in money."

Akseli heard Antto's secret grumbling to the others, although he tried to avoid listening.

"It wouldn't be at all wrong to put a bullet through him."

When such threats became more frequent, he said to Antto:

"Your matter will be taken care of. I think it's right that you get compensation, either new land and building logs, or money. But we can't start taking up such cases one by one. You can wait long enough for a general distribution to be made as soon as this government is organized. If land is given to the landless, then of course it belongs to you too."

"Damn right it does.. But how the hell will that damned suckface pay for my sitting in jail?"

"There's no way to pay for that. But you mustn't start doing anything on your own. No one lays a hand on people."

This last had become clear to Akseli even before the uprising began, for the November murders had forced him to think through the issue. Nothing was to be done by force, for violence against human beings contradicted the spirit in which he had grown up. As deep as his bitterness and hatred lay, the thought of violence could not enter his mind, except as a threat at most. He had also taken a solemn vow against it to Elina, when she had appealed to him on behalf of the family and children. Such a promise did not, however, mean that the enemy were absolved from harsh reminders of their earlier behavior. When he sent his men on errands of confiscation or out on guard duty, these were his instructions:

"There is to be no empty ranting. You are to carry out your mission strictly. And it doesn't matter how high and mighty a person you are dealing with."

As if spontaneously, the "barrack" became the center of the community. Footsteps constantly clumped on its steps, and the snow around it was hard packed by tramping. Scraps of hay and an abundance of horse manure had accumulated near the hitching rail. People moving in and out of the building were clearly in an animated state of mind. They were all happy and enthusiastic. A young guardsman would bound down the steps two at a time. He was in no hurry, but enthusiasm lent him an excess of energy. For the present he went on guard duty gladly and without grumbling. It was fun to stop travelers and ask in an important voice for the password or their travel papers.

From somewhere in the dark recesses of his mind, hero stories he had read or heard would arise. Not exactly the tales of Ensign Ståhl, but stories of the Boers, which they had heard as children from their parents.

Now they were soldiers. One of the younger men might say:

"We have to ask the Lieutenant."

And shortly the "Lieutenant" would emerge into the hall from the buffet door.

"Well boys, there was a battle near Tampere where a lot of butchers died and only one of ours and that was from a heart attack."

"Uh-huh, boys. Listen now. All tenants will be declared free of their masters. The tenancies will be completely in their control."

"Good, good. For once they found a committee that got something done. They didn't have to collect any more statistics."

That gave rise to a lot of discussion and even some little quarrels, for even in their ranks there was a hint of class division.

"Why do the tenants always come first? Others need land just as much. We haven't been fighting just for the tenants."

"We should kill at least thirty of the largest landowners in this parish so that the poor can have land."

"Why not just start shooting them?"

"If they just say the word, this boy will go right ahead. That Manu ought to be hanged ten times over. Many a boy has fainted in his fields."

That evening, Akseli went bustling home, but there his joy faltered. Elina would have given a thousand tenant farms to be freed from her heavy burden of worry. She forced herself to say something to please Akseli.

His father's reply was merely a bitter laugh:

"Ha, ha. Such proclamations mean nothing. What is given by proclamation can be taken away be proclamation. And I've never asked for anything free in my life. I won't take what belongs to another."

His son turned gloomy and said:

"Who owns what then? There was nothing here but raw swamps, and it

166

was common land to boot. But the landowners just took it over as their own... and the smaller farms will get paid."

The explanations had no effect on Jussi. His dream had died conclusively. His long-saved moneys had disappeared, and he consoled himself with the best deal of his life:

"It's good that I didn't buy just one plot for us to be buried one above the other. Useless to pinch pennies there when they spend the money on these wars... at least the graves are decent... And we can be side by side."

Sullen, he watched his sons' comings and goings. They were seldom at home, for they got along better in the village in the company of others. Akseli was home the most often because of his family and household affairs.

Evenings at the workers' hall were the most pleasant when Akseli wasn't there. Somehow his presence was repressive and constraining. If joyful behavior became too noisy and the talk and snatches of song too forceful, Akseli was apt to say:

"Tone things down a bit. People are always dropping in here. It's hard on the ears."

His words did not have a long-term effect, but the hubbub subsided somewhat, for of old they knew that if a quarrel arose, it would lead to more than words. In such cases, a nasty little remark would be made behind his back, as was the case when he checked up on the soup. Going over to the soup pot, he said in a slightly dissatisfied tone of voice:

"Weigh the meat with a little lighter hand. A little less would be plenty."

When he left, someone would whisper:

"Just so he doesn't make Father Jussi the mess sergeant. They are two of a kind."

When on occasion the "lieutenant" ordered Osku to take his place and went home for the night, the buzz of talk in the group of men immediately became livelier. Some of the villagers even arranged to be at the hall for the evening meal. Preeti Leppänen came every evening to see "that son of mine." Aune served food to her father.

"Well, I might taste it, even though I just ate at home."

The carcass of the manor pig was in the cold room in back of the buffet, where all kinds of the workers' hall fixtures were stored. Aleksi Koskela happened to open the door to the room, and saw Aune wrapping up a piece of pork. The considerate Aleksi meant to withdraw silently, but since Aune had noticed him, that was no longer possible. In a confidential tone of voice, Aune explained:

"I couldn't eat any of the meat because it was so fresh. I'll take a little bit home and roast it... I hate pork when it's cooked raw. Don't you?"

"Yeah."

"Then we're just like each other. But don't tell Akseli, he's a little bit of a fusspot. You're altogether different. I've always said that Aleksi is the nicest one of the Koskela boys."

Aleksi just barely blushed, for there was a note of insinuation in Aune's words, and he said in confusion:

"I... I... not at all.."

"You're so nice... I really like you... You're kind of serious... I'm a little bit older than you, but not much, ha, ha..."

Aleksi left the door and walked all the way outside in his confusion.

The men kept up a continual chatter with the women in the kitchen. It was the most fun to tell Elma mildly off-color stories, for she would always answer with an even coarser one. The men did not shy from Arvi's presence, for he would bawl out just as coarsely as the others to his sister. The group had noticed Elma's frequent glances at Aku, and they often "teased" her about it.

"Hey Laurila's girl! Don't look at a man out of the corner of your eye when you're dishing out the soup."

"She put a lot of meat into Aku's bowl. She's a sly one."

Someone would come up to her with a sour look and ask:

"How is Aku Koskela doing?"

"Well... as far as I know."

"That's good. It's good that a man is doing well."

"Go to hell."

For his part, Aku tried to be ready with quips, and it tickled him that Elma was the one they teased rather than he. Sometimes he dropped a vulgar hint to her. He was not aware of how much it hurt Elma, nor were the others, for the girl would hiss back immediately:

"What's Koskela's baby up to... A man like that... He would have to be put under the blankets and made all over again before he would be good for anything..."

III

When the women had cleaned up the kitchen, they too would come out into the hall, where Aune's laughter would soon be heard above the rest. She had begun to hang around Oskari again, but he deftly avoided her. One of the boys from Hollo's Corner took out the Workers' Almanac and began to read from it.

"Hey, listen. You really think you're smart, but this is real science. I mean, a real book-learning explanation. Wait, this is the real dope about sex:

168

"'It has already been stated above that nature has divided the higher animals into male and female so that each has its share in the propagation of the species. This is actually not necessary for said purpose, for the lower animals, as we see, are both male and female, or to put it otherwise, neither.' Wait... this wasn't the place where the passage started... Here's where it begins...'It is generally acknowledged that feeling, that is to say, the sense of touch has the most powerful effect on the feeling of love. In this context, the initiating agent, as we all know, is chiefly kissing. It is for good reason that kissing has been called the preliminary to the effusion of love, for experiments have shown that the mouth is connected to the true sexual organs...' Here's something about doves and their mates but I don't care to read that... 'Likewise a woman's breasts are in physical contact with the same center, and therefore are of great significance in love life...'"

"Boys, there's enlightenment for the people... so that you'll know."

"You're reading such awful things... ah, hah, hah... who writes things like that? I won't listen... ha, ha..."

"Keep still now while I read... 'on the contrary, hearing is of much less significance in love life; however, music seems to have a more potent effect on women. Evidence of the meaning of music in love life is found, for example, in the love story of Richard Wagner and Maria Wesendonk... Like the lips, the nose too is in direct connection with the sex organs, which explains why the sense of smell has some effect as a transmitter in matters of love. A large part of humanity does not kiss with the lips, but with the nose, using the so-called ol-ol-factory kiss, that is, smelling each other, which has also been explained as sucking in another's soul. How great an effect smell also has on human beings, and not just animals, is a well-known fact. Of this we have very many examples, such as Zola's novel Abbé Mouret and Tolstoy's War and Peace. It is claimed that some highly sensitive men can tell from a woman's body odor whether she has an erotic nature, and even if she is a virgin. And it is certain that some women use artificial perfumes for sexual reasons...'"

"I don't believe that. No one has that kind of nose. Goddammit, they don't. Who writes stuff like that?"

"Here it is... on Aino's day, 5.10.1916. N. R. af Ursin."

"He's that old guy with the beard, who was even a spokesman for the Socialists."

"But isn't he a good spokesman? He must be quite a tomcat himself."

"But I tell you, you can't find that out by sniffing. I'll deny that as long as I live..."

"Ha, ha... those are weird writings... Ha..."

Aune's cackle was cut off and the other racket died down also. Total silence prevailed in the room. Someone coughed softly in the doorway. Halme stood there, his cane hanging from his elbow.

"Is Akseli available?" he said.

"No, he went home for the night."

"Who's on duty?"

"Well, I look to be the one."

"Mhmm. Could I possibly use the telephone?"

"Of course."

Osku had already made a humble gesture toward helping Halme, but realized that no help was needed in the matter, and stayed where he was. The reader closed his Almanac, and others surreptitiously hid their playing cards under the straw bedding.

Halme walked into the buffet room with businesslike steps, but his eyes glanced curiously around the entire time. Then they could hear his dry, aristocratic words, spoken into the phone.:

"Yes, yes... Of course not... I'm just an outsider. But it seems to me the shortage is not what people claim it to be, but is of what everyone thinks he has in abundance, namely brains. Yes. Please tell them, if they will listen...How am I... There are old, torn clothes even if new ones are scarce... Ahem. I'm getting along exceptionally well... Yes, let us hope so, let us hope so."

Halme re-entered the hall, stood still for a moment, looking at the sleeping men. Then he said to Oskari:

"Was it cards the duty officer was playing?"

"Yes, we were trying our luck at poker. But for small stakes."

"Uhuh. I would just like to advise you that the hall belongs to the Association and not to the Red Guard, and I would expect the renters to keep the floor in better condition. It's soaked in melted snow."

"There's a little... since there's so much traffic."

Some one started out to get a broom, but one of the men among the group from Hollo's Corner shouted:

"We're cleaning the bourgeoisie out of the country, not sweeping floors here."

"Ahem. It seems to me that a man who can't keep his own feet clean is hardly able to clean anything else."

Halme marched out, and when those inside concluded that he was out of earshot, one of them said:

"Hey boys, he heard what we were talking about. That's why he was in such a lousy temper."

"Goddamned bourgeois, coming around here and giving orders. We should have told him off better."

170

"The poor old devil isn't really living on the surface of Tellus any longer... or whatever it is he calls this earth. He's gotten so damned skinny too, but it's no wonder, since he gnaws on those bundles of twigs like a goat."

Then they took up their cards and the women's question again. When the women were preparing to leave for home, Osku said to Aku:

"Well, boy. Go and see that girl Elma home. She isn't feeding you for nothing."

Aku leaped up with exaggerated haste and said;

"Give me that pistol, otherwise I wouldn't dare. I'll go to guard her life."

Aku took the storekeeper's pistol in order to have guard duty as a pretext. Under the cover of it he was able to leave, accompanied by appropriate jesting. Elma looked asquint at him and ordered him not to come, but the boy did not listen. He winked slyly at the others as he left.

Aune left when they did, but Leppänens' was in the other direction, and she also stopped to pick up the package of meat she had filched.

Aku walked beside Elma, who looked at the ground in silence, until she finally said:

"Where is the mister going?"

"To Laurila."

"Is that so? Does the mister have business with Antto?"

"No, but there is a pretty girl there."

Aku offered to take the girl's hand, but she pushed him away and hissed:

"Don't come shoving over here. Just stay there. You don't have to paw me."

"You mustn't be angry."

Elma quickened her pace, but when Aku did the same, she stopped and stood there. Aku did the same, whereupon the girl started off again. After the maneuver was repeated a few times, they continued walking rapidly, side by side. A path which was a shortcut turned off the road to the Laurila yard, and there they had to walk single file, with the boy behind. When they reached the yard, Elma was about to go inside, but Aku clutched her hands tightly.

"Don't go. Let's talk a little."

"I don't have anything to say to the young Koskela mister."

Elma jerked her hands away, but Aku was aware that she did not use all her strength in doing so, and he began urging her more enthusiastically to stay.

"Let's sit on that sawbuck."

"You sit if you're tired."

The sawbuck was too small for the two of them to sit on, but Aku put a log on it so that there was room for two. Elma sat down, but fended off Aku's every attempt to touch her. At first he was careful. Gradually, however, he strove to get closer. At length he even got his oft-rejected hand to stay around Elma's waist. She sat silent, looking at the ground as if she were unaware of the boy's hand. He tightened his hold. Fragments from the recently read Workers' Almanac whirled through his mind '... the sense of touch... is connected to... breasts are connected to... and the tongue...'

Cautiously he turned Elma toward him, but when he tried at the same time to touch her breasts, she slapped his face.

"Damn, don't hit me. It hurts."

There was outright anger in the boy's voice.

"It's supposed to."

"What are you angry about? What have I done wrong?"

"You don't have to start pawing me here. The mister is going too far... he thinks I'm like... I'll go and cook for the church village guard."

"Why?"

Aku tried to take hold of her again, but Elma stood up.

"Just because... And what business is it of yours?"

At that moment, the girl began to sob, but she quickly controlled herself. Her sobs were drowned out by an angry hiss:

"I don't like you... don't think because... What are you doing here... If you don't go, I'll wake up Antto and you'll see how fast you'll go... I don't care about the whole shitty bunch of you."

"What's gotten into you... what are you really..."

Now Elma became positively wild.

"What are you doing here? A backwoods bumpkin like you. Grown up in the parsonage wilderness. You think you're something but everybody says you're a stupid and tight-fisted bunch. I don't care for anything like that. And you follow me around and imagine things..."

For a short time Aku kept uttering vague sounds of rebuttal, but when he understood the meaning of the girl's words he too became angry:

"Then what are you yelling about? I don't have to chase after any woman's skirts. And listen, there are plenty of them in this world. And as far as we know, we owe nothing to you or anyone else, so that no one else has to suffer for our tightfistedness. We may well be stupid, but not so stupid as to be anyone's laughingstock. What are you railing about? Let's just say goodbye and call it quits."

The boy walked off briskly, but Elma ran a few steps after him, shouting as a farewell:

"Just go. You're not even a man."

As Aku's dark figure was already disappearing behind a copse of alders along the road, Elma shrieked out after him:

"Go and tell your mama."

After the childish, little-girl's shout, she stood facing the road for a while, until she burst into a fit of loud weeping and went slowly inside.

Aku set out hurriedly for the workers' hall, his mind still seething with anger.

"She's crazy... The whole bunch is crazy... and let them be, for all I care. Rips in her skirt too... held together with a safety pin."

As he walked, absorbed in his thoughts, the boy saw two dark figures coming toward him a short distance away. He thought nothing of it until he saw them turn off the road. Even then he merely observed their action, until his consciousness came to a startled halt.

Aku's heart began to pound, and at first he was about to go on as if he had not noticed, but shame succeeded his fear, and he took the pistol from his pocket. The oncomers had gone into the woods some twenty meters ahead of him. He walked nearer to the spot and listened. There was no sound from the dark woods, and the boy's nerves were strained to the breaking point:

"They must be right here. Otherwise I would hear their footsteps."

In a voice thick with tension, he called out, striving for resonance:

"Password."

There was no answer. The boy repeated:

"Password. If you don't come right out with your hands up, I'll shoot."

Two men stepped out at once from the juniper bushes growing beside the road. Aku retreated to the other side of the road with his pistol pointed toward them.

"Excuse us. Who are you? Can you tell us if this is the road to Vammala?"

"To Vammala? This is no Vammala road."

"Then they gave us the wrong directions. A Red Guard road watch back there told us this road led to Vammala. I guess we have to turn around. But can you tell us where we can get a horse to drive us?"

"Do you have a travel permit? And why are you traveling in the dark and why did you go into the woods?"

"We're in a hurry and we couldn't get a horse. We went into the woods because we were a little bit afraid. Nowadays you don't know who you might meet. The Red Guard warned us to be careful."

The man spoke in a familiar and friendly voice, and the boy sensed that his speech was that of a gentleman. His comrade stood beside him with his hands raised. Aku hesitated a moment, and then made a decision:

"Turn that way and walk with your hands up. If you lower your hands even a little bit, you know what will happen. If you have legal permits, you will be sure to get a ride somewhere, but first we'll go to the workers' hall. Those are the orders in effect now."

Everyone woke up when Aku arrived with his prisoners, who were taken to the buffet room after their pockets were checked. Neither one had a weapon. Osku told Aku to get Akseli from home and he himself began to question the strangers. Both were young men, one of them obviously under twenty. The older was a big man, with a brisk carriage; the younger was pale and slight. When he took off his gloves, long slender fingers were revealed, which caught Osku's attention.

"Anyway you're not workers."

"Well, not exactly."

The older man did the speaking and answered questions. The younger one looked back and forth from his companion to the Guards, unable to conceal his uneasiness, unlike his comrade, who acted self-assured and natural.

"What is your profession? Show us your papers."

"We have only ration cards."

"And your travel permits?"

"We didn't even know such things are needed."

"Don't try to fool us. You lied to this man that the Red Guard showed you the road to Vammala. A road-guard would not let you through without papers. You did, of course, pass by him. And besides, this is a strange way to go to Vammala. At night and on foot. Why didn't you go by train?"

"We heard that they don't take civilians on the Pori railroad."

"Why are you trying to go north then? Almost all the weapons have been taken away from the butchers."

"Us? We have no such plans. We're going to meet our relatives."

"Gentlemen, and so stupid. We're not all that stupid. In hunting clothes too. You should at least have traveled in regular clothes. You are butchers."

"So they are. It's useless to question them. Stand the bastards against the wall."

When that shout was heard from the crowd, both men grew serious. Oskari noticed the fact, and it confirmed his opinion. The group gathered at the door began to act threatening. There were repeated shouts of "Take them to the 'hill.'"

"Goddamn, I'll shoot them if no one else is devil enough to."

It was Arvi Laurila who spoke. Osku ordered the men to be silent, but his command was not obeyed. Signs of nervousness began to appear in the

174

older prisoner, replacing his recent calm and assured demeanor. He turned toward the men at the door and said:

"We're not criminals. We ask that we be allowed to speak to some higher officer."

"What the hell officers do we need for you? A bullet in the forehead for you blueblood dogs."

Akseli arrived when the commotion was at its worst. The prisoners began to assure him of their innocence, but he did not even listen to them.

"You can explain things at headquarters. You are traveling without permits and I will not free anyone who is."

Akseli called the church village and was told to send the men there.

"Akusti and Elias can take a horse and drive them."

The prisoners seemed relieved to escape from among the threatening group of men, in addition to which the headquarters sounded like a safer place to them. Relief made them talkative, and they thanked the men for their ride as they were leaving. When the sleigh had disappeared from sight, someone said:

"Why drive them around? We should have shot them full of holes."

"We don't shoot anyone here without an investigation, and besides, it's not our business. They could just as well be telling the truth as lying. People are traveling for other reasons. But the guard should really put in a couple of extra shifts. The men went past two pairs of guards, and no one knows anything. What would you say if someone threw a bomb in through the window when the guards are sound asleep?"

"What could you say? Your guts would be spread out over the hill."

"Wisecracking won't help matters."

Akseli left angrily for home, and the others grumbled to one another before going to sleep:

"The war boss was in a bad mood... And he went home to sleep himself."

IV

At the parsonage, a gloomy and dispirited state prevailed during the first days of the revolution. No calls went through anywhere, and no newspapers appeared, so the only news was the few rumors which the servants heard in the village. The couple were oppressed by many cares and sorrows. Ani had left for a Christmas vacation in Helsinki, and her parents were uneasy for her sake. Where was the Civil Guard? What had happened to the parish forces, whose members they knew to have received an order to assemble in small groups more than two parishes away to the north? The parsonage couple never went anywhere, for they did not want to go to the workers' hall for a travel permit.

The fourth day brought relief. The county physician drove up to the parsonage bringing news:

"All Ostrobothnia, Savo, and Karelia are in the hands of the Whites. The Russians have been stripped of their arms. And Swedish troops have crossed the border in support of the Whites. They say the Whites are approaching Tampere with the speed of motor vehicles. Eyewitnesses have related that they marched in a column of fours for ten hours in a row over a certain bridge. A simple calculation shows that there are tens of thousands of them."

The vicaress wept. She searched for a handkerchief, but couldn't really find it. Tears wet her cheeks as she smiled with joy and blubbered, sobbing:

"I admit... I was already in despair... how could I doubt... the people of Ostrobothnia.. Always... they are always the same... Finland's Dalarna... like with Gustav Vasa... the descendants of Ilkka... real knife-wielders... And I thought their wild spirit was dead... You really brought us news... forgive me, but I was so depressed..."

The county physician wore an affectedly solemn expression, in tactful appreciation of the woman's state of mind. The vicar's voice was also thick, and kept breaking as he spoke:

"That news is worth shedding tears over. They are so near, then... then the Civil Guard must have arrived... at least a part of them..."

The physician went on to tell them the news from the church village. Joy at hearing the news had alleviated their bitterness, and so they spoke of the Reds' activities with amicable mockery:

"The women there are the worst of all. It's not good for us to show ourselves... They drop nasty hints in voices loud enough to be heard. They always gather at the workers' hall when the landowners appear before the staff, for they are forced to show up there in the morning and evening. The master of Yllö, in particular, is subjected to hearing all kinds of things. One cross-eyed witch of a woman shouted at him: 'You didn't get to take my cottage after all, or put me in the poorhouse, you damned prince,' and then something followed that I have to ask pardon for repeating. She stepped up to the master and hissed: 'If I had any teeth left I would bite off your balls.'"

At first they displayed the amusement appropriate to their class, and then they became serious. The vicaress said:

"I don't admit to being mistaken about this people. That grossness has its source in the Russians and above all in our Socialist leaders. Remember what this people was like before the Socialists... Such grave, chaste humility can never be totally extirpated..."

The news affected them so deeply in the midst of their oppression that there was no room to doubt it. They spoke enthusiastically of a victory already achieved. As one spoke, the others nodded:

"Yes, yes..."

At intervals Ellen still required a handkerchief, but her weeping was limited to slight symptoms, which merely caused her to swallow:

"If the Jaegers are home already and take a position in front of the men from Ostrobothnia..."

The thought brought on sobs. One might also fall in the van.

When the county physician left, the two were in a state of enthusiasm.

"But are they coming in trucks then if they are advancing with the speed of motor vehicles? But how, on winter roads... Well, with army trucks, maybe somehow..."

"Of course they will put the bravest ones into trucks and send them on ahead. If Ilmari is in Finland, he will be in the first trucks. It's his nature. How afraid I was when he climbed on the roof even when he was little..."

Then the lady began weeping again.

"I'm beginning to have feelings of foreboding... thinking that this happiness is too great... I'll see him alive, and see the Whites coming..."

Their enthusiasm lasted until the next day, then little by little doubt began to gnaw at them. It demanded that they seek further information, and the vicar decided to go to the church village. He could make up an excuse that had to do with his office.

"But they will still insist on a travel permit for you. And it's otherwise more dangerous for a man to travel too. I'll go."

"They won't let you go either."

"They are probably not as strict with women. And a lot depends upon who happens to be on guard duty."

A horse was hitched for Ellen. It was a cross between the now-dead Star and a domestic breed, for they had given up on the coach horse. The coach had been in the shed unused for years. It was not a rare thing for the wife to drive, and she now trusted that no one would pay any particular attention to her.

Aleksi Koskela and Lauri Kivioja were standing guard at the road juncture near the store. Aleksi carried the parsonage rifle, but Lauri Kivioja was unarmed. The vicaress was walking beside the sleigh as she drove the horse. Lauri stepped into the center of the road and grasped the corners of the horse's bit. Aleksi greeted the woman and asked for her travel permit in a quite confused and troubled voice.

"I don't have a travel permit. I'm on the way to the church village for shopping."

"Well, you should have a permit. You can get one at the workers' hall."

"Doesn't Aleksi know that it is improper to impede the movement of peaceable people?"

The boy shifted his feet and kept shifting the gun on his shoulder.

"Well, since there's such an order... If... I could even run and get one... Or if the lady will stop in herself..."

The woman jerked at the reins, but Lauri held on to the horse. She jerked again, and the uncertain horse began to dance in place. When that had gone on for a while, it began to seem comic, and the woman's anger rose. The news which had arrived the day before had brought her to a mood of actual defiance:

"How can Aleksi Koskela take part in anything like this? Doesn't he understand that before this, only highway robbers have behaved in this way? Hasn't Aleksi been taught proper behavior at home?"

Lauri had been holding the horse's bit in silence, but hearing the woman's angry words, he stepped quickly alongside the sleigh, snatched the reins from the woman's hands, and stepped onto the sleigh runners.

"A road guard has an important duty and doesn't have time to listen to uncivilized people barking in the middle of the road."

Lauri jerked at the reins so hard that the woman had to shield her face from them, and the horse trotted off toward the workers' hall.

The vicaress entered the buffet room escorted by Lauri. She was pale, but exaggeratedly proud and scornful looking. Lauri explained the matter, whereupon Akseli said:

"We will write a slip for you and you can continue your trip."

"I will not take an illegal travel permit."

"Yeah, well then you aren't going anywhere."

Men could be seen through the door that opened into the hall. Some peeped from behind the others in order to witness the encounter. That made the woman even prouder than before, and for a long time the futile war of words continued. The presence of the men had an effect on Akseli. He acted more severe than he would otherwise have been, and became increasingly harsh as the argument continued. Finally he said to Valenti:

"Write the travel permit, whether she takes it or not."

Valenti began to write and asked as politely as possible:

"I beg your pardon. What are the lady's first and middle names?"

"It's not necessary. I won't take a travel permit."

Valenti wrote the slip without a first name, after which Akseli signed it:

"Here it is. The lady can take it if she wants to. I would advise her to take it. Even if we overlook it here, one still can't get through the church village guards without it."

"If I take that paper, it would be the same as acknowledging your rule, and my conscience won't permit that."

"The lady's conscience has permitted a number of things in this world, so I don't put much stock in the lady's conscience."

The men laughed outright. One of them from Hollo's Corner, who, as someone less known, dared to be more shameless, shouted from behind the others:

"Isn't she a proud woman! Maybe it would take her down a notch if we made her scrub the hall floor. For once in her life she could get a taste of a worker's life, since she's been waited on by maids up to now."

"Or set her to washing the turnip dishes with the girls."

The shouting and the raucous laughter did not affect the woman, but when she thought she also saw malicious glee in Akseli's grim regard, the shouts took on more meaning. That harsh look, which seemed to enjoy the clamor of the men, devastated and defiled her. A vague fear stirred in her mind. The experience was such that the instinctive basis of her courage collapsed. In her ignorance she had relied for her safety on being a woman, but she was beginning to lose that certainty. Therefore she exerted her will to bypass her fear, and fear itself increased her pride, while at the same time it made her emphasize her position as a woman and appeal to that for the safety it afforded:

"I repeat that I won't take your slip. I'm a helpless woman, so do what you like with me. I'm ready to wash the floor. I'll even wash your toilets, for no work done for my country and the lawful rights of Finland's people is shameful."

Akseli avoided her eyes for a moment. Then he extended the slip to her:

"Here it is. I've offered you the right to travel, but if it's not good enough, then stay at home. And since you haven't washed even your own toilets up to now, it's useless to talk about other's toilets. The time for those festival speeches is past."

The men added their own words to Akseli's. The woman was silent, her eyes dimmed with tears.

Akseli coughed and said briefly:

"Lauri, take the lady to the parsonage."

Valenti opened the door to the woman:

"Pliis."

The woman nodded her thanks and went out followed by Lauri. There were men in the entry and in the yard as well. Passing them, the woman kept licking her dry lips. She paid no attention to Lauri as he drew the robes over her in the sleigh.

Akseli watched from the window as the sleigh disappeared from sight. The men cracked jokes at Valenti's show of courtesy, and he tried to crush

179

them with a few garbled English phrases. When that did not succeed, he began to fix the knot on his tie, ignoring the others' talk.

"Go into the hall. Everyone has something to do there."

Akseli spoke the words curtly and harshly, and, falling silent, the men left the buffet room lazily. When they were gone, there was a long silence, for Akseli said nothing, and the others did not exactly dare to ask him any questions.

After a couple of hours, the vicar arrived to get a travel permit. He stood on the threshold hat in hand while the slip was written out. He spoke only the words absolutely necessary to carry out his business.

More and more frequently Halme found reasons to come to the workers' hall. He made phone calls to all and sundry, and might even sit for a while at Akseli's request. He took no direct part in affairs, but was glad to hear about them, making little comments in which mockery was plainly evident. He seemed not to approve thoroughly of any action.

"You see how much you're needed now. Sorting out the tenancies won't be hard, but if it comes to a land distribution... And the work needs to be organized. They are sure to start sabotaging planting and stuff in the spring. It may be that we'll have to do the manor planting on behalf of the Association if Manu starts being mulish about it."

After a few more visits, Halme was already saying;

"Civil affairs are of a different nature, of course. I could advise you on some of them."

One day he became absorbed in a certain question and stated his opinion. When an order came from the church village that farm work must be continued, he spoke up:

"Tenants are now freed from their obligation to do day work, but they make up such a share of even the manor's work force that work cannot be done satisfactorily when the men also have to do guard duty. I don't know what you think about it. I don't see any solution except to demand the same amount of work from the tenants in return for prescribed payment in money."

"We're sure to find enough of a work force for that when the men are freed from the Guard. And there used to be men who were unemployed. The Guard can't have changed the situation so radically."

The Guard and the freeing of the tenants have changed it. And can I ask when the men might possibly be released from the Guard?"

"Well, that I can't say. When they get things straightened out in the North."

"And when might they possibly be straightened out?"

180

"How should I know. I'm sure they're organizing an attack there."

"And so matters should be left to such conjecture? Well, it's not my business. I just meant to help Koskela a little, since he has so much to do, which isn't helped at all by the fact that the orders he gets are of every imaginable kind. Like these, one of which makes another impossible."

"Come and give the orders yourself. Why did you drop out then? No one forced you to. On the contrary, we almost begged you on our knees to stay with us."

"I've promised to help you with some civil matters, but that doesn't mean I've changed my position."

Then he checked over the staff papers, telephone messages, and the circulars. A little, dryly mocking smile flickered at the corners of his mouth, and sometimes he muttered an incomplete phrase to himself:

"And what was this one all about..."

A little gust of anger stirred within Akseli, but he did not show it. Halme's presence not only eased things practically, but above all, gave him moral support. For although he was, during the day, a clear-spoken and decisive Red officer, at night he was often a solitary Akseli Koskela, who sometimes had troublesome thoughts. The attitude at home toward the rebellion weighed on his mind, and he could not help feeling some small discomfort at ordering confiscations and searches in his home community. His attitude toward his mentor had always been respectful, nor had he ever approved the mockery people directed at Halme for his juniper-berry and fir-needle drinks. The master's withdrawal had left a small moral gap in him, and with Halme's return, he was even willing to swallow a bit of mockery. When the master left, he opened the door for him with clumsy courtesy, as if he were a little boy.

Halme departed by way of the hall, and Akseli could hear his words from there:

"This floor still seems to be a mess."

"The summer will dry whatever it wets."

Akseli strode quickly into the hall:

"Who said that?"

"Elias."

"Pick up the broom and sweep the floor."

Elias was slow to move, but he did obey. Halme left without intervening further in the matter, and when he was gone, Akseli said to the men:

"If anyone shoots off his mouth to Halme again, he'll answer to me."

His face flushed and his eyes swept the room with such a look that the men's faces became sober. With stiff, heavy steps, he walked into the buffet room and closed the door after him.

In a couple of days, Halme was involved in the actual leadership of the staff. His first task was to deal with the matter of Susi-Kustaa's travel permit, for two men from Hollo's Corner, who did not know the man, had arrested him. He had, in addition to everything else, been carrying a flintlock on his shoulder.

"I won't meddle with your weapon. But you should have a travel permit."

"The gun is mine. I won't give it to you."

"But you need a travel permit."

"Goddamned if I do. I travel my own paths."

Halme would have left Kustaa alone, but the others began to demand that he turn over his rifle to the Guard. There had been talk of the matter earlier, but Akseli had not taken it up.

"I won't give you my gun, goddamned if I will, even if you put my blood in a bottle."

Kustaa stood in the doorway in his jacket, his chest mostly bare, although it was wintry cold.

"It is about time you started to listen to what people say, Kustaa."

"You listen yourself, and goddamn good."

"You've always made a little fun of the workers, Kustaa. That has to stop now."

Halme ordered them to give the gun back to Kustaa.

"It's the way he makes his living, at least partly."

Kustaa got his gun back and left, muttering and grumbling softly. Halme ordered the guards to let him travel freely wherever he wanted to. Not everyone was pleased with the decision, and said:

"He has made fun of the workers so often that he should not be given any special rights."

But the greatest grief for the master were the rumors. Women would come to him and whisper:

"He says so and so... I wouldn't... I don't mean... although he did swindle us out of those ditches, where we always made hay... but he went to the manager and told tales on us... I don't mean... But he's said bad things about the Association before this..."

The master would say some appropriate word which would get the rumor-monger to leave. He knew of old these quarrels over pastures, brook hay, and all those little advantages which revealed the bitterness of the struggle for life among these little people.

Akseli was glad to leave more and more business to the master's care, and he himself concentrated on the training of his platoon. If a matter came up which involved the Guard, Halme refused to deal with it. He emphasized that fact even to the people of the community.

"You have to speak to Koskela about that. I have nothing to do with military affairs."

Having joined the staff, Halme went once to try and persuade Otto to join. Otto had remained silent on the sidelines and stayed at home for the most part. Halme found him in the woodshed. First he explained the reasons for which he had ceased to oppose the revolution. He had by private channels heard Salin's words, upon which the latter based his joining the rebellion, and presented them with alterations which made it unnecessary to reveal their source:

"When one has marched to the same beat as the workers for as long as I have, one cannot abandon them even if one cannot approve their actions."

Otto set a piece of wood on the chopping block and split it with a blow of the ax. Then he picked up the piece, tore apart the halves which were still joined by some fibers, and tossed them into the pile.

"Yeah... that beat seems pretty mixed up right now. Of course, it's everyone's own business... As for me, I've decided to stay and help Anna around the house... And you'd better come inside and drink some chicory coffee... Things may yet turn out badly in that business."

"Well, that would be the last reason for me to stand aside."

"It's enough for me... that alone. I don't think it's my business to go and get myself hanged because of fools. I got tired of being on the governing board... I'll be damned if I'm going to bother my head over matters that are decided by shouting anyway."

He said the last seriously, but then switched to a lighter vein as if afraid of too much gravity:

"It would be better for me to join Wolf-Kustaa's Guard. It seems to me that he is after all the freest citizen. No form of rule has been discovered that will make him obey."

"Ahem. We really can't set up a forest anarchist as our model. And I was the one who saved him. Otherwise he would have been forced to obey."

They parted a little stiffly, and on the way home the master fitted Otto's position into Marxist theories:

"It's because he now has the possibility of paying his rent in money... Ever since he's shown little interest in social questions."

Akseli was drilling his men in back of the workers' hall when Valenti called him in to speak to the master. As he stepped into the buffet room he sensed at once that an unusual atmosphere held sway there. Halme cleared his throat nervously and avoided his eyes. Valenti, Kankaanpää, and Antto were in the room, but Halme asked them to leave.

"I have a personal matter to discuss with Akseli."

Akseli sat and waited, wondering what it was all about. The master was ill at ease, and his voice seemed to quaver as he asked:

"When you sent the two prisoners to the church village, what did you write on the paper they say you sent with them?"

"What did I write? All I wrote was how they were taken prisoner and why. What about it?"

"They have been killed now."

Akseli said heatedly:

"Don't start bringing my name into it... My paper has to be there at the headquarters... Did they say anything about it?"

"Silander called me and said they had been brought there with some paper."

Akseli phoned Silander.

"How do you know what was written on my paper... And who am I to give orders to kill people... If I had wanted them to be killed, I wouldn't even have had to order it, but just left them to my men."

"I haven't said that your paper had an order to kill them. I just wanted to let you know so that next time you'll know where to send your prisoners. I already told you after the strike that I don't approve of such things... I started out in this position on condition that such things would not happen. And orders were also given to take off their coats so there would be no holes in them. They say one of the men is going around in the hunting boots taken from the body. I hate anyone who would plunder a corpse..."

"What are they saying at headquarters?"

"They say they didn't order it. But even so, it shouldn't be left at that. They were killed in back of shoemaker Saari's sauna... and stabbed with bayonets to boot."

"Who were the men?"

"They claim no one knows. One of the men at Mellola's sawmill has those boots, but he says he got them from someone, that he wasn't there. But he must have been one of them, along with Flour-Sack-Mandy's boy. You must know him?"

"What Mandy's boy?"

"Well, the Mandy who used to wear pants made from flour sacks. Don't you remember what they said? That 'Extra Prime' was printed on the front and 'Dainty Grain?' on the rear. That's the story that went around. — It was her boy. And I don't wonder. He's none too bright. But that's no excuse... smarter men should answer for it. And now they're rushing around here getting ready to go to the front. Taking power doesn't seem to be so simple now. If we lose, you know what will happen to us when such acts are committed."

"Well, I didn't do it. Let those who are guilty answer for it.. But no one is going to lay such things on my head... That paper must be somewhere there where it can be read. I even remember the words: 'Arrested hiding beside the road, having passed guards secretly, and without papers.' And that's the truth. There was nothing else on the paper."

Having hung up the phone, Akseli sat looking at the floor. Then he said to Halme;

"My conscience is clear... and besides... somewhere in Lyly they found a workers association chairman killed, with his membership card nailed to his breast. When such news spreads, it's impossible to stop the other side..."

"Did the men who were murdered do it?"

"Of course not... but others have to suffer."

"And if we should lose? Do you feel it right that you should be punished for this?"

"I didn't say it was right... But if we lose, they'll be sure to punish me for many other things I haven't done."

"This makes it hard for me to return... When I can't even imagine killing in a battle...and those men were not at all dangerous."

A long and troubled silence followed Halme's words. Neither man had anything to say. The silence was broken by the ring of the telephone, and Akseli picked up the receiver.

"Valenti, come and write this down. It's a message."

Valenti came and began to take down the telephoned order. Akseli looked over his shoulder at the words appearing on the paper. They were a very detailed order to leave for the front.

"At the station by three tomorrow. Uhuh. That means a lot of work and commotion."

The news completely overshadowed the present question. Akseli asked for more clarification from headquarters and forgot to inquire further about the prisoners. There was so much noise on Salin's end of the line that he could not hear clearly the words coming from the phone.

A lively traffic developed in the village. Those leaving for the front went back and forth between their homes and the workers' hall. Older men were ordered to replace those scheduled for guard duty. People came to the workers' hall, each with a question of some kind.

"Could Koskela come over here?"

"About that boy of ours... He has such poor shoes too..."

"We will try to get shoes for him."

Many of the men were indeed poorly equipped. Many a lunch was packed in birchbark knapsacks and when he held the evening inspection, Akseli saw men in the ranks wearing only jackets with a safety pin holding the neck shut. He called headquarters about the situation, but they could offer no help, merely vague promises that they were supposed to get equipment in Tampere. Arvi Laurila, who was also without an overcoat, boasted to the others:

"We'll get army overcoats in Tampere... We'll be real soldiers..."

When the men heard that they were stopping off in Tampere, they grew more and more enthusiastic:

"We'll see a bit of the world, boys... We'll even get to ride a train..."

Aku had not spoken a word to Elma after their quarrel in the Laurila yard. If they happened to meet, Elma passed by with an exaggerated swing of her buttocks, and the boy tried to pretend he hadn't noticed. But the girl was silent these days. She did not stay at the workers' hall a single evening, but went home as soon as her work was finished. When news of the departure for the front arrived, she disappeared from sight. After appearing at the hall, she remained in the cook shack. Watching from its door, she secretively followed the comings and goings of the men, and if Aku was in a group, she ducked quickly out of sight. But if Aune was not present, she hurried to peep through cracks between the boards.

After the evening mess, Aku went to get wood from the woodshed. Taking an armful of wood, he noticed Elma standing in the door. Inadvertently he began to say something, but then remembered that he was supposed to be angry, and concentrated on his work. Elma entered the woodshed, and even in the dim light, the boy could see how upset she was. When Aku said nothing, she went out, but returned at once, thrust a slip of paper into his hand, and said:

"I wrote a goodbye to the mister since the mister won't talk any more..."

Then she literally ran away, but blubbered as she went:

"...no need to answer... it's not for that... so the mister won't think..."

When Aku came out of the shed with his armload of wood, the girl was nowhere in sight. Carrying the wood, he entered the kitchen. There was no one there. He closed the door, lighted a storm lantern, and unfolded the paper. It was hard to make sense of the wretched writing, but word by word the boy sounded out the letter:

To a mouthy mister.

Since the mister can't stand to say anything any more, I'll write. And everything is true what I said. I don't take anything back so you don't have to think... The mister can go to the front for all I care and I don't even care if the butchers kill him. What is it to me when I'm just a gypsy or something to the mister. The mister is proud and I really hope a bullet hits him. Not so he'll die but so that it hurts a lot and the mister will cry. That would be good for someone who always makes fun of someone who is innocent. I'm just saying goodbye because we have known each other although I never went with the mister. I haven't meant anything like that, only laughed. The mister will read this letter to the men so you can all laugh. I don't care about that even if it's clear the mister will do it since all he can do is be proud and nasty. I won't come to see the men off and I'm going to stay home this evening. I'm going to Pentti at eight to get suet that was promised to Mother, but I won't come to the hall so you don't have to think so. You don't have to answer this or come to say goodbye. If the mister comes he'll get the same kind of send-off as last time. You might have said a good word sometime, but always shot off your mouth with the others. Just goodbye and good luck to the mister on his life's road so that he won't run into any gyp-sies and won't have to be ashamed.

Wishes one who the mouthy mister knows well..

Aku folded the letter, put it into his pocket, and blew out the lantern. Without conscious thought, he sensed the letter's meaning. He went inside whistling and after waiting for the opportunity a long time, he succeeded in being alone with Akseli.

"Tell Mother I'll come home later."

"Where are you going then?"

"It's my own business."

His brother looked at him in astonishment for a while.

"With the Laurila girl?"

"Of course not. Just to the village. I suppose there will be some kind of send-off."

"Humph. It's none of my business. But..."

"But what?"

"Nothing. I guess you know what they'll say at home."

187

"What do they have to say about it? I'm going with the boys."

"Don't lie... the devil... with something like that now... it's really not... a half-idiot bunch."

"If that's what you think, then there are some half-idiots on your staff too."

"So there are. And that should be enough. Hmh. Well, what of it — it's not my business."

The boy left, but even in the midst of the rush, Akseli found time to consider the unpleasant subject. Then he calmed himself:

"He can't really be chasing that gypsy devil in earnest..."

A little before eight, Aku was standing at the Kylä-Pentti road juncture. It was the surest place, for Elma had to travel that road. Laurila's place was not far from the hall, for upon his eviction, Antto had gotten an old hill cottage from Pentti to live in. The boy did not have to wait long. Elma came along walking slowly, but noticing Aku, she speeded up her pace. When she reached the spot where he stood, she turned her face away. Aku stepped quickly in front of her.

"Hi."

"So hi. Have they ordered a new guard post or what is the mister doing here?"

"You wrote that you were coming at this time."

"So I did. What of it?"

"Don't be smart alecky."

"Did you think... Jesus, what an imagination... Do you think that's why I wrote? And get out of the way so I can get the suet for Aliina."

"Don't be long then."

"Of course not. I have to hurry home."

Aku let the girl go on her way. Secretively she looked over her shoulder to see that the boy stayed in place. After some ten minutes she came back with a package of suet under her arm.

When she again mocked at him for waiting, the boy said angrily:

"Don't you dare make fun of me. Why did you write then?"

"To say goodbye. We have known each other since we were little."

"Did you write to all the others you've known since you were little?"

"No, but I thought I would write to you since you're so mouthy. Have you read the letter to everyone already?"

"Don't say that..."

With a half-angry decisiveness, Aku grasped the girl's shoulders, turned her around to face him, and put his arms around her pinning her arms underneath them.

"Now you'll give me a kiss... to pay me for coming."

They were about equally tall, so that the boy could not reach her mouth.

They wrestled around for some time, until Elma suddenly spat in the boy's face. Instantly he released his hold and stepped back, wiping his face on his sleeve.

"You really shouldn't spit... in another person's face... You need a licking."

"If my hands had been free, I would have smacked you in the face with that suet."

"I know a place where that suet should go... and you along with it. Do you think you can make a clown of me. You're mistaken, Miss Laurila. Badly mistaken."

Aku started off, but stopped when he heard a tearful voice behind him:

"It's your fault."

"How is it my fault?"

"If you had sometimes... just once... but always by force... as if I was some..."

Uncertain, Aku went back. Elma wept, and turned her back, ashamed of weeping.

"What are you bawling about? I don't know what I'm supposed to do."

Out of the weeping came the uncertain words:

"You do know, but you don't want to... just one nice word sometimes."

"What kind of word?"

"The kind they say... you know..."

Aku caught the girl in his arms and this time she allowed him to turn her as if she lacked a will. Her head was tilted too as if she would let it dangle wherever it happened to. Her eyes were closed and her whole body so limp that the package of suet fell from under her arm. Aku picked it up and, taking the girl's arm, began to lead her along the road. Elma followed without resistance, her head hanging. Near the road was the Kylä-Pentti hay barn. It had no door, but a couple of poles had been crisscrossed over the opening. Aku kicked them down, and led Elma to a seat on a low ledge of hay.

"What is that good word?"

Elma turned away, wiped her face on her sleeve, and blew her nose. When Aku tried to look into her eyes, she kept turning her face away, so that the boy had to take her face in his hands.

"Say it now."

"You know it. You've never acted the right way. I know all about it. You would come to me that way, but not really the right way..."

"But if I came this way..."

The "good word" was in the tone of Aku's voice. The boy was deluged with such a shower of caresses that he literally got the worst of the encounter. In the girl's caresses there was a passion which resembled an outburst of anger, and when she pressed her head against Aku's breast, a soft grinding of teeth mingled with the whimper that sounded from her throat:

"... don't go to the front... run away... we'll go together... to work somewhere... nowadays no one asks, there are so many people on the road."

"I can't stay away."

"Will you come back then... to me... no matter what happens."

The words awakened the boy's consciousness to an awareness of their surroundings, but they seemed of little significance to him, and he said;

"Of course I'll come."

"You can do what you want with me."

Aku crept to the door and glanced cautiously in both directions:

"I don't think anyone could have passed by."

"What does it matter. I'm not afraid of anything."

Aku returned to the hay and settled down next to the girl. She was lying on her back with her hands clasped over her breast as if in prayer. In a thoughtful voice, she asked:

"Are we engaged now?"

"Not yet. When the war ends."

"Father says we can get land from Töyry. Not the old land, but a new place. We can even grow flax then. Mother is good at weaving and she can teach me. And we have an awful lot of dishes. Even plates with flowers on them that were sold at auction. I can have some of them... Mother says I'll even get clothes when the workers rule and even the poor can buy them."

Aku did not want the girl to go on. Her ideas brought the unpleasant aspect of the affair too clearly to the fore. It troubled him, although he assured himself that Elma was not to be condemned. She too thought of the same thing and said in a whisper:

"I know that Akseli doesn't like me. No one at your place does."

"Don't... that stuff... What makes you think so?"

"I know it very well. But I won't come to your place. Everyone there is proud. Even Elina is so proud she hardly says hello. Akseli hates me because he thinks you've been with me. Your family and the Kivivuori family are the proudest families in this community... They think others are just that kind... I know very well they talk about Uuno's being in jail... I won't even come to visit them."

Elma's whisper became heated to the point of rage, and Aku, troubled, tried to dismiss the whole subject.

"Don't talk like that... you just imagine things."

"Is that so. Father says how high and mighty Akseli is when he's giving

190

all those orders. And he's not really on the workers' side either. He protects butchers and looks after their interests."

"That is rot. No one in the world hates the butchers like Aksu."

"Oho! Father said at the staff meeting that old man Töyry should be shot and he just yelled at Father that no one was to be shot."

"Of course. No one can be sentenced to death any longer. That law has been overthrown."

"But you could shoot old man Töyry without a law... I hate him... I hate them all. It just gripes me when I see any one of them. They have made our life like this. Mother always says so."

"Forget about it. You'll get compensation."

"You don't care for me. You were lying just now."

"What... again?"

"You lied... you said everything in such a tired voice... you try to pass over these bad things... so that you won't have to explain..."

Elma sat up. Aku pulled her down onto her back again and said:

"You're the one who keeps coming up with those things. How in the world can I get you to believe what I say? What kind of voice must I say it in?"

Elma sensed a note of indignation in the boy's voice and it frightened her.

"I didn't... it just seems to me... but swear... let's join hands."

"How?"

"This way. Like horse traders... so that the bargain will be firm."

Doubtful and laughing, Aku agreed, but Elma was completely serious.

"Don't laugh. You mustn't laugh at oaths. Say this: 'I like you, and when I come back from the front I will marry you.'"

The boy tried to restrain his laughter when he saw that Elma was dead serious. He repeated the oath, whereupon Elma broke their handhold with her other hand.

"If a horseman backs out of his bargain when it is made in this way, no one will ever believe him and no true men will ever deal with him again and everyone will mock him. They will all say he doesn't keep his word and they will laugh at him."

Elma calmed down when Aku had made the vow and when he caressed her, she tried from her small stock of words to find fitting statements.

"We are really beloved to each other."

It was morning when they left the barn.

191

CHAPTER SIX

I

Practical preparations for going to war were not very complicated at the Koskelas'. The men equipped themselves for the front very much as they had for going out on jobs that lasted for a week or so. They put food into their packs, along with extra socks and pair of mittens.

Once Aleksi ran from the new place to the old and asked Akseli through the open door:

"Aku asked if we should put on neckties."

"With an overcoat and woolen shirt? What kind of nonsense is that?"

"It's only because... we're going to Tampere."

"Don't start imagining that we'll be staying in Tampere."

All morning Akseli had been nervous and irritable, although he tried to hide it. He sensed the unspoken accusations in the entire attitude and behavior of Elina and his parents. His thoughts phrased the words they left unspoken. He knew that this is approximately what they would have said:

"Leaving when she's about to give birth..."

He also knew that the family's dislike for the whole rebellion was tied to the pregnancy. If he had been leaving for a job that would last a long time, they would have said:

"Don't worry. We can always get help here."

But as always when he was forced to admit deep down that he had wronged Elina, he became annoyed with her. This time, however, he controlled his temper, merely saying to himself:

"She's just like her mother."

It was true. In addition to looking exactly like her mother, insofar as their age difference allowed, over the years Anna's airs and attitudes had begun to manifest themselves in Elina. She responded to Akseli's frequent outbursts of anger in the same way as Anna did to Otto's off-color speech, that is, with a dejected melancholy. In the early days of the marriage she had still tried to fight back, but realizing that it was in vain, she had instinctively chosen another type of behavior. She shrank into herself both spiritually and physically.

Her eyes, still bright, looked off somewhere into another world, and the boys got to hear profoundly sad songs.

Giving instructions on how to manage things during his absence, Akseli sought to be as expressionless as possible, so as not to call attention to the significance of his departure. He also went to explain things to his father, and to ask him to see to things. All morning Jussi had done his usual chores in silence. He came and went, growling out something vague to which he did not expect an answer. To Akseli's explanations he replied:

"I'll take care of it..."

His mother did not show the grief she felt in her mind. Her thin, dry braid hanging down her back, she went to and fro preparing her son's pack. Sometimes she would stare at a sock and then take it to a window to see better.

"Well, there's no hole in it... what did I think I saw?"

Small, chubby, and calm, she filled butter boxes.

"Eat from this birchbark one first... it's older. So the taste won't be spoiled."

When the boys talked about going to the front, their mother warned them:

"It's no cause for joy. You're going willingly into the jaws of death. You don't know what war is like. I remember Grandma telling me she heard people talking about war when she was a little girl. There were still people living in those days who had seen seven men come back to this parish when a hundred had left it."

"This is the last battle. When we win, all weapons will be destroyed."

"Don't take it lightly. No one knows whose last battle it will be."

Before Akseli's departure, he and Elina were silent for a long time. Only when his pack was on his back did Akseli reach his hand out to her:

"There's nothing to worry about."

Elina caught his hand in a quick and panicky way. Her lower lip trembling, she turned all her attention to the boys:

"Come and say goodbye to your father."

Soberly, the boys obeyed her. Akseli lifted them into the air by turn:

"Be good boys now."

"Yes."

"If they ask for any of our animals, then give them Star. He won't turn out to be a good bull, so he's not worth keeping. And like I said, don't worry about anything. I'll write soon."

"I won't... it's just that the boys will miss you."

"You men won't miss me, will you?"

Akseli chucked each boy under the chin and said the words with which he customarily accompanied the action:

"It's shameful to chuck a man under the chin."

Elina hustled the boys with her to the door. Aleksi and Aku shouted something jaunty as a goodbye, but she did not answer. Alma had also come to the yard to see them off. When the men had disappeared, waving, around the threshing barn, she raised her apron to her eyes. Jussi had been standing on the steps of the new place, and now he opened the door and disappeared into the house.

Elina led the boys into the house and said:

"Wait here. Mother is going into the bedroom."

The little men waited in silence. When there was no sign of their mother, Vilho went into the hallway. Returning, he said to Eero in a matter-of-fact voice:

"Mama's crying in the bedroom."

Many people had gathered at the workers' hall to see the men off. Family members ran up with a forgotten pair of socks or mittens, and behind some corner or other a mother put a tenner snitched from the household money into a boy's hand.

"If you're able to buy something more..."

Lauri Kivioja's wife had just given birth to a boy, and Victor declared:

"Don't worry about a thing. We'll take care of mother and child."

Lauri himself did not seem to be worrying about them. Tossing his pack onto his back, he said to his kin:

"I kind of think that Lauri is going to be raising hell."

Elma Laurila surreptitiously thrust a sheet of stationery into Aku's hand, then quickly left, disappearing completely from the workers' hall. Aku had no time to say anything as the girl half ran off with her head down. He put the letter into his pocket and returned to the yard, where Akseli was just ordering the men to line up. Swayed by the mood of departure, they tried to be more soldierly than usual. Their drill was rapid, but for the most part clumsy and incorrect. Halme did not come to see them off. Someone had asked him to speak, but he had refused.

"What befits a Kaiser Wilhelm is not suitable for me."

The platoon stood in four ranks, and Akseli said:

"Think over everything now, so that you will all have your gear in shape."

"Let's go. This boy always has everything with him," someone declared.

Another added an equally boastful comment, and Akseli ordered the platoon to face left and to march. Victor Kivioja burst out in the midst of the farewell shouts:

"Goddamn, nowhere are they sending a better-looking bunch out to the dying fields. If anyone says a crosswise word to you, then tell them boys, that you come from Pentti's Corner, goddamn."

Beside and behind the column of fours marched enthusiastic little boys with crossbows on their shoulders. They escorted the platoon for a long way, and then returned to the community in military formation.

In the church village, the platoon joined the company. From there, a large crowd accompanied them to the station, along with a brass band. The tune of the revolutionary march rang out in the biting, frosty air, and two hundred pairs of boots — Lapland, felt, or other kinds — strove to strike the earth more briskly than usual. The actual departure ceremony, however, had been organized at the station. The company was lined up in four ranks and the workers' associations' flags arranged in front of it. The leadership elite swarmed around the place, and so that all the rules of militarism might be complied with, a few girls from the youth society had been asked to pin flowers on those leaving. The flowers were made of red crepe paper, but the girls were fresh and pretty, for they had been chosen on the basis of their looks. Shyly they pinned the flowers on the breasts of the leave-takers, and these hired hands and cottagers looked a trifle doubtfully at the flower which had appeared on their overcoats. Hellberg spoke to the men who were leaving as they stood silent, looking at the crowd.

The company had its back to the locomotive, and many tried to steal a glance behind them, for there were some in the group who had never seen a train, and even more who had never traveled on one. But they really could not turn their heads toward the strange hissing sound behind them, audible during pauses in Hellberg's oration, which rang out in the cold and frosty air.

The crowd too stood there without a whisper. Only the station personnel, off to the side, moved cautiously and without attracting attention, preparing the train for departure. After the speech, the company commander, Ylöstalo, ordered his troops to board the train by platoons. The bolder ones, who had traveled by train before, stayed on the steps and vestibules, while the others watched through the windows. One of the station workers taking the place of the stationmaster, who had refused to perform his duties, whistled the signal to leave, and then the first faint hurrahs were heard. The band struck up the Internationale, and those leaving and their escorts joined in. The locomotive, adorned with a large red rosette, puffed, and the wheels moved. Shouts mingled with the brass band's melody and the singing.

The short train was soon in motion, and a few of those who had come to see the men off kept running alongside it. As the puffs of the locomotive speeded up, the runners gave up the race and stood watching, joining in the song, while the more enthusiastic waved a last farewell from the train, now disappearing behind cuts in the land. The song ended, and many of the people now smiled in mild embarrassment at their recent enthusiasm.

In the Pentti's Corner coach, the mood remained festive for a long time. Since there was room in the coach, those who were traveling on a train for the first time tried several seats, as if they were greedy.

"No conductor is coming to ask for our tickets, boys."

"Next time we'll go on our own train. Maybe we'll stop wherever we want to."

"If we had our guns now, we'd shoot like hell whenever we came to a station."

Akseli sat near a window in a corner of the coach. Someone tried to talk to him, but he gave such forced answers that the speaker went away. Resting his face on his fists, he watched the landscape flashing by. The last pale light of the February day glimmered on the horizon. The sun, which had sunk out of sight, cast a cold red on high-floating bands of thin clouds. There was something mysteriously depressing in the sight, increasing the worry that was intruding into his mind. Now that he was free of all practical duties for the moment, he thought of his family. Although he assured himself that there was no real cause for concern, his mind would not calm down.

'If only they don't go on the wall side... with that young bull... He's so jumpy. Pins you against the wall... I should have told Father about that bedding... And I didn't warn them about the cover of that well... That the boys shouldn't go near it...'

He listened with one ear to the confused talk of the men. Arvi Laurila was telling an anecdote, one group was playing cards, and another was talking about the revolution:

"...Believe me, boys, they're not taking us any farther than Tampere... I read in the People's Press that Mannerheim has already gone to some unknown place to gather a new army because the old one has run away..." "Osku, you were bluffing, by God. For once Kivivuori's boy was caught in the act..." "Well then, this old man once went to take a bull to the butcher, and he took some turpentine with him..." "No, they're not fighting in Viipuri. Viipuri is in our hands, and the butcher's commander said that if he doesn't get help, he's going to leave the front..." "And that bull got tired, so the old man put some turpentine on his balls..." "They should have sent the girls who gave out the flowers along with us... Goddamn, the best looker was giving flowers to the men from the church village..." "Then the bull started running so fast that the old man put turpentine on his own balls... But the bull's balls stopped stinging before the old man's and when the old man got to the butcher's he handed him the rope and said hold on to this I've still got a ways to go..."

Having finished the story, Arvi laughed loudest of all, and the others laughed at his amusement. Since they stimulated one another, the laughter swelled to such an extent that soon everyone in the coach joined in. Absorbed in his thoughts, Akseli snorted, but soon withdrew into himself. As they neared Tampere, his frame of reference altered. His worries about home faded, to be replaced by thoughts of his imminent tasks.

"They're sure to have a reception for us there... what kind of quarters will we get... Ylöstalo should see to that..."

"You can see the city."

The men rushed to the window, and some of the men explained the sights to the first-timers.

"That's the general hospital... we'll be going over the Sorrinahde Bridge soon..." "Fairgoers say there's plenty of money in Sorrinahde..." "Stop shoving, goddamn... you'll have plenty of time to see it..."

The train did not drive up to the station, but remained farther off on a siding. The company marched to the station grounds, where a couple of other units were assembled. Ylöstalo tried to order the company to fall in, but he finally had to resort to explanations.

"Don't come so far this way. Koskela, your platoon is like a herd of animals."

Akseli verified that it was indeed so, for the men were gawking at units already assembled on the station grounds and at the spectators gathered around. In a low voice, Akseli scolded the gawkers and got them lined up. Apparently there would be some kind of ceremony here too, for a large brass band was standing on the station grounds.

A group of men with a driver arrived, and a whisper ran through the ranks.

"They are officers"... "Is that Haapalainen or Aaltonen there..." "They aren't here... They're in Helsinki... these are other officers."

There were actually some officers in the group. One could tell by their neat wadmol suits, their boots, and above all, the swords or holsters which hung at their waists. However, these military men remained in the background and a man in civilian dress stepped forward. With the assurance of a man accustomed to giving speeches, he began:

"My rural comrades, tenants, and farm workers. With the authorization of the northern front headquarters, I bid you welcome to Tampere. You have come to join ranks with your factory-worker comrades in your common struggle against the oppressive, enslaving herd of butchers..."

The words echoed from the walls of the station. Some of the people walking along the street stopped to listen, but most of them continued on their way. This was obviously all too familiar to them. The rural comrades tried to stand stiff and menacing in their ranks, especially when the speaker raised his voice as he approached the end:

"...when the proud Red Guard marches, the poor rejoice and the hearts of the butchers tremble."

After the speech, the company commanders walked up to the group there to greet them. Greetings were exchanged: a touch of the hand to the hat, reinforced by a handshake and a raising of the hat. The men in the ranks tried to listen carefully to the buzz of talk, but they could make out only unintelligible fragments:

"The barracks commander will be sure to know that... no, no. They are at the school... Food... that's really your affair... Well, you have food with you... That won't do. What's so strange about that... the orders are clear."

Akseli stood before the platoon and could hear Arvi Laurila's half-whispered words behind him:

"Hey, Akseli, hey. Go and ask that guy if we get overcoats here."

Akseli did not answer, but when Arvi began to press his demand in an increasingly loud voice, he said threateningly:

"Shut up there... Everyone will hear your twaddle."

Ylöstalo and the others returned to their companies, and the units marched off, turning onto a bridge over the railroad. Some spectators stood near the street. Comments could be heard from their group:

"They're taking country bumpkins now... hey, old man, don't get your feet mixed up."

Lauri Kivioja happened to hear a sneering remark and barked a reply:

"We happen to have been to Helsinki, goddamn... We've traveled to farther-off places than these alleys."

Lauri could not make out the reply.

Having marched to barracks near the Tammela fields, the men were forced to stand outside in the cold and the evening darkness. Ylöstalo had gone to get information, but he did not return. At first, out of curiosity the men watched other groups coming and going, but when the cold got to them, a muttering began:

"What are we standing here for? Where did Ylöstalo go?"

"He's sure to come back."

"He doesn't seem to be coming. We have to choose a messenger to go and find out."

Finally their commander arrived, and they got into one of the barracks.

Ylöstalo gave a talk, informing them they would get no food and would have to manage on their own rations. When on top of everything he ordered them not to leave the barracks, there was a loud grumbling.

"Why should we have to lie around here hungry? And we'll really be short of food at the front if we already have to go without eating here."

"A worker-soldier should be able to go one night without food."

"A Red Guard man has a stomach like anyone else."

The actual cause of the grumbling was not the food, but the prohibition against leaving. And when the commander had departed, the men declared openly:

"We're going to town, that's for sure."

After a while, Oskari and Elias left quietly, followed by others. The only ones left of Akseli's platoon were Aku, Aleksi, and a few more men. Aleksi was too humble to disobey a command and it was Elma's letter that held Aku back. He had already read it in the toilet on the train, but now he read it again under the concealment of his pack.

Dear friend,

I cried all the rest of the night when I thought fate has separated us and I hope it isn't forever which my heart fears. Don't go into the very front lines but stay back. Even if they all urge you, don't go. And I would like to tear the eyes out of anyone who tells you to. My friend don't think of anything but the faithful one who waits for you. If they order you, then tell them let others go. Just think that we will get a piece of land from somewhere and a small cottage so we can live together then. If the parsonage is divided you are sure to get it from there. I've already been thinking how I'll learn to weave and will make everything. Every evening I leave the hall when I finish the dishes and go home thinking of you. And then when you come you can hold your own one for a long time and do what you want with her.

Written with love by your own friend.

The boy put the letter secretly into his pocket and turned onto his back. It was silent in the large, open barrack room, for the weary men who had come from the front were asleep and the noisiest from Aku's own group had disappeared. From outside came a constant, soft hum of talk and the crunching footsteps as men came and went in the cold snow.

"Well, it's not her fault they are like that... and besides... why is it anyone's business?"

Now here at a distance in the midst of great events, the matter seemed quite simple in essence, and he began to chat happily with Aleksi, until they were interrupted by Akseli's voice from where he lay some distance away on a bunk:

"Go to sleep. We'll have to march anyway. And I'll put Osku and Elku to break trail in the snow if we run into any."

Osku and Elias were the last to arrive early in the morning. Osku was dragging Elias along by the shoulder, urging him to silence. But Elias was imitating a train:

"Choo-choo — hoowhee — hoowheee — choo-choo."

"Who the hell is making that noise?"

"Quiet. Here comes the command locomotive."

Angry heads were raised from the bunks, and someone turned on a light. Akseli ordered Osku to make Elias lie down, but Elias was able to slip out of his grasp. In the doorway was a boot rack, which Elias put between his legs as a horse, and slapping his behind with one hand, he began to gallop down the lane between bunks. The men he had awakened began to curse and threaten to throw him out. He raised an admonitory hand and said:

"Don't shout. You'll scare the horse."

Akseli literally threw Elias onto a bunk, where he flopped in a heap like an empty sack. After lying motionless for a half-minute, he raised his head and shouted:

"All the proletariat of the land, unite!"

Then he passed out, once and for all, as Akseli scolded Osku in whispers. The latter climbed onto a bunk in silence and said indifferently:

"You should have gone too. I wouldn't have told on you."

"And where did you get that liquor?"

"Stop nagging. Give me some more tobacco."

"I won't."

"Goodbye then."

Half-mumbling, Akseli went back to his place.

"Humph... What one has to put up with..."

The next day they marched through the city to the Technical College to get rifles. There the same thing happened as at the barracks the night before. They had to stand out in the cold for more than an hour as Ylöstalo ran from one higher-up to another. Rifles there were, but no one to distribute them. The freezing men wrestled and hopped around to warm themselves. Men came and went. An officer arrived on a black horse. Dismounting, he approached the company and said in a sharp and sour voice:

"What company is this?"

When he received an answer, he said with equal military weight:

"Uhuh."

Nor did he have anything more remarkable to contribute. Finally Ylöstalo came out with a handsome blond man, bareheaded and wearing a jacket.

"Good day, comrades. Don't be upset. You will get your weapons, but the distributors are at the railroad station getting a load of ammunition.

200

They'll be here soon. We've already called."

From the ranks sounded the voice of Arvi Laurila:

"When are the overcoats coming?"

"What overcoats?"

"We were promised clothes from here."

"Who promised?"

Akseli stepped forward.

"They told me that they would give clothes here to those who had poor ones."

"We haven't promised anything. What clothing we have is to be distributed to the city companies. The rural companies already have clothing better suited to the outdoors. But clothing will be sent to the front as soon as it comes in, so you'll have it where it's most needed. You can go to eat now, and in the afternoon a leave-taking has been arranged at the Tammela market. They'll even recite poems for you there. You'll hear the best actor in Finland recite them."

The man departed, and they asked Ylöstalo:

"Who was that old guy?"

"He was no old guy. He was Salmela, the commander of the northern front."

"He's a real bigshot."

Finally the weapons distributors arrived, but they responded to the angry complaints of the men in an equally angry manner.

"We've got our hands full. Come and carry the boxes."

The boxes of weapons were brought up from the basement and the distribution of weapons began. A shade of respect developed in the men for the expertise and the familiarity with guns of the men giving them out, along with a slight sense of inferiority, for the latter paid little attention to the recipients. To the distributors, they were just another rural company which had to be armed these days.

The men examined the rifles enthusiastically.

"Let me see what kind you have."

"They're all the same."

"No they're not. Some have a lighter and some a darker stock."

Then a shot rang out and Elias Kankaanpää fell to the ground. Arvi Laurila's rifle had fired.

"My God... Elku's done for."

"Who fired there?"

Elias stood up, a little pale.

"Did you get hit?"

"No, but I thought I did and figured I should fall."

Fear was released in laughter, but Akseli ordered them not to load the

201

rifles. Even Arvi began to feel like laughing, and he said:

"I just put a bullet in it and it fired."

"Don't mess around with it. You'll kill someone yet."

It was nicer to march in the city now when they all had rifles on their shoulders, but no one paid any attention to them, for the city was full of men marching with rifles on their shoulders. They were fed in the Theater restaurant, but it was only thin gruel and a piece of bread. Lauri Kivioja, however, voiced the feeling of many by saying:

"For once we're eating in a Tampere hotel, goddamn."

After eating they marched to the Tammela market, where groups on their way to different sectors of the front had been gathered for the purpose of raising their fighting spirit. An event of this sort also brought an audience to the place, and a large number of people were stirring near the marketplace.

Speeches followed, and songs accompanied by the brass band. The reciter promised by the commander-in-chief performed, declaiming the words of the Red Guard March in a resounding voice and with grand gestures:

"...then fr-r-rightful spirits come thir-r-rsting for heart's blood..."

The reciter received thunderous applause from the public as well, and when it ceased, a whisper ran through the Pentti's Corner ranks:

"He is Orjatsalo"... "What"... "He is Orjatsalo..." "Who says so..." "It is him... "Hey, it's Orjatsalo...." "Who is he..." "He's the best actor in Finland, of course..." "What actor..." "Well, the one they promised. Didn't you hear, you damned meathead..." "Well, don't start yelling now..." "Let him be, for all I care."

They marched away from the event to the tempo of the brass band. The size of the crowd and the tune of the march really raised their spirits. Music and the buzz of talk filled the air. The arms of the marchers swung more smartly than usual. All this made a Häme tenant farmer raise his head higher, a shade higher than it had ever been before. "We'll push through now, it just has to be."

He looked around. Shoulders swayed ahead of him, filling the whole street, and above them glittered a forest of bayonets.

"This was an army, by God. With units from Turku and everything."

III

The company was marching along an ice road on a lake. The lake was narrow and seemed to come to an end soon, but when they got closer to the imagined shore, the men observed a narrow sound beginning at one corner and broadening out into a new field of ice. The rays of the winter sun made the new-fallen snow glitter so that their foreheads, wrinkled against the light, began to grow stiff and numb.

Sometimes they met a horse or a procession of several horses.

"Is it far to the front?"

"There's still quite a way."

The strange and lovely landscape could no longer arouse any interest in them. More and more of the men began to stare dully at the heel of the boot in front of them as it rose and fell regularly. As their weariness increased, some detail in the step or footgear of the man ahead would begin to annoy them. They would turn their heads away, but their eyes would go back to following that detail again.

"What a flatfoot."

Leaving Siuro, there had been animated discussion in the ranks, but a few kilometers of journeying over the ice had doused that.

"How far is this place called Ikaalinen then?"

"How do I know. It must be out here somewhere."

In the afternoon as they approached the church village of Hämeenkyrö, the head of the column began to stop without a command. After a few jerks, the entire column stopped. When the crunching of footsteps ceased, the men realized the cause of the halt. From far ahead they could hear a soft rumble, which was repeated at brief intervals. First there was a more powerful roar, which diminished into a rumble that grew slowly fainter.

"Now you hear it then. That's artillery fire."

There was total silence as the men concentrated on listening. Someone lighted a pipe, and even the scrape of the match on the box caused his comrade to whisper:

"Stop scraping there."

The roaring continued. Lauri Kivioja raised his rifle to his shoulder and said, breaking the silence:

"The real stuff is coming, goddamn it boys."

His words freed the others too.

"That's a big gun blasting."

"It's the real western front, goddamn it, boys."

Ylöstalo ordered them into motion, and the roar of the firing was lost under the crunching of snow beneath their marching feet. But the men strained their ears in order to hear that strange and solemn sound again, which caused a tightness never before experienced somewhere in the area of their stomach.

In the dusk of evening, they neared the front. Already they could hear the sound of rifle shots more and more clearly. For the first time in their lives they heard the sound of machine guns.

"The bullet sprayers are singing, boys."

Toward them came horsemen, skiers, and horse-drawn sleds, most of them empty. On one of them, however, three men were sitting, and a fourth was lying on the bottom of the sled. One of the seated men had a bandage on one side of his face, through which a bit of blood had oozed. His mouth was oddly twisted, for one side of his face was swollen, drawing one corner of his mouth askew. But nevertheless, smoke issued from a cigarette in the straight corner. Curious, the men looked at their first wounded man, and when the horse was forced to stop a moment because of the congestion prevailing on the road, one of them asked in an oddly soft and humble voice:

"Were you badly hit?"

The wounded man did not answer. For a moment he turned his head toward the questioner, but then went on staring straight ahead. His blank stare had an odd effect on the men. It conveyed weariness and fever, but also an inexplicable detachment from everything. It seemed to say to inquirers: "I no longer care what interests you."

Only once did the man take the cigarette from his mouth, draw a deep breath, and release it with a mumbled moan:

"Ow... god...damn..."

The horse got moving again, and the wounded man's comrade said to the questioner:

"Why do you ask? Can't you see it went through his head.."

The driver was young, fifteen at most, and he declared:

"It was a pretty rough battle."

There was in the boy's tone of voice a self-conscious declaration of experience.

The march went on in silence.

It was already evening when they reached a village. In spite of the darkness, they could see that the place was buzzing with activity. Men came and went constantly. Every possible shelter was full of horses and sleighs and there were even horses standing along fences. The odd speech of many of the men astounded the men from Pentti's Corner, and they reacted to the strange dialect with a slightly contemptuous amusement, for they considered their own to be the one pure tongue. A passerby asked what outfit they were, and Elias replied in a matter-of-fact voice:

"The Hämeenlinna Washerwomen's Assault Company."

"Don't be a smart-ass, you country bumpkin."

Apparently the man took the answer as a challenge, but not daring to quarrel with the whole company, he went on his way.

They were directed to a house on the outskirts of the village, and Akseli's platoon was lodged in the large main room. The rest were settled in the other rooms of the house, and also in the sauna and its dressing room. Exhausted by the long march, the men lay down as soon as they had eaten, but Akseli began to wander through the recesses of the house, partly out of curiosity and partly because, in spite of his weariness, he could not sleep.

With the coming of darkness, the firing had ceased. Silence reigned in the direction of the front. From somewhere in the distance, there was scattered firing, which the ear could barely make out. From the village came the sound of muffled talk. At the corner of an outbuilding, a freezing guard banged his heels together.

The cold had intensified during the evening. The stars shone bright and clear. Looking at the sky and seeing the familiar constellations, Akseli was overwhelmed by homesickness. On hundreds of evenings he had stood like this in the yard at home, stopping to look at the sky and check the weather. For the first time in his life, he had been torn loose from that familiar setting. The nights he had spent away from Koskela could be counted on his fingers. Hauling logs, he had preferred to drive long distances home rather than spend a week away. Standing in this unfamiliar, faraway place, he experienced a vivid consciousness of similar nights in his home yard. In the same way as now he had looked at the Great Bear and Orion's Belt. The sleepy boys dawdling around appeared to his imagination, and although at home he might have scolded them for romping, that was exactly how he missed them now. A warm emotion stirred in his mind when he saw, in his imagination, their small limbs covered by their new flannel nightshirts. The nightshirts were too short.

"Since there wasn't enough of that flannel. So much of it went for swaddling bands... And I didn't remember to tell her to sleep with the boys. It wouldn't be so lonesome."

At that moment, a light flared in the northern sky, closely followed by a roar and then the whine of a shell. Roughly some two or three kilometers away there was another flash and an explosion. Men thronged to the door.

"Where did it hit?"

Another flash and a roar and another explosion in the air.

"Hey, look, ours are answering back."

"No they aren't. It's that shrapnel."

"Or maybe they have delayed charges."

After a few discharges, the firing ceased. The spectators disappeared into the house, and Akseli followed them. For a long time he lay on the floor unable to sleep. Projecting knots on the worn floor dug into his back. The floor exuded a nauseating smell of insulation soaked by scrub water, which at any rate was alleviated by the odor of pitch from the pack he was using as a pillow. The last image in his mind was an excruciating one. They are wading in deep snow and everyone stops. No one gets up.

In a dim half-sleep, he assured himself:

"...if I just don't start to think... then I'll have the nerve..."

IV

There was lively traffic in the village the following day. New units arrived, but they marched past, for there was no room for them. The men from Pentti's Corner wandered around the other houses, and everyone had news on his return.

"There are so goddamned many outfits coming. And the Russians are even bringing artillery."

Later in the day, as they were standing on the highway, they heard a humming in the sky.

"Look, boys. A flying machine."

There was indeed a black spot on the horizon, which gradually grew larger. Everyone watched eagerly. Some called it a flying machine and some an airship. The plane flew over them in the direction of the front and someone shouted:

"It's Rahja. Things will go badly for the butchers now."

There were men from Tampere on the highway, and among them were authorities on the subject.

"It is Rahja... Eppu is flying, boys... Hey, it's Eppu Rahja. He's going to give the butchers a few candies."

"We don't need anything else. That's some machine. He's going to set the butchers' cities on fire."

"He's sort of a wild one. He was a flyer on the Russian front."

The plane brought on a fit of high spirits.

"Will the explosions start soon?"

They waited tensely, but the plane disappeared in the cold blue of the sky, and there were no explosions.

"Rahja is flying all the way to Vaasa."

An artillery piece was driven along the road. It aroused almost the same enthusiasm as the airplane. Some of the men rushed out to push when the horses seemed to be straining. The artillery crew was Russian, and when they said something in their own language, Aleksi smiled;

"They're babbling in Russian."

An older man stepped up to Aleksi from a Tampere unit, and said softly:

"You should have enough class-consciousness not to use that word for our comrades."

Aleksi was so confused that he could not answer. As he left, the man said:

"I was just letting the comrade know. My intentions were good."

For a long time Aleksi watched the man, who disappeared into his own group swinging his shoulders a little ostentatiously. The boy looked around helplessly at those around him:

"What did he mean by that?"

"I don't know... he seems to be pretty class-conscious himself."

Aleksi's brow was wrinkled for a long time afterward, for he could not grasp what the man had meant.

A horse came from the direction of the front, pulling a sleigh on which there were two bodies. They had not been covered, and everyone, curious, rushed to see them. One was a quite old man with a bushy mustache, underneath which his teeth were visible through his open mouth. To the men from Pentti's Corner, he looked very familiar, for his clothing, with its coarse woolen coat and his stocking-legged felt boots, reminded them of a rural tenant farmer. The sight of him was therefore especially ugly, and many of them turned away. At any rate, the old man lay as bodies usually do, but the other body was frozen in a deformed shape, its head bent backward, one hand hooked upward, and the other shoved into the waistband of his trousers, where frozen blood could be seen. Over his breast ran a home-made cartridge belt.

"The boys are quiet."

Someone made the statement in a low voice. The horse turned into a yard and the sleigh vanished from sight.

Ylöstalo was called to a conference of officers. He took Akseli with him, although the order did not affect platoon leaders. But during these few days Ylöstalo had already noticed Akseli's practical and conscientious manner of doing his duty. Ylöstalo had formerly been in the reserves, but had no other prerequisites for being a company commander. He knew it himself, and that made him uncertain, so he took Aleksi along with him for moral support. It was also good to have two to remember what was said.

The headquarters was in the largest farm in the community. There were horses hitched to sleighs in the yard, and along the stable wall were saddled mounts. One could assume from all other signs that this building housed the staff. Men with swords on their thighs and spurs on their boots moved around in the yard. In the other main building of the farm, women moved about. Apparently it was an aid station of some sort.

The conference took place in the parlor. To judge by its furnishings, the house was a rich and powerful one. Although everything was a filthy mess, its former refinement could be seen beneath the confusion. A pair of orphaned homeowners looked on haughtily from a photograph on a chest of drawers. Officers arrived. Many of them exuded a nice sense of their importance. The war was just beginning and their belief in success was firm. Some were armed cap-à-pie, with a sword, pistol, and a bayonet to boot. The commander of the front spread a travel-association map on the table. It showed the roads and the villages, but nothing about the type of terrain. Then he read a detailed order for the attack, on the basis of which the companies were assigned their duties.

The plan was extremely detailed, but nonetheless simple. First one village would be attacked and taken, then another would be taken, and so on, until all together would take the nearest trading center. From there they would go on village by village, sending out units to secure the flanks and to establish contacts wherever and with whatever, crush the butchers' resistance if it should materialize, and keep going north all the way to Vaasa. The roads on the map ran promisingly through all the villages named to their objective, and these tenants, house painters, union presidents, and metal workers who were called company commanders looked eagerly at the road along which their sector lay.

Ylöstalo's company was subordinated to another company, along with which it was assigned the capture of one of those villages. That company's commander, who introduced himself as Myllymäki, became the head of the entire unit. He was a plump, ruddy man, who exuded self-confidence from his entire body and soul.

Myllymäki stood beside the table looking at the map with his lips pursed. He breathed somehow pompously, puffing out his own mightiness with each exhalation. At brief intervals he shifted his weight from one foot to another, always flexing his knee, which bent oddly backward.

"This is where I'll start out from. You, Ylöstalo, will leave one platoon in reserve. With the rest of the company, you will circle along this winter road. It's not on the map, but spies have checked it out, and it leads to the village. It runs roughly this way. From it you will give us support on the flank. A messenger on skis will maintain contact with me."

Ylöstalo told Akseli to check the map also. The latter approached somewhat troubled, first because he was a supernumerary at the conference, and second, because he had really not seen a map after being in the public school. Myllymäki's stubby forefinger pointed to a spot where there were clusters of black dots on either side of a winding red line. That was apparently the road and the village.

Myllymäki explained, and Akseli, feeling uncertain, responded:

"Ya-ah. It seems to be there."

The map made nothing clear to him, for he knew otherwise that from the village they were in a road led on to another, exactly the one they were supposed to capture. The winter road had been found with the help of a guide, for it was not on the map.

"Well then. That ought to be clear. Nothing more to it than let the bullets fly in the butchers' faces so their balls will ring."

The other officers then had their missions explained at the map. A pen indicated points on the map, a lower lip sucked thoughtfully at an upper lip, and a head nodded in token of understanding. From outside could be heard the clamor of troops marching by. They were conferring about the war at headquarters. Underlying their excitement regarding their mission was the warlike spirit imbibed from adventure books read when they were little boys.

After the official conference, discussion turned to the executions at Varkaus, which the headquarters had received word of. They were enraged, and one of the officers threatened:

"I won't take a single prisoner."

"There's no reason to spare many of those bastards. Every tenth man was called out from the ranks and shot on the spot. And not all of them had even borne arms. There were civilians who were not involved at all and who had come to the factory for shelter because it had brick walls and there was shooting in the city. They wound up in the same group. They were told, 'You criminals always have a story,' when they explained that they were not Red Guards."

"We'll put the same law into effect. Even if they beg for mercy on their knees."

"It only goes to show that we have to win. So when you attack, remember that you are fighting for your lives."

Leaving the conference, Akseli was thoughtful and silent.

Ylöstalo was tense and strained too. On the way, Akseli asked him:

"They most likely shot every tenth men in the ranks. Haven't they vowed to shoot every leader right off? From the lowest to the highest."

There was a note of confidentiality in Ylöstalo's voice when he said:

"We just can't afford to lose."

Listening to the headquarters discussion, Akseli had vaguely sensed something which had not occurred to him earlier. Until now he had felt only a responsibility for carrying out his own individual tasks, but listening to and observing the staff, he had realized that there was no mysterious strength or power in the revolution. It was made up only of himself and men like him. His vague and at the same time all-powerful conception of "the whole bunch" became clearer. It was able to do just what he himself could. And if he failed, then they were lost.

His notion of responsibility broadened, causing a mild feeling of perplexity and pressure within him, which was increased by the fact that he sensed Ylöstalo's strained uncertainty. Nor did he have an especially good opinion of the other platoon leaders.

From time to time, the men stepped off into the snow to avoid loads driving along the road, or other marching units. Such a long time had elapsed since Ylöstalo's last words that the latter was no longer able to make the connection when Akseli said:

"Well, it is a kind of relief to know that there is only one way to go. It does no good to turn back. The grave is there."

"But we should be able to clear the way with a bunch like this. And they say the butchers' fighting spirit is none too great. They have a lot of men who have been half-forced to join up."

When they arrived in the yard of their lodging, they were immediately surrounded by men.

"Did you see when the airship went to burn the butchers' cities... the men from Tampere said it was that Rahja... They say he's a wild one... He even flew for the Russians..."

"What will he burn those cities with?"

"I guess he'll throw bombs... I don't know, but that's what they said."

The men were in high spirits, but Akseli brushed off his feet with the broom, deep in his own thoughts, and not listening to them.

V

The snow and the glow of the winter morning lighted the woods only enough for them to see some twenty meters, and that only with difficulty. The units stood waiting on the road. The men hopped in place, shivering with the cold, their blood still circulating sluggishly after sleeping. They did not know why they had stopped. A messenger on skis went by, asking questions which they most often could not answer. One asked for some unknown officer, another about an ammunition sleigh, and a third about some company.

Up ahead a rifle shot rang out now and then. One man was chewing on a piece of bread, another was smoking with the cigarette cupped in his hands. Then a low-voiced discussion sounded from behind. A group of men came from that direction, and they recognized the voices of Myllymäki, Ylöstalo, and Akseli.

"Form a skirmish line in back of the positions. When you hear the artillery fire, you can start right out."

The leaders stopped, and Myllymäki went on giving orders. Finally he said swaggeringly:

"You just push right on, then. And if you can't, I'll come myself."

From in back came Elias Kankaanpää's softly muttered comment:

"You'd better come right away then."

Their leaders could not hear the remark, but the men nearest to him laughed. Elias had been made a bugler. He had been given a signaling bugle, and he had learned the signals agreed upon. The men had demanded the promised equipment, but had not received it. In its place they had gotten the bugle, which seemed to be of great significance to the officers, for in leaving even Myllymäki said:

"You should be able to push off now. You've got a bugle and everything."

Akseli took his place before the platoon and ordered silence:

"The second platoon will pass the first. Get moving."

The platoon in front went off into the snow as the second platoon marched by. Lauri Kivioja mouthed off as they passed by:

"They're putting the strike force up front and leaving the church villagers to bury the bodies."

The road wound through a gloomy grove of firs, but as they neared the front lines, the woods thinned out. On a small rise stood a couple of men, who ordered them to stop. They were a guide and the leader of the platoon designated to check the direction of the road. Akseli had already gone the day before to study the lay of the land where the attack was to take place and thus had little to ask. Silently the men spread out in a skirmish line, Oskari's unit on the left and the men from Hollo's Corner on the right side of the road. Seeing both his brothers wading through the snow in the line, Akseli turned away. Upon leaving that morning, he had meant to warn them, but out of a touchy sense of honor, he had not been able to. He had also thought to assign the bugler's duty, which was less dangerous, to one or the other, but that he could not bring himself to do either.

The glow of dawn grew stronger. The terrain, with its sparse growth of trees, was clearly visible. From the right, in the direction of the main road, a few shots sounded.

"Shall I sound the advance?" whispered Elias.

"Absolutely not. We'll move out quietly. Blow only when ordered. And it's best that you do very little tooting. They don't remember the signals anyway."

The first cannon shot roared behind them. They could hear the whistle of the shell clearly. It whined past them on the right and exploded out in front of them.

"Is the village so close?"

"It's a kilometer away."

The artillery began to fire in pairs.

"They're blowing stone barns into the air."

Akseli released the safety on his rifle and waved his hand. They ascended the slope, where men were lying in a thin line. Only then did the real tension begin. The men struggled to wade through the deep snow from rock to rock and tree to tree. Akseli himself walked along the road, trying to survey the terrain ahead sharply. In the more open spots he went off the road, but since walking in the snow was laborious, he soon returned to the road. They advanced a hundred meters, and nothing happened. The sparse artillery fire died down, and in its place the sound of constant rifle and machine-gun fire began to be heard from the right, along with unintelligible shouting. The nearest men looked at him inquiringly, but with a wave of his hand he urged them to look forward.

Around a corner of the road, there appeared a cutover area. It looked as if the logging had been done that winter, for the branches and treetops were only lightly covered with snow. Alongside the road were piles of pulpwood. Akseli stopped. The clearing looked as if there might be manned positions beyond it. He took a step or two forward, and thought he saw movement among the trees. Immediately, he leaped off the road, and at that instant he heard a shrill sound in his ears. It was an odd pinging, sound mingled with an explosion. Everything seemed to happen without conscious thought. He was not aware of thinking about taking cover, but it was as if his consciousness had expanded so as to grasp everything simultaneously.

Quickly he burrowed into the snow, and only as he did so did he realize that shooting was going on around him. He could hear bullets striking the trees above him, and rifles banged on both sides of the road. He raised his head cautiously and saw Aku lying behind a rock a few meters to the rear, nervously firing his rifle. The boy kept ejecting his shells rapidly and firing almost without aiming, as if the whole object in firing was to do so as rapidly as possible. Some ten meters back lay Elias and the guide. Akseli dragged himself to a more sheltered spot behind a rock. Breathless, he repeated to himself what he had thought through many times before: "You can't panic. You have to look everything over first."

From behind the rock he surveyed his own line. The men lay in sheltered positions, keeping up a hot fire. Further back crouched the company commander with a few men. Making a trumpet of his hands, Ylöstalo shouted:

"What's out there?"

"Butchers."

From in back of the cuttings came a shout:

"Death battalion. Forward!"

212

That brought on a totally wild acceleration of the firing, and there were shouts from his own line:

"They're attacking. There was a command..."

For a long time there was heavy firing, but nothing more notable happened. Akseli had been warned about shouts intended to lead men astray, and understood that the recent one had been just that. He ordered the information to be passed along the line, and it quieted the firing. Then he raised his head cautiously and studied the terrain before them. The opening seemed broader on the right side of the road, and the terrain on the left was otherwise more sheltered.

"Osku."

"What is it?"

"You have to try to move up. They should fire as fast as they can on the left."

Having given the pertinent orders to the right, he shouted to Elias:

"Sound the attack."

Elias blew the appointed three blasts, actually quite unnecessarily, for the men in the skirmish line could hear Akseli's verbal commands very well. Oskari started out first. He fell at times as he ran through the deep snow, but continued in a crouch, stopping behind the top of a pine tree. Lauri Kivioja was standing behind a huge chunk of boulder and was firing as fast as he could from there. As Oskari ran, he stamped in place and let out a horrible bellow:

"Aaaagh... forward... goddamnit... boys."

But no one followed Oskari. Akseli repeated his command and Aku started out. Picking up speed with the first few steps he began to lurch through the drifts, for the branches, stones, and tussocks underneath the snow made progress uncertain. Akseli could plainly hear the bullets begin to whine around the boy and strike the snow near him.

"Down... Hit the ground!"

But Aku went on until he had drawn even with Oskari, and only when he had dropped into the snow did Akseli's tension relax. He gestured with his hand to the next man and Arvi Laurila started off. But as soon as he rose, a bullet hit his coattail, and he sank back down.

"Get going... what are you staying here for?"

"Go yourself goddamn... driving others into something like that. You could have brought machine guns... so you could let fly with them."

Arvi's word stirred a sudden fit of rage in Akseli. He stood up and shouted:

"Any men here follow me..."

He did not even have time to look for his next spot to take cover. He was

213

conscious that the bullets were coming close and that his footing was very uncertain. At times he staggered and had to brace himself with a hand on the snow, but he continued his bounding run. All the while the bullets whistled by, demanding that he take cover, but his rage was stronger, and he ran some distance past Oskari and Aku before fear got the upper hand and he threw himself down behind the first mound he saw. Panting he lay there a few seconds before looking back. Aleksi was running farther back, dragging his rifle behind him by the barrel, and now Lauri Kivioja was coming too.

Akseli heard some shouting from the right, but the din of shooting prevented him from understanding it. Looking across the road, he saw someone pointing forward and now he made out the man's words:

"They're running... in white clothing..."

Rising to his feet, he shouted:

"They're retreating... Move up fast."

As he ran he became aware that the firing from the Whites' side had indeed stopped, and he moved from the snow onto the road. Reaching the other side of the cutover area, he saw the Whites' abandoned positions. There were pits in the snow covered with fir branches, with loads of spent cartridges around them. He continued cautiously along the road. The ground sloped downward. Then he noticed someone with a white cape over his shoulders skiing down the slope on the left side of the road. His hasty shot missed the man, who disappeared quickly into the trees. The sight shook Akseli a little. It was the first White he had clearly seen. During the attack, the enemy had been merely shots and the whine of bullets, but this was a human being, a man on skis, a fact which transformed the rather vague concept of "butcher" into an everyday reality.

The men caught up to Akseli and he ordered them to assemble on the road. Everyone was still in a state of excitement. Lauri "had yelled goddamn" and Arvi showed his coattail, which had indeed been ripped by a bullet. Ylöstalo arrived with the church village platoon behind him, and the battle spirit of the men from Pentti's Corner increased:

"They were shooting back at us, all right. One of them hit a tree right next to me."

"Yeah, but we had them in our sights... I banged away at least forty times, and I tell you I must have hit someone."

There were no fallen to be seen, but it could well be that the butchers had taken their dead with them when they left. Ylöstalo thanked the men for their first victorious battle, but Akseli did nothing of the sort. He said, rather, in a somewhat irate tone:

"Don't start holding a meeting here on the road. Osku, put the point security in order and let's go... And the command to attack applies to others besides the unit leader. It's good to remember that next time. Just banging away does no good."

"I did go... And I... and I... and I..."

They continued to advance cautiously. The noise of a battle continued without interruption in the direction of the village. Now and then a cannon roared on either side. The guide informed them that they would soon reach the open fields around the village. They knew that from the sound of the firing.

"Now there's hell to pay, boys..."

"You really got us into some kind of spot..."

"We're all caught here... facing a machine gun in this kind of snow."

The assault across the open fields had stopped. The men lay burrowed into the snow, their only protection a row of willows growing in a ditch. The first casualty, one of Hollo's day laborers, was being dragged to shelter along the ditch, although in vain, for he was already dead. The shocked shouts resulted from just that fact. The machine-gun fire continued without interruption, but it was inaccurate owing to distance.

Ylöstalo was crouching at the corner of a rundown little hay barn in the field, shouting exhortations:

"Try it along the ditch... Soldiers of the revolution, forward..."

The shout angered Akseli. After the skirmish with the outpost, they had advanced on the village and reached the edge of the fields. There he had seen at first glance the danger of an attack. The guide had explained to him that "there is a little bit of open field, all right, but there are willow bushes growing there." However, there was altogether a half-kilometer of open field, even though there were willows growing in spots along the ditches. Akseli had spent enough winters crawling through logging woods to understand even without military training what an advance through waist-deep snow would be like. He said so to Ylöstalo, but the latter ordered the men to attempt it.

The platoons had been formed into a skirmish line at the edge of the woods, except for the men from the church village, who were left to secure their return. At first they had advanced without difficulty, but as the willows thinned out, the fire of the Whites became more effective. From the stone barn of the farm nearest them, a machine gun was firing, and their own fire had no effect.

Luckily the cultivated strips ran across the path of their advance, and they were able to move forward strip by strip. For the entire time, Akseli led the attack, in spite of its hopelessness, darting from one strip to the next and getting the others to follow by his urging. He had mainly Osku and Aku to thank for that, for they followed him, bringing the others along with them. Osku had indeed demanded that they stop at the very beginning, but nevertheless he charged forward from strip to strip. When Akseli had responded somewhat tautly to his demand to stop, Osku had said:

"Well goddamn. Do you think it's up to me?"

Aku followed Osku, and when Akseli saw the boy running across the strip, he opened his mouth to shout a warning, but restrained himself. It was not fitting to stop his own brother and urge the others forward at the same time. Lying in a ditch, he studied the village. It was made up of three clusters of buildings, into which the Whites had settled. From in back of the village he could hear the din of Myllymäki's company's attack, but that too did not seem to be progressing. His consciousness, throbbing with effort, sought to consider options. They were limited, however, to two manure piles near the stone barn, but it seemed impossible to get behind them. Akseli's shirt was soaked with sweat, melting snow jammed in through the cuffs of his mittens was causing his wrists to sting nastily, and despair began to dampen his spirit. The entire attack had been badly planned. He cursed and mentally berated the headquarters and the guide; "'A little bit of field...' it's the same as 'a little way' when you're asking directions. Goddamned map readers... It looked easy there... Couldn't we have got to it through the woods somewhere?"

At least not through the nearby terrain, for the fields ended at a bay to the right.

Should they give it up? Simply refuse to go on? His thoughts demanded that he do so, but his feelings refused to.

He took a bite of snow into his dry mouth, sucked on it until it melted, and leaped up. The sharp whine of the bullets sang in his ears as he bounded to the next ditch.

"Come on, boys. One at a time. The rest of you fire."

He fired his rifle, aiming at the windows of the stone barn. Because of the distance, he could not even tell which window the machine gun was firing from, and so he fired at all four in turn. But perhaps it was firing from somewhere under the eaves. He could not be sure.

"Goddamn... Can't you hear the machine gun there... How do you think we'll get there?"

"Forward... at least try."

Osku came so that the snow flew, and a couple of others followed. Arvi Laurila also rose. He was halfway to the next strip when a burst from the machine gun struck him. He screamed as he fell, and fear made the others shrink deeper into their ditches. A burst from the machine gun sent up spurts of snow around the fallen man as if to finish off its prey for good. When it subsided, they could hear Arvi's blood-curdling shriek. It resembled the bellow of a strangled cow. Then they could hear his inarticulate words:

"Help... boys... help..."

He moved, and the machine gun took immediate note of it. No one rose; instead there were shouts of dismay;

"We're not going on... Let those headquarters bosses come themselves and try... Go and tell them... If you won't go, we're going back right now."

"Stop the goddamned whining... Try to get him into a ditch."

"Try it yourself."

Akseli turned in his ditch. Arvi lay obliquely behind him, and he crawled to the spot in the ditch. Taking a few deep breaths, he rose, but ducked down again immediately, for a burst from the machine gun raked along the ditch from the left. It seemed to have realized the situation. Akseli's courage abated. His body would not obey his commands. It was dangerous enough to run over the strip by himself, and he would have to stop and drag Arvi with him. An image of a machine-gun burst striking him penetrated his mind. It would strike his body and the world would turn black. Perhaps he would let out the same kind of scream as Arvi.

"Help... where are you... I'm bleeding... ohhh..."

Akseli took off his mittens and stuck them in his pocket. He could get a better grip with his bare hands. When Arvi's moan was repeated, he leaped up from the ditch. In two bounds he had reached Arvi, and in one continuous motion, he grabbed him by the foot. He gave a brutal jerk and dragged the wounded man with him into the ditch by one foot. As he settled Arvi deeper into the bottom of the ditch, the machine gun kept firing at them for the whole time. When it was silent, he turned toward Arvi and asked:

"Where did you get hit?"

Arvi did not answer. Only the whites of his eyes showed under half-closed lids, and Akseli shouted to the others:

"It was a lot of trouble for nothing."

Then he turned over onto his back in the ditch and lay staring wide-eyed at the cold blue sky, trying to settle his consciousness so that he could think clearly.

"Someone has to make a decision... Ylöstalo isn't able to.... But how then... How can we get there..."

The situation spared him from having to make the difficult decision. Firing began to sound from behind them, along with unintelligible shouting. The men in the ditches raised their heads.

"What's that? What's that shooting?"

Akseli shouted at the top of his lungs to keep the men from rushing blindly to the rear. The shooting and yelling came from the woods behind and to their left, where the church village men were posted. Ylöstalo waved from the corner of the hay barn, and Akseli could faintly hear him shouting:

"Get out of there... get out..."

"Get back, one at a time... But in order... No confusion..."

There was no need to repeat the command. At first the men darted a ditch at a time, but soon the movement swelled and when they reached better shelter among the willows, the whole platoon ran back without taking cover. A man would be seen to fall, but he would get up and continue his blind running. Over the din they heard the tooting of Elias's bugle, and someone shouted as he ran:

"Boys... a long and short... long and short... let it go... that means withdraw..."

Akseli was the last man running. He tried to see to it that no one was left behind, but his greatest concern was the shooting they heard from the woods. What was there?

Ylöstalo was at the edge of the woods. Hands cupped before his mouth, he shouted to the retreating company:

"Form a skirmish line... along the edge of the road. They're attacking on the flank... Easy boys..."

The men arrived panting and crouching at the edge of the woods beside the road. Bullets were still flying from the direction of the village, although the distance made any hits accidental. When the men reached cover, they stopped, but a bullet whizzing close to them made them rush on a little farther. Akseli realized that they had to form a skirmish line to the left of the men from the church village, so that the Whites would not be able to cut off the road. He gave the relevant order, and the men gathered reluctantly on the road to form the line there. The men from the station village drew back through the woods behind them, and Ylöstalo shouted to them to go back along the road to secure the retreat. But the men of that company were too spooked. The commands produced only a helpless milling around, and everyone was ready to race away along the road. The firing of the church village platoon could be heard some hundred meters from the road, and the bullets of the Whites sped through the thick woods, crackling in the branches of the trees along the road. Beyond the shots they could hear shouting, which had to indicate an attack by the Whites.

A man ran out of the woods. Then a second and a third.

"Leppäniemi was killed... Hey, the platoon leader is dead... The butchers are coming."

"You can't retreat. Men... into a line..."

Ylöstalo's voice was panicky too, and the first men ran. Men from

218

the church village came pouring out of the woods, and they responded to Ylöstalo's and Akseli's orders with gasping shouts:

"What the hell is there? How can we fight with men on skis... They go around us... It's best to go... Leppäniemi died... and some wounded boys got left there."

"Are they on skis?"

"Yes, they are... And they have sheets on their backs... They'll circle us if we don't go."

The company left. Ylöstalo took a few helpless steps and shouted:

"You can't... Shape up... soldiers of the revolution... shape up... Long live the revolution!"

When a few rifle shots were heard from the woods, the rest ran off too. In a panicky voice, Ylöstalo said to Akseli:

"They are really running... What shall we do?"

"We have to try to stop them a short distance from here... we can't stop them here..."

They set out after the men. Osku stayed with them as a third man, and they ran crouching, sometimes shooting blindly behind them. They were also being fired upon from the woods on the right, which made clear how dangerous their position was. The White skiers might get ahead of them at any moment, and they ran abreast, panting.

The company retreated to the positions they had jumped off from. Only there did the herd, which had been acting only on instinct, feel itself safe, as if sensing that terrain taken by force was dangerous. Ylöstalo tried to restore order in the confused gang. Sometimes ordering, sometimes explaining in a commonplace way, he was able to organize a firing line. The men were silent and depressed, and eyed the terrain before them uneasily.

After a time, a white-cloaked skier appeared at the roadside. He fell at the first scattered volley. The wild firing continued for fifteen minutes until it gradually died out. The Whites returned the fire sporadically, and their faint response finally brought an end to the shooting. When it stopped, soft voices and the crunching of snow could be heard from their side.

"They're starting an attack."

A period of tense waiting followed, but the continued silence finally calmed the men. Akseli went back and forth along the line to make sure that the men stayed put. He was not afraid of an attack, which could be repulsed, but he did fear their skiers. Nothing would have been easier for them than to repeat their recent movement: to ski off the road to their rear.

He did not dare say so to his men, but bore the burden of fear himself. The extreme strain he had been under since morning began to ease gradually, and with that he began to feel the weariness which the tension had masked. He sat next to Osku at the foot of a tree in a pit he had kicked into the snow and concentrated on listening to the sounds of the battle farther off. They had died down at the village, but somewhere beyond it, they were still fighting. "Has Myllymäki taken the village... Has a messenger been sent to tell him about our retreat?"

For a moment he worried about the matter, but then thought that Ylöstalo must surely have seen to it. Around him he could hear the men stamping their feet and rubbing their limbs. The February day was dying, and the cold was intensifying. Akseli himself felt the chill. His shirt, wet with sweat during the day, was not dry yet, and it pressed a nasty chill into his skin. The warmth of his feet had melted the snow on his boots; they too were wet, but well on their way to freezing. "But some of the men have only ragged felt boots... And not all of them even have overcoats... What would come of this?"

Oskari was some five meters away from Akseli. He studied the terrain before them, occasionally rubbing his arms. Akseli felt like going over to him, but abandoned the idea when he remembered that Oskari had been angry at him during the day.

Oskari turned toward him and said:

"What do we do now?"

"I don't know. Ylöstalo must have sent a messenger to ask for orders."

"I just mean that if we have to stay here, it's going to be one helluva night. Our clothes are wet and it's so cold. You should at least go and see if he's done anything."

Akseli went. He found Ylöstalo sitting on the side of the ammunition sleigh a little way back. Near him squatted the messengers and the medics, on branches broken off from trees.

Ylöstalo looked downcast. He did not look at Akseli as he spoke, but gazed at his boots, the toes of which he kept banging together:

"There's no better place to go... And everything is a mess all along the line. They took a couple of villages and reached the edge of the market town, but got no farther. We've been ordered to hold these positions temporarily... I don't know for how long."

"If we're going to be here for the night, we have to get some warm food."

"Well, yes... if you would go and get it."

Because of Ylöstalo's dejection, Akseli did not dare leave, for he saw that a man in that state would not be able to repel an attack should one come. He suggested that Ylöstalo himself go, but the man refused. Understanding that Ylöstalo did not want to make an appearance at the unit's headquarters, Akseli ceased to urge him and ordered Elias to take care of the matter. Elias took a horse from one of the medics and left. Akseli returned to his platoon, and the hope of a warm meal mollified the increasingly loud grumbling among the men. From the positions came a constant sound of crunching and clunking as the freezing men moved about and hopped. Akseli urged them to silence, but got Lauri Kivioja's words in reply:

"Goddamn if I don't go on jumping when I'm cold."

The darkness thickened. Moving along the line, Akseli tried to console the men, but that had no effect on chattering teeth. Aleksi's jaws were so stiff that he could not speak properly, and seeing that, Akseli made a decision:

"We'll make a fire in back of that hill. Better to die from a shell than slowly freeze to death."

A fence of sorts was made from fir branches on the side toward the enemy in the hope that it would prevent the glow from being seen. When the argument over who should first stand guard was settled, the men gathered around the fire. Food was dug from packs, and when the worst of the chill was over, a quiet discussion arose. Aleksi warmed a piece of bread over the fire and said:

"Will the butchers bury Arvi's body?"

"Why? It won't smell in the winter."

"This is some war. I'm not going into anything like that again. They put you out in a field to face machine-gun fire."

"We seem to have come here to take a beating, boys."

"But they are pushing ahead at Vilppula. They said in the village last night that many houses are burning there. And when they spray them with machine-gun fire, the butchers are sure to go."

"What does it mean if a few houses are burning? It's all stupid talk."

Akseli listened to the talk without taking part in it. Sometimes he wanted to say something, but he controlled himself, wary of offending the men. When Elias returned, bringing some kind of pale tea, the angriest men began to pour it on the ground, but the others managed to save it.

"Goddamn. We could just as well have melted snow."

The tea warmed them, however, when it was heated in Lauri

Kivioja's water dipper, which he had with him as a mess kit. Elias brought them news from the village:

"Sleigh loads of corpses kept coming toward me all the time, boys. The chimney-sweeps took a real beating. They even shot three prisoners. One gentlemanly-looking type raised his hand and babbled something about an international convention, but Myllymäki told him we're observing the Varkaus convention. One of them yowled badly. They must not have hit him well, because he kicked for a long time... I watched while they killed them by the light of a storm lantern."

"Good for the devils."

Gradually they all fell silent. They could not sleep, for the campfire did little to warm them. Some of them nodded with their eyes closed, awakening just as they were about to topple over from their sitting position. Once Osku declared, as if to himself:

"I think this first fight was a real flop. I wonder what the last one will be like."

"I don't know. But at least the bugle was blowing. All day long I blew 'On to Vaasa, boys.' The trouble wasn't in my playing, anyway."

The flames of the fire flared and around it the shadows of the nodding men danced a ceaseless, ghostly dance on the snow. The front was almost completely quiet. The distant roar of a cannon seemed only to emphasize the silence.

And overhead shone the icy stars of a February night.

VI

The torturous, numbing night finally lightened into morning.

Akseli and Osku went forward to assess the situation. There was nothing to be seen except some spent cartridges and ski tracks. A dead scout lay face down on his skis. The rifle was still on his back, and Akseli picked it up. They turned the body over. The body was that of a big young man. He wore a visored cap pulled so low over his ears that it had not come off when he fell. There was a thick, hand-knit scarf around his neck. Under the snow-cloak he wore an ordinary civilian overcoat and there were Lapland boots on his feet.

"Well, he's no special butcher. No bigshot anyway."

"The Ostrobothnian Farmer Johns have put their hired hands out in front. They have forced conscription there. There has never yet been a war fought by the bosses. They just gather up the spoils."

When the men on the line saw that there was no danger out front, they too came out, curious to see the body.

"The butcher is in a deep sleep, boys."

"Good boots. Let's see if we can get them off."

With great effort, they stripped the boots from the stiff feet of the corpse.

"New woolen socks. I'm taking them. My own are all wet."

"Whose are dry? You have no more right to them than anyone else."

A quarrel over the ownership of the socks ensued, and Akseli had to decide who got them. The boots he gave to a hired hand from the manor, whose footgear was the most wretched of all. Lauri Kivioja got the socks. The overcoat was also good, but there was a lot of blood on its breast area. Nevertheless one of the men from Hollo's Corner stripped it off and tried to clean off the clotted blood with snow.

"When we get into the village, I'll wash it. And it will be easy to sew that bullet hole."

They found nothing in the man's pockets but a wallet made from a goat's bladder, a piece of newspaper, and a match box.

"What paper is that?"

"I don't see a name. What does it say there... An appeal to the farm people... 'The specified amount of grain is to be turned over to the local officials without delay...' You'll have tough quotas to meet, boys, just when you need the grain yourself... Wait a minute... 'against those barbaric gangs of bandits who have risen to overthrow the lawful order of society and the right to private property. We are not fighting against people, but against wild beasts. They kill all their prisoners, they strip the bodies of everything, and mutilate them. Bodies have been found with the eyes pierced and the protruding parts cut off...'"

"They're laying it on thick, boys. Protruding parts. What are they?"

"It means your balls. That they cut them off. But it's said elegantly."

"Protruding parts... ha, ha... Shall we see what kind he has?"

"Lauri will take a look, boys..."

With the tip of his bayonet, Lauri drew open the underwear of the body.

"Just leave him alone... what kind of foolishness is this?"

The laughing men were thrown into confusion by Akseli's words.

"And go to your positions."

The men went, leaving the body, stripped to its underwear, behind. Akseli and Osku advanced cautiously. Osku glanced at the body once more and said with a snort:

"Well, I have to say that the girls in Ostrobothnia will be grieving."

He dropped that line of talk, because Akseli's grim face put an end to his inclination to joke. When about ten minutes had passed, they heard a few shots up ahead, and soon the two of them went back along the road:

"They're still there. In the same positions as yesterday."

Akseli went to Ylöstalo with the information. The latter told him that a new attempt would be made, but that they were to remain in their positions temporarily. In the morning the front came to life again, and the men followed the phases of the firing, trying to determine the course of the battle in that way. At four in the afternoon, the din died down, and there had been no movement of the front.

Since another night was coming, the company began to demand that they be allowed to go to the village.

"We're not spending another night at the fire. Go and tell headquarters. The units there have been sleeping in houses."

At first Akseli explained the situation gently, and urged the men to stick it out. But when the loudest ones began to grumble, he said sternly:

"We're not going anywhere from here. You can't just leave a position like that. You can't just drop everything after one go at it."

For a short time his words had an effect. Those with a more practical bent and a stronger sense of duty agreed that he was right. But they too grew silent, shivering in the cold. Their vague dreams had already crumbled. Here there was a snowy woods, a temperature of twenty-five below, and an uncertain, stagnant situation.

Ylöstalo went to the village, returning after an hour to tell them they were being relieved. He drew Akseli and the other platoon leaders aside and told them:

"They've decided to call it off... At least temporarily. In places they've had a hard time to repulse the counter-attacks, not to mention advancing."

When the company marched to the village after the exchange had taken place, there was a lively buzz of talk in the ranks, but Akseli walked in silence at the tail end of his platoon. Although he was just as cold and tired as his men, he could not rejoice at the return to the village. He could think of nothing but the events of the past day.

The men's joy made him bitter.

"If all they ever think about is getting into a house, what will come of this?"

He slowed his pace on purpose, so that the distance between him and the men increased.

The road through the village was filled with men returning from the attack and others going to take their place. From the front came horses drawing sleighs with the dead and wounded. There was a hum of talk and the sound of shouts:

"Hello there, Hautala. You're still on your feet. "Well, it was nip and tuck... "Goddamn, there was no sign of our medics all day... When we find them, they'll get a beating from the outfit..." "One of them came down on skis and I thought, 'You'll get yours, at least.' I let him get close and then I popped him..."

Beside the road stood a group of officers, one of whom was explaining to the others:

"I threw the machine gun away at the brewery.... The men from Vesilahti came and said there was no horse to haul it. I said take it in a hell of a hurry even if you have to carry it. A rider came up and said we need a machine gun because the butchers are rushing us. I sat on a stump and said I have only a barrel and I'm burning it now."

"Damn it! I said... the men are wading in snow up to their balls. Come and try it yourself, goddamn... it's the lack of skis that drove us back. The men are going through the snow in black overcoats. One said he was getting snow in his shoes..."

The uproar along the road died down as the men settled into their quarters. The group from Pentti's Corner got back into their original room. In spite of their weariness, the men seemed lively and relieved. The quieter ones lay down as soon as they had eaten, but the others went on talking about what had happened in the attack. The homey warmth of the room felt good. Clothing and footgear were arranged around the stove to dry. Someone asked Akseli a question. He sat in the corner with his pack, chewing on dry bread, and between bites, he said:

"Why ask me when the others seem to know so much."

The men noticed his restrained anger, and for a while the discussion flagged. Akseli's annoyance stemmed from the men's lightened minds, and he thought as he chewed:

"They have nothing else on their minds except getting near a warm stove."

When the talk perked up again, the situation was discussed:

"Those in the next house said that they advanced a long way, but when the others didn't come, they had to fall back."

"Do you think we'll attack again?"

"Maybe we won't need to. The drivers said there was tough fighting at Vilppula. Maybe they're pushing ahead there."

Akseli had finished eating and said, as he closed the ties of his pack:

"They won't get through at Vilppula either if everyone depends on a breakthrough somewhere else."

"And if they put them in the kind of place we tried to go through. You can see for yourself. We couldn't get anywhere."

"There would be places enough, if there was will enough to try."

He lay down on the floor. Amidst the snores could be heard the whispering of others. Akseli had fallen asleep, but he panted in his dreams, and those nearest could hear him say:

"...death comes at us... through every hole..."

CHAPTER SEVEN

I

Smoke still curled up from the chimneys of houses, cottages, and shanties in Pentti's Corner as it had done before. After the Red Guard's departure for the front, things were quieter. Even less of the customary work was done. The older men did go to work at times, and "stood watch" at others.

Sleighs loaded with hay, straw, manure, and logs drove past the guards, their drivers stopping to smoke and chat. Even Preeti Leppänen had received a rifle, for more weapons had arrived at the village. He had even fired it at a target.

"Just take it easy with the gun. Be sure not to point it at anyone."

Preeti seldom did guard duty. Mostly he helped Elma and Aune in the kitchen or went to "carry the word."

After Akseli's departure, Halme was forced to reconsider his anti-militarism. He had to take part in the organization of watches and in the Red Guard's confiscations. From day to day, his position changed. When he heard via rumor what some master or farm owner had said against the new regime, he was likely to make a dry, biting remark. Although he tried to carry out the confiscations as fairly and courteously as possible, there was talk, and when he heard the word "thievery" he would say briefly:

"When we take something, we leave a receipt. They, on the other hand, just assumed that everything belonged to them."

Sometimes he visited the Koskelas, chiefly to take them news of the family's men, whose doings he heard about from the staff in the church village. To Jussi and Alma he spoke noncommittally, since he knew how they regarded the rebellion.

"I consider it a great misfortune, but I also view it as my duty to alleviate the situation."

To Elina he was kindly, asking how she was doing, and saying as he left:

"Your condition is a beautiful answer to this killing. When the great moment approaches, have Jussi bring word to the headquarters. I'll send it on by phone, and send a driver to the church village."

His mind was full of arrangements for the community's spring planting. He was no farmer, but with the advice of Antto and Kankaanpää, he planned how to use the work force. And beyond that he saw greater tasks in the future, which he sometimes revealed to others:

"Perhaps there is still time for me to see this community filled with happy homes."

Thus would he speak during some more solemn moment, when the discussion touched upon future goals, so that such a remark was a fitting conclusion. He could also use it to defend his right to have abandoned his former opposition, in which case he would accompany the words with a slightly melancholy sigh at having to travel this road, which he could not approve, but which he could not avoid either.

When news of Arvi Laurila's death reached the headquarters, Halme decided to bear the tidings himself. He could have told Antto when the latter came to the headquarters, but "Poor Aliina is in need of words which are perhaps lacking to Antto."

While still outside the Laurila home, he set his face in an expression of sympathy. In the doorway he took off his hat and remained standing there. Those inside saw from his expression that something strange had happened. His appearance seemed all the more remarkable, since Antto had just returned from the headquarters.

"My good friends. I have always been glad to stop in here, but this time I would rather not have come. I have heavy news."

Aliina sat ready on the edge of the bed.

"The church village headquarters informs us that Ylöstalo has sent news of the company's dead, and your son is among them."

Elma left the room and went into the bedroom. Antto looked at the ground and mumbled:

"Yeah... yeah... uhuh..."

Aliina raised a corner of her kerchief to her eyes. Head bowed, she rocked back and forth, but no sobs came. Halme continued standing in the doorway, but when the silence demanded some comment from him, he said:

"If my presence bothers you somehow, I'll leave. But I would like to say a few words:

"Death, and not least, a sudden, violent death, is a human being's severest trial. It is, so to speak, like weighing while using only one end of a balance. Everything has its counterpoise, summer and winter, fall and spring. Let us take some so-called concrete examples from the realm of life. One could list such things as a sled and wagon, night and day, wind and water, and so on. Life is the counterweight to death, so it is believed. But I don't believe so. Death does not mark the end of life, but a change in its form, that is to say, a change in life's essence. It is childish to believe that our mortal senses should dictate the quality of life. For my part, I believe that beyond their sphere of observation is a huge, unknown, higher world, but it is merely the low developmental stage of our senses which prevents us from being aware of it. As you know, I'm not what they call a religious person, although I do acknowledge the great Nazarene as the greatest teacher in the world. My belief in immortality has a slightly different basis, but with regard to the main point, that is not important. And to you Aliina, you who have suffered so much, I wish to say this in your latest grief: your boy is not dead, but he lives. I hope you will find consolation in this assurance. And you too, Antto."

Aliina did not reply, but sat as before with her kerchief to her eyes. She had not listened to Halme's speech, nor could she have understood any of it. Antto coughed from time to time and muttered something unintelligible. Then his jaw began to shake:

"...that too... the third already..."

After a brief pause he continued:

"That goddamned iron balls will pay for this yet... they put one in the poorhouse and the other in jail... they killed the third... That devil should be sent to meet his maker... The boys said when they went to get hay from the station that he was watching them the way the devil did Mikko Jeltti from behind the fence..."

Halme rose:

"I'll leave now. Perhaps a visitor is too much at this moment."

He bowed goodbye. Antto's words had confused him slightly, but he was still feeling the mood induced by his own speech when he arrived at the workers' hall. Valenti said that he had been asked to call the headquarters, and Halme put through the call. It was Hellberg, who ordered him to go to the parsonage and warn the vicar. He had given a sermon, the tone of which Hellberg described, concluding the call with:

"Tell him in earnest that he is not to do it again. They have heard of the butchers' early successes and have gotten bold. And take your gloves off when you go there, or I'll come myself. And we have to start taking measures with that whisker-face at the manor. He does as he likes there."

"For the time being, everything is fully in order here. And I believe it will continue to be, insofar as it depends on me."

Halme spoke in a constrained and indignant tone. He did in fact go to the parsonage, but changed into his best clothes before leaving home.

When the news of the swift advance of the Whites proved groundless, a mood of silent dejection prevailed at the parsonage for a few days. The couple realized that they would have to continue their quiet, isolated life. They were a little frightened on hearing of Yllö's imprisonment and continued to go to the church village for news, but after the first disappointment, they had become less credulous. The master of Töyry visited the parsonage. He brought news of his sons and other members of the Civil Guard, Arvo having stopped in at home one night. The men were living in a wilderness between parishes, for only some of them had made it through the front lines. Others had been caught and immediately executed, so the boys had stopped trying to get through. Töyry had taken food for them to a hay barn in his back fields, but since the Reds kept close track of the farm's supplies, they no longer had enough food, and Töyry asked for more from the parsonage. A common shortage would not be as noticeable.

The visit produced a flurry of activity in the shut-in and listless life of the pair. Food was filched and sent secretly to the Töyrys. The vicar's wife began to knit socks and mittens. She had never liked handicrafts, but now the matter involved much more than merely knitting.

"I can at least do something. No matter how little."

The situation had turned the vicar into a thinker. When the Whites did not arrive straightway, doubt began to gnaw at his mind. Might the rebels still win? Was there some justice in their cause?

When news of some setback to the Whites arrived, his doubts increased immediately. On such occasions he had begun to put his thoughts down on paper. He reflected on points of Socialist doctrine, and to dispel his doubts, he had to rebut them. First he would write down some Socialist thesis:

With the abolition of private property, classes will disappear, and evil in society and human relations will disappear along with them.

Underneath that he wrote:

Can this be true? It cannot. For the following reasons:

Society is not a primary but a secondary cause. An evil society cannot have made people evil, since society is created by people, and that evil which exists in society naturally has its source in people. This being so, must not a change come from people then? Absolutely. If we divide everything equally today, tomorrow the stronger will have taken from the weaker his share. Absolutely. This results from the fact that in spite of everything we are biologically unequal. This does not mean that there are not many undeserving people holding positions in society. (I count myself among them, since I have not earned even this modest station.) Can a change in society make us equal then? No. With what idiocy have those poor workers been urged on. (For they are poor things, although it is hard to forgive them.) In contrast to this, one can see more and more clearly the profound truth of Christ's proclamation. The evil is within us, and it will disappear only on condition that we destroy it ourselves. How else could the Word have lived for two thousand years, if it did not contain the essential truth of mankind and its soul. Society as such is not evil but you and I — all of us are. For what is society? It is nothing. It is the relationship of people to one another. Change yourself and your relationship to society will change, and then society will change. Unequivocally. (I thank the trials I am undergoing. Otherwise I would not have come to think this through clearly.) What a doctrinally weak shepherd of souls I am then, when I have to witness my Lord and Master's truth to myself on paper. The time of my trial has come. Thus it is my duty to sustain the courage and hope of those to whom I have been appointed shepherd. Lord, you know my weakness, therefore You cannot deny me your strength. I, poor eternal Peter, pray for a shard of strength from Thy rock, for I need it now, not for my sake, but that of my lambs. I must now be the one who lifts the despairing to hope. And thereafter, Thy will be done, not mine. Amen.

Having written, he felt emboldened and at ease. That in turn made him happy and confident. Thrusting his thumbs into the armholes of his vest, he paced back and forth across the office floor. Vaguely he imagined himself before a firing squad. Wife... children... all life... what about his own life. I have no right to remain silent. The pulpit is the only place from which one still may speak the truth... He who is silent there... he commits treason.

On Sunday he preached, actually in a veiled fashion, but still clearly enough. And when through the window he saw Halme approaching, he had no doubt what his business was.

There was some slight confusion in their greeting, since they were accustomed to shaking hands, but then both men realized the tension between them and omitted the handshake. It was for the same reason that Halme refused the proffered chair.

"To my sorrow I must take up a matter I would rather not. I have been assigned the task of warning the vicar regarding his sermon last Sunday, which has aroused bad blood in certain quarters. I would courteously request that the vicar not continue to aggravate an already heated situation."

The vicar drew a breath and said in a calm and affectedly humble voice, afraid that Halme would interpret his answer as a threat:

"My sermon dwelt with the same matter as the earlier ones. I spoke of the truth whose servant I am. And I don't believe it would inflame any decent person."

"Since the vicar knows me, he must realize that I am not interfering in the vicar's sermons. But in a time like this, when feelings run high, we all should try to calm people down."

All this time, the vicar's wife had been staring openly and piercingly at Halme. Her protruding eyes seemed to challenge him to a mental duel. When Halme turned, her eyes followed him. But her look did not have the effect she was hoping for, and she asked:

"Shouldn't Halme rather be calming those men who killed two young men, whom Koskela sent from here to the church village to be murdered?"

"It is difficult to control enraged people, who are also subjected to continual provocation. Nor did Koskela send those men to be killed. That rumor is totally unfounded."

"There was a paper with them which ordered their murder."

"Please go to the church village and look into the matter. I believe the paper is still in safekeeping there. Ahem. And further, I did not come here to quarrel but to give you a kindly warning."

The vicar's face turned slightly red:

"Is this a threat?"

"It is not. The vicar apparently wishes to misconstrue things on purpose."

A nasty thought had long been in the vicaress's mind, and she smiled as she said it out loud:

"Why is Halme now involved in the rebels' affairs when at first he refused to go along with them? Do their chances of winning seem so much stronger to you now?"

Halme stiffened. The shot caused him to look somewhere above the pair, and his voice had a chastising condescension when he said:

"As you know, the revolution began against my will, nor do I approve of it more at this time. But a man of honor does not abandon his comrades to misfortune. I have been marching with the workers until now, and I cannot leave them when they are acting stupidly. I believe it impossible for the gentry to understand my motives in any other way than the one just expressed by the lady. That is their affair. I would, however, wish to inform them that victory is not now as certain as it might have seemed then. I might also inform them that I pay no attention to personal insults, so in that sense their words are pointless. But if they somehow afford internal satisfaction, be my guest..."

The vicar coughed slightly, and the insolence in his wife's eyes became somewhat veiled. The vicar adopted a more friendly tone, but soon reverted to his original one, which annoyed Halme, for it seemed as if the vicar had stolen his role. It was indeed difficult for him to come on strongly and give orders, for he found the greatest satisfaction in the role of a victim of injustice. For a time they both declared their martyrdom to one another, and wound up as angry as when they had begun.

"I find it difficult to hold a religious service if I am forbidden to speak freely according to the beliefs for which the church and religious services exist. I can, of course, be prevented from doing so... but... as long as it is possible, I must continue to do my duty."

Halme prepared to leave, but turned at the door as he shaped an idea which had come to his mind a few days ago:

"Nothing prevents the vicar from continuing religious services if he stays within their boundaries. But this late-awakened sense of duty angers the working class. For hundreds of years it has sought aid from the church, for it has heard there the words of the great Nazarene regarding those who labor and are heavy laden. But they have been left to lament beside the church in the manner of the mourning women: 'They have taken away the Lord out of the sepulcher, and we know not where they have laid him.' Indeed. They saw only the empty stone grave. I do not intend this as a personal attack, for that is not my weapon. Nonetheless I hope it will clarify the substance of my warning."

He left quickly in order not to give the vicar an opportunity to respond, and contented, he marched through the hallway, straightening his posture to achieve the maximum effect when he reached the lane of birches — he had, you see, conjectured that he was being watched.

The vicar laughed, striving for a contemptuous and scornful tone.

"They do remember the words of the Bible when they need them for their nasty ends."

When Halme had disappeared from sight, they drew back from the window. The vicar, however, felt that he had spoken too scathingly of Halme, and hurried to amend his words.

"Although as an individual he is not bad at heart."

"That's just where he is bad. What is wrong with him on the surface then?"

"Every time I meet him, I feel as if he has had some kind of effect."

"I know what it stems from. His imposingly slow and controlled speech. He has that ability. And I've never denied his intelligence... To the contrary... But is that a virtue in a rebel? Doesn't it make him all the more blameworthy? I do acknowledge his merits. And with age he has also developed further."

The vicar's wife happened to look out the window.

"Look... Look quickly. Our new government is passing by."

They went to the window. There went Preeti, shambling along the road, his fur cap tilted to keep it on in the wind. A rifle dangled from his shoulder, from the barrel of which a long, rat-tail bayonet thrust upward.

They took note of Halme's bad temper at the headquarters after his visit to the parsonage. He was silent, and curt whenever he spoke. It was his habit to withdraw into himself when he was offended. He sat looking out the window, not listening to the conversation of others. The deepest cause of his ill humor was not the parsonage pair's behavior in itself, but the disappointment he had suffered. On the way there he had lived in the imagination of being thanked for the warning and of appearing as some kind of protector. He would have been benevolent and protective in response to the humility of the elite.

Thus the vicar's controlled animosity and his wife's spiteful insolence stung him so much that he thought angrily:

"...it's the same old story... always... They assume the right to debase me because I am a tailor... Since I have made my own way ... since I have worked for what I have... Is their victory so certain... People like that... Shamelessly taking land another man has cleared. Enjoying a large income from poorly managed duties... And such people accuse me of a lack of ideals."

He turned away from the window:

"Valenti. There are still four hundred kilos short in the hay they were supposed to send. Write up an order for the parsonage to send that amount. And you, Kustaa. Order a man with a horse to drive it to the station."

After the slip was written and the order issued, the master maintained his severe silence until the telephone rang. Hellberg inquired about the results of his visit, and Halme replied:

"I don't know what effect it had. I did warn them in plain words. But they still felt compelled to shame me."

"Well, they will continue to shame you as long as you keep presenting propositions to them. Such people will believe you only when you bang your fist on the table. And now you'll go to the baron and ask about those weapons again, and get a written assurance that he is not plotting against the rule of the working class."

Hellberg's insolent words alleviated Halme's bitterness at the vicar and his wife slightly, for a portion of his wrath turned to Hellberg. But nevertheless he walked to the manor in a proud and determined state of mind.

The baron rigidly refused to sign a statement, and when Halme asked about his planning for crops, he began to grumble:

"What you mean... I plan?"

"We should perhaps take part in organizing the work. We should see to it that the land is tilled according to our current needs."

"I... I... not know... Who does all new... Who bring new cows? Who teach village planting? It is me. I not need advice. If you do... do alone... I away... not with you... Take away whole manor."

But this time Halme was proud too. He spoke in short, precise phrases, as if to demonstrate the power of his words. The baron's self-control collapsed and he roared:

"I old man... I not need... You do like you want... I order you out of my home... I write no papers."

Halme telephoned Hellberg about the visit.

"I'll send men there to straighten the matter out. We can send the district headquarters' investigation unit."

Hellberg's words were angry and threatening, and Halme's regret grew as the day went by. Perhaps he should not have presented the matter in just that manner... He could have softened the picture.

He called Hellberg again.

"Are the men of the investigation unit up to the task? I don't want them to start using any pressure tactics here."

"Those boys know their job, all right. If he does not bind himself in writing, he is to be arrested. It's about time for that bullying devil to do a little thinking."

Halme calmed down, trying to suppress the feeling of pleasure that strove to rise within him. At bottom he did not think it bad if the baron were given a little scare. Nor would it be too much for the vicar.

"They are insolent because they trust in my good will. Well, they are not wrong in that. But what kind of people..."

The baron was sitting in his study, checking a list on which all of the headquarters' compulsory requisitions were written down. Although he submitted to the requisitions superciliously, letting the members of the Guard take whatever they wanted to, the overseer kept an accurate record of them. He refused to take receipts offered in return in order to avoid giving any hint of approving the confiscations. When his tenants refused to do their rent-work, the headquarters ordered men who were not serving in the Guard to work at the manor. Them he had to pay in money. But a record was kept of the neglected rent work. It would be needed when the Whites arrived, and the tenants who had broken their contract would be sent on their way.

The baron believed firmly in the victory of the Whites. It was merely an idea stubbornly implanted in his head, for he did not know even as much as the other Whites about the true course of affairs, since he lived apart even from them. He did know that the front was somewhere north of Tampere, and he needed no further support for his belief. The Reds had to lose, for they were scoundrels, every last one of them, and such people were not able to govern a country.

He put his book away and went into the baroness's room. She was reading the Bible, as she had done every night during the uprising. She had had little contact with the outside world even before this, and that little was now completely broken off. Frightened, she had deliberately tried to curl up and separate herself from the course of events. Sometimes she even spoke of it to her husband, recommending that Magnus stop being angry with the leaders of the rebellion and leave everything in the hands of God.

"Why should we old people care about it? If they take our property, we can surely live somehow. If it's God's will, we must bow to it."

"God doesn't want what that gang of scoundrels wants. And it's a question of more than property."

The words were spoken so rigidly and threateningly that the baroness fell silent.

Now when the baron entered the room, the baroness closed the Bible. She hesitated whether to tell the baron of a dream she had had the previous night. She believed in dreams and premonitions, but she did not really dare to speak of them to her husband, for she knew that he despised them, although he tried not to show his attitude. The baron sat down, stretched his legs straight out before him, and began to stare at the floor. The baroness waited for a moment, but when her husband did not speak, she opened her book again and began to read.

When a pounding was heard on the front door, they both rose. They could hear a servant's steps in the hallway and a knock on their own door after a moment.

"There are men out there."

The baron himself entered the hallway. He asked through the door who the knockers were, and a strange voice answered:

"The landless people's subcommittee. Open in the name of the law."

The baron opened the door and, by the light of the half moon, he saw three men. Farther out in the park lane stood a horse and a sleigh in which a man was sitting. The baron drew back from the door, whereupon the men stepped inside. The first arrival, apparently the leader, was a smallish man under thirty. He wore a Russian soldier's cap on his head and a new uniform of coarse woolen cloth. On his feet were high-topped boots, but those tops had been folded far down, so that the upper edge nearly touched the spurs which jingled on his heels. From his waist dangled a sword held up by a braided straw thong. He was slender, but moved briskly, and his features were regular. His mouth was sharp and he had a small mustache, split in two by a shaven strip under his nose.

He looked at the baron for a moment with an odd smile in his eyes, trying to meet the baron's glance at times, and then quickly averting his eyes, always smiling that mysterious smile. He was followed inside by the other two men with rifles under their arm, to the barrels of which red rosettes had been tied.

"What you want?"

"We heard that the gentleman has begun to make hiding places and we're going to look around a little to see where they might be, ha, ha, ha..."

The leader of the men laughed and continued looking at the baron as if examining him more closely. The baron sensed that he was in a tight spot; the man seemed to exude something threatening, nor was his smile at all calming. There seemed to be malice and mockery underlying it.

"Please look."

"Maybe we'll take a breather first."

The baron led the men into the study. The riflemen remained standing in the doorway, but their leader sat down at the desk in the baron's chair. The baron began to sit down too, but the leader said, accompanying his words with a dry, short laugh:

"The gentleman will stand. This is an interrogation. When the gentleman's old friends, the gendarmes interrogated me in their day, I had to stand. For three hours straight, ha, ha. When I started to get weak and asked for a chair, they told me that the person being interrogated stands. So we have to obey the regulations, ha, ha..."

The baron rose calmly and straightened up to his full height. He did not really understand the leader's mockery, but he sensed the malice in his tone, so he put on a stiff face and gazed over the leader's head.

"Well, then. Tell me where the manor's weapons are."

"I give away. I said so."

"Are you sure?"

"I said so."

"Who were they given to?"

"Men who go away."

The leader had been fingering the holster of his pistol under the desk. Suddenly the pistol appeared in his hand, and he aimed it at the baron. This time his perpetual smile disappeared:

"Where are the manor's weapons?"

The baron closed his eyes a moment as if expecting a shot. When it did not sound, he opened them again. His voice shook a little when he spoke:

"I give away."

The leader continued to point his pistol at the baron. He looked at the baron in silence for a few seconds and then said:

"So you have armed a counter-revolutionary organization. Good. That's a grave crime. As a precaution for the future, you will sign a statement that you will refrain from counter-revolutionary activities. Here it is."

The leader put his pistol away and took an already filled-out paper from his pocket. He read it aloud, slowly and clearly. The style of the wording was deliberately offensive. It used such words as a "plea for pardon for shameful and criminal counter-revolutionary activities." In the end it demanded a vow of loyalty to the people's delegates, or rather, to the decrees they issued.

"I can promise be not active. I can't promise obey laws which is not law."

"Sign."

"I can't."

The leader looked at his men. One of them stepped up to the baron, and with a quick movement, placed his bayonet point against the baron's breast. His leader roared:

"Sign, you goddamned bloodsucker!"

The baron took a step backward and drew a couple of deep breaths. A concentrated, inward-looking gaze appeared in his eyes.

"I can't."

The man thrust his bayonet point right against the baron's breast. At that moment the door opened and the baroness stepped in. Seeing the situation, she pressed a hand to her heart and screamed in terror. The baron ordered her to leave in Swedish, but she did not answer him. In a shaking voice, she began to speak in Finnish:

"He do nothing wrong... good men... you leave old people be.... I begs you. I pray you... I know weapons is gone away. The guard men took them in fall time... You believe it..."

The trembling and frightened baroness looked back and forth from her husband to the men as if seeking support from each of them in turn. The leader rose and bowed graciously to the baroness:

"The lady will leave. She must not disturb the interrogation."

The man bowed again and clicked his heels together so that his spurs jingled. The other bayonet wielder caught the baroness by the shoulder and said, mocking his leader's courteous gestures and tone of voice:

"Let's go now. I mean, we don't touch women."

But the baroness did not obey. She sensed that the bespurred man was the leader, and so she began to speak to him in a prayerful voice:

"You have mercy old people... you too mother and father... Don't you believe God..."

The man caught the baroness by the arm again, but she broke loose.

Then the leader ordered the man to leave the baron alone. The effect of the baroness's presence was apparent in the leader's behavior. In spite of his humble bow, he jingled his spurs and straightened his posture, looking proud and all-powerful. He explained to the baroness that the baron would not agree to sign a declaration. The woman rushed to her husband's side and seized his hands, ignoring the others, and began to beg him in her broken Finnish, for in her panic she did not think to change languages:

"Magnus... write their paper... I begs you... write them..."

The baron shoved her away and said softly:

"I can't."

The baroness began to sob and went on begging in Swedish. The leader assumed a stance, placing a hand on his sword hilt, and said:

"I am placing the gentleman under arrest. Get your clothes on. You're coming with us."

But the baroness did not calm down.

"You leave him home... He is old... Why you take him? You do bad to him..."

"Since he won't promise not to oppose the strivings of the working class, he must be arrested. No harm will come to him. The lady need not worry."

The baroness seemed to sense that begging was useless. Sobbing, she helped the baron to dress, handing him a scarf. In her nervousness, she tried to help him button his overcoat, but did not manage to close a single button. Once more she tried to get her husband to sign the paper. The baron did not dare meet his wife's eyes, fearing he would yield to her look. Anxiously he patted her shoulder and said in Swedish:

"Don't be afraid... Nothing will happen to me. I can't sign... Don't ask me to now..."

The baroness followed them to the steps. Without looking back, the baron walked to the sled between the two bayonet wielders. The baroness stood on the steps until the sleigh turned onto the road from the lane of lindens and disappeared from sight. The servants, who had been hiding at the other end of the house, now dared to come forth, and they led the baroness inside. Half senseless, she let them do so. Wringing her hands, she walked between the servants, confusedly repeating her husband's and God's name.

The baron sat in the back of the sleigh. On either side sat a rifleman, his legs dangling over the side. Their leader was up front with the driver, turned sideways to the baron. In place of his recent courtesy, his attitude was now one of malicious mockery. The men too were behaving more harshly. The same man who had threatened him with the bayonet inside leaned a little away from him, and looking back at him over one shoulder, said:

"The nobleman doesn't seem to have noticed the change in the world."

The baron stared straight ahead, and did not answer. He was nauseated by the nearness of the men and tried not to lean against them. The leader laughed at the rifleman's words and added a supplement to them:

"The gentleman does not know history... that feudal society has become a capitalist society and now it will become a socialist society. The nobleman thinks we are still in a feudal society."

There was a hint of smug self-conceit in the young leader's voice. The nobleman ought to discern that they were educated men. When the baron did not answer, the leader continued, after a pause:

"The gentleman probably knows nothing about such men as Marat and Robespierre. They were able to humble the nobility a little. We happen to have a little bit of learning. Now is the time for Finland's lords to think a little bit about their ill deeds. Perhaps the gentleman doesn't know about such a man as Babeuf... Nor about the Paris Commune."

When the baron still remained silent, the leader cackled his dry laugh, this time more threatening and nasty, for he took the baron's silence as a demonstration of his feelings. The baron, however, had not heard a single word. He had been concentrating on controlling the tumult in his own mind. He was not afraid. The hardest thing to bear was the thought of his wife's distress and helplessness, in the face of which his will threatened to collapse. But when he thought of signing, and the humiliation it signified, his entire nature rebelled against it. What would life be like afterwards? Shamed and humiliated, without a shred of self-respect. He did not fear his own fate at all. During the rebellion he had considered this possibility often enough, so his thoughts and his attitude were traveling an old course. Age had decreased the significance of his own life, so that his own death did not seem terrifying. But thinking of his wife made him choke up. Especially since she had lived her entire life like a child, with no will or responsibilities of her own.

They came to a small bridge which crossed a narrow stream. The leader grasped the driver's hand and told him to stop.

"Let's stretch our legs a little."

The baron rose slowly from the sleigh along with the others. A powerful premonition assailed his mind: it will happen now. But the men began to walk slowly as if limbering up. The baron stood on the bridge looking at the moonlit landscape. The leader and one of the riflemen were walking behind him. He was about to turn around in the grip of an instinctive foreboding, for the steps seemed to be coming significantly nearer. But he did not have time to do so. The bayonet struck him in the back, and raising his arms, he

240

fell to his knees, then onto his face. For a couple of seconds, he understood everything. His thoughts fumbled for a prayer, but then went black as he felt an excruciating pain spread over his entire body. The bayonet had struck right next to his backbone.

"Throw the body into the brook... There's enough of a melt there... It's sure to sink."

The men grabbed the body, but one of them interrupted the lifting and said:

"Not yet... Let's look in his pockets."

He began to grope through the baron's pockets, but found nothing.

"No watch or wallet... But hey, he had a ring on."

There were even two of them. A wedding ring and another decorated with a coat-of-arms on his index finger. When the rings were pried loose, the baron moved, and a rattling whimper came from his mouth.

"Hit him once more. The goddamn thing is whining."

The bayonet rose and struck, piercing through the body all the way to the bridge planking.

"Hey, I'm taking that scarf before we throw him in."

The leader watched in silence as the men hoisted the body over the rail and threw it into the brook. It broke the thin ice at the edge of the current and disappeared into the black water. The driver, who had been silent the whole time, said:

"Big Manu went to join his forefathers, goddamn."

He was from the church village and he knew the baron. His words, however, seemed affectedly harsh and actually had been spoken to cover a silent horror. They were accompanied by the leader's cackle. Briskly he sat down in the baron's place in the sleigh and said:

"We're off now."

The riflemen sat down in the back of the sleigh with the leader. One of them put the baron's scarf around his neck:

"It smells of the bosses."

The leader sniffed it casually. Then, looking straight ahead, he began to whistle, tapping his foot in the air emphatically, but soon the whistle changed into a song. He had a clear tenor voice, and when he sang softly, his voice sounded very much like that of a woman:

> *To the barricades, brothers and sisters now,*
> *persecution threatens anew,*
> *and all too many have died.*

Now brothers, seize the avenging sword,
and march against the oppressor.
Fight the great and noble battle
for the rights of man.

The leader interrupted his song and shoved the man on his right away from him:

"Goddamn, don't sit on my leg. It's starting to ache."

III

Preeti Leppänen found the baron's body the very next morning. He had been on the go about headquarters' business, and noticed blood on the bridge. At first he thought someone had killed a rabbit, but then he happened to see a fur hat on the edge of the ice. Looking at it, he also noticed the body in the brook, the head of which was under the ice. Preeti bustled back to the headquarters and announced:

"There's a dead man in Lonkka Brook and there is blood on the bridge and a fur hat on the ice."

Halme and Valenti went along with Preeti, who was unable to explain what the body looked like.

"And he had an overcoat on... but his head was under the ice..."

Halme walked ahead in a state of nervous agitation, with Valenti and Preeti following a few steps behind. A grievous conjecture made Halme hurry, and when they reached the bridge, he said:

"Take a pole and try to get him up."

Preeti fetched a pole and he and Valenti descended to the bank of the brook. Preeti thrust at the body to straighten it in the stream, for the current had turned it crosswise. Valenti stood in the snow, his hands reaching toward the pole, but not grasping it. He lent only moral support to Preeti's efforts, for he was afraid that the ice would give way, and stayed too far back. After thrusting for some time, Preeti got the body to turn, and the baron's head appeared from under the ice. At his first glimpse of the gray hair and beard, Halme let out a small sound and turned away. Then he said to Preeti, making his voice heard only with the greatest difficulty:

"Let it go... We have to get help."

Preeti and Valenti climbed up to the bridge. Halme walked back and forth, first taking a few steps toward the manor, but soon returning and looking into the brook again.

"Who has... who has done this?"

At times Halme tried to pretend he did not know, for the knowledge was too heavy to bear. Looking important, Valenti studied the bridge and the traces of blood.

"Don't trample the tracks. Come off the bridge, Master. We have to start a thorough investigation. There has to be an interrogation at the manor."

Preeti stepped aside, and he too looked at the tracks.

"I think it would be best to get a police dog right now."

Valenti waxed enthusiastic about secret-police work and began to plan an investigation:

"The same kind of thing happened in Rock Springs. The mining company's cashier was robbed and thrown into a ditch. The brook was bigger, though, and there was no ice on it. And the body wasn't thrown off a bridge, but carried farther off. But the police solved the crime through the tracks.

"A police dog would be the best thing, for sure. It wouldn't take long. And a man can't do anything when the dog gets ahold of his lapel. It pins a man down."

For a moment, Halme hesitated. He had a strong desire to join in with Preeti and Valenti's plan and pretend ignorance of the whole affair. But that seemed impossible, and he said:

"Valenti, go and tell the overseer. Let him bear the news to the baroness since he knows her... he's better able. And send me a horse at once... Immediately."

Valenti departed, and Halme was left alone with Preeti. Preeti went on explaining and talking continually, but Halme, who was walking back and forth, merely said occasionally:

"Yes... just so."

"Where do they have those dogs? Don't they have them in Hämeenlinna, if not nearer... We should ask at the manor, since he left there... Did he go for a walk or... He was one of those wanderers. He used to go for walks, even late in the evening. Especially when he was young, and the maids said he always went when he was angry with his wife... Would they have had a quarrel now? Who can tell how it was with him. But a dog would clear it up... There are all kinds of things like this now... In times like this all kinds of things happen... Execution would be the right punishment... but an old man... And jolly in his own way. But with his tenants... I don't mean that. But once when I asked for mattress straw and the overseer offered old, rotten stuff, he happened to go by and saw what was going on and said, the way he talks, Leppänen is no kind pig to lie in litter... So at bottom he was a good man... If we could only get a dog now."

Preeti's babbling was a torment to Halme, and when the horse Valenti had sent arrived, he sat in the sleigh and said to the driver:

"To the church village. As fast as you can."

Since there were many men at the headquarters, Halme asked Hellberg to step aside with him. Hellberg looked sleepless and worn out and was more irritable than usual. He took Halme into a separate room, where the stage properties for the workers' hall were kept. Closing the door, he said:

"Well, why all this secrecy?"

Halme's lips trembled:

"Your interrogators have murdered the baron. This is getting to be... I can't continue working with you if this goes on... Are there no longer any limits? I demand an honest answer. Was that your intention?"

"Are you going to start interrogating me too? I told them to find out about the weapons and get him to sign an oath or to make an arrest if it wasn't forthcoming. Apparently the old man started raising a row, since that's the way you've taught him to behave. If you had been firm at the start, this kind of thing would never have happened... And you always seem to be more worried about the safety of the bourgeois than about the revolution."

"Killing an old and harmless man is no revolution... I regret not having stuck to my decision... I have to say it... It seems to me you have nothing against such actions..."

Hellberg sat down on an old and dusty chair which apparently belonged to the stage furnishings. He drew a breath as if to calm himself and began to speak like a teacher attempting once more to explain something to a hopeless pupil, with no expectation of results but in order to fulfill his duty:

"Now listen, Aatu. I have never in my life killed anyone or had anyone killed. I don't pity those bastards, but I don't approve of killing because for one thing such rumors alienate people from us. But we are fighting for our lives. Things are not going well, attacks have failed on all fronts. That is a truth we have to face squarely. That being the case, this kind of moaning won't do. I don't think it's my business to start punishing my men. The refugees from Varkaus have said that every tenth prisoner there was shot at random. At Seinäjoki they have a regular slaughterhouse where they collect the workers from Northern Finland to be killed. And you blubber about one man, who furthermore has tortured the working class all his life. No, listen. The only thing we can do is gather new companies from the parish. My good man, you must understand that victory is our only possibility. No matter how severely you punished those murderers, it wouldn't save you if we lose. I can tell you kindly that those to be killed have already been named, and you are among them..."

Hellberg emitted an oddly grating laugh and studied Halme as if to check what effect the information had. It had none, and Hellberg went on:

"I am on it, Silander is, Ylöstalo is, Koskela is. When the landlords and the gentry meet here, all they talk about is who will be killed when the butchers come. I know. I keep abreast of things. You walk around as if you were dreaming and worry that something bad might happen to them."

Hellberg laughed again, but then immediately had a fit of rage which he had difficulty in controlling outwardly.

"And if this doesn't stop, I will have to take Draconian measures. Kalle Silander is trying to tack, but it's no use. You strayed into the wrong business. Revolution is no summer festival."

Hellberg ended, panting with agitation and rage. He stopped looking at Halme, as an indication that he no longer wished to discuss the matter. But when Halme's counter-arguments drew him into the quarrel again, he shortly repeated the word, "draconian." The word seemed to please him greatly, and he especially emphasized its baneful sound value. He had an aversion to educated diction, but the ring of this word in his vocal cords seemed to resonate profoundly with his state of mind. After quarreling for some time, he said:

"I will notify district headquarters. Let them do what they want. Let them know in the village that the matter will be investigated and the guilty punished. And if they aren't, that is the district headquarters' affair. I have no more time."

Halme departed by way of the kitchen door. On the way, he alternated between feeling chilled and oddly warm. His legs felt at times as if the circulation of his blood had been cut off, and then again, the soles of his feet began to feel actually hot. In his confused mind, one thought kept hammering:

"Did Hellberg interpret my call to mean...?"

Horrified, he tried to reject the idea.

"I specifically warned him..."

But that was followed by another thought:

"Why did I warn him? Didn't I, in my warning, reveal that I was cognizant of that possibility?"

At times he strove to be hard and repeated Hellberg's word "draconian," but the word did not at all suit his mindset. The baron's body had already been taken away, but nevertheless Halme could not look at the brook as he drove over the bridge. He only stopped in at the workers' hall and ordered people to be informed that the matter would be investigated and the guilty punished. Then he drove home.

Emma was worried about her husband's state of mind. Although she herself had been horrified by the event, she soothed her gloomy husband. Together they blamed Hellberg, and the more Halme accused him, the easier it was for him. But he was unable to sleep in spite of that fact. His mouth felt dry, and he drank glass after glass of a drink made from raspberry leaves and juniper berries. At night he developed a high fever, and the next day it was the talk of the whole village:

"Halme is deathly sick. His temperature was over forty last night. He must have gotten chilled on the sleigh when he went to investigate the baron's murder."

At first the village buzzed with the big news of the baron's death. But when people heard, as the day progressed, that it was not an ordinary murder, but that the Red Guard had gone to get him from the manor, the hubbub died instantly. The matter was discussed confidentially, in subdued tones. People were silent when in the village, but at home they pondered the matter freely.

When Preeti presented his idea of the police dog, people averted their eyes and made some broad general comment:

"Well, yeah, that would solve it all right."

And Preeti explained to everyone:

"I couldn't think what it was at first. But when I saw the hat, I thought, this is foul play... There's something in this now. I didn't know him, but then when the master told me to shove him with the pole, his beard came into sight... They say the men wore the Guard's markings... But a dog would clear things up... That's what I think."

Henna had to go to the village too. She communicated her message to everyone she met:

"They wouldn't have found him if Preeti didn't happen to look at the ice there. He's so sharp... Preeti told them to get a dog right away, but then the master got sick... Preeti knew him right away... If they could get that dog... Doing a thing like that... And he just made the overseer get better mattress straw for us... He said the Leppänens had to have it... He always took Preeti's side in everything..."

When Antto Laurila heard about the matter, his first words were:

"Good, goddamn. In this case the poor people got their wish, to deal a death wound to a bourgeois."

Others did not approve of the matter so publicly. Some merely said in an indifferent tone of voice:

"They did have the Guard's markings on them, but who knows. His rings were taken, though, so it's a robbery-murder."

But a silent horror prevailed in many a cottage and tenant farm. The news did not arrive at Koskela until the evening. It was Otto Kivivuori who brought it, and he spoke his mind very clearly:

"They weren't really unknown men. Some people know very well who

246

they were."

Elina was mute. Alma too was silent, for the event afflicted her because of the boys. Jussi stared into a corner and muttered to himself.

But that wasn't all. For Otto related what Janne had told him of the weak position of the Reds, that the much-vaunted offensive had come to nothing. He also drew a conclusion from that fact:

"If it comes to an accounting, then the innocent will suffer for this too. The landlords in the church village are gnashing their teeth."

Elina responded with angry torment:

"What do the innocent have to do with it?"

Otto realized the girl's fear and said casually:

"Well, it shouldn't..."

Before leaving he tried again to lighten the mood in the family. He did get the boys to laugh by singing funny songs, but their elders could not shake off their dejection. When Otto had left, they all busied themselves with their own chores. Elina was already having difficulty with hers. She had to sit on a bench at intervals to catch her breath. When she carried some pail or other, Jussi would come and take it from her hand:

"...I ... no reason to... with that..."

They went to bed early. Their lighting facilities were still poor. The headquarters had offered them kerosene, but Jussi had categorically refused it:

"We have never lived on stolen goods up to now... If you take it, that's your business."

He said it to Elina, who did not reply. Their relations had become strained of late, for Jussi openly criticized Akseli. No breach occurred with Alma. When one evening Elina stopped while doing her everyday chores and began to weep without saying a word, Alma came to her and said:

"Poor child."

She said no more, and left Elina alone. The next day they were a trifle uneasy, recalling that little moment of intimacy, but in the scant everyday remarks they exchanged, there was a closer tone than previously. Alma even offered to sleep at the old place, but Elina did not want her to:

"Vilho can come and tell you if you're needed."

She slept with the boys. When they were already asleep, she lay awake. In the evening, she could not seem to find the right position for sleep, and propped herself up on pillows against the head of the bed. On the upper pane of the window in the back bedroom, there was a strip free of frost, through which she could see the tops of fir trees and a piece of the sky above them. She gazed at them as she leaned back against the pillow. The trouble in her mind added to her bodily distress. Her father's recent words

247

had openly revealed a premonition that had slyly intruded into her mind on occasion. What would happen if Akseli lost?

She understood defeat only as Akseli's defeat, for to her the rebellion had meaning only with regard to her husband's fate.

In the wake of her agonized thoughts, she prayed. The thoughts associated with the prayer were none too clear. The strip of sky which could be seen between the frost and the window frame somehow became God's representative in her consciousness. The stars, the sky, and God somehow belonged together. Somewhere out there it was, a huge, unfathomable power that took away and gave. And that small strip of heaven, in which a couple of faint stars twinkled on the horizon, made her feel relieved and more restful. She slid down from her half-sitting position and breathed easier. On the fringe of consciousness someone seemed to reassure her that all would turn out well. She straightened the covers over the boys lying beside her, and their peaceful sleep affected her so that she felt tears in her eyes and a tremor in her throat. Smiling in the dark at the faintly distinguishable boys' figures, she said in her thoughts:

"You sleep, anyway..."

Then she felt the first weak pang. Uncertain, she waited for it to be repeated, but only after the fourth was she sure, and she carefully awakened Vilho:

"Will you go and tell Granny and Grandpa to come here."

"Yeah."

The boy hastily threw on a few clothes and disappeared through the door. Jussi and Alma came, and Jussi rushed out to hitch up the horse. Elina was a little troubled at having to bother him at night, and she said:

"Halme did promise to phone... but since he's sick.."

"We don't need anything like that here..."

Jussi had no travel permit, but fortunately the guard at the church village knew him, and, being Akseli Koskela's father, he was allowed to pass. At midnight he arrived home with the midwife, and after one o'clock, Elina gave birth to a third son.

IV

They were unable to contact the baron's relatives, and the vicar took charge of the burial. When told what had happened, the baroness fainted, and was not really in her right mind when the body was brought to the manor. She covered the body and spoke as if she did not fully understand what had happened. Once she recovered from the shock, she took to her bed and became totally apathetic.

No funeral procession could be arranged, but a large crowd of Whites gathered at the church, and the funeral took on the nature of an overt demonstration. It was an ordinary weekday in the church village. Men of the Guard stood watch, and off-duty Guardsmen wandered through the village with their rifles. Landlords and gentry congregated at the church, whispering to one another and glancing cautiously at the Guards standing around the church. The coffin had been driven to the church on an ordinary sleigh and carried to the altar in advance.

The vicar entered slowly from the vestry. He refrained from looking at the audience deliberately, in part because he would not have known all of them well but also because he had decided to speak out, heedless of the consequences.

During the hymn, he weighed what he would say in his mind. He had not written it out in advance, as he did his sermons, but trusted that a full mind would supply him with the words to say. At the very last moment, be began to feel his assurance failing him. His hands were sweating, and a voice in his consciousness whispered: What good will it do?

The same thought had caused him to hesitate even before the ceremony, and then he would force himself to reflect on the baron's murder. He had no idea of what the men were like, since the manor servants had not seen them clearly, and the baroness was unable to describe them. But in his imagination he saw them as animal-like beings with low foreheads, who growled savagely as they thrust their bayonets into the baron. That image gave him courage.

His cheeks were unnaturally pale, but his ears were a glowing red. When he looked out over the audience, the coughing and the rustling on the benches ceased. Holding his breath, the sexton tried to close the damper on the stove without rattling it.

"Do not fear, for God has set a limit to Satan's days. Do not fear, for he can only get our body and not our soul. And above all, do not fear, for we have no right to fear."

The vicar's voice rose with each word. At first there was a slight uncertainty in it, but it grew clearer and firmer as it rose.

"...pity invades my mind, outweighing the shock. Pity for such beings, whose first and only resource is brutality and violence. What a testimony to their ignorance. It is the ultimate acknowledgement that they understand nothing else. Faced with such deeds, we have the same feeling as when viewing the evil wrought by instruments of nature. We cannot hate an animal which has gored its caretaker to death, for we know it has neither a soul nor a conscience. But what can we say of those who have deliberately turned the beast loose? We can say that because of them, the earth is cursed. Because of them a woman gives birth in pain. Because of them the serpent stings our heel, and because of them cold and heat torment us.

"Let God forgive them if he can. He can do what we small human beings cannot. For this innocent blood cries out from earth to heaven. We know what Cain said: Am I my brother's keeper. Thus he replied, and washed his hands, imagining that none would see how red the wash-water was. But we also see the mark on Cain's forehead, and we are firm in our belief that as an exile from God he will wander strange lands plagued by the shame of his crime.

"My friends. Oppression and fear have been the gloomy guest in our homes during these times. Any decent person no longer knows, when he goes to bed, if he will see the morrow. But here beside this coffin, we cannot fear. The civic courage shown by the deceased is an example to us of what justice and truth may demand of us. But it is also an example that justice and truth cannot be drowned beneath a wave of terror. For every martyr makes it shine more bright and clear. If we have had doubts earlier, now before this coffin we know clearly what is right and what is wrong..."

As the vicar spoke the blessing, the sobbing of women could be heard in the church. As the coffin was carried to the church grounds, with the crowd following quietly, some of the people came up to squeeze the vicar's hand. The landowners were gloomy and withdrawn. Ellen wept constantly and glanced uneasily at the Guards lounging about the church grounds. The vicar himself was still in the grip of strong emotions. He too noticed the guards and grew more and more nervous, but forced himself not to fear.

The landowners filled in the grave. Even Mellola worked along with the rest, but, breathing heavily, he began obviously to slow down. About to take a shovelful, he drew back and muttered:

"You do it now... although I could have..."

As the grave was filled in, the mood of those present became more prosaic. Now and then words were exchanged that had to do with the trip home. One whispered to another asking for a ride home, or about straw for bedding.

On the way back from the grave, someone thanked the vicar for his talk, to which Mellola's words came as a counterpoint:

"But how will things go with the confiscations at the parsonage now... They use them as a kind of punishment... They took a third pig from us the other day... Uhhuh... That's what they are... Cains is what they are... They would like to have my bull... it'll likely be the next to go..."

Before the group had time to disperse from the churchyard, two unarmed men from the Red Guard arrived, one of whom said in a rather troubled voice:

"If the vicar would come to headquarters. They have some business with him there."

People exchanged significant glances, and the vicar's wife immediately stepped to her husband's side:

"You're not going alone. I'm going with you."

The vicar tried to deter her, but she stuck to her decision. Escorted by the Guards, they walked to the workers' hall, but the vicar's wife was detained in the hallway. The vicar was taken into the hall, where members of the staff sat at a table in front of the stage as a kind of tribunal. Having greeted them, the vicar stopped near the table and waited. He received a few careless nods in reply. Hellberg looked first at the tabletop and then began to stare at the vicar. After a brief silence, he said:

"The vicar has turned the baron's funeral into an occasion to agitate against the revolution. We don't exactly approve of such behavior here."

All the way to the hall, the vicar had prepared himself for this encounter. At first he had intended to come on strong and emphatically, but had rejected such a stance. Instead, he strove to be calm and controlled.

"It was impossible to avoid the issue during the service. I have condemned the murderers... I did not expect the staff to have anything against that."

The expression on Hellberg's face revealed that he had understood the innuendo. The other members of the staff looked off in different directions. The vicar did not know all of them, and he tried to recall if any of them had been in the church. Hellberg controlled his rage and said in an almost friendly voice:

"The vicar is in no sense an investigator or judge of these events. He should stick to the gospel and not start interpreting the law. Since the vicar appears unable to restrict himself to the day's text, but has strayed from the church into politics for the second time, we have to hold him temporarily. It is a precautionary action. Your safety is guaranteed, perhaps better in our custody, since such talk may lead excitable people into unconsidered actions. Your family can visit and bring additional food from home if the Guard rations are unsatisfactory. You can have bedclothes brought from home if you wish."

He looked at the vicar as he spoke, but turned toward the window as he continued:

"We do not do this willingly. It is also a dishonor to the parish when we have to imprison our minister."

Having said that, he smiled, but only with his face. His eyes remained the same. The vicar stood opposite Hellberg, looking at his black hair. There were a few scattered gray hairs in it that had a silvery glint. Hellberg was in his fifties, but age did not seem to affect him. Strong, yellowish teeth showed from beneath his black mustache when he spoke. His hands were clasped in front of him on the table, and thick black hair grew on the backs of his short, stubby fingers.

When the vicar did not respond, Hellberg turned halfway toward a member of the staff and said:

"Ahlgren, take the vicar to his destination."

Then he went on talking, with no sign that his words were addressed specifically to the vicar:

"Formerly the masters put the poor in the poorhouse. So now it's fair for the poor to put the masters there."

Then he took up some papers, a gesture indicating that the matter was settled. Ahlgren rose and muttered something to the vicar, who took it as an order to leave. When in the hallway, his wife asked to go with him to the poorhouse, Ahlgren stopped her:

"It's no use... And there's nothing to fear... This is just a precautionary measure... the workers are in an agitated state of mind..."

The vicar's wife calmed down when she heard that she would be allowed to visit her husband. They said goodbye in the churchyard, and Ahlgren diplomatically moved a little way off.

Ellen blinked her eyes and swallowed.

"What do you want me to bring?"

"You can bring food... but you can leave the bedclothes. First we'll see what they are like there. And bring the Bible. The small one that's in my study drawer."

"Yes... I'll come first thing in the morning. I'll take a horse... Is there anything else?"

"That's all... And don't be upset... I'm perfectly calm myself."

"I won't... Goodbye... try to sleep..."

"Go home now. And don't worry about me. I don't regret it the least bit..."

They both went their way, without looking back. The Guards standing around watched their farewell:

"Uhhuh. They're putting the preacher into mothballs too..."

The vicar was put into a "madman's cell" in the section for the mentally ill in the community home. It was like a jail cell. There was a peephole in the door and bars on the window. A chair was fastened to the wall, as was the cot. A short time after Ahlgren left, a guard's face appeared at the peephole.

He wanted to see how the vicar would adapt to being here.

The vicar sat on the cot, then clasped his hands in prayer. It had such an effect on the guard that he drew back from the wicket.

Having prayed, the vicar lay down on his back. Now that it was all over, a heavy weariness spread over his body and soul. Nevertheless he felt a faint joy regarding his sermon. His dry lips moved as he said to himself:

"I could not rest easy if I had not done it."

Then he sank into an apathetic silence. He could hear someone walking back and forth in the passageway. From the next cell he could hear the soft jingling of chains and a confused gibberish. Only when he had heard it a number of times did it dawn on him:

"Why, it's Laurila's boy..." Frowning, he recalled the affair, and sighed:

"Well, at least he doesn't understand this..."

When the guard brought food in the evening, the vicar was sleeping soundly, with his coat over him and his hat on his head.

The tension of the first few days' imprisonment gradually relaxed. Ellen came once a day to bring food. A guard was always near at hand, but by means of slips of paper put in with the food, Ellen briefly explained what was going on in the outside world. After a few days they even had a chance to talk to one another when the guards became more familiar with them and purposely withdrew farther into the corridor.

There were other prisoners in the poorhouse, but the vicar was not allowed to see them. They were not taken for walks at the same time as he was, but Ellen was able to tell him that the apothecary was a prisoner too, along with his wife. There was also a certain Lieutenant Granlund, who had arrived from Russia, and, having tried in vain to reach the Whites, had hidden in the apothecary's house. In addition to Yllö, a few of the parish's more notable landlords had been imprisoned. Töyry too was afraid of being arrested or murdered outright, now that Halme was ill. Laurila had made some threats in the village.

One day the vicar's wife informed him that Jussi Koskela had offered to speak on behalf of the vicar's release on the pretext that Elina's child must be baptized.

"I thanked him, but I don't think it will help. Your assistant is free. And they won't listen to him... And in spite of everything... It would be difficult to have recourse to their help."

"Old Koskela hasn't done anything wrong."

"Yes, but the child is Akseli's child... If you wish, we can of course try."

"It is useless, of course. A thing of that sort will have no effect on Hellberg... Halme perhaps... but he is helpless now... And it would be even more repugnant to depend on him for help."

The vicar's imprisonment made the bond between the two particularly close and heartfelt. When the guard was absent, Ellen held on to his hand the entire time, and they embraced in parting. Age had made their relationship deeper and more spiritual, and the fatefulness of the situation made them forget convention. Looking into each other's eyes, they understood everything, and there was no need to speak.

When his wife left, the vicar would begin to eat. The guard also came to the spot, for through a spontaneous, unspoken agreement, the vicar gave a part of his food to the man on watch. It was not the same with all of them, but several of the guards were old tenants and laborers on church village farms, and when they were alone, their attitude toward the vicar was humble and respectful. If the guards were young, discussion produced no results, for they obeyed orders zealously. But an actually friendly relationship developed with some of the older men. When the vicar offered them his food, they objected at first, but then gladly ate the choice fare.

Sometimes they spoke of the rebellion, guardedly at first, but as their trust increased, more openly. It was evident from their talk that one or both of them were beginning to have doubts:

"I don't... I think things could have been worked out... If they could have done something about the worst cases... I for one have behaved well..."

Someone might, in veiled words, ask for the vicar's help when it came to a settling of accounts, which, they already speculated, might be coming, but the horror of which they could not foresee in their wildest dreams. The vicar promised, but consoled them by saying that such intervention would not be necessary. Only evildoers would be punished, so he believed.

This mildness was awakened only when he saw an old laborer in a patched coat humbly and clumsily thanking him for a meat sandwich and eating it shakily, afraid to show his pleasure.

It was different when the guards were young boys, many of whom, the vicar recalled, had just finished their confirmation school. They shouted covertly spiteful comments in loud voices or sang dirty songs in the corridor. When Ahlgren came for an inspection and asked about his wishes, the vicar informed him of the boys' behavior. It changed for a couple of days, but soon was the same as before. The vicar asked Ahlgren that he be allowed to do some work in place of walking, and the latter arranged for him to cut wood in the woodshed. The boys on watch arranged for him to have a lunatic as his partner, and the vicar could see from their smiles that they had done so on purpose. He tried not to let it bother him, and spoke to the fool as straightforwardly as possible.

"Are you a priest or a provost?"

"I'm a priest."

"Yeah... You don't know how to saw... you jerk at it like that... The saw should run from one end to the other... Isn't that so, Provost?"

"I'm sure it is. But I'm not used to it."

"Ha, ha, ha, ha... I can see that."

After a while the madman asked in a whisper, glowering at the guards from the corner of his eye:

"Who put you in here?"

"I'm here by order of the headquarters staff."

"Ha, ha, ha, ha, ha... That's only what you think... That bailiff put you here the same as he did me. And old man Yllö is behind of it... I'll kill both of them. Ha, ha, ha."

The madman got angry and began to explain in a loud voice:

"When you see him coming with a block of wood in his hand, then turn your ass to the wall. He's crazy... He tried it once with me and I told him you won't stick that up there at least not until you round it off a little. Ha, ha, ha..."

The boys laughed along with the fool, and the vicar concentrated on his sawing. The madman began to whisper again:

"Let's kill them and escape... I already have a sack to put our things in... It is torn, but I have a needle to patch it... just as soon as we get thread we'll patch it... We'll go to North Tornio..."

When they left the shed, escorted by the mocking smiles of the boys, the vicar said to the fool in a friendly voice:

"Goodbye, Heikkilä."

"Ha, ha, ha."

He did not look at the boys, but went into his cell as if they did not exist.

In his cell he started to read the Bible. He had begun to underline in it the passages he thought fitted the situation. The boys had gathered in the corridor, and the guard was secretly watching through the wicket. He whispered something to the others and a voice called out in the corridor:

"First commandment. Pack and prunes."

The vicar looked closely at his book and tried not to hear.

"Second commandment. Boots and prunes."

"Eleventh commandment. Don't panic. What is it? A woman's envy is worse than a thief and the greedy have a shitty end."

The shouts came from some distance down the corridor, but the vicar knew they were meant for his ears. When he could not manage to ignore them, he tried to overcome his rising anger by relating them to a larger context, for he knew that his helpless rage was slightly comic.

"...it is too superficial... but has the situation evoked it, or is it truly a deep-seated vulgarity... of course the one shouting knows what the bystanders will appreciate... Alone he would not do it... in the first place, the group makes him bold... and in the second place, their admiration inspires him..."

"Well, boys, there was this preacher who was drunk in the pulpit, and he told the people to do as I say, not as I do."

"All the preachers are like that. The people are told to do good, but they themselves do evil. They fool the people with mysteries. It would be nice to know, for example, how all the animals fit onto Noah's ark. And where Cain got a wife from. If someone can answer, good."

After a while the boys tired of shouting and moved to the door of Antti's cell. Antti made enthusiastic noises and clanked his chains.

"Antti, show us what kind of equipment a man has."

In a moment there was a roar of laughter from the corridor.

"We ought to get some nut from the woman's side as a partner for him. We could see if he knows what to do with it."

The vicar rapped on the door of his cell. The boy on guard came to the wicket.

"Shame on you. I'll tell Ahlgren about this when he comes. You could at least leave a helpless lunatic in peace."

There was silence in the corridor for a while. The vicar returned to his cot. The boys could be heard to whisper among themselves, until one of them said in a loud voice:

"Have you heard, boys, that all the bourgeoisie prisoners will be shot?"

That was followed by a restrained giggling, and the shouter broke into song:

> The battle grows sharper.
> Ever stronger in the ranks of the poor
> the feeling of freedom swells.
> The state is helpless now,
> its torture, rack, and pain.
> Heroes die singing freedom's song.

"... they know not... they know not what they do... But mercy does not help... the Old Testament must be enforced... in all its severity."

The vicar tossed from side to side on his bed, for he could not lie in peace in one spot.

256

For a week Halme struggled in the jaws of death. A doctor was sent for, but he was of no avail, for Halme refused to take medicines.

"You have pneumonia. You were badly chilled."

"I am not chilled."

"You can't stand much cold, for you are very weak."

Emma had told the doctor about Halme's selection of foods, and the doctor maintained that the entire illness resulted from it.

"Juniper berries and raspberry leaves are not dangerous, but it is doubtful that one can live on them."

"I have eaten all vegetable foods. Master Doctor is drawing the wrong conclusions. I am not weak because of my food selection but because I have ignored its regular observance recently."

The physician did not argue further. As far as he was concerned, Halme could just as well die, and it would be wiser of him to do so before the government troops arrived. He wrote prescriptions, which Valenti fetched from the church village, but in spite of Valenti's explanations and Emma's pleas, they were left untouched.

"In addition to everything else, they even contain alcohol. And that is what their effect is mainly based on. Medical science violates nature. Only the curative methods of children of nature are genuine. It is precisely alcohol which is a good example of the way in which a human being's strength may be temporarily increased by robbing him of it, but the contrary effect nevertheless does occur. Medicines are the same... No, I don't need them... This is another matter... For the first time the specific spiritual gravity of the soul of a being named Adolf Halme is being tested. Will it conquer matter or not... Thank you, Emma, for your care... but I beg you... Let it be... Nature is the greatest chemist... medicine is quackery... nor is illness essentially a material phenomenon.. it is a disturbance of the spirit... a state of weakness..."

After a couple of days, he became delirious in the evening. His fever exceeded forty degrees, and on two evenings it reached dangerous readings. But he was sufficiently aware during the day to refuse medication. It seemed as if all his colossal stubbornness were concentrated on that end.

During strangling fits of coughing, Emma held his head and tried to wipe the phlegm from his mouth. When he could speak, Halme would say:

"Who are you?"

"I'm Emma... don't you know me?"

"Good... go and tell them at headquarters that the slip is in safekeeping... I didn't write anything on it..."

"What slip... what slip are you talking about?"

"Your slander doesn't bother me... my conscience is clear... If you want to know a secret... although you're not worthy of it... it happened one night... I'm sure I was awake... and I left my body... Go ahead and doubt... I didn't get far, for doubt and fear invaded my mind and I returned to my body... I wasn't ready... there was something unclean... This is all true... an ant... it bit my foot this summer... I picked it off... for the sake of principle..."

"Aatu... sleep... don't talk... I'll give you some juice... will you have some...?"

"...it was for the sake of principle... when it came to mind... You could live without biting, you know, I said to it..."

"Sleep now... shall I put a compress on your head?"

"But Socrates was the greatest of all..."

"Aatu, don't you know me... I'm Emma."

"Emma... well... thank you... Am I somehow sick?"

"You are, but you'll be well soon."

"Is that so... we should make an arrangement... if there's a change... we could make contact... well. Let it go this time."

When the fever went down, a state of grave weakness followed. The slightest effort caused his heart to pound and his chest to ache. For a couple of days, the invalid was unable to speak. His skeletally thin hands rested motionless on the bed covers. Sometimes when she looked at the bed, Emma was frightened, for at first glance her husband's face bore a great resemblance to a skull. Loss of weight had caused the lower part to shrink to almost nothing, and combined with the clearly defined, bulging forehead, it had the effect of a skull.

Recovery began slowly, but Emma joyfully noted signs of improvement. If the covers slid off or became badly rumpled, Halme immediately asked her to straighten them. He also asked about his letters and other personal possessions and took pains to see that everything was in the right place. And when for the first time Emma heard a note of dissatisfaction in his voice, she felt an inexplicable feeling of relief.

"Why have you hung my black coat on the nail next to the door? You know it doesn't belong there."

"I didn't think... since you don't need it now..."

"But my dear. If I needed it, I would of course be wearing it. But since I don't, it should be on its proper nail."

Emma put the coat back where it belonged.

"Thanks."

Emma was absolutely correct in taking her husband's return to excessive fussiness as a sign of improving health and was not offended by his remark.

Gradually Halme began to question Valenti about headquarters matters.

But his interest was a mere formality. And although his health was already fairly good, he appeared sicker than usual when such matters came to the fore.

"I can't think now... Ask in the church village..."

VI

Uuno Laurila had gotten out of jail. He had been freed on condition that he go to the front, to which he had agreed, but he stopped at home on his way. Somewhere he had managed to clothe himself well, and he also had large quantities of cigarettes. He gave Aliina a lot of money, and when she asked where he got it, he said:

"Day money from the jail. I took it all when I left."

The boy listened quietly to the family's talk of happenings in the village. They did not seem to interest him much. He asked a few idle questions about Arvi's death and accepted the fruits of Aliina's and Elma's bustling preparations in a slightly gruff and indifferent manner. Aliina made the dishes he had previously liked, and Elma pilfered ingredients from the Guard's kitchen for them. In the past, the Laurila children had even gotten a limited portion of meat, and if they yammered for more, it brought on a storm of grumbling and recrimination. Now Aliina heaped the boy's plate with more than he could eat. When talk turned to leaving for the front, Aliina said:

"You could just stay at home now."

Then she turned aside so that the boy, embarrassed by his mother's nearness, would not see how moved she was.

The mother grieved in secret because the boy seemed alienated from them. He wandered around the yard in his hard-topped boots with his hands in his pockets and gazed off somewhere. Even after eating, he sat with a faraway look, dug at his teeth with a toothpick, belched, and withdrew into himself. Elma now fawned on her brother, with whom she had continually fought before. Self-important, but blushing with pleasure, she hinted to him about Akusti Koskela. A small trace of interest appeared in Uuno's gloomy eyes, and a sort of smile crossed his face, but that was followed by a snort and the words:

"Watch out that he doesn't pump you full."

"Pooh... we do what we do."

The boy had longer discussions with his father. They had a common topic of conversation in the jail, and they spoke of it as men who know more on the subject than others.

"Did they still take you to church there?"

"They did, all right."

"You should have told them, goddamn, the way I did, that it's enough of

259

a religious service for me to have chains on my legs like Daniel in the lion's den."

Immediately after that, Antto recalled:

"They've promised me new land, but that won't be the end of it... I sure have a few words to tell that goddamn suckface."

Uuno went to the church village and returned with some bootleg liquor. Father and son drank together, and when a slight intoxication began to spin around in Antto's head, he said to his son:

"Just between the two of us, I tell you, goddamn, that we can take care of ourselves. I used to wrestle in my day... I was still under twenty when I was in Korri's malt sauna. They shut the door, but I pulled on it so that the hinges squealed. Three of them came at me, but when I threw haymakers the nettles crackled as the men fell. Even the maid ran off shrieking, and I went and brushed the malt down onto the floor. Oh, Jesus, I was black that morning... I'm a little old, but there's still a man here. I'm a little wild, like you."

After a short time had passed, Antto gave his son a significant look:

"We should go and pay that ironballs a little visit... They have to give half of their seed-grain. The order came to headquarters. Let's make the goddamned thing drive a load to the church village."

"Good."

They went by the workers' hall and picked up their rifles. Uuno walked quietly, but Antto's step was hurried and eager, and he spoke in a low voice:

"I would have had them singing cunt-songs in Latin a long time ago, but that goddamned pantywaist was in the way."

His son did not answer. He was one of those men who said little and did not boast.

When at Töyry they saw the father and son coming, the woman of the house frantically tried to hide her husband. During the entire time of the rebellion, Laurila had not been at Töyry, for Halme had not let him go there. Therefore the visit seemed so threatening that Töyry actually intended to hide, but was too late. There would have been time enough, but pride prevented him at first from accepting the notion of fleeing and hiding, and when he did bow to it, the Laurilas were already standing in the main room. Töyry thought it best to go openly to meet them.

"Greetings, Kalle. We thought we would come and see if you're getting old. We haven't seen you in such a long time."

Töyry realized at once that both of the men were drunk. He said softly and uncertainly:

"Well, don't we all get older at this age."

"You don't, goddamn it. You're still the same suck-face."

260

Antto was trembling with suppressed rage, for he wanted to play a cat-and-mouse game, but could not control himself. Banging the butt of his rifle on the floor, he said:

"Listen now, Kalle. Stand there and listen now. Stand there very nicely and be still. This time I speak and you listen. And hear what you are now... You're one of the world's devils, a Finnish wolf, you're such a devil of a man that there's none like you on earth. Your father was a swindler too, but you could get along with him somehow. But from the time you took over the farm, my life has been a hell. Do you remember the rent-work contracts you laid on me even though you knew a man couldn't finish them in a day... You were trying to get rid of me, and thought they would give you a reason... I knew damned well what your schemes were. You accused me of brawling, just another way of trying to make me go... There is a way of paying you back, but let it go this time... a bullet through you, that would be the right punishment."

Töyry's wife had been wailing the whole time, but Antto's threat caused her to step hurriedly to her husband's side:

"Now don't... we haven't done you any wrong... we've always given the headquarters what they've ordered..."

"You keep your mouth shut too, you high-and-mighty bitch... You don't deserve any better... The right thing for you would be to pour melted tin into your twat... And you, Kalle, hitch up your horse and take a load of grain to the church village headquarters... You've been ordered to turn over half of your seed grain... You'll make the load yourself and you'll drive it nicely yourself. That will be enough for this time, for I know it burns your tightfistedness like hellfire, ha, ha, ha..."

Antto tried hard to sound mocking, but his forced laugher was merely an empty cackle. Töyry listened to the outburst with a cold, expressionless face. In the same kind of voice, he asked:

"Is it the headquarters' decree?"

"Yes. And this time we're all the headquarters you need. Hitch up the horses right now."

The landowner put on his hat and went out. Weeping, his wife watched from the window as the men went to the barn and then to the storehouse. Töyry bagged the grain and carried it to the sleigh. Uno was silent all the while, but Antto spluttered from time to time. When the load was finished, Töyry took the reins and was about to climb onto the sleigh, but Uno said softly:

"Now go stand up on the load and shout: 'Long live the Revolution!'"

The landlord did not understand the order at first, and when he did he laughed in disbelief:

"There's really no need to start playing games here now."

"Move. As I recall I told you to shout 'Long live the revolution!' from atop the load."

When Töyry hesitated, Uuno swung the rifle from his back and aimed it at the landlord:

"Just so you know it, old man, I have an itchy trigger finger."

From the window, Töyry's wife had seen the rifle leveled at her husband and ran to the storehouse. Töyry climbed up on the load and said weakly:

"Long live the revolution."

"What kind of cheer is that? Just like from a rejoicing breast now."

"Long live the revolution."

Töyry's wife rushed up to the storehouse:

"Have mercy, for God's sake... Is there no justice left in the world?"

Antto roared at the woman:

"Don't you whine, you stuck-up bitch... Remember the kind of sniveling you did about the rent-wool... and remember when my old woman was almost full term with a baby how you whined because her work was worth nothing... I still remember your words, you old bag, couldn't I get someone to replace her... Jesus, woman, where would I get money for a substitute, when I had to do gift days for nothing... God, why don't I just put a bullet through such devils?"

Uuno took one of the landlord's mittens from the load and set it on the branch of a large birch tree alongside the storehouse in the yard:

"And now old bag, you will bark at those as a pay-back. Have you barked at a squirrel before?"

"What, Jesus bless us... I don't understand..."

His face pale, Töyry stood on the load and said:

"Do whatever you will with me... but you ought to be men enough not to lay hands on a woman..."

"We won't touch her... but bark at the squirrel or the old man will fall from the load like a heath grouse..."

The woman understood and, panic-stricken, began to bark at the mittens.

"Cock your head to one side like a dog when it barks up a tree..."

Töyry ordered his wife to stop, but she did not obey and kept up a kind of yelping mingled with sobs. Antto essayed a laugh, but he totally lacked the ability. Since he knew that a mocking laugh was appropriate, he let out a cackling with a slight resemblance to one.

"Goddamned lousy dog... the squirrel isn't scared... he just sits there... ha, ha... the squirrel isn't scared... ha, ha... lousy squirrel dog..."

Töyry stepped down from the load.

"If... go ahead and shoot me... here I am... but don't..."

Uuno's hand touched the sling of his rifle, but he dropped the idea and said:

262

"Stop it, goddamn... since even a squirrel isn't afraid of you..."

The woman stopped, and her husband told her to go into the house. But she did not go until she saw her husband leave with the load. Antto and Uuno slowly followed him, and when they were alone, Antto said:

"Jesus... where did you think that up... I laughed so goddamn much..."

And Antto guffawed, an angry guffaw, totally lacking in even the joy of malice.

One evening Töyry went to get hay from a barn on a back field. He had scheduled these visits to coincide with the use of hay so that the trips would not attract attention. Sitting on a sack covered by a horse blanket, he drove along the woods road, studying the tracks on it and the woods around him.

Reaching the barn, he again surveyed the surroundings. From the woods came the swish of skis and a voice:

"Is it OK?"

"Just come on out."

Arvo Töyry and Uolevi Yllö skied up to the hay barn. They did not use their poles, to avoid telltale packing of the snow. Both men were sooty and bearded, and their sunken eyes peered nervously around them. They did not relax for even a moment, but continued to look around, tense and alert, ready to leave at any moment.

Uolevi stood watch at the door of the barn while Töyry and Arvo emptied a sack into the boys' backpacks. In soft whispers, the two exchanged information:

"Your father is in the poorhouse, and the vicar has been arrested too... But their new attack is said to have failed too. Silander said to someone in private that the morale in the Guard is poor... They leave the front on their own."

The boys told about their conditions. There had been little change in it. They lived in the woods, but three of them at a time could stay at a forest cottage on a tenant farm. The owners were Whites, but they associated with the Reds in the next parish, and could thus find out if anyone had caught wind of the guerrillas. Potatoes they got from the farm, but they lacked other foods. And the constant vigilance exhausted them. They had even planned some sabotage as the Whites began to move south, but they dared not do it prematurely because it would reveal their existence.

Töyry told of the Laurila's visit in a voice that shook, for even telling about the humiliation seemed difficult. Arvo asked his father to go with them, saying they would come to the barn in the evening to get him, but Töyry said:

"I won't leave Mother alone... and she isn't able go anywhere."

The boys made ready to leave. As they stood on their skis, Töyry said softly:

"If it is so... that... my... if there's no protection... then... they have lost... any right to live... Not a seed of that family... should be left to trouble the earth... If I don't live to see that day... It will be left in your charge..."

It was hard for him to say the words. Arvo did not answer, but Uolevi's sooty and stubbly face twisted into a kind of smile.

"The time for the last waltz is sure to come...There are twenty-two boys out there who have been waiting for that day... So there's no need to grieve... Let them dance and celebrate now. They're having a ball before the end. But just try to keep a low profile. It doesn't pay now... And if you can, send my greetings home. And tell them we'll meet again..."

The boys disappeared into the dark woods, and Töyry began quickly to make his load of hay.

CHAPTER EIGHT

I

A faint glimmer of dawn shone as the March night neared its end. Akseli's smarting, bloodshot eyes could discern the outlines of the landscape as he walked crouching along the line from one man to the next. The clear night thundered with the noise of a battle which had lasted for three days. From his own line, a rifle muzzle flashed from time to time, and the sound of a shot rang out. Return fire came from a wooded ridge opposite them. There the muzzle flashes could be clearly seen. An occasional burst of machine-gun fire crackled and whined in the treetops. Sometimes a bullet whistled very near, but Akseli did not take cover. He was in a slightly crouching position, which had little significance in the random firing in the dark.

No one spoke to him, and he had nothing to say to anyone. He walked merely to check that men were not asleep on line and to keep himself from falling asleep if he stayed in one place. His boots were wet and his clothes stiff from the night's cold, but he did not feel chilled.

He sensed the suspicion and bitterness that prevailed in his relationship with the men. No one was grumbling now, because they were unable to. His own despair was no less than theirs, but he shook it off. Ylöstalo had already gone to staff headquarters in the late evening, and there had been no sign of his return. "It doesn't matter... The men are no longer good for anything. Why does he hop around the headquarters to ascertain the situation when they don't know there what it is? And even if they did, it would mean nothing... What good are resounding commands when no one obeys them."

Akseli stopped and leaned against a tree. "It's really cold out here."

The thought turned his mind to the sound of intense firing coming from the right. The thunder of artillery could be heard over the undulating rattle of small-arms fire. From somewhere behind he could hear talking and vague shouts, made unintelligible by the sound of the firing. Soon someone came running and panting toward their position, and Akseli heard Elias's voice half-shouting:

"Akseli, hey, where's Akseli?"

"Here."

"Hey, tell the men to retreat, quick... we'll be surrounded."

"Who gave the order?"

"No one, but two of the machine gunners said there's a whole mob of men coming and the butchers are chasing them."

"It's a lie... everyone stay at his post."

"Listen, it's no lie... Three skiers went by here, and when we asked who they were, they said they were coming back from watch because their company disappeared somewhere."

The nearest men had heard Elias's words and they came crowding around.

"We really ought to go."

"We're not going anywhere..."

"Don't yell, for God's sake... For three days you've kept repeating we won't retreat, and you yourself know that they've been coming back from there the whole time. ..and you can sure tell from the shooting too..."

"We're not going anywhere because someone saw three men on skis. Go and find out more. Come back only then."

Elias left and the men returned to their positions, but the news traveled down along the line. Some men from farther off came to inquire about Akseli's situation, but he drove them back, cursing in annoyance. Continuing to lean against the tree, he tried to ascertain the course of the battle from the din, with no better results. But he clung rigidly to his decision, for he knew from experience what a war of rumors this rebellion was. During their entire time on line, every possible kind of word had spread throughout the units, all of which he well knew to be based on totally false and misleading information. Since there was nothing solid and reliable to go on, every rumor which circulated was wilder than the last. A long time ago he had decided firmly to pay no attention to hearsay. Under no circumstances would he order a withdrawal on the basis of a rumor.

And he repeated in his mind the same thought he had repeated innumerable times during these three days: Someone has to hold his ground.

For the White attack had been going on for three days now, and one position after another had been lost. At first the resistance had been stiff, but then the men's powers of endurance had failed. Sleepless, and dependent upon chance for food, the men who had battled for three days were in a perilous state of mind. Yesterday evening Akseli had been openly threatened. Actually not by his own platoon, but by men from the station village. For in truth he had commanded the whole company during the entire battle. Ylöstalo constantly found reasons to go to the rear.

"You take charge of things here during that time. I'll try to get food for the men."

No food came, nor did Ylöstalo. Yesterday food had been hotly demanded, and Akseli had told the men to wait, but that had started an uproar. The men had threatened to leave their stations and go and get the food themselves. At that point, he had lost his temper and threatened to shoot anyone who left the line. And he had been told:

"Listen, it'll stop at one. You'll be the second."

Thinking these thoughts, he felt his eyelids closing by force, and he decided to start moving again. But there was a shout from behind him in the woods. He concentrated on listening, and when there was a brief pause in the shooting, he heard an unfamiliar name being repeated at brief intervals:

"Aumaoja... Aumaoja... Aumaoja..."

The voice sounded panicky, and during another brief break in the shooting, he clearly heard the voice wailing:

"Aumaoja... where are you? Don't leave me... I can't... Tampere medics... where are you?"

Akseli stood still, holding his breath. The shouting sounded strange. Apparently someone was wandering around behind their lines.

"Osku, go find out what that movement and noise are all about."

Oskari left, growling out something vague. He had advanced perhaps a hundred meters when they heard a few shots from his direction. Then his voice rang out:

"Butchers... Over here, men."

Then someone else shouted:

"Bayonets in line on the right."

There were more shots and another cry from Oskari, but he could no longer be understood above the shooting. Suddenly, Akseli grasped the situation. It was true then. But he tried to keep his voice as calm and measured as possible as he gave orders to the men. There were panicky questions and some of the men darted back and forth blindly. But the dim light of the morning caused the men to draw nearer one another rather than flee in complete panic. Akseli got his own platoon together and into some sort of skirmish line.

"Osku is ahead of us... look out for him..."

But Osku soon came to meet them.

"Goddamn, there are butchers out there."

"How many?"

"How do I know? Someone ordered bayonets on the right, and a dozen were firing."

Akseli ordered the men to move ahead, but they advanced very cautiously. Even before they got close, the enemy opened fire and they hit the ground. The bullets crackled in the trees. Then they heard Lauri Kivioja shout:

"Goddamn, we're in for it now, boys. Lauri is not going to stay here and get killed.

That started the panic.

"To the road, everyone... we're surrounded... the others have run away..."

Akseli roared at them in a hoarse voice to stay put, but his words were drowned out in the crackle of fire from the Whites. He managed to get Oskari and Akusti to stay with him, since they were the closest, and he ordered them to pass on the command to withdraw to the rest of the platoon, since he realized the situation was beyond remedy.

The two started out, but the panic had already spread the length of the line. Everyone repeated the same shout:

"To the road... everyone gather on the road..."

The men could see only about ten meters, so there was a continual shouting as they called to each other. Amid the noise, it was futile to give any orders.

Fortunately their position was a familiar one. The men's sense of direction led them to the road, and the entire company assembled there, although in total confusion. Akseli tried to get the platoons organized, but whenever he found a platoon leader, he saw there were only a few men with him. Shouting their names, he got this answer:

"Where is Koskela?"

Everyone was looking for everyone else, and at the same time the entire mob was walking back along the road, stopping now and then as if to listen. Having ascertained that all the company's platoons had left their positions, and having met Oskari again, Akseli said to him:

"Go quickly back to the hill where the Russian cannons were. Stop everyone there, and try to get them into position. Maybe they'll calm down enough there. Take as many men from our platoon as you can get together and put them in a line. I'll try to get them into some kind of order on the way."

Oskari left, gathering up as many of the men from Pentti's Corner as he could, but the others followed close on their heels. A powerful impulse to retreat was driving the men. Sometimes they stopped as if hesitant, but a shout or the sound of a shot in the vicinity immediately put them to flight.

Akseli stopped shouting and tried with the aid of his squad leaders to achieve some order in the platoon. His commands had no effect on the men; no one obeyed them. A muddled herd of dark figures, the group charged back in the gloom.

Then Elias came toward them.

"Your orders are to delay them. You have to stay as a rear guard and hold them, so the cannons and supplies can be gotten away."

"Where is Ylöstalo?"

"He's in the village... organizing the withdrawal... everyone is falling

268

back... It's a goddamn mess there."

"Humph."

There was a bitter, tearful rage in Akseli's voice as he roared:

"Listen just a little bit... We're in no great danger. They can't come in the dark like wolves... We have time enough now."

He rushed on ahead in order to arrive at the hill where he had ordered Osku to organize a position before his company arrived. Beyond the ridge, the fields began. The main road, along which the real breakdown had occurred, ran there. Akseli had a clear grasp of the situation. He had to get his company to stop before they reached the road in order to cover it and to secure the area between the roads. He did not believe the enemy would charge into it at night, but dawn was already glowing on the horizon.

Oskari had gotten the men from Pentti's Corner into a line and stood on the road, ready to stop those who were retreating. Akseli stopped beside him, and when the first of the men arrived, he began to direct them into a line along the road. At first, when they came singly, they obeyed him doubt-fully, but when they came in larger groups, they stayed on the road.

"We're not going to stay here, boys. We'll be surrounded."

"We're not going to be surrounded. Who the hell started all this? What the devil are you doing? We haven't heard a shot for hours, and you're run-ning like a pack of wolves."

"Yeah, but don't you understand? The butchers are right on our heels."

"They plan to sacrifice us. I know. So the others can get away. The offi-cers are leaving us here so they can escape."

From the main road and the village behind them, they could hear shouts and the din of moving troops. In the darkness of night, the sounds increased the feeling of confusion and uncertainty. Then they heard the crunching of snow and soft voices from the woods on the left. It turned out to be their own men, however, and from them they inquired about the situation.

"Everybody go if you mean to save yourselves. We're done for. We had to leave the machine guns and everything back there."

The men continued on their way. The last to come was an oldish man who was dragging through the snow at a half-trot, looking in fright at the men on the road, and saying as he went by:

"Run for it. Just run for it."

"Let's go, boys."

Akseli stood in the middle of the road and spread his arms as if to stop the men from leaving. But no one obeyed him. He begged and roared out commands, but the only result was shouts from the group:

"Stay and be killed yourself if you want to. We're going now, all the way home."

Trying to stop them was futile, and Akseli tried to get at least his own platoon to stay. But Oskari refused:

"We're not staying. What can a few men do here?"

Oskari's voice was angry and harsh. It was a bitter blow to Akseli, and he retorted just as angrily:

"We have to stay... If the butchers come after us, you know what will happen in the village. It must be a complete mess there, and everything will be lost."

But his words had no effect on Osku. In his own carefree way, Osku had been ready during the entire war to go into the worst straits, so Akseli had ordered him into them. But now even his measure was full. Exasperation engendered by weariness made him say:

"Stop shooting off your mouth, for God's sake."

The men from the skirmish line gathered on the road. Aku and Aleksi stood behind the others, troubled by the situation. Not knowing which side to align themselves with, their brother's or the group's, it was difficult for them to take part in the quarrel, and they were silent. Lauri Kivimäki resolved the situation by throwing his rifle over his shoulder and being the first to start out:

"Goddamn. The noble people's finest troops are leaving now. If you want to, then fight all you please. Lauri's leaving now."

And all of them went. Elias raised the bugle to his lips and softly blew one long and one short blast: the signal to retreat. But Akseli snatched the bugle from him and gave him a shove:

"Go, goddamn it... Go all the way home... You'll see then, when the butchers put a rope around your necks..."

"Stop yelling there... We're not staying here to be killed."

Akseli stood alone on the road. The horizon reddened in the glow of the March morning. There was a continual din and shouting from the village, in which commands and curses were distinguishable. The soul of the revolution crunched as it shattered. And since it was a Finnish revolution, it had its own sound.

"You bastard, you and Seppälä go and collect your traitor's pay together, and stop giving orders. The Vaasa bank will be sure to pay you."

"Shut your mouth, you son of a bitch... Headquarters can kiss my... go yourself, you bastard."

Akseli started walking slowly toward the village. Suddenly he took a couple of steps to gather speed and then tossed the bugle violently into the woods. It rang out bright and clearly as it hit the side of a tree.

His clenched jaws quivered as a hiss mingled with a sob escaped them:

"Go, you bastards."

When Akseli reached the village, confusion raged at its height. The road was a chaotic stream of men and conveyances. Men shouted curses and demanded the right of way. The wounded groaned on their sleighs. Officers gave conflicting orders. Akseli heard Ylöstalo's voice from the road. Going in the direction of the voice, he found Ylöstalo arguing with a couple of drivers. He was demanding that they wait for the wounded, begging and pleading:

"Revolutionary soldiers do not leave their comrades. Men, remember your wounded comrades."

Farther off, Myllymäki was shouting out. He had stopped a loaded sleigh that was driving from a nearby house onto the road:

"Able men off the sleigh. The horse goes to get the wounded from the Red Cross."

In the dim light, Akseli saw Myllymäki seize the horse's bridle and two men get off the sleigh.

"Let go, you goddamned old man."

Then he heard Myllymäki curse and a shot ring out. One of the men fell to the road. Shouts ensued, followed by more shots. Myllymäki staggered a couple of steps and fell beside the road. The horse drove off after a group of men, which scattered to the roadside at the last moment.

Akseli stepped in front of the men Ylöstalo was detaining.

"If one of you leaves without the wounded, I'll shoot the horse first and then the man."

The men contented themselves with grumbling softly. The wounded from the retreating troops stopped at the horses, and when a load was completed, Akseli let the horse leave. Undoubtedly some uninjured men got into the bunch, for it was impossible to get everything straight in the rush and the dim light. The wounded kept arriving, some on their own, some supported by comrades. A few were pushed by their comrades on water sleds or kick sleds they had found. These troops had held their position on a ridge to the very last, and had been forced to withdraw under heavy fire from the surrounding White troops. They knew nothing about their leaders, but had broken out in small groups under the cover of darkness. They were much less subject to panic than the troops which had left earlier, simply because they had been in such a tough situation that moving off had seemed a relief.

The last three men to arrive were calmly smoking, and when Akseli asked how matters stood, they explained calmly:

"There are no more of our troops there. We are the last. But a lot of dead and wounded were left behind."

"Where is your commanding officer?"

271

"The company commander was already dead by evening, and the platoon leader shot himself when he was wounded."

The men continued on their way. The road was empty in the direction of the front, but fugitives were still coming out of the houses. Akseli stood in the road as the last sleigh drove by. An old man, apparently a supply man, stood on the runners. When the horse began a slow trot, he fell off the runners and shouted, as he tried to get back onto them again:

"You'd better go now. Mannerheim has landed at Ikaalinen from an airplane. He has six thousand men with him."

Akseli set off along the road without looking around him. In passing he glanced at the body of Myllymäki, who lay face down on the shoulder of the road. Beyond the village, two artillery pieces minus their front wheels had slid off to the side of the road.

II

Siuro, Nokia, Tottijärvi, Vesilahti.

The company held a meeting, demanded a leave, and granted one to itself.

"We've been on line so long. It's someone else's turn now."

At first Akseli spoke to the men individually. The man addressed would answer in a troubled manner:

"For myself, I would... but the company has decided..."

There were also thefts. The strange surroundings freed the men, and on their own they took food as well as clothing that fit from houses along the way. If someone tried to stop them, a rifle butt would hammer the floor. The company split into small groups, for the men avoided their officers and traveled by themselves. No one actually spoke of his destination. It was somewhere in the background of their consciousness. But when they saw a road sign with the name of their home parish, they turned in that direction without a word.

Local commanders ordered the men to stop and form a new front, but Akseli's shows of temper and Ylöstalo's high-faluting speeches fell on deaf ears.

"Goddamn, the Tampere headquarters sold out the whole front... They let the butchers through on the flanks... They secretly opened the lines at Kuru..."

The men latched onto such rumors easily, since they lent moral support to their own retreat. It was whispered that Salmela, the commander of the northern front, was involved in a plot with the butchers, and when Akseli took issue with the rumors, the men said:

"I don't know... But that's what they said in Siuro..."

During the retreat, one thing slowly became clear to Akseli. For the first time in his life, he began to think of human actions and behavior in isolation from their rightness or wrongness. At first he had explained angrily that retreating was to be condemned, that the front must be re-established. Gradually he came to realize that it made no difference. The men admitted it, but kept going. The question was not whether the men were right or wrong in retreating, but of the means to stop them.

First, he had to find time. He had Oskari suggest a day's pause, and that was agreed to. The company was quartered in a village. During the day, Ylöstalo and Akseli spoke cautiously to the men who could most easily be persuaded to side with them, and they continued working on the platoon. A meeting was called for the evening.

The first demand was for a new commanding officer, and Ylöstalo gladly acceded, although it meant humiliation. He suggested that Akseli replace him, and the latter was chosen, although not without opposition. When the choice was made, Akseli stood up on a sleigh in the yard of the house where they were meeting.

"I'll take on the job. But if we mean to go on as we are now, we don't need a commanding officer. We can get home in one herd."

There was silence in the group. The men looked here and there. They did not feel entitled to grumble, for Akseli had the right to speak. No one could remember his ever having become unnerved for a moment, ever having spoken a discouraging word, or ever having spared himself at another's expense. Everyone remembered his gray overcoat well, for he had actually been the company's commander in combat situations. Not because he had sought to be, but because he had been the most conscientious of the platoon leaders.

He stood on the sleigh, his body thin, his weathered cheekbones prominent, his deeply sunken eyes bloodshot with weariness, and spoke:

"After something like this, many of you think it's not worth it. I don't blame anyone for wanting to go home. I have a family, and I would like to go and see it too. But now it's a question of whether we can afford to. Have you thought about what follows from leaving? That the others will take care of the front? What others? My good men. There are no others, we are the same kind of company as all the rest. I know it's been whispered that the butchers will demand only the leaders and that the rest will be pardoned. Here I stand, let him who wants to turn me over, step forward. Make a clear proposal. If it will save you, then I promise that I myself will go to the butchers. It's better that a few die than that everyone die. But believe me now, I'm not speaking to save my own life, when I say that it won't be

273

enough. At Varkaus they killed all the officers and every tenth man from the ranks too. How do you know which one of you will happen to be the tenth man? If you think that you can just go back to work now like before, you still don't know the Finnish bosses. You already know that I'm a poor speaker, and I don't have much to say to you. Two words will do, win or die. It's no longer a case of the workers' question, it's a case of life or death. Make up your minds. I can't force you to do anything. But figure things out a little. And take everything into account. I mean, face the truth."

He stepped down from the sleigh, and there was a low murmur of talk among the men. A few of them rose to explain:

"We didn't... we would... but we have to know what the situation is... What happened in Tampere... If we could only get an honest explanation... But the lying has to stop."

Akseli stepped up onto the sleigh again:

"Tell me one time that I've lied to you. If I did, it was because I had the wrong information myself. I try to get things straight."

The meeting dispersed. In silence, the men returned to their quarters.

Ylöstalo prepared for his journey home. He had first offered to serve in the ranks, but Akseli recommended that he head for home. It would be unpleasant to give orders to his former commanding officer. He wrote a letter home, a few meaningless lines. He himself sensed their lameness, but it was better not to reveal his state of mind.

The roads were thawed in many places, but Ylöstalo traveled by sleigh. His plan was to go by way of snowy winter roads. The late winter evening was already dark, when the two men said goodbye in front of the headquarters building.

"I'll try to get replacements. If only the situation were clear enough so that I could know where to send them."

Try to... If you see anyone... give them my regards. Tell them I'm well... Tell them along with the letter. It's nicer that way."

Ylöstalo left. For a long time, Akseli stood on the road and gazed after the departing horse. Sometimes the sleigh runner struck a rock, causing a spark to shoot out.

He went to the local village headquarters. No one there knew anything about anything, and only then did the full extent of the collapse become clear to Akseli. He had to call many headquarters before he got any sensible explanation. At Toijala he finally found a headquarters, where he was ordered to take his company to the front "goddamned quick."

The company assembled without complaint. Standing in formation, they listened to the rumble of artillery in the direction of Tampere. The dark horizon flared. Gradually the shimmers merged and spread. A blood-red glow shone over the treetops.

274

"Tampere is burning."

"Move out."

Feet crunched on the thawing road. Sometimes there was a metallic clank when a rifle bolt happened to hit a mess kit hanging at a man's waist.

Shells whirred over them at nearly treetop level. When one crashed into the woods some two hundred meters ahead of them the men ducked their heads lower. From the nearby rail line, they could hear machine-gun fire and the sounds of cannon from an armored train.

Akseli was lying behind a rock. The spring dampness of the earth, now bare of snow, felt unpleasantly cold through the clothing over his knees and elbows. In the crannies of rocks and in thickets there was still snow, and underneath the dripping-wet moss there was ice. But surprisingly the spring sun already shone through his overcoat onto his back. Akseli listened carefully to the din on his right, for he was waiting for the command to attack to come down the line from that direction. His company was ready, so that he had a moment to himself. He was tired. His eyes burned and his mouth was so dry it stung. His mind fumbled through the details of the plan of attack and in that context, he felt a defiant bitterness.

"The weakness of the rural troops' command." What did they think they were then... I'll go anywhere they will.

They had been attacking for many days already in an attempt to help Tampere. There were many troops from Helsinki, and failures gave rise to accusations and distrust. And of course they, the leaders of rural troops, were not able to hold up their end.

This attack had to succeed. At night they had watched the glow of fires over Tampere. It was a sign that the city was still holding its own, but the word at headquarters was that it could not last long.

There had also been rumors that the Germans had landed, and that made even the most optimistic feel depressed.

Akseli could not help thinking of that, although he tried to concentrate on his duties.

"If that is true, even this will do no good... No matter how grandly we break through... It's the end of everything."

But with bitter determination he stared ahead through the fir woods, into which they would soon have to thrust. He strained his ears, and in the intervals between the cannon fire from the train, he heard a repeated shout:

"Helsinki shoemakers. Forward... Shoemakers forward... Helsinki shoemakers, attack..."

A rapidly intensifying fire ensued. Akseli stood up, and shouted in a voice that was hoarse from the cold and days of shouting commands and hurrahs:

"Forward... and this time all the way to Tampere..."

He went quickly, crouching behind trees and juniper bushes. The heads of men advancing in a skirmish line flashed into view here and there. The rocky woods began to thin out. Among a grove of young birches, a red cottage with its outbuildings came into view. A wagon road ran past it, along a pasture fence toward a field on the right, at the edge of which a gray log hay-barn could be seen. Clumps of seedlings grew around the cottage and there were small potato patches near it. Reaching the edge of the open pastureland, Akseli crouched down and studied the surroundings of the cottage. An artillery shell had landed in the yard. The windows were shattered, and in the walls were holes made by shell fragments. There was no movement around the cottage, but someone moved on a hill in back of the pasture fence. Akseli hit the ground quickly and gestured to the nearest men to take cover. He began to study the hill again, and now a white fur cap rose clearly into view behind a hillock of dry, brown grass. He raised his rifle and aimed. After the shot, the fur hat disappeared from sight, but very close to the spot, a machine gun began to chatter. Then they could clearly hear a voice shouting in Swedish:

"Reds out front. Fire."

A din of firing erupted immediately. Akseli saw the men hugging the ground and pouring a hot fire at the cottage.

"Don't shoot at the cottage. There's no one in it... Their position is on the hill behind the fence."

"What?"

"Don't shoot at the cottage. They are behind it, on the hill."

He took in a lungful of air and shouted so loudly that he felt a nasty twinge of pain in his inflamed throat: "Forward," and dashed ahead until he reached the corner of one of the outbuildings. Only in its shelter did he hit the ground. Firing a few shots from behind the corner, he got a burst of machine gun fire in response, which spattered the board walls of the building. In the midst of the excitement, he was able to note the homey-looking fishing rods and the half-rotted fyke net on the outbuilding wall. He turned, shouting and gesturing to the men behind him to follow. They shouted exhortations to one another and continued firing until the boldest started out. Akseli saw Yllö's day laborer, the same "Ugly Santeri" who had brought him the command to rebel, start running in his footsteps. Suddenly the man fell, emitting an audible yelp. A few times he moved, trying to rise, but then he sank face down on the ground. A few men got behind the sauna and beyond them a few others crossed the road and disappeared into a patch of alders. Akseli rose cautiously and peeped around the corner. The machine gun had apparently forgotten him, for now it was firing frantically into the patch of alders in back of the sauna.

"Where is it?"

The low chatter continued from the hill, but Akseli could not see the machine gun. From behind the corner, he surveyed the yard, searching for suitable cover. In the shadow of the cottage he would be able to reach the fence behind it.

He did get there, and then he saw the machine gun. It was in plain sight under the roof of a root cellar. He could even make out the man's face, the strained and frightened face of a very young lad. He thrust the barrel of his rifle cautiously through an opening in the fence and took aim, trying to control his panting. The man firing, who was upright, fell behind the machine gun, and Akseli rapidly emptied his rifle. Two men were left at the machine gun, but others crawled away in flight in back of the pit. He could vaguely hear shouting:

"Come and help... boys..."

Akseli reloaded his rifle and to reinforce a sudden decision he had made, he said to himself:

"And now, goddamnit..."

The rotting fence collapsed in a heap as he grabbed a post for support and stepped over it. Having cleared it, he shouted:

"Come on, boys..."

He felt something hit at the base of his ear with a snap, and felt a burning sting in his neck.

"I'm going to die..."

He threw himself behind the nearest rock for shelter — there were many of them on the root-cellar hill — and felt at his neck. His hand was smeared with blood, but barely, and he realized that the bullet had only grazed the skin of his neck. A defiant joy filled his mind, replacing the recent frozen horror of death, and shouting wild hurrahs, he stood up and ran to the shelter of the root cellar. The men who had been lying behind the sauna followed him over the fence and up to the root cellar. They could hear Swedish language commands and shouts from very near, but the only words they could understand were the 'goddamns.'

Akseli dragged the machine gun out from under the roof of the pit and turned it around frantically. Bullets ricocheted from the nearest rock, and Akseli fired blindly in the direction the bullets were coming from. He emptied the remaining bullets from the belt in the machine gun and shouted to the men lying behind him to get the boxes that were in the root cellar. Feeding in the next belt, he shouted at the top of his lungs:

"First platoon... Come on... There's nothing to be afraid of here... Lehtimäki. Forward. I'm the one who's firing here... This isn't a butchers' machine gun."

Having gotten the belt in, he loosed a long burst into the juniper growth, and saw that it caused movement on the hill.

Finally the men understood the situation and moved forward. They climbed over the fence, and seeing that the Whites were not returning the fire, they continued on to the hill.

"Hey, look. The men from Helsinki are going through that field."

On the edge of the field, there were indeed men to be seen, running crouched over and firing. The firing from the armored train and the sounds of the locomotive seemed to have moved forward along the track. The front was advancing then. But Akseli knew from past experience that once the first objective was attained, the men would be content with it. Now too they gathered on the hill around the root cellar to check the bodies of the dead White machine gunners. It was always difficult to continue an attack. One of the men noticed the blood on Akseli's neck and said:

"You've been hit."

"So I have. But form up the line and move on. We can't give them a chance to stop."

Lehtimäki got his men moving again, and the advance continued. Walking behind the skirmish line, Akseli bandaged his neck. He was still breathless and excited. The roar of shots along the entire line added to his enthusiasm. It seemed to express a power with whose impetus they could finally move forward.

But they did not get far before the shots from scouts ahead of them indicated that the enemy had stopped.

But the initial success still had its effect on the men. Encouraging one another, they continued the advance. The firing flared up again throughout the woods, and the continual waves of shouting repeated the name of the distant, unattainable goal:

"To Tampere... to Tampere... to Tampere..."

Messengers from the next company brought them the first warning. Mounted men arrived, crouched over their horses, trying to protect themselves from stray bullets.

"Company commander... Where is the commander? The butchers are attacking the shoemakers and the militia. You have to continue to attack, even to the very last man. You are ordered to break through."

Other such commands and exhortations continued to arrive. But nothing came of attempts to continue the attack. For to the left, in the direction of the Pentti's Corner platoon which Osku was now leading, the same kind of commotion erupted. Soon Elias arrived from there, frantic and panting.

"Osku is asking for help. The butchers are right in his face."

Akseli could do nothing, for an attack also began at the point held by men from the church village and spread across the entire company's sector. Akseli ran toward Oskari's platoon, where the pressure seemed greatest.

The first of the fleeing men came toward him. It was Aku, staggering backward, sometimes falling, but struggling to his feet again. His unearthly pale cheeks showed through the grime and stubble on his face.

"What's wrong with you?"

Aku sank to his knees, hugging the trunk of a fir tree as if seeking succor from it.

"My leg won't hold me up. Don't leave me to them. They'll kill me anyway..."

Gritting his teeth and supporting himself on his rifle, the boy tried to rise again. Through the trees, Akseli could see the crouching figure of Osku, who was just jerking the ring from a hand grenade and hurling it with a curse at the attackers. They had just gotten the hand grenades, and Osku was fascinated by them, while others were a little afraid of their unpredictability. Aleksi was crouched behind a tree near Osku, passing a new hand grenade to him.

Akseli ran to them and told Aleksi to take Aku to the rear. Ducking low, the boy ran back. Akseli made sure that the two were able to leave. Osku crawled backward, dragging the box of hand grenades, and shouted to him:

"Goddamn, get out of here, there are only two of us... But let's throw these first."

"Take them with you."

He took the box from Osku, who still snatched up a grenade and hurled it violently toward the crashing and shouting that could be heard from the woods. Then they ran low, side by side, with bullets constantly striking the trees around them.

Half-formed thoughts whirled through Akseli's throbbing consciousness. The men were nowhere to be seen. How far had they gone? He had to get his company to stop. Otherwise they were lost.

They first caught up with Aku and Aleksi. Aku was hopping on one leg, leaning on the shoulder of Aleksi, who kept repeating:

"Try to go on... Try to go a little farther..."

Oskari stayed to help the boys, and Akseli went on. Only near the red cottage was he able to get some on his men together. They stopped there a while to get the wounded to the rear before they resumed their flight. For Akseli's shouts and pleas were in vain. His hoarse voice pulsated like the bark of a winded hound on a scent. The nearest men did obey him, but his influence worked only on those he could call by name or point out with a finger. Elsewhere the men bunched up, and from group to group circulated

279

a rumor they could never withstand:

"The butchers are surrounding us. The line has been broken."

It was true. The line was broken, and the White counter-attack was in full swing. With a handful of men, Akseli reached the main road after his scattered company. There, men from other scattered units had assembled. What followed was a duplication of scenes already familiar from the collapse of the front at Ikaalinen. The cursing of commanders. Groups of men who, not listening to anyone, went on fleeing although there was no longer any danger. Wounded who groaned beside the road, begging for help and getting none. Here boxes of ammunition were flung aside. There a loyal soul dragged a machine gun all by himself, until he shoved it off the road:

"To hell with it... I'm no goddammed horse..."

Two frightened looking prisoners were brought to the place.

"What the hell are you dragging them here for?"

Two shots, and two bodies writhed by the roadside until mercy shots rang out.

The retreat continued for some ten kilometers. Akseli did not rant or rave. Calmly he gathered up his company and got to rest for the first time that day. In the evening he sat outside alone and watched the fires at the front. The horizon over Tampere no longer glowed red, for the city had fallen. And from a company commander he knew, Akseli had received the certain news that the Germans had landed.

There was no reason for further striving. Dully his eyes took in the flashes of artillery fire, which his wearily drooping eyelids soon shut out from view.

The news of the Germans' arrival set him to thinking of Aku's fate, and along with Aleksi, he went to look for the hospital train. He found it on an overpass. Having procured a horse to drive, he went and got Aku from the train.

"I don't know how far you would get on it... And are there even any hospitals there at all? They can take care of the wound just as well at home."

His face pale, the boy sat on the wagon. The bullet had only gone through the flesh of his thigh above the knee, but he had lost a lot of blood.

"What will I tell them at home?"

Akseli's face twisted into a kind of smile.

"Tell then whatever you think best. Try to explain somehow... It won't pay for them to look for graves now... Mine will probably be somewhere around Kymijoki. If we're still able to get there."

He gave his money to Aku.

280

"Take this home. I don't need it... I have to keep my watch, since I will need that."

As Aku was leaving, he added:

"You should make out all right... at least, there's nothing on your conscience... If you would sort of take care of them..."

"I will. 'Bye now."

"'Bye."

The company had to go on line again, but attacking was called off with the fall of Tampere. Uuno Laurila also returned to the company, having come by way of many units. He reported to Akseli and told him the news from home, although it was already three weeks old.

When the order came to pull back, the men in the company demanded that they go home first. Akseli got permission for them to do so, since it caused only a small detour in their journey. He had to debate the matter with himself, but the more he thought about it, the more eagerly he himself wanted to visit home once more.

Marching toward his home parish, he thought of nothing but his family. One night at home. Against that background, the black despair of that day and the days to follow vanished.

III

A lamp "turned down low" shed a dim light in the Koskela main room. No one wanted more light. There was no longer anything to do. Akseli's pack was ready. Conversation was forced. When the silence began to seem alienating, someone said something. During the periods of silence, the distant roar of artillery could be heard in the room. Alma went to the window and looked out over the swamp from it.

"What is that strange kind of glow?"

"They are houses burning."

"My God."

During the evening the glow spread wide, and Akseli looked at it, conjecturing:

"They will break out from there come evening at the latest, and by that time we have to be out from under."

He returned to the table and said, not actually directing his words at the listeners:

"They say that there are plenty of roads, but these days they are likely to be pretty crowded."

Alma was sitting on a bench with her hands in her lap. She rocked back and forth from the waist up to indicate her mind's unrest.

"But what if the boys go too."

The remark seemed to be meant for Akseli, and he replied:

"I won't tell them to go or stay. But I think it's wiser for anyone whose life is not in danger to stay. I, of course, have ordered everyone to leave, but I will not force anyone to go. Nothing bad will happen to the boys. It's more dangerous if they fall into the hands of someone who doesn't know them."

He was silent for a moment, and then he said softly:

"It's different with me."

That brought on a long silence, infused with an oppressive gloom. Jussi rose in turn to look at the glow of the distant fires and said as he gazed at it:

"What if I should at least try... I would speak to the vicar."

Up to this point everyone had spoken in soft and faint voices as if honoring the sad and heavy feeling of the evening, but now Akseli's words were resolute and vehement:

"You will not. You will not beg him on my behalf. You can speak on behalf of the boys, but not for me."

"Don't, don't, boy... There's no use in being proud."

Akseli did not answer his father, but said to Aleksi:

"Go and see to that horse."

He had taken a saddle horse from the church village headquarters, although his riding skills were very weak. Aleksi went out and stayed for some time. Returning he said:

"Aku. They're asking for you out there."

Akusti went out, using a cane. When he was gone, Jussi muttered:

"That Laurila girl is hanging around like a bitch in heat. Going with someone like that... she won't even come inside... It's best for that family to go... They pulled such a stunt at the Töyrys'."

Aku descended the steps with difficulty. Elma stepped out from the darkness of the threshing barn. She came to meet Aku, and helped him by propping him under the arms. They sat down on the threshold of the threshing barn.

"Are you leaving?"

"Nothing will come of it."

"We'll take a horse from somewhere and I'll drive."

"Akseli says it's hard to get to Russia. Nobody knows how far the Germans have come. If they catch us, they will take the horse away... and then what will we do? But why are you going? They won't do anything to women."

"I don't know... Mother is making me go. But she herself is not going, nor Father. They say they can't go into something like that when they're so old... when they don't know what they might run into. But I have to go with Uuno..."

Elma began to cry and clung to the boy's neck, blubbering:

"Because they're going to kill us all... Töyry's dairymaid said so... and Father won't go... no way... they're staying. They're going to find out."

Aku calmed the girl with assurances and explanations. She stopped crying and they sat in silence. The thunder of artillery was silent for a time, but the glow of the fires was brighter than before.

The night was calm and the sky was bright. From the direction of the village came the sound of unintelligible speech and the rattle of wagons. Elma listened, motionless:

"What is that sound? Is the wind blowing out there?"

Aku listened too. Far off in the direction of the main road there was a strange humming. One could not distinguish individual sounds, but it reached their ears as a single buzzing and murmuring. They could not make out what kind of hubbub it was. They had never heard anything like it before, for it was made up of the footsteps of thousands of horses and people, of the rattle of wagon wheels, of commands, curses, pleas and prayers, the crying of children and the singing of drunks, even of a brass band's playing.

It was the head of a column of refugees. The cauldron of misery was bubbling and boiling over, until its sound was drowned out again by the roar of the cannons.

"Well, this had to get straightened out somehow. Come back home then."

Elma did not answer. She began to hug and kiss the boy, panting with passion, which changed on occasion to sobbing.

Indoors they were going to bed. Jussi and Alma went to their own place, but Aleksi stayed in the main room. Elina and Akseli went into the bedroom They were both silent, for they had said what they had to say. At most, they whispered a few words about some trifling matter. They had to be quiet because the children were asleep.

When Akseli had arrived in the evening, they had greeted each other with a handclasp, for others were present and closer caresses were therefore unsuitable. Only now when darkness had eased their shyness did they embrace. A two-month separation had somehow estranged them, so that closeness made them both feel shy. The gloom of the situation also had the effect of making them feel ashamed of too much passion.

'You've gotten thinner. I can feel your bones so easily. You don't even spread out after having a child like the others."

They lay awake for the few hours that Akseli had. When the time to leave approached, Elina said:

"Don't think about us, then... it'll be easier on you... We will have enough..."

Elina paused for a moment, turned her head away, and then continued with some difficulty:

"...protectors..."

"The worst thing for me is to think that you'll grieve for me here... I could make it by myself... if I didn't have other things... I would go and hide out for the worst days... But the people... Hellberg is leaving the refugees to me too. I have to take the Guard and a gang like that... If the Germans want to, they can be in Kymijoki a week before we can with this caravan of refugees... But it's all over in any case."

"What will you do then if that's the case?"

"We have to try to get through to Russia... But I will come back. When it's possible. I won't stay there. And I can't live without you."

It was three o'clock. Akseli put off the decisive word from one second to another, but then it had to be said. They got up and began to dress.

"Shall I wake up the boys?"

"Don't... it's better."

Throwing his pack on his back, Akseli went over to the boys' bed. He stroked the blond hair on both of them and swallowed hard.

"Don't come out... there's no reason... I'll go over to the new place."

His words were succeeded by Elina's sobs and her faltering words.

"Goodbye... there's no use in crying... We have to go on..."

Hurriedly, almost running, Akseli rushed out. Aleksi was standing in the yard.

"Bring the horse to the yard. I'm going to see Father and Mother."

Akseli was back in five minutes. Hastily he extended his hand to Aleksi:

"Well then. So long... And help Elina and the boys. I'll pay you if I make it back."

Clumsily, with difficulty, he got up into the saddle.

"Where is Aku?"

"Near the threshing barn."

Two dim figures appeared from the darkness of the threshing barn. After a brief handshake, Akseli said:

"If Elma means to go, it's time for her to get a little something together. We have to be in the church village before twelve."

Then he twitched the reins. Leaning against the entry door, Elina listened to the thudding of the horse's hoofs, which changed to a rapid gallop on reaching the road.

There was a light in Halme's window when Akseli rode into the yard. Tying up his horse, he knocked at the door. Valenti came to open it, and Akseli hurried in.

"Have you made a decision?"

"I have. I'm staying."

"I'll arrange a good ride for you. You can have your own horse and driver."

Halme looked at the wall.

"I'm too old and sickly for such a trip... And if I die here, at least I die at home..."

"Well, goodbye then."

"Goodbye. I wish you luck on your journey..."

Having squeezed Emma's and Halme's hand, Akseli said to Valenti:

"Take the necessary number of horses from the manor. I'll write a slip for Osku. You can take what you need from the store."

When he glanced back as he went out the door, the image of Halme lingered in his eyes, emaciated cheeks, gray hair and mustache, and a faraway look in his deeply sunken eyes.

People were in motion on the roads and in the yards of the village. Those who were leaving were making provision for the journey, and those who were staying were hiding their scant possessions. As Akseli rode toward Kivivuori, someone came toward him on foot, whom he recognized as Victor Kivioja by the raucous blowing of his nose, a characteristic of Victor's. Akseli stopped the horse to take leave of him. Victor spoke in a whisper, although his whisper was rather loud:

"The boy is leaving... it's no good for him to stay... I found out... Don't tell anyone, but I went to see the storekeeper. Although I only... I did a little butchering for their Guard, since they asked me to. He said to me first that I had some of the Red spirit in me, but I said Jesus, boy, remember the past, a few animals and loads of grain. Remember when we covered the sauna window with a sack and you kept watch while I butchered some rams. That shut him up a little. But he said he couldn't do anything for my boy... Don't tell anybody... I told the old lady that Victor will come out of this okay like from many other tough spots... Is that a stallion under you? Let me feel him over a little... How old is he? He hasn't been starved for oats. He feels like silk, goddamnit... The other day I made a deal with a man from Pori in the church village... I don't know if it was stolen, but they were strangers... Yeah, he said it wouldn't work for the boy because he carried a weapon. But I told the boy to go off into the woods and live there as long as his sweet life was in danger. Socialist blood will soon be cheap, boy, goddamn. Do you believe it?"

Akseli started off, but after riding for some twenty meters he heard Victor shout something he could not make out:

"What?"

"He has a good gait, I tell you... but he hits his hoofs together... otherwise he looks to be quite an animal..."

The door at Kivivuori was shut, and when Akseli knocked, he heard Osku say from in back of it:

"Who is it?"

"Me."

He wondered at the caution. Janne was watching him from the open door of the room off the entry, and Akseli saw him shove a pistol into his pocket.

"What are you doing here?"

"I ran away from those military outfits of yours. They are said to be killing the revisionists and bourgeoisie as they leave. I thought we would be safer here in our home corner."

"Who's been saying such things?"

"Who? The kind of men who are walking around the church village with rifles on their backs. What kind of men are they?"

Ignoring the sarcasm, Akseli went into the main room, followed by Osku and Janne. Otto was sitting at the table and Anna was lying on the bed with a wet towel on her forehead. Pack on his back, Akseli stood in the middle of the floor and looked at her. She turned her face toward him for a moment and groaned softly:

"Are you ill, Grandma?"

"It's because of you... Because of your evil-doing... and bringing misfortune on the innocent too."

The words came from Anna as heavily as if she were breathing her last, and she turned toward the wall. Akseli sat down and handed Oskari some signed papers, with which he would be able to carry out confiscations.

"Although it makes no difference. But for appearance sake."

Otto slouched against the table and said:

"Wouldn't it be wiser, boys, to cut out the confiscations? People will be staying here too, and someone will have to pay for them."

Akseli said, his eyes on the floor:

"It has to be done. How can we take care of such a mob of refugees... We need food and horses."

"Uhuh. I was just thinking... The worst of it is the business with the baron, though."

"The only ones involved in that are the ones who killed him. Let every one answer for his own deeds."

Janne was leaning against the stove plucking at a hair in a nostril without success, making little sounds as he thought things through. The hair did not come loose, and as if he were coming to, he rubbed his nose and said:

"What will you do with those prisoners then?"

"I'll set them free."

"Hand them over to Silander. They'll be a little trump in poor old Grandpa's hands."

"He can have them."

An awkward silence ensued. It was so troubling that Akseli thought of leaving. Osku broke the silence:

"Hey, old lady. Don't be sad."

He rose and began slamming and banging his things into a heap.

"What the devil good is thinking now..."

Anna responded with an angry complaint, but it eased the oppressive mood. Akseli rose and shook everyone by the hand. At the door he stopped and said rather clumsily , fumbling for words:

"I would ask you... if the boys get into something... to sort of look after them... I'll repay you... if there's a chance... See to it that you're in the church village by eleven at the latest."

He said the last words rapidly to Osku and left. On the rise in the yard stood Preeti with a rifle on his back.

"Are you on guard?"

"I'm sort of watching..."

"Give the rifle to Osku in the morning. Don't in any circumstances leave it at home... And tell them they forced you to join the Guard. And goodbye... try to get through this somehow."

Then he hurried his horse into a gallop. Because of his inexperience, he was forced to focus all his attention on the horse. It helped him to get rid of the images of Elina and the children, which kept forcing themselves into his mind.

IV

That night lights burned in every cottage and shanty in Pentti's Corner. And in every cottage and farmhouse they wept. Families scattered. What little money and food there was, was divided among those who were going and those who were staying. Plans were made to go and bow down to their lords and masters. Fearfully they went outside to listen to the roar of the cannon and the glare of fires on the southeastern horizon. And toward morning the strange humming from the direction of the main road grew stronger. And with the dawn its sounds could be distinguished, the rattle of wagons and the shouting.

They were awake at Töyry. The master was of two minds: to go off into the woods or to stay at home. His wife urged him to go, but he did not want to leave the house.

Nevertheless, he was fully dressed and went outside from time to time to listen and to look at the fires. Each time he returned, he would say:

"It sure seems to have moved, sort of."

His wife was uneasy. She went back and forth into the rooms of the house to see that nothing of value had been left in sight.

"What about that wall clock? Maybe we should put that away too."

"I don't think they'll take anything like that."

"If we could just get through this day... I've decided that I will go and take communion the first Sunday I can. My heart is so heavy with those ruffians..."

A stamping in the entry interrupted the woman's speech. Töyry hesitated for a while, then went to the door and opened it.

"Let's make a little trip to the headquarters."

Uuno Laurila was standing outside.

"What business would they have there in the middle of the night? I won't go until morning."

"You have to go. It's an order."

Töyry's wife was standing at the inner door, and when she heard Uuno's voice she too came out. Weeping, she begged that her husband be allowed to stay at home. Her pleas and complaints were extraordinarily bitter and angry. Her thin, pinched voice was thoroughly unsuited to melting pleas. Her husband kept on refusing to leave, but then Uuno took the rifle from his shoulder and said curtly:

"Well, if you don't come you'll die in that doorway."

Töyry went. He thrust his now hysterical wife back into the entry, but she followed them out to the yard screaming continually:

"Father... father... father..."

Töyry turned his head once to look back at Uuno, who was following him:

"I don't care about myself... but if you are a human being, you might think of her."

"Hurry up. Move it."

Before coming to the store, the road to Töyry ran through a small patch of woods, where Uuno ordered Töyry to stop:

"Think about some old matters a little bit... Now is the time to."

"I haven't... to my knowledge I haven't done anything wrong."

Töyry's voice shook and there was a trace of pleading in it. Uuno, on the other hand, spoke in an absolutely cold and steady tone of voice:

"You've been waiting for this day the way a horse waits for summer. But listen, you won't get to see this butchers' celebration day."

A bleating noise escaped Töyry. He took a few hasty steps, but then seemed to grasp the situation and stepped to the side of the road, pulling his fur hat down over his eyes. The second word of the Lord's prayer was cut off by the bang of the shot.

Uuno waited until the body stopped jerking and then walked off toward the village, but he returned after going a short distance and bent over to check the dead man's pockets. When he found nothing in them, he kicked the body and grumbled as he left:

"I might have known, the goddamned miser..."

When Töyry's wife heard the shot, she started running toward the village, but turned back and went to awaken the servants in their building in the yard.

"Jesus... Jesus... Jesus... Come quick... They took Father..."

In her shock, she used the word "Father," although she had always particularly avoided any kind of familiarity with the servants and so had always called her husband "Master," as an intuitive means of keeping the necessary distance from the servants in everyday dealings. The sleep-befogged servants did not quite know what was up, and without waiting for them, their mistress began running toward the village again. She was bareheaded and coatless. Panting and stumbling over her long skirts, she ran on, paying no heed to mud puddles. Perhaps she would not have noticed her husband's body if her eyes had not happened to spot his white shirtfront. She sank to her knees beside the corpse and stared at it like one awakening from sleep. In a pleading voice, she repeated:

"Father... say something... Father... I'm here... say something..."

Gradually she realized the senselessness of it, and sank weeping onto the body. Her hands were stained with blood, and when she pressed them to her tear-streaked cheeks, they too became stained with blood.

Staggering she returned to the house, where the servants stood helplessly in the yard. The body was fetched with a sleigh and carried onto a bed in the main room. Only in the lamplight indoors did the woman notice her bloody hands. A servant brought her water and she washed herself. They undressed her husband and wiped off his body with wet towels.

The servants vanished into the kitchen, for they were somewhat in dread of the corpse. Beside the bed the woman sat leaning and weeping over it. Feeling a cheek with her hand, she whispered:

"Cold... cold..."

Having calmed down, she began softly to sing a hymn. As she did so, her mind regained some degree of composure. When she stopped singing, she sat for a long time, her head atilt, staring at the face of the dead man. Then she went to the kitchen door:

"You come and see too, what a nice smile he has."

The servants came in and mumbled their agreement. Their mistress sat down on the chair again. The faintness of her voice seemed to cast doubt on the truth of her words.

"When I was singing the hymn... it was as if someone went to the head of the bed... I don't know what I thought I was seeing... but it was as if something white fluttered by... Did they come... to let me know... or was I seeing things. But if someone... then our father... near God... the best of men..."

As their mistress bowed her head, sobbing, the servants, troubled, crept from the room. She did not notice their departure, but went on talking to herself as she wept:

"Five heads will not pay for this... Really and truly, someone else could have died in his place... A curse-word never crossed his lips..."

Throwing herself on the body, she burst into uncontrolled weeping and blubbered:

"...maybe... he sometimes said... pa-pagan..."

V

From early morning on, a continuous stream of refugees poured through the church village. One wagon followed another so closely that those sitting on the one in front had to keep fending off the heads of horses from the one following. The men who were driving walked alongside the loads, and their families sat on bundles, wrappings, bedclothes, spinning wheels, sewing machines, dishes and grain sacks. The littlest ones, worn out from weeping, sat on their mothers' laps, and the bigger children, blue with cold, looked around with sober eyes, shocked by the strange developments. The clunking of the wagons, the pounding of horses' hoofs, the crying of children, their mothers' shushing lullabies, and the high-spirited romping of the young blended into one continuous roar.

An old man driving a horse asked one of the residents of the church village who was standing beside the road:

"Do you have any idea where they're taking us?"

"Aren't you supposed to be going to Russia?"

"Well, that's what they said... But they say you can't get there any more."

Alongside the stream of refugees galloped horses ridden by men of the

290

Red Guard, asking all kinds of questions:

"Where are the men from the Lautta headquarters?"

"The Lautta headquarters... We haven't heard of it... but there's supposed to be some headquarters behind us."

The rider jerked the reins of the horse so fiercely to turn it that the frightened animal pranced in place for a moment.

"Have those bastards run off too...?"

Jabbing his spurs into the sides of his mount, the man rode back to ask anew, but got the same answer.

In the morning, the movement within the church village increased. Groups of refugees from this very parish gathered in yards and open places with their escorts. People came and went. Horses, hay, grain, and goods from stores were confiscated, if there was anything left in them. Families gathered in some corner to spend their last hours together. Even at the last minute, someone could be heard to say:

"Maybe I should try to go and see the master..."

"You know what he'll say..."

Then there was a brief silence as they waited for the mind in which a small spark of hope had been kindled to submit.

"Wear your woolen nightshirt if you have to sleep out in the open..."

From the moment he arrived in the church village, Akseli had been busy. There was constant traffic through the doors of the workers' hall.

"Six families without horses are coming from Salmi. Where can we get animals for them?"

"From Salmi, of course. We don't have enough here."

"There's a family coming whose children have scarlet fever."

"Drive them back. They'll die on the way."

When the pressure increased during the morning, he began to drive away those who asked useless questions. And if he had a moment free, he growled:

"What the hell obligation do I have to take care of this by myself... No one is helping..."

The headquarters staff had disappeared. Several of them, as old men with families, stayed at home, not wanting to be visibly active at the last minute. During the night they had already sounded out their masters' inclinations. Many were doubtful, for refugees coming from conquered areas spoke of a bloodbath, but even the smallest spark of hope detained them. Hellberg had already left the previous day. He said he had been summoned by the Viipuri People's Committee, and ordered Akseli to take charge of the entire caravan.

Akseli had turned over the prisoners from the poorhouse to Silander.

Hearing threats that the prisoners would be executed when the refugees left, he had seen to it that they were taken to safety in the morning darkness. Silander chose a guard for them from among men who were staying, and Akseli could see how relieved he was.

"If something happens to them, it won't do for anyone to stay here."

Akseli himself knew that very well, nor was he sure that things would be any better even if the prisoners' safety were seen to. The crush of work, however, kept him from thinking of anything but the immediate task at hand. Only when the people from Pentti's Corner arrived and Osku told him of Töyry's murder, did he explode:

"What were you doing there? You were left to look after things."

The pointless accusation angered Oskari, and he said:

"How the devil could I watch every ass? Why are you talking that way, big man?"

After thinking for a while, Akseli said:

"Might it be better after all to go and get the boys?"

"What do the boys have to do with it?"

"Nothing... But will they ask about... And why didn't that blockhead at least go into hiding... And I didn't think... when Antto stayed I thought they wouldn't dare..."

He turned away and barked:

"Tell that goddamned scum to stay out of my sight..."

Osku left, and Akseli began writing confiscation orders. A couple of times his pen stopped:

"Should I still send a horse to get them? But how would Aku manage with that leg?"

Nor did departure seem any safer. A new front at the Kymi River had been planned, but although his inquiries had received vague answers, he knew it was doubtful that they would get to Russia, not to mention establishing a new front.

His pen began to move again. In his awkward schoolboy hand, one signature after another materialized. A. Koskela. Confirmed. Seal.

In the afternoon he began phoning nearby villages to ask the size of the stream of refugees. He had tried to get at least a general idea of the number of people and vehicles in their own caravan, and calculated roughly how long a stretch of road they would require. When he had to read the result in kilometers, even he was astounded. When he learned that there was a sizable gap in the line at one point, he sent a rider to stop the rear column at a bridge. The line could be closed up for a while before a crunch developed at the rear, and their group would have the stretch of road they needed.

When the road was clear, he gave the order to leave. From yards and hitching rails, one vehicle after another started out. People said goodbye and wept, but they tried to hide their tears, for to weep in the church village seemed too shameless. In addition, the shamefulness of tears and emotions had been instilled in their consciousness since childhood. A hand was extended, a face tried to assume an everyday expression:

"G'bye now."

Then lips moved, seeking some word of release, which was not to be found however. The load departed, and when the distance was sufficient so that one was no longer ashamed, a hand was waved on either part. The long road of suffering for the people of byway and hillside had begun.

Akseli stood beside the road checking the departure of the loads. Villages left in united groups, the members of the Guard traveling with the civilians in order to take care of their own families and relatives. When he judged the stretch of road to be long enough, Akseli sent word that the stoppage could be released. He had chosen young horsemen as messengers, in order to manage the long column with their help, but seeing old men traveling on foot in the crowd of refugees, out of some sense of shame he had given his own horse to a boy.

The last of the loads made the turn around the cooperative store, and Akseli set off walking behind them. From beside the gateposts an old woman stepped out onto the road. Shy and fearful, she mumbled:

"Sir Commander... may I... ask..."

Akseli stopped. The woman was clutching a clean handkerchief in her fist and was otherwise dressed in her best for her trip to the church village. She was apparently from some out-of-the-way community, and to her a Red Commander was a bigwig to be shy of. To Akseli's look she responded by asking humbly:

"What about coming back... Since two of our boys... They say that the leaders know..."

Akseli looked into her eyes, but he could not sustain the gaze. In her eyes was a distraught plea for some kind of hope, but he did not have the heart to tell her the truth, and even lying was difficult. Turning aside, he said as he left:

"When the situation settles down a little... it won't be long."

Looking back he saw the woman raise the handkerchief clutched in her fist to her eyes and walk away with her head bowed. The sight opened Akseli's mind to experience in a second what the day's uproar and haste had thrust into the background. The boys' blond hair and sober blue eyes flashed before his eyes. After a short distance, he turned and looked back again. The church and the church village always brought to mind a vague memory of red and blue paper covering a bottle cork. In his childhood, the church village had been associated in his consciousness with his father's liniment bottles.

It was a sunny afternoon. The spring of 1918 had come early. There was already green grass on the ground, and dust from the road hovered over the column.

The church tower gleamed in the sun. The sunlight seemed to gild everything they were leaving.

He turned to go and did not look back again.

CHAPTER NINE

I

In the evening the last of the Red Guard units marched through the parish. After that a silence reigned in the villages. There were no travelers to be seen on the roads and no sound of human voices. Everyone withdrew into himself. In the cottages of the Reds, a silent, gnawing fear prevailed. The whole northern horizon seemed to exude a threat of death. The masters and the farm owners also remained in hiding or shut up in their houses.

The only sound in the villages that night was the barking of dogs.

Antto Laurila was hidden in the attic of his sauna. Kankaanpää carried food into his hay barn. Emma Halme urged her husband to hide too, but Halme was reluctant. Emma suggested the root cellar as a place of concealment. It was filled with straw, and one could hide there. After hesitating for a long time, Halme agreed to crawl in under the roof, where he dug a hollow for himself. Emma gave him a blanket, which he spread on the floor.

Soon, however, he clambered out from under the roof, brushing the straw and dirt from himself. He was troubled and confused about this plan of concealment. Lying in the top part of the root cellar seemed so ridiculous that he had agreed to it with great reluctance, and only at Emma's insistence. The couple stayed awake late into the evening. Halme sat absorbed in thought. To Emma's painful conjectures, he replied with consoling remarks, making light of the whole matter. He refused to eat, insisting that he was not hungry. But his reason for not eating kept running through his mind.

"If the worst happens... it will be easier... The weaker the body... the more ready the soul..."

To Emma he spoke in generalizations, not revealing the relevance of his remarks:

"There is a saying, 'A sound mind in a sound body.' At one time I believed it myself. But it seems to me that there is no soul at all in a sound body... That kind of statement may arise from the fact that the name of soul is given to all human mental activity... But that isn't always closely related to the soul... I would say that in human beings, only that is soul which is ready at any given moment to separate from matter..."

He was happy that he still felt weak as an aftermath of his illness.

"For the soul is there for the sake of immortality."

He kept repeating the pet ideas that had taken possession of his mind in his later years.

"Fear. Well, fear is the feeling which reveals the extent of our wretchedness. Only our material being feels fear. To a pure soul, on the other hand, it is a non-existent conception, since it can deprive us of nothing."

Emma did not participate in these monologues. From time to time, Halme went outdoors to listen to the silent night. Restlessly he paced around the yard in the spring evening, breathing a heavy, constricted sigh from time to time.

They went to bed late. Years ago they had moved their twin beds to opposite walls, beds with high ends, decorated with knobs turned on lathes, which the young master tailor had obtained as an indication of his superiority when preparing "our common nest."

In the early hours of the morning, Halme rose and sat on the side of his bed.

"Emma."

"What?"

"Would it bother you if I sang a little?"

Emma rose uneasily.

"Why would you sing?"

"I don't know. I'm restless. I can't get to sleep. It always calms me down..."

Halme began a hymn. Emma lay down again and turned toward the wall to hide her tears. The thin, shaky voice grew gradually stronger:

> *A wretched worm, a traveler only,*
> *many the troublesome road I have trod.*
> *Estranged, I searched for my fatherland,*
> *my evening hours will soon be at hand.*
> *Not to my sorrow, I have no home here,*
> *I hasten there to the land of my hope,*
> *where rest eternal enshrouds me.*

Halme moved his chair to the corner of the room and sat with his face turned toward it. His lips nearly touching the wall, he continued to sing, shifting his head until he found the best distance from the corner, where his voice was altered by the echo; it took on a tone that reminded one of an organ playing in the distance.

> *Life here is a shadow, a dream,*
> *restless as a roaring rapids,*
> *disappearing in sands like the water.*

The song did indeed calm his agitated nerves. The tuneful vibration of his skull raised his spirits, and he felt a kind of well-being tinged with melancholy.

Having finished the song, he lay down again. But the recently achieved peace did not last long. He tossed in his bed, then got up a couple of times and walked from window to window. But the dawning morning was completely inscrutable. There was nothing to be seen or heard.

Otto Kivivuori stood in his yard watching two riders who were cautiously approaching along the road. He went to the gate, whereupon the two rode more boldly up to him. They kept their rifles trained on him at all times. They were young men, twenty years old at the most, and when one of them spoke, there was an intentional manly gruffness in his voice, with which he covered up a shade of fear.

"What geezer are you?"

"I'm just a man named Kivivuori."

"Are there Reds in the village?"

"They already left yesterday."

"If you're lying, you die."

"Go and look for yourself if you don't believe me."

The boys continued to point their rifles at Otto. It was plain to see that they did not enjoy holding and pointing rifles. When a white-capped mounted officer appeared around a corner, followed by a marching column of fours, the two riders waved to them and rode forward. Otto remained at the roadside to watch, and the officer riding by repeated the question about Reds. His marching men were mostly young boys, whose faces were grumpy with strain and fatigue.

Some of the men looked at Otto as they marched by, but most of them paid no attention to him. They were dressed in pretty much the same way. Most of them wore gray army overcoats, but there were also civilian clothes to be seen, and even a few visored caps. Many of them were wearing fur hats, and drops of sweat ran from beneath them, streaking their dirty faces.

"Hey, Yliluoma. Give me a drink of water."

"What the hell water-carrier do you think I am."

"Kiss my..."

The newcomers took a break on the manor hill. Some people gathered around to stare at them curiously, and when the news of their presence spread, the vicar arrived with his wife. Noticing that they were gentry, the officer rode over and saluted. The vicar's wife wept as she greeted him, and kept repeating:

"How we have waited for you... How we have waited for you..."

Then she asked the officer if he knew an infantryman named Salpakari, who had gone to Germany, for she imagined that all the Whites knew Ilmari. But the officer shook his head and repeated the name:

"I have probably heard the name but I don't remember. Perhaps he isn't on this front but somewhere else. They've been scattered throughout the army."

The vicar was moved. He had come home only that night. The traces of his imprisonment could be seen plainly on his face. It was thin and gray, and the tense sleeplessness of the last nights had increased his weariness. He turned to the nearest soldier and began speaking, but gradually raised his voice, intending his speech for the entire company.

"Good soldiers and Sir officer. I am the minister of this parish, and by virtue of that position, I wish to welcome you. Welcome you noble sons of Ostrobothnia, you descendants of free men, who have demonstrated that your fathers' spirit still lives in you. The free farmer of this country, whose neck has never bowed to the yoke of slavery to the land, has risen up. Fear of God, love of his native land, and respect for the law still live beneath the homespun coat of the Finnish farmer."

The soldiers looked at the ground as the vicar spoke, and their expression of sober bitterness, caused by weariness, intensified. The vicar's wife went to the manor to speak to the baroness, who had sunk into a state of apathetic dullness after her husband's death. She had taken to her bed, and was almost visibly drying up and wasting away. When the vicar's wife announced the arrival of the Whites, the baroness seemed totally indifferent. The vicar's wife asked if milk from the manor could be given to the soldiers, and she agreed with equal indifference. She did not seem even to understand the matter properly. The vicar's wife went to speak to the overseer, who gave the servants orders to distribute the milk. The milk cans roused the soldiers from their numbness. The vicar's wife herself began to hand out the milk busily and enthusiastically, while farther off the vicar spoke to the officer.

His wife poured out the milk for the men, who, sullen and ill at ease, listened to what she said, and quickly disappeared with their mess kits, disconcerted in the presence of a fine lady and her admiring and friendly remarks:

"Here is something for a Finnish soldier. Alas, are you wounded?"

The soldier, who had a bandage on his hand, mumbled in confusion:

"A little scratch..."

He ducked quickly behind the others. Having drunk their milk, the soldiers looked for a possible second helping:

"Let's get in line again. That old woman won't remember our faces."

"That devil is bound to spot us with those popeyes of hers."

More milk was brought, the yield of one entire milking at the manor, and soldiers even filled their canteens for future use. Then the officer ordered them to fall in, and raising their weapons, the men formed ranks.

"Forward, march."

With a salute, the officer spurred his horse and took his place at the head of the marching column as the pair waved a farewell.

In the afternoon the Töyry brothers arrived in the village. The members of the Civil Guard hidden in the woods had gone to meet the Whites as soon as the front began to move and now arrived with them in the parish. Aaro went to the church village with a horse and brought back weapons. That same night the arrests began. Even the master of Kylä-Pentti appeared with a rifle on his shoulder and a white ribbon on his sleeve, but he did not take part in the arrests, merely guarding the prisoners at the fire hall where they were brought together. The arrests were carried out by the Töyry brothers and the storekeeper. The manor overseer also took up a rifle, his Swedish citizenship notwithstanding. The foreman, who had been forced into many dealings with the Reds in connection with the confiscations and had borne many insults, accompanied them enthusiastically.

First they brought in Antto Laurila, who had been found immediately in the sauna attic. Arvo Töyry had ordered him to come down, put a Mauser to his temple, and asked:

"Where is Uuno?"

"You must know that he's gone."

"It doesn't matter. He won't get far enough away so that he won't be found. And I tell you Antto, that you're going through that narrow gate."

Arvo was calm and controlled. The words came from him with entire calmness, but they were translucent with a hatred that no show of emotion could purge. Antto glowered at the earth and said:

"Well, go ahead and shoot. Why walk me around for nothing?"

"You'll have a little time to think about it. Start walking, you bull."

Kankaanpää's hiding place was also located. Through the window, Halme saw him being taken away, and Emma urged him to hide quickly. Halme walked back and forth uneasily with a divided mind, and finally consented to go into the root cellar. He went down on all fours and crawled in among the straws. His position was as uncomfortable as possible, and on top of everything, he hit his head on a roofing nail that had come through a crosspiece. Emma placed some straws over the hatch.

"I'll tell them that you followed the others at night in case they've heard that you didn't go with them."

Halme lay sprawled on his belly, the scent of incipiently rotting straw in his nostrils. In a minute he was thoroughly fed up with his position and the whole hiding place.

He clambered back out and replied to Emma's panicky questions:

"First of all, there's hardly any use in it. They are sure to find me. And I haven't done anything for which I should have to hide."

He went into the house and took off his overcoat. Emma begged him to eat something, but he refused. He drank a little honey mixed with water, but he would not abandon his fast. When they heard from the yard the sound of a group of men approaching, he forced himself to be calm, and assumed a more dignified expression. Arvo had left the conduct of the matter to his uncle, for because of his youth, he was a little shy of confronting Halme. The storekeeper had no such inhibitions.

"Uhuh, uhuh. Throw on some clothes, Halme, and let's go."

Halme stood up, looked at the men for a moment, and then said:

"Are you looking for me?"

"Didn't I say so already. Let's get going."

"But why so many men and rifles. You know that my principles forbid me to fight."

"Is that so, ha, ha. Well, let's go anyway."

Emma did not make a scene of any sort, but controlled herself, knowing that Halme would regard any demonstration as unfitting and unworthy. She offered him some food, but Halme took nothing but a little honey. As they walked toward the fire hall, Halme still had his cane under his arm, for he would not surrender it even on this journey.

Because of its out-of-the-way location, Koskela was left to the last. The men went first to the old place and Arvo asked Elina:

"Is Akseli gone?"

"Yes."

Noticing the men coming, Elina, urged by an instinctive cunning, had taken the little boy into her arms. It increased her feeling of security, for she felt a vague fear for her own person, and tried to withstand the harsh looks of the men calmly.

"But the boys are at home."

"They must be there."

A nasty smile flickered on the storekeeper's face:

"What about it now, I say. Does Elina know where our goods are? I mean the ones that Akseli confiscated."

At first Elina did not understand what he meant, and she replied:

"As far as I know, Akseli hasn't confiscated anything."

"Yeah, uhuh. I just happen to have a lot of those theft papers with Akseli's name on them. We've come to check up, and if we find any of my goods here, I tell you things won't be very nice for you either..."

Now Elina understood. Her voice a mixture of weeping and indignation, she said, plucking nervously at the child's swaddling bands as if calling the men's attention to them:

"You can check all you want to... We've never lived by robbery here."

"Well, well. Let's be a little... For three months, I say, there's been robbing and stealing and not much else... Different men are running things now. Elina should take that into account. There will be no more orders from your side, so it would be better, I mean, if you changed your tune a little."

Elina was not made of heroic stuff. She was timid and shy, but indignation made her say hotly:

"Go ahead and search. We have no locks anywhere. Every place is open... and if you want, here I am... with the children."

The last words of defiance were immediately succeeded by fear. She squeezed little Voitto tightly in her arms and looked at the boys, who, withdrawn into a corner, were looking at the riflemen.

The men went over to the new place.

"Uhuh, boys. Let's take a little trip to the church village then."

The boys began to dress. Jussi sat gloomily on the bench, trying to start speaking, which was very difficult for him.

"As far as I know, the boys have done no wrong, so there's no point in taking them..."

The men did not act harshly here, since respect for Jussi restrained them. Arvo mumbled a little evasively:

"If nothing, then... Everyone's affairs will be checked... that's all..."

Alma prepared a package of food. She appealed for Aku to be left because of his leg, but the storekeeper said that if he was unable to walk, a ride would be sent for. Then Arvo added as they were leaving:

"I can't say about the boys. But I tell you this, even if it isn't your affair, that it won't be good for Akseli to show up..."

Jussi and Alma did not reply. The boys said goodbye, and Alma put a fifty-markka piece in Aleksi's hand.

"If you need it. We will come and see you."

Aku took his cane and went ahead of the others, limping. Aleksi followed with his package of food under his arm. Vilho and Eero stood watching from the steps of the old place.

"Hi boys," said Aku, but they did not reply because of the visitors. Aku took a few steps, but then stopped again.

"Vilho, come here."

The boy came hesitantly, scowling continually at the riflemen.

"This is for you."

It was his uncle's bone-handled jackknife with two blades, a large and a small one, a corkscrew and the tiniest of clawbars. Aku had noticed that the boy would like to have had the knife, although he had said nothing, for he never asked for anything. He gave Vilho the knife. The boy clutched it in his fist and ran back to the steps beside Eero. From there the two watched the group of men until it disappeared around the corner of the threshing barn. Later the boys recalled the sight well, for it was the last image of their uncles in their memory. Uncle Akusti always returned to mind in just that form, walking stiff-legged with a cane, and Uncle Aleksi with the food package under his arm!

The boys hurried inside. When their mother wept and did not exactly notice them, Vilho clung to her knees and said:

"Mother... uncles went with the gunmen..."

Made shy by their mother's weeping, the boys tried to break loose when Elina drew them to her skirts and said:

"They will come back..."

But although she tried to control herself, afraid that she would frighten the boys, her body shook with weeping as she stared over the boys she had drawn into her arms.

II

Ilmari arrived home at the parsonage. He came on horseback, leaped directly from the saddle to the steps, and ran straight into the house. A bout of hugging and weeping followed, during a pause in which Ilmari asked:

"Is everything OK... Where is Ani... Has anything happened to you?"

His mother did not answer, but kept on repeating something unclear, so that Ilmari began to wonder if something might have happened to Ani, since she was not present. His father finally managed to explain that Ani was in Helsinki and that thus all the members of the family were safe. When his mother was at last able to speak rationally, her first question was how long the boy would stay:

"You could stay a week... or two weeks..."

"I can stay only till evening. I'm here by permission of my commanding officer."

"How did you happen to come right here... as if you were guided."

"It didn't just happen. I asked to get into these troops."

For a long time, the parents were so muddled they did not know what to ask first:

"What rank do you have? Is that a major's or a captain's insignia?"

"It's a lieutenant's rank... A Finnish name and the Finnish language are no recommendations when it comes to promotion."

An expression brought on by some annoying and unpleasant memory crossed Ilmari's face. For his parents, the lieutenant's rank was quite sufficient. Their son was somehow of the age to be a lieutenant. Major and captain were somehow more commonplace, and such ranks were not befitting a hero. Heroes were always lieutenants.

Neither of them had any notion of what a war is. They imagined their son as a kind of Lieutenant Zidén, riding into battle against the enemy with his sword raised on high. The image brought to their minds a subconscious memory of Edelfelt's illustrations for *The Tales of Ensign Stål*.

The discussion was scattered because there were so many things to talk about. Ilmari answered his mother's and father's naive questions politely. They kept looking him over ceaselessly. Even his father's voice took on a note of humility and respect, and he accepted his son's opinions without qualification.

The vicar's wife saw to it that foods which she remembered Ilmari had liked the most were prepared for him. But she did not linger long in the kitchen and soon returned to the parlor. She studied her son's expressions and gestures, enjoying even the most minute of them. It felt as if all her wishes had been fulfilled at once. Ilmari was wearing a green infantry uniform with leather leggings and spurs on his shoes.

How manly the set of his mouth was. And how a brush haircut became him.

For his part, Ilmari was interested in his parents' adventures during the rebellion, and the vicaress proudly told of his father's speech at the baron's funeral. His father was modest and said quietly to indicate that there was more to the matter than a mere speech:

"Speaking wasn't difficult. The difficulty was to achieve the state of mind where one could speak."

"But I refused to accept their travel permits. I didn't take one until I had to, in order to see your father in prison. And they threatened to make me clean the toilets, but I promised to do that before I would take their permits."

"Who threatened you with that?"

"Akseli Koskela. He was all-in-all here. He ordered all the robberies. And he sent two young men to the church village from here to be killed. And Töyry's wife said that Laurila's boy spoke of an order from headquarters when he came to get his father. I don't doubt it at all. I've always known there's something horrible about him... Something beastly... Have you ever seen him smile? Do you remember anything like that?"

No one remembered.

That led to a discussion of other murders by the Reds, about which news had already reached them. The first White newspapers had described them in detail, and the vicar was especially affected by the murder of many clergymen. Superficially, his words did not convey that information, for a thirst for revenge did not suit his position and attitudes, but when he recalled the details of the murders he had read, he could not control his hatred:

"I don't care how I was treated. I have no right to feel personal hatred. But when old, honored shepherds of souls... who have sacrificed their lives for the good of the congregation. No, no... not for my sake. But no matter how you look at it. One cannot even understand such savagery... But when pure hate has been sown for some twenty years. Hate, hate, day after day. Not for my sake, but one has to ask, has society the right to be merciful now?"

Ilmari's stance was calmer, for it was more direct. There was no sign of emotional turmoil in him, merely a cold, observant practicality, along with a sense of aristocratic superiority. His lips were tightly pursed as he sliced the meat, and he emphasized his words slightly, giving them the same energy required in cutting the meat.

"Such questions are pointless. The stink of the Russians has infected them and that's enough. We have only one law for such types: line them up and shoot them. I haven't run over the heaths of Lockstedt and crouched in the marshes of Courland in order to come here and ponder whether we should be merciful to traitors."

The father sensed this dispassionate ruthlessness in the boy, and felt himself somehow smaller and more insignificant, since he himself was never able to relate to matters in such a straightforward way. Besides, he felt the boy had outgrown his former self. In earlier discussions he had been somehow evasive and uncertain, but now their relationship seemed to have been reversed. But that did not trouble the father; on the contrary he admired the boy and felt proud of him. When the lad had been younger, he had often worried about his nature. Now he felt the proud joy of a father. In the midst of it all, he was able to imagine himself in some esteemed group with his son. When the boy spoke, he listened as if to the word of God, and his mind was tickled by the boy's aristocratic self-confidence.

"We believe that we cannot afford to divide the land among them again. We have come and found it a nest of anarchists. We need spurs and curb bits here. We will organize along military lines, and we'll see if this may yet become a state. Even among the bourgeoisie there seem to be a lot of people who need to be told: Line up in a column of fours, and then left, left, hup, two, three. Down with the nonsense about the rule of the people. All this stems largely from the fact that we haven't had an army. The people have no concept of discipline. And above all, its leaders have not understood the leader's stance. They want people to obey, but don't know how to command. All politicians should be called into army service during the summer. We infantrymen will teach them how to govern a country."

The father was somewhat troubled by the boy's words, but he was not offended. After all, it was his son speaking.

"Yes, youth is often looked down upon, but few young people have gone through the kind of school you have. Undoubtedly the responsibility for the country will rest on your shoulders... Certainly... certainly we older people have been badly mistaken. We have almost thrust the right to vote upon them, and spoiled them... Indeed, one who grows up without discipline dies without honor... How true it is. It applies so well to these people."

"In any case, they will die without honor."

His father sighed sorrowfully, out of a sense of duty toward his ministerial office:

"Indeed... what misfortune they have brought upon themselves."

His mother took little part in the discussion. She herself waited on the table, for she did not want the servants to disturb their togetherness. She merely looked at the boy. How manly the creasing of his eyebrows when they drew together over his eyes as he pondered some answer to a question of his father's. She was seldom silent, but on this occasion her entire soul was topsy-turvy. She contented herself with merely nodding as the father spoke:

"Of course you will do as you see fit. And there's no point in even talking about continuing your studies after so long a time... And we now need soldiers much more crucially than we need lawyers."

They linked the entire future of the country with the boy's future, and the vicar said:

"The young country badly needs a work force now in all areas."

That ended the discussion of affairs of state, and they returned to more commonplace matters. Ilmari rose from the table, and his parents listened enchanted to the sound of his spurs. All the refinement they had achieved was now banal in the face of this martialism and their esteem for it. For now spurs were jingling in their dining room. And had he not actually commanded the boys from Vaasa like Lieutenant Zidén.

Ilmari straightened out his green uniform after having sat in it. He jerked at its tails, straightened up, and twisted his neck a little inside his collar.

"Mother, do I have any underwear here, or were they all left in Helsinki? Mine are so dirty, and besides there are some alte Kameraden in them."

"Bless us. You don't mean you have vermin?"

"What soldier doesn't have lice? But I wouldn't like to leave them here."

His father had been wearing Ilmari's underwear, and he turned over a pair of his own to the boy. Mother and father gazed in admiration at the boy's dirty underwear. Their soldier son had vermin! The dirty undershirt and pants were taken out to the garden and burned.

"Look at that. There's a real old one. With the Iron Cross on his back too."

"Ugh! How could you stand to be in such clothes... Do you have an Iron Cross?"

"No, I didn't even have a chance to get one. The Swedish boys saw to that. But my buddies came to a hot end. I pity my old comrades... you are flesh of my flesh and blood of my blood..."

The comment was followed by a delighted laugh from mother and father.

Before the boy left, the telephone rang and the vicar went to answer it.

"Indeed he is... Many thanks... Yes, we are so happy in the midst of all this grief... Yes, that would make us very happy... I'll have to ask him."

"That was the master of Yllö. He asked me first to congratulate you. He said that the parish should arrange an official party for you when there is an opportunity... He recommends some kind of post command or something for you ..."

"I'm in the service and no landlord can decree that I be made a commander. And I don't under any circumstances want to be anything of the sort."

But the thought was so pleasing to the parents that they tried to persuade the boy to agree. The security force headquarters could take care of the formalities. The boy refused bluntly. On the one hand, he would like to have stayed at home, but the plan did not fit in with the great future he visualized for himself.

"A command. I would miss my opportunity."

"But the war is over. You can no longer accomplish anything there... Stay home now... I've waited three years for this and now you're leaving..."

The master of Yllö had taken care of the matter. Ilmari was ordered to organize the parish Civil Guard, and to supervise the call-up of recruits, specifically because he knew the locality. Ilmari did not resist forcefully, since the command was temporary and would last only until the Civil Guard were organized. And the war, since it would in fact end soon, did not offer many opportunities. He still had to go to his unit, but on the following evening, he was already being addressed as commander in the church village.

The empty cells in the poorhouse filled up. There were not enough of them even to hold all the officers. Prisoners began to be collected in its fenced-in yard. Man after man was thrust through the gates. Silent, shivering with cold, having already gone hungry for a day, the prisoners stood freezing in the yard. At night they tried to sleep huddled together, but another's body-warmth did not suffice against the chill of the spring night. In soft whispers, rumors spread within the compound.

"Security force headquarters is checking everything. Men in positions of responsibility will be kept in prison, but the rest will be freed to go to work."

"Mellola said that everyone who belonged to the staff will be shot."

"They won't be shot. The Germans have issued an order not to. That if even one man is shot, they will go and leave the butchers in the lurch."

Preeti Leppänen was jailed too, but within a day he was put on a work detail. He was even allowed to go home and to have other liberties. The men of the Civil Guard considered him a fool, even gave him a soldier's cap, and Preeti told people he was in the army.

Women were imprisoned as well. It was whispered among the group from Pentti's Corner that Aliina Laurila had been brought to the "women's side." On the third evening Wolf-Kustaa was thrust into the compound, and acquaintances rushed up to ask him the cause of his imprisonment. Kustaa did not explain. He withdrew into the farthest corner and sat there. Knees drawn up to his mouth and arms wrapped around his calves, he sat immo-bile like a wolf fallen into a trap, and when people from Pentti's Corner tried to talk to him, he drove them off with a couple of curses.

Kustaa had wound up in the compound because of his gun, and had come within a hair's breadth of losing his life. On the very first day, a proclamation had been nailed to walls, which ordered everyone to turn in all weapons to the Civil Guard on pain of execution. When Kustaa's rifle did not appear, and since its existence was known, the storekeeper went to get it. The door was hooked on the inside, and Kustaa barked in answer to the storekeeper's knock:

"Why the hell are you banging around people's houses?"

"You have to give your gun to the Civil Guard."

"To hell with your Civil Guard. No one takes my gun. It's mine and it will stay mine."

When the storekeeper began to press the matter, the barrel of the rifle appeared in the window:

"I won't give you my gun, but you'll get the charge from it if you don't leave right now."

The storekeeper left as fast as he could, for he did not doubt Kustaa's word. But later in the evening they went in a group. They advanced in a careful skirmish line, taking shelter behind rocks.

"Here's how it is now, Kustaa. If you don't open your door, we'll let fly through it... The laws are in force again..."

Kustaa had time to fire his muzzleloader once without hitting anyone, before Arvo Töyry got in through the window and laid hands on his uncle. But only when the manor foreman rushed in was the wildly struggling Kustaa subdued.

Then he was taken through the village with a man on either arm. Kustaa's oft-patched pants were short, so that between the dirt-black foot rags sticking out of his shoes and his pants cuffs, a piece of his grime-encrusted legs could be seen. At brief intervals he would dig his hob-nailed clodhoppers into the ground, but the foreman would jerk him into motion. Behind them came the storekeeper with Kustaa's gun on his shoulder, babbling:

"Now I tell you... There is to be no more bucking society... Everything will be put in order now... It was a bad business, Kustaa... That shot could have killed someone... and I don't know... just shooting like that may be a capital crime... Society is in the saddle now."

People watched the procession fearfully from their windows, and it further increased their sense of oppression. If even Kustaa was taken, who would be spared? And seeing the people, Kustaa roared:

"Look at that goddamned black marketeer taking my gun... He used to trade on the black market and now he's started stealing..."

"I... I... I'll tell you only once that society won't listen to that kind of talk."

It was Ilmari who saved Kustaa's life. Those at the Civil Guard headquarters were firmly convinced that Kustaa should be shot as a warning to others, above all for his disobedience and his armed resistance.

Ilmari understood the comic side of the affair, which the landlords could not comprehend. The idea of shooting was abandoned, but rather than being released, Kustaa was led to the enclosure. And there he sat like some pagan idol, sullen and solitary, indifferent to the cold and hunger.

On the third day the prisoners got a small piece of bread. Their family members circled the fence with food, but the guards drove them away. Sometimes a slippery-moving little boy or girl got up close to the fence.

A whisper ran through the group of prisoners:

"Lehtonen... Lehtonen here."

The child handed her father a package through the fence and whispered, looking fearfully toward the guard:

"Mother told me to tell you that the master said we have to get off their land."

Small feet flashed in hasty retreat, nor did the child hear her father's faint shout:

"Go and ask... if maybe in Kantola's sauna room... they have their own lot."

"The field court will sit in the county building."

The rumor increased the gravity of the expression on the faces of the prisoners. Soon, pale and sleepless, they began a trek from the poorhouse to the county building and back again, with a rifleman on either side.

The court consisted of a certain judge, described as a military judge, along with Yllö, Mellola, Pajunen, and with Lieutenant Granlund as a member of the armed forces. The last was a brother of the apothecary's wife and a deserter from the Russian army. The same group served both as prosecutors and as the sentencing agency, for the same landlords served on both, nor were the death sentences actually decided upon in open court, but by the landlords in private discussions. There, ideas and opinions were crystallized, which were then made public via the headquarters and the court. The first case handled was that of Silander, for whom the death penalty was demanded. The landlords were slightly troubled. It had not been many days ago that they had thanked him for their safety and their lives. The judge and the military representative soon dissipated the landlords' doubts. Lieutenant Granlund was a particularly eager advocate of the death penalty. When the landlords half-heartedly testified to Silander's moderation and his actions on behalf of the White prisoners, the Lieutenant said in his broken Finnish:

"Is him a Red or ain't him? Is him a Red or ain't him?"

"Well, he has had the Red spirit from the very beginning."

The Lieutenant remembered a certain autumn day in the Kiev railway station when a drunken gang of soldiers had made him touch the ground with his forehead and say three times: "I am a pig." For days thereafter he had contemplated suicide, unable to eat or sleep, with the soldiers' mockery and laughter ringing in his ears. And there had been many people watching.

"Him a leader and agitator. Who come to die if not him?"

"Right. He helped the Whites out of fear. If he had won, what would have happened to us?"

So Silander had to die. He came out into the hallway as white as a sheet. To the questioning looks of those awaiting their turns, he could answer only by pointing to his forehead. From then on the men knew there was no point in entertaining vain hopes.

The judge was staying at Yllölä, and after Silander's sentencing, the anxious families of the prisoners tried to get to speak to him. Finally it was necessary to station guards before Yllo's steps. And a constant stream of farm owners kept appearing at the headquarters.

"That's what he said. They took three loads of hay. Here are the slips. You can see what robbers they are. He has no business being a member of society any longer. You can give him his last dose of medicine. And he cursed so vilely in our house."

Töyry's widow also went to the headquarters and to Yllölä. The judge himself received her out of respect for her grief. She wept after a while and said to the judge:

"No better man could be found... Not a Sunday went by that he didn't listen to me read the Word of God... If we didn't go to church... And a beggar never had to leave without a slice of bread..."

"Do you know if there was talk of this matter at their headquarters? Did you hear of any threats from there?"

"I know they were in back of it. That head agitator, the one who really whipped them up. Lying sick to death, but still able to carry out murders... But that gang urged the boy on too... He didn't have anything against us... He was in jail, that was nothing... That wife there is a real... She has behaved so shamelessly to me..."

The woman wept and blubbered:

"Five lives won't pay for this..."

As he spoke to the woman, Yllö's dry face assumed a sad and sympathetic expression.

"Kalle was enough of a good friend to me that they will pay for it. We were like brothers. And I don't recall that we ever had any differences of opinion about county matters. Nor about the congregation either. But what about Koskela there? We've thought about evicting that boy's family. Doesn't old Koskela have his own place to live there?"

"He has. And you should send that family so far away that they won't be seen or heard. He was the one who asked us about guns in the very beginning and threatened our boys."

"It's been said that he announced publicly that he would no longer do any rent work. That means breach of contract, and the law no longer applies. The father can stay, of course. To my knowledge, he is a decent man and has opposed his son."

"But he's been a leech on the congregation too. He's swindled woods and pastures from the parsonage."

That evening Janne Kivivuori asked to speak to the court. After a brief hesitation he was admitted to Yllölä. The master told him to sit down, but asked in a forbidding, official tone of voice:

"What is Kivivuori's business?"

"I came to say a few things about my father-in-law's sentencing and a little bit about this whole court procedure."

"What is there to say about them?"

"There is a lot to be said. First of all, their legality is questionable, and secondly, it would be nice to know the basis for my father-in-law's sentence."

Yllö had hastily explained the nature of Janne's legal career to the war judge before he entered, and the judge asked:

"What basis is there for your claim?"

First of all, the constitution of the tribunal. There are out-and-out plaintiffs as members of it. Or are you going to argue that the master is an unbiased judge in this affair?"

"Heh, heh. Can Kivivuori find a law-abiding citizen in this country who is not in some way a plaintiff? Who among them has been spared from this banditry?"

"Then you should postpone the judgments for a little while. Until feelings have cooled down a little. And besides, isn't it true that crimes against the state are tried in the Court of Appeals and not in this sort of field court? As to my father-in-law, no matter how strong your legal rights may be, it is hard to find the basis for the sentence in the law. The clauses dealing with death sentences do not apply to him. He has not killed anyone or taken part in a murder, he has not usurped judicial authority, nor even municipal authority, but took it on only upon pressure from the Guard, partly because there was no one else to do it."

"Heh, heh. It was hard to exercise authority when we were driven from the county building with rifles."

"So it was. But my father-in-law was not there driving you. He did take power from the usurpers, but under extremely mitigating circumstances."

"This time matters are such that Kivivuori can stop twisting the law. Does Kivivuori remember ordering people to bare their heads to criminals sentenced by the court? That was an incitement to crime, and since you are a lawyer, you ought to know what the law says about that."

"It says nothing on the matter. It was an action taken during an eviction by which I prevented a dangerous scuffle from developing. But to return to the Silander case. If the sentence is carried out, it will be a judicial murder."

Janne was ordered to leave. He went, but said at the door:

"The master has reportedly said that socialism will be laid so low that it will not rise again in a hundred years. But the directions to judges say nothing about laying socialism low, so that the master has rather a wrong conception of his office. And that is the greatest illegality. Go ahead and push things to the limit. There will be bodies and graves to bury them in, but that will not kill socialism. But you will get to do what makes you happy."

With a sly smile, he added from the door:

"I have wisely steered clear of the rebellion. I have even opposed it much more openly than the masters have dared to do. Therefore I am a law-abiding citizen with a good reputation, and have some degree of practical legal experience. I would really be a much more suitable member of this court than Mellola, for example, whose legal knowledge is based upon the fact that he was sentenced last winter for breaking the law. So you might consider changes in the constitution of the court. Or what do you think?"

"If I recall, I ordered Kivivuori to leave."

At home, Janne sat sad and sullen. Sanni's hysterical outburst of weeping had already abated somewhat. Her husband did not console her, but growled:

"What good does that howling do?"

He did, however, try to calm his son with a few playful words. When the Civil Guard arrived, he said with a nasty laugh:

"It took you a long time although it isn't far."

When one of the men's bayonets struck the door frame, Janne said:

"Don't mess up your walking stick."

"Shut your mouth for once."

"Don't you order me around."

In the dark yard there was the sound of a rifle bolt opening and closing as the man put a cartridge into the barrel.

"Will you keep your mouth shut?"

That time it did stay shut. His angry captors pushed Janne so violently into the enclosure that he had to take a few steps to keep from falling on his face.

Halme was half-led to the county building, for he was staggering from hunger and fatigue. Actually it was only a fever that kept him upright, which he had developed while shivering in the compound, and which stimulated the last shreds of his vitality. Stand he could not, but he asked for a chair. One was brought to him.

The fever elevated his state of mind into a kind of wavering unreality, in which everything seemed somehow insignificant to him. On hearing of Silander's death sentence, he was at first upset, but soon regained his equilibrium. He understood that there was no use in defending himself because of the nature of the judgment, so he concentrated completely on maintaining his composure.

"Do you admit to having gone to the manor on the fourth of March at about three or four in the afternoon?"

"I did go there at about that time. I don't exactly remember the day."

"What did you discuss with the baron?"

"The organization of work on the manor... spring planting and the organization of the work force."

"And what else?"

"I remember asking him to sign a binding agreement which was demanded of him."

"Did you quarrel?"

"Not on my part. The master baron did get excited, but then he had quite a temper. I remember that he was offended by my suggestion... I did present it courteously."

"Did you threaten the baron?"

"That has never been my custom."

"According to the account of the servants, you were heard to say something like this to the baron: 'I warn the baron not to provoke the people. Anything might happen.'"

"It is impossible for me to remember my exact words. But I may have said something of the sort, because I had heard rumors of murders in different places. In my opinion, I was doing my duty in warning him..."

"Does it also follow from this that it was also your duty to phone the church village headquarters? Ahlgren, a member of the staff, states thus: 'Headquarters received a call from Tailor Halme of the Pentti's Corner staff. Former member of the parliament Hellberg answered the phone. From his words, Ahlgren got the impression that the intention was to send some men from the investigation unit to search for weapons and demand his signature.' Do you claim that your own comrade's testimony is a lie?"

"I don't claim that. Insofar as it concerns Representative Hellberg's words. But it was not my recommendation. I called again after perhaps two hours asking if the men were up to their task... I mean, as far as their behavior was concerned."

The judge responded with a knowing little smirk:

"Why those doubts? I suppose you didn't know that these investigation units were really terrorist organizations?"

"I did not know that. And I still don't know. And I also got the impression that it was not at all Representative Hellberg's intention that the baron be murdered. The men had orders to arrest the baron if he did not sign the binding agreement."

"Binding agreement. He would have been arrested on account of that meaningless agreement?"

"Master Judge. Where the baron was concerned, it would not have been meaningless. Whatever his opinions may have been, his word was always binding... We believed in a man of honor's word."

The landlords snorted, and Lieutenant Granlund muttered something in Swedish.

The judge spoke in a clear voice as if to emphasize thereby the factual nature of the testimony:

"On the following evening three men arrived at the manor, along with a driver assigned by the church village headquarters. No search for weapons was conducted, but after raising a row for a time, the men took the baron with them and brutally murdered him on a nearby bridge. What do you say to this?"

"The gentlemen know what I have said to this... My principles are so well known to at least some members of the court that I consider such questions meaningless."

"Well. We've wondered a little here what kind of man Halme has come to be known as."

It was Yllö who said it drily and angrily, then turned his head away.

"Do you admit calling the church village headquarters and asking them to send men to wring the agreement from him?"

"I admit calling them. I said nothing about wringing an agreement, so I cannot admit to doing so."

"It is not a question of your tone of voice, but of the actual content of the words. Do you admit participating in this murder?"

"The gentlemen know that the accusation itself is senseless."

"Guards. Take him to the hallway."

After five minutes had passed, Halme was summoned inside. This time he was not allowed to sit down.

The judge's words reached his feverish consciousness from a great distance:

"...for rebellion against a lawful government and organized society, for complicity in robbery and murder, for illegal deprivation of freedom, you are sentenced to be shot by decision of the field court."

Halme's already rapid breathing accelerated slightly, but otherwise he tried to stand erect. All his wavering will power was concentrated on one point: he had to stand straight. He had to stay calm. The only thing he had to lose was his dignity and honor. The basic uncertainty of his soul, as a cover for which he had woven the great role of Adolf Halme during his lifetime, undercut this effort of will. Momentarily despair was already breaking through to the surface. He had planned a speech, but was doubtful whether to ask permission, fearing that his strength would fail him. There was, however, so much to be said that he could not forego the opportunity.

"My good gentlemen. I know that I cannot complain about your decision. But permit me to say a few words."

"Haven't you given all your inflammatory speeches by now?"

When no further prohibition was forthcoming, Halme began:

"My good gentlemen. I speak for no other reason than out of an obligation to truth and justice, the only sovereigns I acknowledge as the supreme judges. My insignificant life has perhaps been far from perfect. At the end of the journey I see much that I have not previously understood as wrong. But my good gentlemen. Why don't you let me die for the sake of my ideals? Why do you have to shame me with the name of murderer, an accusation the senselessness of which you yourselves understand? Perhaps before the highest judge I am partially responsible for the evil of my fellow men and for those deeds which you accuse me of. But before you, I am innocent. The rules of earthly justice do not apply to me. I am guilty insofar as I am a human being along with you. But your judgment does not touch me. I die because you want me to. My task is to try to bear it, and... and I... I admit it isn't easy... But when you accuse me of agitation and incitement, then have mercy on those I have agitated and incited, for as my guilt increases, so theirs diminishes. Think of their children and wives. Control your anger, for within three weeks you may yourselves wish you had. My good gentlemen, you yourselves bear the guilt for this rebellion. Therefore, have mercy on yourself with light sentences. For you are punishing yourselves. You are shooting the ghosts of your own greed and haughtiness. As I recall, I have already said that they don't die by shooting. You did not believe my words. I understand that. But in back of my insignificance is a great witness. It is the inevitable course of life. And the coming decades will make you believe my words. My good gentlemen. You smile. Let that be permitted you. I will soon finish, for I am tired and cannot go on. But finally I wish to inform you that the first great teacher of mankind, the first socialist, the son of a Nazarene carpenter, was condemned by law to die for the sake of truth and justice. Today every confirmation child must know this by memory... he sits at the right hand of God and will come from there to judge the quick and the dead."

Halme stopped when he felt his strength give out, for he had many more thoughts, which had arisen and taken shape during periods in the night as he shivered in the poorhouse enclosure. His mouth too was so dry that his tongue could no longer shape his words properly. The effort of will had so exhausted him that he went out without being ordered to, for he could no longer stand in one place. In the hallway, he said to those awaiting their turn:

"Per aspera ad astra."

His lips trembled, uncertain as to whether to shape themselves into a smile or a sob. Nevertheless he straightened up for the benefit of the security men standing in the outer hallway.

"There goes one of the head agitators... He must have got a death sentence."

Halme did not react to the words, but walked cautiously down the steps. Only near the apothecary did he succumb. And with his will, his body collapsed too. He reeled into a picket fence soiled with road dust and remained leaning against it. The guard, who was gentle when alone, urged him to go on, and Halme, ashamed of his weakness, stammered:

"I beg your pardon... Illness... if you will wait... I'll take a little honey."

He dug from his pocket a porcelain container that had once contained some apothecary's salve, and a teaspoon wrapped in waxed paper. His dry mouth would not really melt the honey, and Halme sucked on it for a long time, speaking to the guard as if he were asking his pardon:

"This restores your strength quickly... it contains secret nutritive ingredients... ancient philosophers already knew that... a product of nature itself... the great chemist..."

With a troubled smile, he panted for a while against the fence, and then struggled to his feet.

"Why did they take my cane away?"

After a short time, the guard heard him mutter to himself:

"I would really have needed it now..."

After Halme's departure, the members of the tribunal were silent for a short time. His speech had troubled them. They had not listened to his thoughts, but the tone of voice of a man going to his death seemed to have had an effect. Pajunen broke the silence:

"Now we even got to hear the word 'God' in a socialist's mouth."

"He should have become a schoolteacher, like I told him long ago... uh... yeah... He always had those hunks of verse and those sayings... he had a schoolteacher's style."

Mellola felt some pity for Halme, but the judge quickly set their minds at ease:

"He seems to be an old fox. He wasn't just speaking out stupidly. He had thought it all out... If people were only as innocent in their actions as they are in court."

After the Halme case, they took a lunch break. The tribunal went to Yllölä to eat, although all of them lived in the vicinity. But at Yllölä they could talk over many of the cases in advance.

316

Mellola dragged along as the last one in the group. When they reached Yllö's garden, he whispered to Yllö…

"Listen, Artturi..."

Yllö dropped back without the others noticing, and Mellola nodded at them, turned off the path, and opened his fly:

"Let's pretend to piss... I have a little matter to talk over with you... I can't get any out... but they won't notice.. I don't want to whisper. About this Jokinen case... It seems as if Granlund badly wants him to be shot... For my part, I wouldn't care if they were hard on him, but we don't have any-one else who can run that machine."

"Hasn't the Lepistö boy used it?"

"Sometimes, with Jokinen keeping an eye on him... but I don't trust him with it alone. And I've got all the winter's logs to saw... since nothing got done. It does no good if the work suffers... we have to go on living from now on."

"But he's been so outrageous... And he said that the two murdered strangers got what they deserved."

"Well... as to that... He's the one who took my grain by the sackful. One Red held the sack and I had to put the grain in myself... And during the strike he sneered at me... But I have sawing to do for the farms, though there is no rush with logs for market."

Yllö thought a little while:

"Well, let him stay, if that's the way it is. We can order him to do compulsory work under your guarantee."

Mellola was relieved and wheezed as he walked behind Yllö to the main building:

"I'll pay him wages too... And then he can be shot if I find someone else... But there aren't likely to be many after this hullabaloo... But is that a wagtail already... Look at it... You know them better."

"It's not a wagtail. It was just otherwise rocking."

"Yeah... I thought it looked so much like a wagtail... But there was no reason for you to block Kivivuori's shooting... He deserved it more than many others."

"Yes, yes, but he spoke out against them too openly. We have to watch out a little..."

"But he said all kinds of other things."

Mellola was angry about the autumn decision in Janne's case, but Yllö would not agree to having Janne shot.

IV

Kankaanpää was saved from a sentence of death, although he had been a member of the headquarters staff. He was saved by Pajunen, who was a distant relative:

"He's such a lump of a man that he's not worth killing. His socialism will go when there are no others around... He was a socialist because others were."

There was not even a hearing for Antto Laurila. He was informed of his sentence on the basis of the staff's testimony. Antto glowered at the members of the court from under his brows and said, after hearing the sentence:

"Just let it come. But even if you fill a trough with blood, the day will come when you'll beg for mercy on your knees. And that's a goddamned fact."

He did not have time to say more, for the guards led him out.

A long discussion arose over the Koskela boys. The master of Yllö wanted to save them.

"A little because of their father. He's a decent man."

The judge was of a different mind.

"We do not condemn a father for his son's deeds, nor can the father's decency save the sons. And didn't the oldest brother start the whole rebellion in the village?"

They called the parsonage and asked about the boys' characters. The vicar put in a good word for them.

"They have always been led by their older brother. By themselves they would hardly have joined the rebellion at all."

The vicar's statement made the decision so close that a hair would have altered the balance. But Lieutenant Granlund asked:

"They not lead men. But they are weapon in hand. Good character. Maybe good character in peace. Real devil in war. They Guard rebels."

The strike riots, for which they had not been punished, were also a disadvantage.

The sentences came up for a vote, and the boy's fate was decided by three to two in favor of death. Those voting in favor of death, the chairman, Granlund, and even Mellola, felt a slight regret when they saw Aleksi before the tribunal. The boy stood shyly fingering his coat hem and asked when he had heard the sentence:

"Well, may I go now?"

The brother's cases were successive, and when Aku saw Aleksi coming, he knew everything from his face:

"What?"

318

"Nothing... we'll talk about it later."

Aleksi went quickly, for he was afraid to talk to anyone close to him. Even though Akusti gritted his teeth, the tears still came to his eyes. The rage brought on by his brother's sentence made him behave furiously, which eased the compunction of those who had voted for the death penalty.

"I have no regrets... except that I didn't do what I am accused of."

Mellola's wheezing voice could be heard:

"Oh my, oh my, oh my..."

There were many people standing in the yard of the county building, although they were shortly driven away.

Passing through the crowd, Aku noticed Otto.

"The death penalty... for both of us... Tell them at home... but don't come to watch."

"I'll go and talk to them... I'll go to the headquarters."

Most of the people in the crowd were the silent and fearful kin of the condemned, but there were also members of the Civil Guard and other Whites who did not hide their malicious glee. One of the men who heard Otto's words was a farm owner who was standing with a white ribbon on his arm. He had earlier belonged to the workers' association, but having married the limping daughter of a farm owner and having become a land-lord by that route, he had left the association. Now he was a member of the Civil Guard, not out of conviction, but out of fear because of his past, and for the same reason he now said to Otto:

"No use talking now. Other tools are speaking out."

Otto had already been leaving, but now he came back and said, as if happily surprised:

"Well, if it isn't Valprii. So you're here too. But your ribbon is so badly faded."

Otto's face was smiling, but there was a burning hatred in his eyes. Valprii took a couple of steps backward in an effort to maintain his aplomb, but it was difficult, for people were laughing aloud. In addition, there were members of the Civil Guard present, who knew Valprii Rautala.

Otto was not admitted to talk at the headquarters, and when he returned to the county building, Uolevi Yllö came after him.

"Kivivuori is going along with the others," he said.

"No he isn't."

Two of the security men grabbed his hands, and so Otto was taken away. Valprii had gone to the headquarters and said:

"He defamed the Civil Guard in a public place."

"Is that devil free? Why hasn't he been arrested? He was a member of the Board and he was on the strike committee."

And so Otto arrived at the poorhouse compound.

However, Otto did get word to Koskela. When a stranger from the church village appeared in the yard, Elina knew immediately that it spelled trouble. When he stood hesitating about which building to enter, she went out.

"Are you Mrs. Koskela?"

"I am."

The man began to speak a little painfully:

"I have bad news. Your husband has been captured."

"Why... in God's name... he hasn't been anywhere near here."

"He has been captured. He's in no great danger now. But there's another matter that's a little worse... It's this way... your boys have been given a death sentence... And something has to be done quickly if they are to be saved... I don't know when they will start shooting them, but it may even happen soon."

Bursting into tears, Elina looked toward the window of the new place:

"How can I say it... to Grandma... What will I say? Oh, my God..."

Sober and troubled, the man looked away and prepared to leave in order to escape the unpleasant encounter.

He departed and Elina went to the new place. Halfway there, she stopped, intending to ask the stranger to stay. In her fear and helplessness, she imagined he might be of some assistance. She was already thinking of calling him back to come with her and talk about the matter, but then she realized that he could not change anything. She tried to control herself as she stepped inside, but could only stammer repeatedly:

"The boys... the boys..."

Then she sat on the bench and burst into loud weeping. Alma's face went white but she said nothing. Tears rolled from her eyes and she stared straight ahead while her lips moved as she silently repeated the Lord's Prayer, the first one that came to her mind.

A grunt escaped Jussi. He was sitting on the edge of the bed, and little by little his shoulders sagged lower and lower. Elina explained the matter more fully, and that awakened the old man's energy:

"I'll go to the parsonage... and to the church village if need be..."

Alma fetched Jussi's Sunday clothing from the attic. It was the same suit he got from the Vallén boys, almost thirty years old. Jussi changed his clothes and left. The two women were left alone. Although the boys had not been very close to Elina, she was completely crushed. The horror of the death sentence was hard to bear in itself, but that made her think of Akseli's fate. If the boys had to die, then there was no possibility for Akseli, unless he managed to escape.

In the midst of her own sorrow, Alma tried to console her.

"You poor child, don't cry like that... One has to learn to endure in this world. A person can't give in like that..."

Elina asked her to come to the old place to wait. The afternoon and evening passed, and Jussi did not appear. The children were put to bed, but the women waited up though the long and dismal hours of the April night.

Panting, Jussi traveled toward the church village, walking one step and running the next. He was breathing heavily, and kept repeating fretfully to himself:

"If I only had a horse... but in that rush..."

On Tammikallio Hill he was forced to sit by the roadside. He had been told at the parsonage that the vicar and his wife were at some kind of freedom celebration in the church village, and without further thought, Jussi had started off toward it. Only when traveling became difficult did he remember the horse, but it was too late to go back and get it. Having caught his breath a little, he continued his journey.

Seeing the crush of people in the church village, Jussi became more and more panicky.

"Where can I find them... what on earth is going on here?"

The Civil Guard had organized an oath-taking ceremony in the churchyard, and the crowd was thickest there. Jussi thrust into the throng, his panic making him bolder than usual. He shoved people out of his way to get closer to the group of gentry. The vicar, however, was at the very forefront of the Civil Guard, and Jussi could not get close to him. Almost every member of the power structure was present; even the field court had suspended its session, for the war judge was administering the Civil Guard' oath.

Jussi watched the proceedings, expecting as every speech ended that it would be the last. But there were plenty of them. The apothecary had been named head of the Civil Guard, but Ilmari was in charge of the oath taking. There had been secret plotting for positions of command, and the gentlemen had had uniforms made for themselves, with homemade insignias of rank. The apothecary had managed to get a Swedish garrison cap from somewhere. The county doctor had already had a uniform secretly made for him during the rebellion. He wore leggings and had spurs on his brown brown oxfords. Many had asked if Halme might not be put to work making uniforms for them before his execution, but he was said to be too weak to do so.

The war judge was continuing to read the oath, which the members of the Civil Guard repeated, holding two fingers in the air. Jussi was amazed. In spite of his perturbation, he wondered crossly:

"Really... really... Don't people have anything else to do. Fingers in the air and mumbling stuff like that..."

After the oath, the vicar spoke of its meaning. Affected by the military nature of the audience, he stood stiffly erect as he spoke:

"...you have sworn a sacred oath to your country and to the lawful organization of society. You have asked our Lord's help in fulfilling it. We have seen that God has not left unanswered the prayers of those who asked his aid in the oath they took on going into battle. He has blessed the weapons of justice with victory. Today we can feel ourselves free citizens, but free also from that fear and oppression which has weighed on us so heavily during these gloomy months. After severe trials the sun once more shines brightly on the people of Finland. The rule of anarchy has been crushed by the strength of our proud sons, but let us not forget that they have merely been agents in God's hands. He has supported the weak with his strength, and on this beautiful day, which can be compared only with that day in Lapua of which the poet sings, we raise our thanks to that God of Hosts, to whom the people of Finland have always had recourse. Let us strike up the hymn of praise to him, a hymn which our forefathers have sung countless times in the morning before a bloody battle and in the evening when it was over. There beyond that stone fence lie our fathers, and when they hear that hymn, they will sleep in peace, knowing the their spirit still lives in our sons. And they will say to each other as the old soldier said when he greeted the victor of Alavus: 'Our fathers' spirit lives on, there are heroes in Finland still...'"

Aaa... migh-ty fo-ortress i-is our Go-o-o-o-d...

"Oh Lord... and there will be prayers too..."

Jussi moved restlessly, but every time he tried to approach the group of gentry, his nerve failed him:

"I can't... barge in..."

Jussi was mistaken; after the hymn, there was no prayer, but a show of honor to Ilmari. The apothecary took over and asked Ilmari to step forth from the ranks. Ilmari went and stood at ease, gazing with calm sobriety at the audience, his leather-gloved fists loosely closed at his sides. The apothecary stepped up to him.

"Sir Infantry Lieutenant. I have been honored with the task of greeting you on behalf of our parish. In you we see the personification of the infantry code. That ideal, of which we may now say, that no country in history has ever had the like. From generation to generation, you will continue to be the proud model for Finland's youth. Mothers will tell their children about you, and youths and men will hold you up as an example. In our country's difficult days, you were not disheartened. Taking your future into your own hands, you went to a foreign country for the military training needed to free your country once and for all. Those three years you spent in the German army will be inscribed indelibly in the pages of history. But the proudest page of your history will, however, be written about those battles which you went through in order to free this beloved land from the Red plague. As young leaders, you forged in our army the unflinching will that carried it from victory to victory. I ask you: what were Leonidas and his Spartans compared to this? Sir Infantry Lieutenant. On behalf of the parish, I bid you welcome home."

The apothecary saluted and Ilmari responded. A few attempts at cheers were heard from the crowd, but shyness smothered them. During the talk, Ilmari had stood calmly, maintaining a stiffly soldierly expression in order to prevent his gratification from showing on his face.

After the honor ceremony Jussi believed everything to be over and moved toward the vicar, but a new number followed on the program: Two white-clad maidens carried a huge bouquet of flowers to Ilmari.

"To the Finnish infantryman. From a thankful people."

The girls glowed and blushed, and a tiny unofficial expression flashed in Ilmari's eyes, as if he were winking familiarly to a girl he knew. Then he took the bouquet, squeezed the girls' hands, touched a hand to his cap, and said in a loud and soldierly voice:

"I thank you."

The wife of the county doctor was standing beside the vicar's wife. Envy distorted her features into an ugly mask, and afraid that the woman would notice, she hid her state of mind by hugging the vicaress and whispering:

'May I say... can a mother ask for more?"

The vicar's wife did not answer, but swallowed a sob. Jussi was again working his way toward the vicar, but this encounter frightened him. And then the apothecary shouted:

"Please clear the way. Now the troops will pass in review."

The Civil Guard carried out some sort of review on the way to the fire hall for the "oath" coffee. For the occasion, coffee had been collected from the gentry's hiding places, and many had given from their little in the spirit of common sacrifice. Jussi imagined that he could speak to the vicar on the way and started to follow him. From the group of gentry he could hear enthusiastic talk:

"Is it true that the Germans are in Lahti...? They took Helsinki on the day they promised... That shows their organizational skill..."

The vicar noticed Jussi, but managed to avoid him before their glances met. He tried to pretend he had not seen him, and feeling bothered, he darted into the fire hall before Jussi, who was trying to rush onto the steps, was able to call his name.

Jussi stood in the hallway. The members of the Civil Guard walking back and forth looked at him in surprise but left him alone. From the hall could be heard the confused hum of talk and the clinking of coffee cups.

"My brother at the taking of Tampere... he shouted: 'The Vaasa March' boys... the Reds are getting to be horribly afraid of it...' But my cousin wrote that they were right in the front lines, and it was very dangerous. Then he and a few of his comrades decided to sacrifice themselves. They started to fire very fast and the Red Russians took to their heels..."

"Pity is the greatest weakness now... What would come of an operation if the doctor pitied the patient? Yes, yes. It is awful... But first one has to ask if they are even human beings... Have you read the descriptions in the papers... protruding organs cut off with dull weapons..."

"I did read one article... It said that among our people there hasn't been the kind of purging as for example in the War of the Roses in England and the Thirty Years War in Germany or among France's Jacquerie. It said that the violent and anti-social elements have disappeared from among civilized people in such civil wars..." "But so much violence is occurring among us..." "Yeah... I don't know about such writings. But there has to be a clean-up now. I thought so already when they showed me a bayonet and told me your bull-calf or your life."

"Sir Lieutenant has surely moved in larger circles there in Germany."

"We simple country folk..."

"Just like Sven Tuuva... You must have noticed that I haven't spoken very kindly to him."

Arvo Töyry came into the hallway and Jussi asked him to tell the vicar to come out. Arvo looked at him angrily at first but then went back into the hall. The vicar came out and Jussi bared his head.

"Would you... just so much... a few words..."

"Let's go out."

They went a little distance off from the building and Jussi began:

"I... because of the boys... as the vicar knows, they're not bad boys..."

"My good Koskela. I tried my best, but the sentence will not be revoked... I gave a statement for the boys... A good statement... But they say those strike riots were such an aggravating factor... I know how hard it is on you... and I assure you, I have done what I could... But they say that one revoked sentence without new testimony would invalidate the others... And the hatred is so bitter... those murders..."

"But not our boys... what shooting they might have done in the war..."

"I'll try to speak again. But I want to warn you against vain hopes."

The vicar went inside and returned quickly:

"I can't help you."

324

Seeing Jussi's distress, he began a hasty explanation:

"But you yourself can go to explain... Now is not the right time, but when they go to Yllölä, try then."

The vicar squeezed Jussi's hand:

"I wish you good luck... they will listen better to a father...."

Jussi tried to say something, but the vicar departed hastily.

After the celebration, Jussi tried to go to Yllölä, but they refused to receive him. Evening arrived, and the despairing man went from door to door, but they were all closed to him. The fear of death made the frightened rustic go even to such doors as he would never before have dreamed of knocking on. They were not opened, and if they were, the answer was:

"It's not my business. Speak to the judge."

The spring evening grew dark as the man dragged himself toward home. His step, which before had always been nervously eager, was now weary and apathetic. A couple of kilometers from the church village he came to a stop:

"Why go home... when I know nothing..."

Jussi went back again. But he was unable to try anywhere else, and stood leaning against the hitching rail. The dark church village was silent. Here and there footsteps and low voices could be heard. A cigarette glowed in the darkness. The silent church tower rose into the darkness.

V

At four in the morning a clamor arose in the mental-case wing of the poorhouse. The men condemned to death, who were held in two incarceration cells, knew what it meant. There were footsteps, the murmur of talk, and the clunking of rifles. Doors were opened and the condemned ordered out into the corridor. There stood Ilmari, Uolevi Yllö, Arvo Töyry, and a few other men. The condemned squinted after emerging from the dark cells. Pale-faced, they shivered with cold, although it was warm in the cells. The chill resulted from poor circulation wrought by numbness. Gradually the painful thoughts induced by the fear of death had abated, and they had sunk into a kind of protective torpor, with the aid of which it was easier to endure. Along with it even the functions of life had become weaker. Ilmari took a paper from his pocket. He stepped in front of the group, but looked over their heads. It was clear that he had adopted an exaggerated attitude of callousness. In a low, uninflected voice he said:

"The sentences will be carried out. I have the duty of overseeing them and I want to say in advance that all demonstrations are futile. It is best to bow to the inevitable."

Then he read from the paper:

"Silander, Kalle August."

"Here I am."

"Everyone will answer by saying, 'Present.' Halme, Aadolf Alexander."

"Present."

"Leivonaho, Armas."

"Present."

"Laurila, Anton Kustaa."

"Mm...hmh..."

"Koskela, Aleksis Johannes."

"Present."

"Koskela, August Johannes."

"Present."

"Ylöstalo, Kalle Armas."

"Present."

"Ahlgren, Edvard."

"Present."

Ilmari folded the paper and put it into his pocket. A brief silence ensued, broken by smothered coughing. Amidst it all there came to the men's ears the sound of chains clanking in the nearest cells. From in back of a barred opening in a door they could hear a jerking and the babbling of Antti Laurila:

"Aaa... Aaanttii... Gruel... gruel..."

"Column of twos. Move!"

They went out. Riflemen stationed themselves alongside their line. The morning was dawning, and the raw air affected their breathing, causing them to cough weakly. The procession followed a side path from the poorhouse, crossed the main road, and turned onto a small road through the fields. The outlines of the landscape were already visible in the dim morning light. To their left gleamed a single light from the county hospital window.

Halme and Silander were at the head of the column. In spots where the road was uneven, Halme began to stagger and stumble, and Silander grabbed his arm to keep him from falling. The Koskela brothers were walking side by side. They had been in separate cells and had not spoken to each other since the sentencing. Now as well they were careful not to do so. Both felt that it would have stirred painful emotions and therefore they remained silent. It was difficult for Akusti to walk, for his thigh had become swollen, but he limped along manfully with the aid of a cane, which he had been grudgingly permitted to keep after many battles with the guards. Once he stumbled, whereupon Aleksi took a step toward him and said, extending a hand:

"I'll... help..."

"No... by myself..."

Both mumbled their words, turning away from each other. When they approached the edge of a woods, Halme began to sing in a voice broken by his gasping breath:

A wretched worm, a wayfarer only...

Ilmari said angrily:

"Quiet. No singing."

"We are no longer under your command..."

Halme went on singing the hymn, and Silander joined in. Their song was broken and stumbling. The others did not join in. Aleksi did shape the words to the song with his lips.

Then he will find his home city,
having suffered his earthly fate...

"So the socialists are singing hymns now?"

It was one of the escorts who said it, but Ilmari ordered silence. They came to the woods, to an old, abandoned pit from which men given relief work during the years of famine had taken gravel to build a road. There were vague rumors about the pit, according to which the bodies of people who had starved to death were buried there. The rumors had caused the headquarters intuitively to choose this pit as the place of execution, for people still remembered the rather gloomy repute of the place.

...when this body is turning cold
and death seals up my eyes...
take me, O God, to joy in Thy presence...

"Halt!"

The column stopped. Those at the end took a step after the others were already standing still.

"Silander and Halme. Stand over there. You can turn your backs if you wish."

Halme walked a few painful steps and turned toward the executioners, who also lined up. Uolevi was a member of the firing squad. Pajunen's day laborer, usually regarded as a half-wit, also strutted to a place in the group. Apparently the course of events had been agreed upon in advance.

"Silander. Take your place."

Silander did not move, but one of the men grasped his arms and led him to Halme's side. Silander did not resist. He had merely been unable to take those last steps. He turned his back to the executioners. The rifles rose, and the clack of their bolts was accompanied by Halme's words:

"Until we meet, comrades... I die taking refuge in God's mercy, innocent in the eyes of men..."

"Fire!"

Silander's croaking scream mingled with the roar of the volley. Halme fell without a sound, as if struck by lightning. A few sounds came from the group awaiting their turn, and someone covered his eyes with his arm.

"Leivonaho and Laurila."

The two went to stand beside the fallen. Antto kept up an unintelligible grunting and mumbling, and looked straight at the executioners. Arvo Töyry, who had been watching the prisoners during the shooting, stepped into the group of executioners:

"I have business with this pair too."

When Arvo raised his rifle, Antto opened his coat buttons and said:

"Let fly, goddamn, and bury me standing so it'll take less land."

"Fire!"

"Next."

The brothers went in their turn. Aleksi asked in a breathless and hoarse voice:

"Which way shall we face?"

His younger brother snapped in a singularly angry voice:

"Forward..."

As they stood in their place and the executioners prepared to fire, Aku suddenly hurled his cane toward them with all his might. It caused confusion in their ranks, and brought muttered curses.

After the disturbance the rifles rose again, and Aku whispered:

"Goodbye. Don't be afraid."

"Fire!"

Aleksi did not fall at once, but staggered for a few seconds with his hands outstretched, before falling at last onto the heap of corpses. Even here he continued to move. Aku drew his hands quickly to his breast when the bullets struck, fell to his knees, and from there onto his face.

"Next."

Ylöstalo took his place, but Ahlgren had to be dragged to his side. When they got him there, he fell down and pressed his face into his hands. He was shot there, and Pajunen's hired hand finished him off with a bayonet.

Ilmari took his pistol from its holster and went to check the heap of corpses, one of which still was moving. From underneath the pile came a stifled rattle. Ilmari shot each one in the head. As the bodies lay in a heap, he shifted one of them with his foot, in order to bring a head into view from underneath.

"Did I count correctly? Did I fire eight shots?"

"You did, but why shoot them again?"

"It is the usual custom. Bullets shot into the body do not always cause instant death, and someone might suffer."

"No matter if they do suffer a little... But they do teach you everything in Germany. No one here would have known that."

"Granlund would have known. He was in the Russian army."

"Two men will stay on guard here. No one is allowed to come near the place. I'll send the gravediggers as soon as it's daylight. And remember what was said. You can't talk about the details of the execution."

Dawn's reddish tint was already glowing on the horizon when the Civil Guard returned to the village.

Since only the boys meant anything to Jussi, he imagined the first shots to have been their death volley. Starting off for home at a panting half-trot, he heard the succeeding volleys as well, but paid no attention to them. The shuffle of his footsteps mingled with the heavy, wheezing sound of his labored breathing.

Otto, Preeti, and Wolf-Kustaa were among those ordered into the gravediggers' gang. They belonged to the group for whom the masters thought this was sufficient:

"To throw a little scare into them."

Otto was actually counted among the leaders, but his steering clear of the rebellion had moved him into the group of those to be "scared." Burying the dead was considered a suitable means of scaring.

They dug the grave in the hard gravel while the guards stood around them. Over the bodies buzzed flies enlivened by the morning sun, their flight still clumsy from the cold. Distorted faces and bare hands shone yellowish in the sun. Otto noticed that Aleksi Koskela's good boots had been stripped and taken away, but thought it best not to say anything. Pajunen's day laborer, who had been left to guard the bodies, had taken them.

The work of the weakened prisoners was poor, and the guards barked angrily at them. Otto replied that he was not able to work because he had gone almost without eating for many days.

"Just get on it. Gravediggers have been promised extra pieces of bread."

Kustaa did nothing. He pretended to dig a little, and he replied to the guards' commands by arching his wing-like eyebrows and pursing his mouth. The grave had to be dug deep, for the plan was to bury the bodies in many layers, since, according to headquarters' calculations, the number to be executed amounted to nearly a hundred.

When the grave was deep enough, the bodies were carried to it. Preeti humbly took hold of even the bloodiest places, which the others avoided.

"Let's cross the master's hands a little."

"Goddamn it. They haven't been crossed before."

"I just thought. Since it's done with the dead."

And ignoring the prohibition, he crossed Halme's hands over his breast and covered his forehead with his hat, which had been badly mutilated by the bullet from Ilmari's large-caliber pistol. Preeti fingered Aleksi Koskela's good coat:

"Would it be all right to take this home... I guess I could do that..."

Otto saw that Preeti would like to have the coat, and he said:

"I guess you could send it home for him."

The guards agreed, and Preeti took off the coat.

"Maybe I would buy it... if they agree to sell... Since they wouldn't have any use..."

As if in thanks, Preeti gently straightened Aleksi's body, and crossed his arms over his breast as he had done the master's.

They shoveled a ten-centimeter layer of gravel over the bodies, and the guards also told them to cover the blood that had flowed at the spot of the executions. A guard was left at the grave when the others returned to the poorhouse.

Preeti was allowed to go home that evening, and the prisoners asked him to do errands for them, to which he agreed:

"If I could get a slip of paper and you could write them down. My memory has gotten so bad in my old age."

Otto drew Preeti aside and advised him:

"Don't let them see that coat. And if you ask for it, don't wear it for a while. And if you see them, don't say anything about the boys' bodies. Just say that they looked peaceful, as if they were asleep. You yourself understand what to say. And go and ask for food at our place if you can get it to me through the gate."

At home Preeti put the coat in the entry closet, but shortly he and Henna went to look at it.

"I'm sure they'll sell it... I might even go and plant potatoes to pay for it... Since they don't have people to work... We can make one for Valtu from this old one..."

On her departure, Aune had left Valtu in her parent's care, and Henna cared for the child alone while Preeti was in the "army." But later in the evening Preeti began to hem and haw:

"Would it be... Kivivuori did give me permission... Although it really wasn't his to give. Even though he is related and stuff..."

Preeti had to go to Koskela. Things had calmed down there already. When Jussi arrived in the morning with the news, Alma had shut herself up in the boys' bedroom. In an hour she had come out calm and said no more about the matter. During the day she and Elina had sung hymns together.

Jussi had been seeing to it that the seed grain was in good condition in the storehouse. The boys had come to see their grandfather, but had not enjoyed their visit for long. Jussi had answered them gruffly, not really aware of their existence.

Preeti's arrival broke the tranquility they had achieved. Alma wept quietly while Preeti explained:

"They looked just like they were sleeping. There were no marks of bullets on them or anything... The master was just the way he used to be... The boys looked as if they were sort of smiling... I thought... I took that good coat of Aleksi's... If you sort of want it... I could really buy it... Henna might even come to plant potatoes... Or maybe you don't need her..."

"I'll give you Aleksi's other coat... It's so... to see it on someone else. But keep it for now..."

Alma gave Preeti one of Aleksi's coats and Preeti thanked her over and over as he was leaving. On the woods road he opened the coat and looked at it:

"Well, the other one is sort of better cloth... But then it had those bullet holes."

VI

The next day the storekeeper arrived at Koskela with a rifle on his shoulder. The whole family was in the old place, for Alma and Jussi had moved there to live, since it seemed easier to bear their trouble and pain in the company of others. Jussi looked at the storekeeper and laughed a nasty, nervous laugh:

"Did you come to get me? As far as I know, I'm the only one left to shoot here. Unless you start on those youngsters..."

"I have some business with you, Elina."

"Are you going to shoot me?"

"You don't have to be afraid for your life. But take a rag and pail and go and clean up the workers' hall a little bit. They've left it in such a mess."

Elina dressed and went with the storekeeper. On the way, the man tried to make conversation, but Elina would not say a word to him.

The wives, daughters, and sisters of the Reds had been gathered at the hall to wash and clean out what had been left there by the Red Guard, for the Civil Guard were taking it over. The cleaning was also a method of punishment. Anna Kivivuori had been excluded, but Emma Halme had been ordered to take part, in spite of her advanced age. When Elina saw Emma's eyes red from weeping, tears rose into her own. They were not allowed to say anything that did not have to do with the work, but Elina shook Emma's hand and curtsied to her on the sly. The curtsy was nearly instinctive, a girlish demonstration of respect. They scrubbed the floor while the men of the Civil Guard looked on from the door. The well-brought-up Töyry brothers were troubled by their uncle's gross comments:

"Raise your skirts a little higher so they won't get wet... We're not afraid of bare knees... We have the weapons..."

"Do you still sing that song that says there is no other ruler nor Creator but the almighty people?"

When the hall was scrubbed and work on the kitchen and hallways began, the storekeeper said:

"Uhuh... Elina Koskela has her own job now. Since she's the wife of the leader, she gets a special task. By special order of the commandant."

Elina was taken to wash the latrine. Men gathered around her partly because of the nature of the work, but also partly because some traces of her old beauty could still be seen in her, and beneath the joking was an unconscious undertone of courtship. Elina merely stared at the rag as she rubbed the seat of the toilet. Once she said, in response to the men's laughter:

"We do this at home every Saturday... and no one... laughs at it."

The laughter died away at the tremor in her voice. The master of Kylä-Pentti arrived at the workers' hall and seeing the situation he began to sputter:

"I say, this is improper, I say. Go home, I say."

"It is the commandant's order."

"Even if it's Mannerheim's order... it is, I say... improper."

The master's cheeks were red, and he hawked angrily. The others laughed in embarrassment, and Elina was told to go home. The master of Kylä-Pentti had been left entirely in peace by the Reds, for no one bore him any grudge, and as a man of good will, he had also begun to speak out against the punitive measures. In his own village, people listened to him, but his words carried no weight in the church village, and in spite of his efforts, he was unable to save anyone there.

His anger did have an effect on the others, and there was even some kindness in the men's commands when they told Elina to go home. The master of Kylä-Pentti also told Emma Halme to leave, along with another of the older manor worker's wives.

Elina returned home with her rag and her bucket. For a long time she tried to battle against despair, but at Matti's Spruce, she collapsed. Slumped at the foot of the spruce, she wept like a babe in arms, first drawing in a

deep breath, so that the sound of the weeping was heard only when she began to expel it. She was not weeping at having been shamed. Her panic centered around a man who was journeying somewhere far away:

"God... Lord God... that he get to Russia... help him, God...

Ellen had established a women's auxiliary for the Civil Guard and had had a "field dress" made for herself. Everyone who had the slightest possibility of doing so was to have one like it made. There had been an argument about the color, but Ellen had her way:

"Gray has been the color of Finland's army throughout history. It isn't pretty, but it cannot be the intention to appear as any kind of sexual being in that dress."

She used the words "sexual being" contemptuously, under the influence of the old "women's question." But when she got the dress, she was dissatisfied with it, because it was terribly ugly.

"That seamstress is getting old. She doesn't make as good dresses as she used to."

"Heh, heh. But there have been some changes in your figure too."

The vicar laughed and patted his wife's shoulder:

"We're getting old. Yes we are, mamma dear."

The lines around Ellen's lips tightened and she blinked a couple of times:

"Well, a seamstress should be skillful enough to fit an older body too. And don't call me 'mamma dear.' 'Mamma' is a word of Swedish derivation, and I've never liked it."

"Now, now, you shouldn't take it like that... I was only joking... You don't show your age. And what does it matter. You could get a little rounder. Especially if there is any basis in those ideas about your becoming the wife of a parish dean. A dean's wife has to be a little plump. It goes with the position. Although I don't quite believe it yet."

"If you keep on being so self-effacing, then they won't give it to you. Everyone else is parading what they did during the rebellion, but you speak of your sermons and your imprisonment as if you were asking for pardon."

"But it would be improper for me to start presenting such things as merits. Since it also looks as if there are so many deserving people around... To many the rebellion already seems to have been a good thing... Misfortune has its good side where some are concerned. Now many people have even helped out and hired the jaegers, whom they still called traitors a year ago. When you listen to them, it seems almost as if they had been in Siberia..."

The vicar sat thinking, and then after a short time, he said in a quiet and uncertain voice, as if he were afraid of his own words:

"I've been thinking... We shouldn't have forced Ilmari to stay here...although really it was Yllö's fault."

"Why shouldn't he have stayed?"

"Just because... His position. You understand."

"If you mean, because he is commanding executioners, I don't understand. He himself told me that he stopped one of the firing squad from abusing a condemned man. He obeys the law."

The vicar said, as if to himself:

"Nevertheless I wish he wouldn't."

"And someone else would be more lax. Is that so? If a judge, for example, thought that way, what would become of the justice system?"

"Of course that is true... And otherwise I don't... But I can't really understand the sentence of the Koskela boys. Perhaps it is according to the law, but mercy is also justice."

"Did Akseli have mercy on those two unknown men? He did not even have the nerve to carry out the sentence himself, but sent them to the church village for execution."

"The boys aren't responsible for Akseli's deeds. But it does seem to me that they had to answer for them... And we have to talk about the eviction. Not otherwise, but for old Koskela's sake."

"The eviction? Akseli himself broke the contract. You are a strange person. All your life you've lacked a sense of balance. You've got a strange habit of tormenting yourself by imagining things. You are not evicting old Koskela, but Akseli. I'm afraid you're soon going to start asking if you might possibly be to blame for this whole rebellion... And Elina wouldn't be able to run the tenancy, and you know that Akseli will never come back alive... Just look at this bag of a dress... I could make a better one myself. I said that it had to be simple, but I didn't mean it should be a sack."

The vicar glanced at the dress in passing and uttered something consolatory. His troubled state of mind continued for a while, but when his depression had hit bottom, the rebound began, and after a time, he said:

"What was that church, anyway, the one where they led a bull to the altar and administered communion to it...On the other hand, it is really... They surely are in the right who say repentance must precede pity. But it's so difficult even to believe that people can be such beasts..."

Ellen gathered the fabric into her fist at the waistline, but then, angry and chagrined, she took the dress off. The maid came in to announce that the old mistress of Koskela was asking to see the vicar.

"I wouldn't care to see her today."

"Tell her we have to be at the ceremony for the presentation of the colors."

"It's best to speak to her right now. Why put it off?"

Alma entered the chancellery in her Sunday dress.

"I came to talk about the boys."

"Well. My condolences... I put in a good word for them... but what happened happened."

"I just thought that... into consecrated land... a blessing at least..."

The vicar said uneasily:

"Wait for a while... I can't arrange it yet... There is opposition to their being buried in church land."

"But we have the grave we bought for Father and me... They could be there."

"That's right. You do have a grave... But it's entirely a question of whether the headquarters will allow them to be taken from their present grave. And for the present, I think it is impossible. Let's wait now... until this rage subsides a little."

"Yes... but even beyond the grave... And the boys did nothing to anyone... They weren't that kind..."

The vicar's wife had also come into the chancellery.

"To my knowledge, they weren't accused of anything but armed rebellion. And this is a awful for all of us. Their judges didn't want to condemn them either... It is sad that it should cause grief to entirely innocent people like you, and it is exactly for your sake that my husband did all he could."

In spite of the assurances, Alma sensed the coldness in the woman's voice, and she fell silent. It was improper to bandy words with the vicar's wife, and so she prepared to leave.

"Listen madam... I have another very unhappy matter to bring up. Since Akseli has neglected to pay the rent for the tenancy and publicly announced that it will no longer be paid, the congregation considers that he has broken the contract."

"Oh."

"That doesn't involve you. It involves only Akseli. I've even managed to see to it that you will get the provisions Akseli supplied you with from the parsonage."

"Uhuh."

"Tell Elina about this... And perhaps you understand without my saying so that we had no part in this... But I could do nothing about the bitterness Akseli aroused."

"I see."

Alma departed. The vicar's wife left the chancellery, but the vicar stayed there alone for a little while. He was sad and silent when he rejoined his wife. Ellen took the "field dress" from the back of a chair and dangled it in her hands, gazing at it appraisingly, with her head cocked to one side:

"But we have to get dressed. Tell me if I can wear this."

"You have to. Since you gave the order yourself."

"But I will have to turn over the flag and give a speech. I'm not frivolous, but there is certainly no room for comedy on an occasion like this."

"Why did you choose the lynx for the flag?"

"Why, it's on the shield of Häme. And the lynx symbolizes alertness and speed."

The hired boy drove the sled up to the steps, and they started off. On the trip, the vicar still spoke only a few reluctant words. Ellen guessed that he was still troubled by Alma Koskela's visit, but she did not broach the subject again. As they approached the church village, there were many travelers on the road. The members of the Civil Guard were coming to the ceremony with horses and bicycles, some even on foot. The parsonage couple shouted a few words to many of them as they passed by. Meeting people made the vicar more animated too, and when they reached the church village, he was lively and cheerful in greeting his acquaintances.

The ceremony was at the county hall, which was packed with people. The couple from the parsonage immediately became the center of the hubbub, not only because of their position, but also because, as the parents of an infantry lieutenant, they shared in the effulgence of his glory. Those who were not on familiar terms with the parents referred to Ilmari as "Sir Infantry Lieutenant" when speaking to them.

"Is the Sir Infantry Lieutenant going to the Helsinki parade?"

"Yes. He is going with his unit, but will come back for a while yet. He does badly want to be free of his Commandant's duty. He has more youthful energy than he can use here."

"We were just saying how smart and energetic he is. My husband said that within ten years he will be addressed as General Salpakari."

The vicar laughed, but then said with genuine gravity:

"Yes indeed. The young state needs a work force in all areas."

Alma brought the news to Koskela, but they had endured so much that it did not seem significant. Jussi said to Elina:

"They can't evict me, and I have the right to keep anyone at all in my

336

dwelling. You'll come and live in our place. I don't know how I can get along... the money is all gone... except for what little Akseli has there in the bank. But at least there's a place to live. And we'll find a way."

"But they say the Reds have to pay for their confiscations. And that Akseli too will have to pay for those slips."

"Maybe they'll take the cattle and anything else that's loose... But we will manage to raise the boys."

"I think I can go home. The baroness has refused to evict the families of rebels. I'm sure I can stay at home."

But Alma rejected that idea.

"We will get along here. Even if we have to do handwork. It would be bad for you to go there. And we don't even know if your father can stay... And you belong to us. We'll live somehow or other..."

"I can't stay. I can't stand to live around them..."

Elina stuck to her decision, and they began planning her move immediately, although under the terms of the breach of contract, it was still possible to plant and harvest that year's crops. But there was no one to do the work, so Elina thought it best to give up the tenancy at once.

Every night series of volleys rang out in the famine pit. In addition, there was talk about one incident or another: He tried to escape from his escort, so they shot him.

People got used to the dying. Even the condemned got used to it. There was seldom any sort of display. Silent, expressionless, they left the poorhouse between the riflemen for "the hill." Elsewhere, in the more thickly inhabited places, they stood people "against the wall," but here in more sparsely inhabited Finland, those who were to be executed were taken to "the hill." Someone was said to have shouted "Long live the revolution," as he was shot, but more often one could hear the singing of hymns from the incarceration cells. In the pit, they mainly looked at their executioners with eyes full of gloomy hatred until the very end. And the shooters stared back over their sights, which were hard to see in the summer-night gloom, with the same expression.

No one shouted or made a scene. They merely looked at one another, for this hatred was genuine Finnish hatred. It was like a swamp pond: black, cold, deep, and turbid.

Aliina Laurila's execution gave rise to jokes in the village. She had asked for a hymnal in the night, and one of the poorhouse women attendants had brought it to her. However, Aliina had not sung any hymns, had not even read the book, but held on to it with her hands clasped around it. As she was being shot, she had pressed it to her breast. She had been ordered to turn her back, but had refused. When forced to turn around, she had immediately spun back again, all the time saying nothing, but clutching the book to her breast, mute, her eyes wide and still.

"She's become civilized to that extent... In the past she showed her rear end even to the sheriff."

The prisoners who were not condemned to death were sent to a prison camp in Tampere. Others were freed to work on their master's recognizance. Preeti Leppänen and Wolf-Kustaa were freed, but Otto Kivivuori as well as Janne had to go. Each prisoner tied to a long rope by the wrists, they traveled to the station. The Kivivuoris, father and son, were next to one another, and when the guard did not happen to be near, one of the angry prisoners whispered to them:

"Now you see. What good did it do you to side with the butchers?"

Janne did not intend to answer at first, but then he said lazily:

"My rope is a lot looser than yours. Take a look at it."

The guards, though, hovered assiduously around father and son, for they had come to know their ready tongues, which had to be watched. The father was generally quiet, however. Age made it difficult for him to endure, and he did not want additional difficulties. But from Janne's locale, every so often one would hear a guard say:

"Isn't Kivivuori going to learn to keep his trap shut? Pretty soon he'll get it shut for good."

Janne fell silent, but when the guard left, those nearest him heard him mutter:

"This game isn't over yet... The spirit of our fathers lives on."

CHAPTER TEN

I

Along the road leading from Hämeenlinna to Lahti, the people wandered in an endless column of vehicles and marchers. They still had some room to move, but around them the ring tightened day by day. Families crouched in their vehicles, numb from the chill of the dank spring nights and their mind's crushing despair. Ahead and along the sides of the column moved the Red Guard units, smashing their encirclers' roadblocks and protecting the refugees' flight. No one was leading them any longer and there was no one they could turn to for answers. They were making the pilgrimage on their own, and when they encountered the enemy, they hurled themselves at the obstacle with the whole strength of despair. With grave and fearful eyes, the children in the vehicles listened to the strange din, the shooting and explosions, and their mothers tried to calm them, hiding their own pain. Then they started off again, perhaps through a hail of bullets, and continued on their way. From the vehicles, uneasy questions were directed at the returning Guards:

"Where is our father?"

When the answer was, "He got left there," the wife grasped the reins. The load consisted of a little food, the bedclothes, some article or other of value from the home, and the widow's and orphans' inconsolable grief. And ahead of them lay the only alternative to death: the march to Russia.

Thus this homespun folk continued on its pilgrimage of defeat. They had begun to wax arrogant about their fate, and fate had struck them down, as the gods are in the habit of doing with the defiant. They were now alone. The Dantons, the Robespierres, the Marats, the Babeufs — they were all gone. Only Koskela, Lepistö, Salo, Kuoppamäki, Lahtinen, and Ruotiala were left.

And over the despairing caravan floated the dust of the spring highway.

His eyes puffy, his feet rubbed raw, with a long growth of stubble on his face, Akseli led his horse by the reins. Two small boys sat on its back. Vacantly his eyes took in some dried codfish lying on the road, which someone had discarded there to make a load lighter.

They were no longer able to advance along the road they had meant to take, but had been forced to turn farther north. In an open area to the east, the advance of the column ahead of them had been cut off by fire from the Germans.

There was talk of parishes whose names Akseli had heard Victor Kivioja mention in his youth: Hauho, Tuulos, Lammi... Victor had even bought a wagon from Hauho.

Near the next wagon, the laughter of Aune Leppänen rang out. He could also hear Valenti, Osku, Elias, and Uuno Laurila there. Elma was with the same group, but he never did hear her voice. One night Akseli found the girl crying behind the wagons.

"What's the matter?"

"Nothing."

"Well, you're not crying for fun."

"What goddamn business is it of yours? Go to hell. I guess I can cry if I want to."

And angrily the girl went her way. The large men's trousers she was wearing flapped in time to her stride as she walked. But on the Alvettula Bridge, Elma had taken a rifle and asked how to fire it. She had been told how, but had not yet gotten to use it.

Aune's laugh and the hum of the boys' talk came to Akseli's ears indistinctly, mingled with the rattle of the wagon wheels and the sound of the horses' hoofs. He felt as if he were only half awake, his consciousness not fully alert. He was awake only to the extent that his mechanical walking demanded. He had not been able to sleep even as much as the others. During pauses, he always had his hands full. Actually the marching was easier for him, for then he did not need to care about anything but his own movement.

The sound of shots penetrated his numb consciousness. At first they did not matter to him, but when they continued, he began to listen more carefully, and once he had them placed, he awoke completely. The firing came from some three kilometers ahead of them.

People on the loads began to ask questions.

"What is that... Is the road cut again? Doesn't anyone know anything?"

The column kept on advancing, but soon it began halting temporarily, each halt longer than the last, until the road refused to ingest it further. Taking the boys down from the saddle, Akseli told them to go to their families, and he rode ahead along the roadside until he was closer to the firing, which had now subsided to an occasional shot. For a long time he got vague answers to his questions, but when he got closer, someone came riding toward him. The man shouted as he went by:

"Men forward... the road is cut... The Germans are ahead of us... Where are the officers..."

When Akseli got closer, there were new messages.

"It's ugly up there... children's bodies on the road."

340

Akseli rode as far as he dared because of stray bullets, then tied his horse to a tree and asked a man to watch that no one took it. Traveling in a crouch along the side of the road, he came to the edge of the woods and saw a village opening ahead. The head of the column had turned back, but there were vehicles and fallen horses left in the road. Beside the vehicles there were indeed the bodies of women and children.

"Where is there an officer here?"

"We don't know. Our commander got left there."

Finally some officers were found, who began to organize the men arriving from farther back into a skirmish line. Akseli went to fetch his company. His horse was still there, and he rode back as fast as the roadside, now congested by the column, permitted.

"What's out there? Are the butchers there?"

Questions rained upon him, but he did not have time to answer. Reaching his company, he ordered the platoon leaders to assemble their men and be ready to march.

"Every last man who is able to fire a rifle."

Osku stood on the road, rifle on his shoulder and a slice of bread in his hand, shouting to the men from Pentti's Corner to form a column of twos. Carefree and giddy Osku, who could make even the widows and orphans in the column laugh. The children a mile ahead and behind in the column knew him, for in Hämeenlinna he had finagled a keg of caramel paste, which he distributed to children on pieces of new shingling he had taken from the wall of a hay barn.

On this journey the men were usually quick to form up. They took their rifles, cartridges, and a chunk of bread from the load. There was no grumbling or even questioning.

Uuno Laurila was in the first row of the group. Silent, with a cigarette in the corner of his mouth, he watched the commotion among the others as if in contempt. Valenti Leppänen fussed with something unnecessary near the load and, mumbling discretely, moved away from Osku. But Osku shouted:

"Valenti too. Join the gang."

"I don't even have a rifle."

"There's one on the load. You might even take two."

Looking troubled and confused, Valenti dug out a rifle from the load. Akseli noticed what was happening, and said:

"Let Valenti stay and take care of the loads... See that everyone doesn't follow when we start out."

During the journey, he had often felt pity for Valenti. If Aune had not taken care of her brother, he would literally not have gotten a piece of bread to put into his mouth. Although the horses needed to be spared, Akseli had given Valenti permission to ride on the wagons, for after the first day of marching, there were huge blisters on his feet. Shivering with cold, carefully shielding his clothing from dirt and filth, Valenti crouched at the foot of a tree during breaks, humble and depressed by his helplessness. Sometimes he would take a pen and paper from his pocket.

"I just thought of something... Nothing will come of it... but I'll put it down on paper."

Relieved at Akseli's words, he put the rifle back on the load, but Elma picked it up.

"Give it to me... I'll go... You gals come too..."

Swinging the rifle on her shoulder she stepped over to the platoon, but did not take a place in its ranks. Osku looked at the large men's trousers she wore, which made her look laughably fat, since their waist was wrapped twice around her.

"Well, at least the gal won't get cold. But put that rifle away," he said with a laugh.

"Keep your mouth shut. I'll go into anything you will... If you weren't so useless we wouldn't be here..."

"Come along then... And if you come out of it alive, you'll get a kiss. So on to St. Petersburg. Let's go."

Elma urged the other women to take up a rifle too, and got several of them to go with her. The young girls had been given some instruction in handling the rifles if need arose, although not many had fired one.

The company set out. Their dear ones stayed with the loads, waving goodbye and preparing for another painful wait.

The company marched past the jammed-up column. Panicky people asked questions which no one was able to answer. Wives thrust their children into the wagons beneath covers and bundles, for German artillery shells had begun to fall up ahead. In one spot someone shouted to the marching company:

"Don't go up there for nothing... There are no Germans there... They are Englishmen and Americans who have come to help us..."

"What is that firing?"

"The English must be fighting the butchers."

Some of the men in the company began stopping doubtfully. There was joy mingled with a slight doubt on the faces of the refugees crouching in the wagons and on the roadside.

"That's what they say... Hey, the English have come... Who said so... A rider went by and said..."

The people looked at one another. A slowly rising sense of relief brought tears to the eyes of frightened mothers. Then Akseli's voice rang out:

"Why are you stopping? Don't believe such things... I've been to see for myself. Get going."

"Who said that... who went to see... Some officer shouted that it's a rumor. Then why did they..."

Heads drooped.

Stray bullets made the company duck down. Along the road stood men who pointed and shouted:

"Over to the right. No one is there yet... Ask for Tilda Vuorela. She's the commander of a women's company... and then go on to the right..."

The glow of fires illuminated the night. Burning buildings collapsed in a heap, sending eruptions of flame and sparks into the air. But their crackling was drowned out by the roar of shots and the shouts of rage from thousands of throats. In the wavering light from the fires, the final assault began. What started it, no one knew. Who gave the order — even that was unknown. Perhaps there had been no more specific command than the exhortations the panting refugees had shouted to one another the entire evening:

"Forward... forward... forward, boys..."

What probably happened was that from the fringes of the circle of light around the fires, some man with initiative started forward. Another joined him, and a third, and they drew the others along. Perhaps in the consciousness of that mass of humanity, there had dawned a communal, instinctive realization that this was the final moment, and with group despair pressed to the limit, they had launched the assault. No one led them. The darkness and the total confusion of the units turned the remaining officers into ordinary riflemen, who commanded only the area they could see around them. The companies became mixed up, and during the battle they formed new ones. Somewhere a seventeen-year-old boy gathered some ten men around him and shouted an order:

"Company, advance."

And he started off. A leader brought forth by the situation, with whose youthful defiance there was combined the tension caused by the fear of death and perhaps joy at his position of command, which could end in the middle of his first charge.

Akseli fought with the men from his home village. Strange men had become mixed up with his company, and some of his own men had been lost somewhere. Panting, thirsty, and sweaty, he shouted to those nearest him, pointing out where to move ahead to and where the German positions were.

They had advanced along a pine-clad heath to the edge of a village. Fifty meters ahead of them a cottage was burning, the home of a Häme grandmother, where the old woman had perhaps been living out her dove-like existence with two lambs. Near it grew two rowan trees, and there were lilacs by the porch. Bullets punctured the walls of the cottage. The fly-spotted picture of the Savior with its passage of Scripture flew from the wall to the floor. And from the vicinity came shouts:

"Achtung...Achtung..."

A German officer's whistle blew a signal blast, which was followed by a roar of rage:

"Christ... goddamn."

Akseli saw Osku rise in a crouch and start toward the burning cottage along the edge of a potato patch. But he saw something else which made him yell out frantically:

"Osku, down..."

Behind a small outbuilding which had not yet caught fire, he caught a glimpse of a helmet in the firelight, and at that moment, Osku fell. Lauri Kivioja and Uuno Laurila had been following Osku to one side, and they threw themselves down when they heard Akseli's shout.

"They are behind that shed..."

Akseli fired a few hasty shots and circled around, avoiding the circle of light. As he went he uttered the shout he had repeated hundreds of times that evening and night:

"Forward!"

In the shelter of the rowan trees and the well sweep, he reached the corner of the shed. A face beneath a helmet came into view, distorted with tension. Another man was in back of the first, and he was on his knees, firing through a crack in the board wall. Akseli's rifle bolt snapped on an empty chamber, and he saw the flash of a bayonet around the corner. For a timeless second a thought lingered in his consciousness: "This is it."

Afterwards he could never remember what he thought or did. Not even how he had avoided the bayonet. What he recalled most clearly was how his rifle butt struck the German's helmet and how, with a rifle without a stock, he watched the German run a few steps in flight until Uuno Laurila's shot cut it short.

He threw his broken rifle aside and ran to Osku's side in the potato patch. He turned the body over and said Oskari's name twice. Oskari's open eyes gleamed blue in his dirty, bearded face in the light from the fire. But it was a lifeless gleam. His hat with the red ribbon had fallen off his head.

Akseli made a sound. Some memory from home moved in his mind, but it was blotted out by a burst of machine-gun fire whining across the potato patch. Quickly he took Oskari's watch and wallet, although he knew the act was unnecessary. Snatching up Osku's rifle too, he ran crouching to the cottage, behind which he could hear Elias's voice:

"The highway, boys... The highway runs there... watch out..."

Near the outbuilding, he looked quickly back. The cottage roof collapsed, and a bright flame lighted up the night. Osku's blond hair could be seen plainly against the black earth of the potato patch.

He joined in the shouts of hurrah that had begun around him and ran across the road. Beyond it could be heard Elma Laurila's shrill shout:

"This way, men... what are you afraid of..."

Around this rural community in Häme a battle raged between the German Uhlan Guard, on the one hand, and units made up of Finnish tenant farmers, day laborers, loggers, and their wives and daughters on the other. The Germans had come into this village, as into many in Poland, Belgium, and France. They had knocked around the fronts of the big world war, fighting now against one country's army and now against another's, stealing chickens, singing their songs, and smoking their poor cigarettes. But this was the first experience with anything of this sort.

From the dim light of the flames appeared visored caps and felt hats, and underneath them shone raging, dirty faces, that came and kept coming right into one's face. The Germans could hear shouts of hurrah and curses, which they had learned to mock, but whereas they said them with amused laughter, their enemy roared them through gritted teeth. And when a Uhlan saw a rifle butt raised to strike and sensed the last, horror-struck moment of death, one of those grating curses rang in his ears.

Nor was it only caps and hats that came at him, but tightly wrapped babushkas under which gleamed the frenzied eyes and mouth of a girl who essayed to sing in a shrill, panting voice:

"Now forward our native sons... "

To the right of a narrow lake, along a pine-clad heath, and across the main road, the assault advanced as one melee of crackling, roaring, and shouting. Mingled with the hurrahs were attempts at the Marseillaise, sung to the Germans in hoarse, panting voices. The shrill shouts of young girls were cut short by broken screams when a bullet struck.

There was no native land for them in the snows of the North, but behind them black death reared up, and so they achieved in that night attack such a despairing crest of fury that the Uhlans could not withstand it.

Around the burning buildings, remnants of the Germans who had become separated from their own forces battled for their lives, for they knew no mercy would be granted them. The others had scattered into the woods.

Silently, from hour to hour, the crowd of refugees listened to the continuing sounds of the battle.

"Will they get through? Have they taken the village yet?"

"Not yet... the like of it has never been seen even in hell."

The shivering children looked at the blood-red glow of the fires which spread over the treetops against the paling morning sky. When a mother was asked a timid question, she could not conceal her distress under a consoling reply, and the children sank back into their own mute world, in which their imagination sought to weave an explanation for the glow of the flames, the explosions, the shots, and the far-off shouts, the like of which had never been heard before.

From the head of the column, the wounded flowed back. Some came crawling, some more lightly wounded leaning on shoulders, begging for bandages and water. The medics who were there bandaged them with the help of the refugee women, but in the midst of their pain, their only concern was the course of the battle:

"...doesn't it seem to be moving that way..."

People clustered around them:

"Did you see our Martta there? She has a kind of red-striped kerchief..."

There was still shooting near the buildings when shouts came from the head of the column:

"Forward... What, what did they say? Forward... they said to move forward..."

The first vehicle started off. Bullets still whined through the air, and the man stopped his horse doubtfully. The road was blocked with vehicles and horses which had fallen in their shafts, goods fallen from loads, and human bodies. After a moment's hesitation, the man shouted:

"Hang on, hang on."

Beating his horse, he drove to the side of the road, the wagon rocking, and his wife crouching over the children on the load to shield them from the bullets and to keep them from falling off the wagon as it hurdled the ditch. They were followed by a second and third wagon. When a German machine gun began to rattle from somewhere, confusion ensued. Those in the lead stopped, but the pressure of those behind thrust them forward.

"Go on... we were ordered to move forward... Who's blocking the road? We'll be left here to die..."

The road ran between burning buildings. Snorting horses, shouts and curses, exhortations and commands. But the column moved, and in the wagons, even the children repeated the shouts of their parents: "Forward!"

A vehicle drove by a burning building. A man stood up on the load with a spinning wheel hoisted over his head. Hurling the implement to the roadside with all his strength, he shouted:

"Goddamned spinning wheels... now it's a question of life or death..."

There was a burst of fire from the roadside, and the horse fell. The man still kept on beating it as it lay there, until he shouted:

"Get off the wagon."

His wife and children got off the load, but again the machine gun rattled:

"Jesus Jesus... the children..."

The last one left standing in the road was a little girl wearing a grown-up's coat and with a kerchief on her head. From a load driving by came a shout:

"Away... run... girl... run..."

The girl's stupefied consciousness seemed to rouse. She ran a few steps, but then returned to the road where her mother lay writhing. Then there was only a brief, frightened cry:

"Agh."

One family's journey had ended.

The firing dwindled. Again the road drew the column forward. Even the fire subsided, and the morning dawned. A few isolated shots echoed around the village. Someone wounded during the night heard the rumble of the advancing column. He was no longer able to call out for help. Raising a Mauser to his temple, he fired.

The journey continued. Gradually the procession returned to its established order.

"Hasn't anybody seen Onni?"

"Not since Artturi saw him about three o'clock."

"Have you seen a little boy with a knitted woolen hat... of gray yarn?"

"I haven't seen him."

"Did he die for sure... so that he wasn't left to..."

"He was as dead as dead can be. I said his name many times and felt his heart..."

Akseli walked alone. Someone had taken his horse, but it didn't matter. He had sent men to care for families that had lost their father, but otherwise he avoided places where he would hear the weeping of widows and orphans.

From ahead the sound of artillery fire carried over the column.

Elias hurried abreast of him from behind.

"Did you hear. What are those... They say you can't get through Lahti any more."

In a tired and soft voice, Akseli replied:

"I know exactly as much about the matter as you do."

II

"If a weapon is found on anyone from now on, it means an automatic death sentence."

The Finnish interpreter gave the orders, and the Germans watched alertly with their rifles ready to fire. Akseli walked slowly in the line toward the pile of weapons. He had thrown his rifle into the woods before the surrender, but he still had a pistol. He had kept it when he had seen the bodies of men lying by the roadside, and had heard the rumor:

"Every tenth man was taken from the ranks and ordered to reveal his commander... And the boys say..."

No one wanted to die for the sake of another, and Akseli kept his pistol to the last. The temptation to suicide was exceptionally strong. For a long time he had sat beside the road with his head in his hands. Would it not be better to die now, tired and numb, choosing the moment of death himself rather than have others do so after a tormented period of waiting? The numbness of his mind was so great that the instinct for self-preservation had to seek out its best weapon.

"If there is the smallest possibility... for the sake of the boys..."

But even as he dropped the pistol into the pile, his hand held on to it uncertainly, causing a German soldier to growl something nervously in his own language.

Akseli dropped the pistol.

"Boolet... boolet..."

"The last ones are in the clip."

He moved on to the group of prisoners waiting farther up the road. Now that the decision was made, he felt easier. His relief also resulted from the fact that only now did he feel freed of the responsibility for the fate of his company and the refugees. He was pleased at having happened among a group of prisoners who were strangers. It was good to be alone, surrounded only by strangers.

They were taken toward the city, filling the whole road. Beside the files marched Germans in steel helmets with bare bayonets, the prisoners walking gravely between them.

After a while a man was waved out of the crowd of prisoners. He was made to strip off his boots and hand over his watch. One of the Germans looked at Akseli's boots for a long time. Having made a decision, he motioned him to one side:

"Boot... boot..."

Akseli took off his boots.

"Uhr... Uhr..."

He gave the man both watches, his and Osku's. Both wallets went as well. They seemed useless, but the boots were another matter, and he pointed to the German's boots and his own feet. When the man understood his meaning, he laughed in a friendly, cheerful manner and said:

"Nein, nein..."

In his stocking feet, he continued his journey toward Lahti. Closer to the city, civilians thronged the roadside, among them a landowner, who stood with reins in hand and suddenly began to beat the men traveling in front of Akseli with them.

"Goddamned Red bandits..."

Akseli tucked in his neck when he reached the spot. Two painful blows struck his back before the German soldier ran in between, shouting angrily, and shooed the man away with his bayonet. From behind they could still hear the landlord's panting voice:

"Took my best horse just the other day. The bastards are going to pay for it with their lives."

Then there opened before them a broad field full of people and vehicles.

In the field Akseli found people from his home parish who had arrived earlier. No one had footwear to give him, but he found a sack and a cord on one of the loads. He tore the sack in two, wrapped the pieces around his feet, and tied them with the cord. Getting a piece of bread, he ate it, leaning against a wagon wheel, half asleep. Then he stretched out on the ground and fell asleep immediately.

At some time during the night he woke up.

"Where is the shooting?"

"Shhh... they're taking people from here."

"Where to?"

"To that hill... that's where the sound is coming from."

Akseli sat up. The sounds of thousands of people moving and their soft talk filled the air. Again came the sound of a single shot, and the people nearest him fell silent.

Akseli rose and went shuffling closer to the edge of the field. Some sense warned him not to go where he could be seen, but curiosity got the best of him. It demanded that he find out how things stood and thereby what his own fate would be. Four prisoners were brought out of the crowd of people, three men and one woman. The woman wore clay-stained men's clothing.

"Five men are to go with them. Are there any volunteers?"

The officer looked at the group of soldiers. A young boy tossed his rifle by the strap to his shoulder:

"Let's go, Niemelä. We'll show the Germans how you shoot a man..."
Akseli drew back quickly, and Elias came toward him, saying:
"Don't be a fool nd go out there... there might be someone you know."
"They took four of them."
"They've been taking them all night. Go over to that wagon, we'll cover you up there. They'll come to ask for the leaders in a little while... And someone may open his mouth."
They went over to the wagons, but Akseli gave up the idea of hiding.
"I won't... let them take me then... I'm going to sleep."
He lay down on the ground. The afternoon sleep had not nearly banished his weariness. He twitched slightly when shots echoed in the woods nearby.
"I wonder if they were the ones... the woman was crying..."
He looked directly up at the spring sky, which was beginning to shroud over with the darkness of night. The hum of talk was soporific. Somewhere nearby a child was crying and he could hear the mother soothing it.
"Tomorrow you'll get water, child... tomorrow the men will bring it to you... try to sleep... go to sleep now, child."
He was already asleep when the next execution shot roared. The sky disappeared from sight, and Red Officer Koskela slept on his back on Fellman Field, a sleep as sound as death, overcoat collar raised around his neck and shapeless sack wrappings on his feet.
Around him the tragedy of ten thousand people played itself out in the quiet hum of concerned talk and subdued weeping.

One day, a second, a third, fourth, and fifth. Hunger and thirst, Civil Guard members moving through the camp, and panicky farewells.
"They took our father."
Women's skirts were in demand, for a rumor ran throughout the crowd of people.
"Women, take off your trousers... everyone in men's clothing will be shot."
They got a skirt for Elma by the simple expedient of Elias's stealing it. He also managed to get something to eat now and then, but day by day the food decreased and hunger increased. Valenti had developed a fever, for his overcoat had been stolen and he had caught a chill. Elias did get him an overcoat, for if anything at all was obtainable, Elias had a trick to get it. When officers going through the camp happened to come near, they hid Akseli in the wagon under horse blankets, and the men leaned idly into the wagon to conceal him from view. For the Finnish Red Guard was perhaps the only army in the history of the world whose officers were forced to comply with the first duty of a commander. They did not do so voluntarily,

but under bitter compulsion. Throughout the day, but particularly in the evening, series of shots rang out in the surrounding woods.

On the fifth evening, a disturbance arose in the Pentti's Corner group.

"The apothecary... hey... hide him, boys..."

But it was too late. The arrivals had come too close.

"There's Arvo too... and Yllö's boy."

"Ahaa... So here you are?"

There were officers with the men, and the apothecary pointed to Akseli.

"We want this man first."

"Do you know him?"

"Very well. Uhuh, Koskela. There are many people who would like to see you at home."

Akseli rose and stood up. The other man they took was Uuno Laurila. A discussion arose between the officers and the men who had come. Akseli noticed that he was being looked at, and could make out these words:

"You can't take him... if what you say is so, he will be a valuable person to interrogate... You can give us written information about him... you would shoot him right away, but through him we may find out about many others."

Akseli heard the words without actually understanding their meaning. Uolevi explained to him.

"Koskela's case will be dealt with here. But Laurila will come with us."

The words seemed insignificant to Akseli, although they meant a slight prolongation of his life. His strongest emotion was actually to ask something about his home, but he understood that no one would answer anyway. He stood motionless, staring at the earth. Should he ask? Perhaps he could ask Arvo. But there was no need to inquire, for Uolevi said:

"There would be some little matters to clear up there, but they can be taken care of here too. Although you really belong with Halme and your brothers."

"And where are they?"

"Under the ground, and you'll soon be there too."

The knowledge did not greatly affect his benumbed mind. His consciousness was somehow frozen. He watched without expression as Arvo said to Uuno:

"We have a little matter to settle between us."

Uuno stood with his hands in his pockets and said as he had once said when leaving Ketunmäki:

"Let's go."

There was restrained rage in the eyes of the men who had come for them. The apothecary again pointed a finger at Akseli and said in a low voice to an officer:

"He has at least two murders on his conscience. He's one of the most dangerous."

Then they asked where the church village men were, and Elias answered:

"We don't know. We were with our own outfit."

"We'll find them well enough. And we won't forget you either."

When they were leaving, Uuno turned to Elma. When she heard Uolevi's words, she had drawn back into the shadow of the wagon and wept there curled up in a heap. Uuno called her name, and she turned:

"Don't feel bad about it."

Uuno said it softly, thrust his hands into his pants pockets, and left, swinging his shoulders with exaggerated pride. Elma curled up again and thrust the corner of her kerchief into her mouth.

One of the officers said to Akseli:

"You are a company commander. Why didn't you tell us?"

"Nobody asked."

"Hmm. Follow me."

The officer spoke in a normal tone of voice, without anger or sharpness, and Akseli shuffled after him.

There was tumult at the end of the camp. Men came and went, prisoners were assembled into different groups, and then set off in different directions. The officer gestured to Akseli.

"That way."

They were taken up a hill away from the city. There were many people at the roadside, scolding and threatening the prisoners. A woman, well-dressed, with the air of an upper-class person, screamed hysterically:

"Kill them, kill them..."

Akseli pulled his hat over his eyes to escape the sight of those angry faces. There, under its brim, was the only chance for the solitude he yearned for. In his dull and empty mind, there was only one hope:

"If they would just shoot me soon."

III

"The sound is coming from in back of the fifth barrack."

The prisoners never got used to it, although they heard it more often than they saw their daily bread.

They lived in a crowded cell. They tried to take turns sleeping on the cement floor, for there was not room enough for them all to lie down at one time. Every day, names were shouted out and men taken away, but that didn't help matters, for new ones were thrust in. There was really not time enough to get acquainted.

It was Akseli's turn to lie down. He lay with his face pressed to the wall. The stone wall was cold, and he kept his lips against it, trying to breathe cooler air from its surface. He could not actually swallow, for his throat burned dryly. Hunger and thirst had already become a bodily pain. An hour ago, a man had begun to take a sauna bath leaning into a wall. Shouting and cursing, he had pretended to beat himself with a whisk. Thirst and the stifling air had caused the man, whose mind was going, to imagine himself in a sauna.

Sharp pangs of hunger rose from Akseli's bowels. They resembled a stomach complaint, and to many they were just that. A finger-sized piece of bread made of chaff and three small, yellowish herring once a day changed in many stomachs to a green paste mixed with blood, which came into one's pants of its own accord, before a sick man was able to make it to the barrel in the corner by the door. The air, polluted by the reek, was lacking in oxygen, for they were not allowed to open the window. Once it had been opened without permission, and one of the prisoners had bent over to breathe at it. He had had time to draw two breaths when the guard shot him there. The body was dropped out.

Skin turned yellow and bodies exuded a cold sweat. Time crawled slowly. When names were called out, many actually waited for their own to be called. But in the cell they protected one another's lives. When someone tore strips from his clothing and begged for hanging, it was not allowed.

For many days, Akseli had awaited the interrogations mentioned in the field, but when he entered the barrack, they had only taken down his personal information and no such interrogation had occurred. He was getting to be the only original occupant of the cell.

The door opened. A dead silence prevailed in the cell.

"Are the following men here?"

Names were read out, and Akseli's was the fifth.

"Koskela, Akseli Johannes, born March twenty-sixth, in the year one thousand eight-hundred eighty-seven."

It was him. Painfully he struggled to his feet.

Only when they were on their way to the yard did he really feel how weak he was. He had to focus all his energy on moving his feet. With every step he had to make sure that his leg would bear the weight. What he saw as he went by stirred a slight curiosity in him. Red-brick army barracks, yards full of prisoners huddling on the ground, barbed wire, and soldiers and officers going to an fro.

He could not sustain an interest in them.

They were told that they were being taken to maximum-security cells, and they entered the same kind of building they had left. But the cell was even smaller, apparently being originally intended as a closet for brooms and other supplies.

They could already hear a quiet sobbing from the cell.

Days became confused. Akseli could not remember the number of days he had spent in the cell, but he judged them to be six or seven. Once he asked the men who had brought him if his name hadn't been on the list, but got only a barked response:

"What business is it of yours?"

Men were taken from the cell one at a time, and finally it was his turn. It was not a long trip, "turn right at the corridor."

Behind a table sat a big man with a shiny, bald head and thick, black eyebrows. Other officers and soldiers stood nearby. When Akseli staggered painfully to the table, angry eyes glared at him, and the bald-headed man glowered at him and growled:

"Ahaa. How many murders do you have on your conscience?"

Akseli's eyes fixed on a club and a length of chain on the table. From here the faint sound of screams had carried to the cell, and rumor told of men being carried out.

"I asked, how many murders do you have on your conscience?"

"No one... not one."

"Maybe not, goddamn, since you don't have a conscience. Which do you want, to be sent to your home parish to be shot or would you rather die here."

"Here."

"Few are so badly wanted by their home parish as you. Just looking at you, I can tell you're a criminal."

One of the men stepped forward, took him by the shoulder, and shoved him:

"Stand at attention in the presence of an officer."

For a second it flashed through Akseli's consciousness that he was doing something he should not do, but bodily pain and weakness clouded his reasoning. He felt the blood burn in his eyes and cheeks. A shaky roar of rage burst from his lips:

"Don't touch me... by God..."

Blood rose to his head and things went black before his eyes. The floor began to rock, and he fumbled for the edge of the table. Then a fist struck his face. A flash of red sparks was the last thing he remembered.

He was clubbed while already unconscious. A boot stamped his face, and blood streamed from his mouth and nose.

The baldhead growled:

"Number one."

The soldiers grabbed the unconscious man and dragged him along the floor.

"Empty the corridor. Everybody out."

The session of the court had ended.

The first thing he saw was a dim light, which grew clearer and became a wall. Then his ear began to distinguish sounds. From nearby he heard someone babbling as he sobbed:

"Not for myself... But I have eight children..."

His cheeks felt clumsy, and in his dry mouth, his tongue was encumbered by congealed blood. Thirty centimeters from his eyes was a plaster wall on which there was writing. His eyes read it, but his brain could not take part in the reading:

I die tomorrow. Ordered to be shot, Frans Wilhelm Laakso. Born in Karkku. Going to join his father or changing food plan. Wife shot. Three boys left, Heikki, Matti, and Lauri. There are 12 of us and we are all free. We die free.

Akseli closed his eyes. Gradually he began to feel pain in all parts of his body. Behind his back he could hear the quiet movements of several people. He tried to turn over, but his strength did not suffice, and a rattling moan came from his mouth.

The face of a young boy, blond hair falling over his forehead, appeared above him. His face too was swollen:

"Hey, our buddy woke up. Does anyone have a rag?"

The boy wiped his face with the rag and dug the blood from his mouth with a corner of it.

"Is that better?"

"It is... a little water."

"They won't give us any."

"Where am I?"

"Are you afraid to hear?"

"No."

"This is the death cell... from here you go to the swamp in back of number five... just so you know."

The boy said it almost boastfully. Then he turned away:

"Hey, buddy. Give me that fur hat so we'll have something to put under our buddy's head."

The boy put the hat under Akseli's head as a pillow, for he was lying on a cement floor. Akseli mumbled some kind of thanks, and the boy went away. Bit by bit, he began to listen to the sounds around him. From the corner of his eye he saw the round, weathered face of a young woman. She had a turned-up nose. Hands materialized over the face.

He tried to turn again, but could not. Mumbling, he begged the others to turn him. The same blond boy came and turned his aching head and body so that he could see the whole room. It was dimly lighted. The light which struck the wall came through cracks between the boards over the window, and just happened to fall on the writing. The rest of the room was much darker. People were sitting on the floor, leaning against the walls. In the dim light he could make out another woman, already up in years, a farm wife wearing a kerchief on her head. When his eyes adjusted to the light, he could see details more clearly. People with bowed heads, their eyes on the floor, some of them weeping quietly with their hands over their faces. The blond boy was leaning against the wall near Akseli, and he said to the girl with the turned-up nose:

"Don't cry, girl... And don't pray... There is no heaven up there. The bosses invented it to make the people humble... When you flop into the swamp, that's it, goddamn. Your body will grow worms, and your soul will go off into the winds of hell and you won't know a thing... It's no use to be afraid... And it doesn't even hurt."

"You stop that too."

It was an older man, speaking in an exasperated voice.

"Don't think about it... Think about old things... that's what I do."

The young man brushed the hair from his forehead. He seemed restless. Sometimes he clutched at objects and he would speak every so often:

"But then there's this song, boys:

Our country lies in the northern snows,
on its shores our hearth fires blaze.
Wielding the sword our hands grew strong.
Our minds burned with honor's creed.

"Stop it."
"Don't get all worked up."

We watered our mounts in the course of the Neva.
They swam like fish oe'r the Veichsel.
They brought our avenging swords to the Rhine
and drank the king's wine from the Danube.

The boy stopped and said with a slightly nostalgic sigh:

"I was in the Turku cavalry, goddamn. We used to ride like hell with the boys... The bastards won't give us water..."

He walked to the door and kicked at it:

"Don't kill us with thirst, goddamn... the bosses talked about shooting."

The kick did not produce any movement in the corridor, and he returned to his place.

"I don't give a damn... But if my sister would bring a package so I could eat once more."

Then he sat for a long time against the wall with his arms wrapped around his knees, thinking, until he began talking again. He apparently had to say all his thoughts aloud before he was able to think them:

"The bald head asked if I shot that gentleman... I said no... I thought I wouldn't say anything to those bastards... And I got a fist in the face that made my ears ring... But I'm glad I did, and I'll tell them even on the rim of the grave that I did shoot the bastard... I asked him if he would give me work now... He said let bygones be bygones. I told him it wasn't all that long ago... He fired the old man because he belonged to the association, and my sister too, and he wouldn't hire me. He told me Reunanen, you even were in the factory children's choir when he tried to cozy up to me... Yes I was, I said, and a good singer too... many other people say so and not just me... But I let the daylight through him... I really was one of the brats in the choir... They gave us towel bibs... boys and girls got the same kind... And we sang. I have a sonorous voice. They were nice songs:

> *Child of Finland, don't trade away*
> *your own beautiful land.*
> *For the bread abroad is bitter,*
> *and harsh the speech on foreign strand.*

After his song, the boy went to kick at the door again:

"Water, you bastards... Those goddamned fuzzy-headed Kainuu louts can hear this well enough but out of deviltry they won't come..."

Returning to the wall, he began to reminisce again:

"If my sister knew, she would bring me a package. That is, if they haven't killed her... She was in the Red Cross, and they killed all the Red Cross women... And all the men with low foreheads... They wrote in the papers that all the Red women had to be shot so that they wouldn't breed new pups... and all the men with low foreheads because they were hooligans... But if my sister were alive, she would bring something... I wouldn't care so much about the others, but I would like to have seen my sister

357

again... Water, you goddamned burr-heads... Our buddy wants water..."

Akseli moaned for water. His tongue was thick and unwieldy in his blood-sticky mouth. His shapeless, swollen lips were burning. Pieces of chaff left in his gums from the bread prickled and stung.

The streak of light shining on the wall from the crack in the boards shifted slowly. They guessed at the time of day in low voices, and the later the time, the greater the uneasiness among the occupants of the cell. Only Reunanen seemed to become more talkative and gay.

The door opened. A nervous movement arose in the group. Someone tried to get behind another's back.

Both women were taken out, along with Reunanen and the old man who had wept for his eight children. The girl braced herself against the doorframe, weeping and bursting into high-pitched screams. A soldier grabbed her braid and dragged her into the corridor with one jerk. Reunanen turned around in the doorway, raised his hands, and said in a resounding voice:

"So long, buddies... You won't hear when I sing in the pit... But you'll hear the shots, and then I want you to say the singing boy is gone... And if you see anyone who knew Jalli Reunanen, then tell him that my last wish was that someone should sing at his grave the song that says: 'Don't weep, Mother, don't weep, mother dear...' So long, boys."

The door was closed and they heard Reunanen's words from the corridor:

"Don't shove me, you goddamned burr-head."

The words were followed by the thump of two blows.

Akseli was now strong enough, and turned back toward the wall. The same writing struck his eyes again... "three boys were left, Heikki, Matti, and Lauri..." He moaned softly with pain, but the same moan gave vent to the grievous knowledge that remembering the boys would be the worst part of his torment.

In a half-hour, new prisoners were thrust into the cell.

IV

The Hennala barracks were at the edge of a wooded pastureland, with a part of them on a field of clay. The Russians had just recently constructed them and they were only half-finished, ugly buildings of red brick masonry. Even the surroundings were raw and neglected. A barbed wire fence had been strung around the area, and in these barracks the prisoners were collected from Fellman Field, from the foundry, the schools, and other collection sites.

Many were already staggering from weakness on arrival, for in the collection sites, they had had to make do with the food they happened to have with them. They were divided into groups and had identifying marks painted on or labels affixed to their backs. A constant stream of groups arrived from distant home parishes to identify them:

"This man."

If a group did not take a man with them, soldiers at the barracks would take him out in back of "number five," where there was a ready-made mud pit left when soil had been hauled from it to enrich neighboring farms.

The men from Pentti's Corner were in the same barrack. Only the women had been taken away. Board partitions divided the large barracks into smaller rooms, which were crammed so full that the occupants had to take turns sleeping. During the first days they had to stay in those cells without any food. Those who were weak from the after-effects of wounds or illness died in a couple of days. Suddenly a man who had been standing would stagger and sink at the feet of the others. His body would be towed through the crush to the corridor and collected for hauling away. Valenti's fever was gone, but he was so weak that he was allowed to lie down continually. Thin and dirty, he lay there on the cement floor. On the very first day he had been nicknamed "Yankee" because of his speech.

When they were let out during the day, Valenti grew somewhat stronger from the fresh air, and the bits of food that Elias managed to scrounge for him. Many of the prisoners squatted in the yard, afraid even to move, for no one knew the regulations, and in addition the guards came up with all kinds of whims. The smallest violation was cause for shooting, and the bursts of machine-gun fire and single shots heard constantly from in back of "number five," sustained the terror. But Elias adjusted quickly. In one day he learned what one could and could not do. He learned to move and to observe, and in a pinch, he could be frightened and humble:

"Sir soldier, can one go into that barrack's yard?"

"It isn't exactly allowed... but go on then..."

He would wiggle through a swarm of prisoners, ask and observe. He stole one guard's cigarettes and traded them to another for bread, then returned from his mission with the bread hidden under his coat. Meantime Lauri had kept watch over Valenti, who, because of his weakness, got all kinds of notions.

Once when lurking near the barbed-wire fence, Elias saw Aune walking on the other side of it.

"Aune."

"Jesus, is it you, Elias?"

"It is."

"It's weird. You're so dirty and skinny."

"Where are you?"

"In the women's barrack, but I go to clean the room of a soldier from Pori."

"Couldn't you get a little bit of bread... Valenti is in bad shape."

"I'll ask the soldier... if he'll give it... He's awfully nice... He's a gentleman..."

They arranged a time and place to meet. Aune was not allowed to come to the other side of the fence, but she could give him the bread through openings in it. She told him about Elma too. They were in the same barrack but in separate rooms.

"I saw her... But she doesn't really say anything... She's mourning for Akusti and her family."

The guard approached and they parted.

A bachelor top sergeant had indeed chosen Aune as his housecleaner. He lived outside the camp, and Aune was given a pass which allowed her to move about. There was really no cleaning to be done in the little room, but the sergeant laughed his bachelor laugh, for the war had upset his customary life-style too. At first he went through a few preliminaries. Aune would stand in the doorway.

"Is this good enough now?"

"It's fine... But if you would fix that a little more."

Aune did some trifling thing.

"Now that bed cover..."

Finally the sergeant pinched Aune.

"Teehee... Sergeant, you're so awful."

Aune covered her eyes with her hands.

"...aa..."

The threshold was not a high one, but even though the sergeant was stingy, he had to promise bread before he could cross it.

" I don't... but I'm so awfully sick too... there's so little food..."

"Well, I can give you a little..."

"And my brother is in the camp too, and he's about to die... I can't even think..."

The sergeant's forehead was sweaty. The look in his eyes darkened, and the dry past of his scrimping soul vanished, shattered by great events.

"...he has even gone to America... and he's an American citizen... And he wasn't any kind of Red... he's just a refugee, teehee... you mustn't, I'm so ticklish... he's a big reindeer owner..."

The sergeant no longer heard Aune's word, although they were spoken almost into his ear:

"...he's a little more refined... a kind of American... he's that kind..."

Valenti grew a little stronger on the extra bread. But in a few days it dwindled and then ceased entirely. The sergeant had come to his senses and realized that he had the power of life and death over people. In addition, Aune tended to handle his binoculars and other things, about which the sergeant was jealously solicitous. When Aune asked to look through the binoculars, the old face of the sergeant took on a dissatisfied expression. He did let her look, but wisely held on to them as she did.

"It makes everything so awfully nice... One end makes things bigger and the other end makes them smaller."

The sergeant grumbled something, and always checked everything carefully after Aune's visits. Having glanced cautiously out of the window, he even counted his money.

And Aune, offended, said to Elias:

"A girl from Kotka has been there a couple of times... And she isn't at all good-looking... I don't mean... but it's so awful... to go just for the bread..."

Keeping an eye out for the guards, Elias looked around.

"Don't bother him too much... just ask once in a while..."

There was a gloomy and serious expression on his face as he said:

"...ask the kind of soldiers who look at the women but don't say anything... many of them are from the northern backwoods and they don't understand the situation..."

The next day Aune brought a piece of bread and a chunk of baked curds. But she was upset, and there were tears in her eyes.

"Elma was put in isolation... they called out her name... they must have got it from home... They always take them from that room..."

Elias snatched the gifts she brought with her, mumbled something unintelligible, and, glancing around, vanished into the group of prisoners.

Elma sat on the cement floor leaning against the wall. She had recently been brought from the chief guard post at the field court. She herself did not know that it was a field court, for they had asked her nothing but her name, age, and place of birth. After that she had been sent to this large room filled with weeping women, most of them young girls, but with a few older women among them as well.

The door opened and an oldish, gray-haired civilian stepped in. He wore glasses and looked through them at the women, blinking his eyes.

"Would God's word be suitable now?"

He spoke in a kindly voice, but nevertheless there were shrieks from the group of women:

"My God... Are they going to shoot us..."

One of the girls curled up in small heap in a corner.

"I'm not the one to decide that, but at my own request I have permission to say a few words to you. If you wish..."

The women were silent, and the minister took it for agreement.

"Perhaps we'll sing something first."

The minister began a religious song, which a number of women's voices joined in, their singing mixed with sobbing. Elma remembered only parts of the song, and these she sang with the others. The cool stone wall felt good against her burning cheek, down which an even hotter tear soon rolled. Crouched in the shade of a wagon in Fellman Field she had wept her eyes dry. Finally she had merely clenched her teeth on her kerchief, for tears no longer came. Arriving at the barrack, she had finally achieved a kind of equilibrium amidst the strange hubbub. Only at night, awake in the heat and constriction, in the grip of a gnawing hunger and of thirst, surrounded by the buzzing whispers of many women's voices, she heard, as if from somewhere far off, these words ring in her ears: "He is under the ground, and soon you will be there too."

Then she had covered her face and wept.

Here among these frightened women, her firmness of will had broken down again. Leaning her head against the wall, she listened to the song, joining in the stanzas she happened to remember. When her mouth was dry, she dug a dirty rag bundle from her pocket. In it she had a few half-rotting, leathery turnip peels, from the insides of which she sucked through her teeth the little moisture they contained into her dry mouth.

She was not afraid of death. She feared only the moment of execution, but she did not want to live. Her most powerful emotion was a poignant yearning for everything she had experienced with Akusti. While the song of the minister and the women rang out, she saw Aku coming, leaning on his cane, in the darkness of the threshing barn. In her mind she repeated the words the boy had said: 'Dear, darling, beloved.' Hunger had enlarged her dark eyes as her face shrank around them. Her hair was a mess, the dress Elias had stolen for her was too large, and the men's shoes she wore, tied with packaging string from a store, were covered with clay. Her hands and face were so dirty that streaks from her tears could be seen on her cheeks. At intervals she hummed along with the rest, but lifelessly and in snatches:

> *...like a rose which puts forth petals and fragrance,*
> *like a bubble which gleams and disappears...*

The other women sang devoutly, their voices sometimes breaking down into weeping. The same girls who, at Syrjäntaka, Lahti, and at these same

Hennala barracks, had charged German machine guns, shrieking madly. Dirty, ragged, shamed, and hungry, they were living the last moments of their lives. Their thoughts revolved around the approaching horror or the place where they had once learned this song: at home, their mother humming along with them, in a faintly lighted little cottage during long, dark winter nights as the spinning wheel hummed and the carding combs rasped.

> *Only joy in the Lord is from everlasting,*
> *a rose that ne'er lets fall its petals.*
> *Haste to secure it while you are still young,*
> *the one rose beyond all compare.*

As the minister recited the Lord's Prayer, whispering voices repeated it, and when he left, the women seemed calm. Then the door was torn open.

"Up and out in the corridor."

Panicky whispers and sounds. One of the bolder ones asked:

"Where are you taking us?"

" Don't ask useless questions."

They guessed what was going on when they saw the soldiers with rifles in the corridor. Curious glances fell on the women, for almost all of them were young, although many were in wretched clothing and filthy from head to foot. One of the soldiers winked at his companion. The women sensed in the soldiers' glances the unchecked brutality directed at them, and that knowledge, which did not rise to the level of thought, added to their horror, for it stripped from their consciousness the fiction of a woman's inviolability.

The air in the corridor was stagnant. The odor of cement and plaster was mingled with those of human sweat and excrement emanating from the cells. The doors were closed, with a guard standing before each one, and the corridor was otherwise empty. The women, uncertain and helpless, were lined up in the corridor. At a gesture from the officers or soldiers, they would take their places, but they might continue to shift, uncertain of whether they had understood the gesture correctly. Clearly not understanding their situation, they moved with a frightened humility, as if to please their guards. But it was in vain. The expression of harsh and brutal lewdness did not leave their faces. Aune happened to meet the procession at the outer door. She saw Elma in the group and asked an officer standing by the doorframe:

"Where are they being taken?"

"To a German soap factory."

The officer had just coined the witticism, and it seemed so clever that he answered Aune, which he would not otherwise have done. Aune drew back frightened, but Elma noticed her. The girl took the turnip peels wrapped in the dirty rag from her pocket and tossed them hastily at Aune's feet.

"Take... them... and goodbye..."

In her fright, Aune was unable to reply, but gazed with open mouth. Elma hurried on with her head bowed as if she were fleeing from Aune.

Elma walked in the van of the group. The low evening sun gilded the barracks and their surroundings. She gazed at the ground. The laceless shoe of the woman in front of her flopped badly, and she often looked as if she were about to fall out of weakness. They reached the gate and turned there along a trail into the woods. Clouds of insects roused by the springtime rose and fell in the sunlight. The damp fragrance of the swamp woods nearby struck their nostrils. Echoing in the clear evening air over the noises of the camp could be heard the laughter and shouts of women and soldiers standing along the road leading to the gate. They made Elma quiver, for with them some poignant but vague memory intruded into her consciousness. A smothered sob escaped her.

The path through the fir trees was much traveled, and bare tree roots protruded from its muddy bottom. A shoe had been left in a soft spot. Spent cartridge shells gleamed along the trail. Many garments were also to be seen. Hats, gloves, and a woman's ripped blouse.

The woods were marshy , and insects buzzed in the damp air, coming to attack the lagging column. The farther it went, the more staggering became its progress. There were growled commands, and the sobs had changed to storms of weeping. Someone fell and was ordered to get up.

Before them appeared a black, muddy excavation. The trunks of trees around it were torn by bullets. Someone babbled a prayer and someone screamed when they saw the machine gun and the man who was fingering it.

"Break it off here. You others stay here and turn your backs."

There were twenty of them, but the division was not equal, for there were eleven in the first group.

Not all of them were able to go. They were shoved and dragged to the edge of the pit. One was on her knees, her hands clasped, begging for mercy, and on her knees she was dragged to the place. The soldiers were brutal and angry, as if fending off their horror by that means. Clothing tore with a ripping sound, and there were curses.

Finally they were all in place. Elma looked into the mud grave and saw a woman's shoulder there. The grave had been poorly covered the last time. Next to her was an older woman, who kept repeating hysterically:

"Jesus... take your children into your care... Jesus, take your children into your care..."

The lock of the machine gun snapped, and Elma caught hold of the lamenting woman. They stood abreast, their sides to the machine gun, Elma hugging the woman with one arm. The girl next to them was whispering a plea for the Lord's Blessing.

The machine gunner had made a mistake in feeding the belt and was still poking at his weapon. He was not too skillful at it, for slight drunkenness had made him clumsy. He had been given alcohol from the camp hospital. With the slyness of an alcoholic, he had pretended to be too sensitive for his task, and so had gotten the doctor to relent. The officer said something to him in an impatient voice, and the soldiers looked at the women, trying with their brutally mocking faces to expel the pity and horror that was stirring somewhere deep in their souls.

Elma turned her back to the machine gun and embraced the old woman passionately.

"Don't... don't..."

She panted heavily as she said it, and held the woman as if to shelter and protect her, but when she heard the rattling of the machine gun and the screams and the rustle of falling bodies behind her, she clung to her like a child. Even when she fell she was clutching the woman so tightly that she dragged her down with her.

Once she returned to the threshold of consciousness. She saw a little reddish light and felt an inconceivable pain in her body. Then that too went out.

It happened when a soldier fired the insurance shot into her head before throwing her into the grave.

V

Akseli was already able to move. But there wasn't much opportunity for it. The room was always full, even though the people changed. There seemed to be no sort of plan in the executions, for some who were brought in during the afternoon could be taken the same evening, but for his part, he had been in the cell for many days. He was totally concentrated on waiting to die, and often he wished to because of the tormenting hunger and thirst. They got water only by happenstance, and that was very seldom. Once a day they were given a stinking soup with a piece of dried cod in it, with sometimes a vague taste of some root vegetable. When one ate it, it screeched in one's teeth. Every few days they were given a piece of bitter-tasting bread made of chaff and vetch, from which splinters stuck in their gums and palate. Their other food was either small yellowed herring or sardines, which gave rise to a thirst, not the kind that he had sometimes known on a sunny summer work-day, but a pain in his mouth and throat and in his whole feverish body.

He had his own regular place on the cement floor in the corner. Those who had been with him longer in the cell did not really bother him. They already knew that the man with the surly stare wanted to be left alone.

After a short time he was forced to change sides, for his bones, which protruded more and more, were compressed against the hard floor. Sometimes he raised his hand to the shafts of light shining through the spaces between the boards. Their joints were knobby. He could plainly see the bones and tendons of his wrists under the chapped skin.

He could not see his bearded face, the cheeks of which dried up and shrank between his teeth once the swelling had gone down. His eyes sank into their sockets. But he guessed at his own appearance by that of the others.

Like many of the others, he suffered from a bloody dysentery. At first the others helped him to get to the barrel. But as soon as he was able to move at all, he refused their help. Supposing that the moment of truth would come soon, he tried to get to his feet. Slowly he rose on all fours, then to his knees, and painfully exerting all his strength, he stood up, leaning against the wall. And along the wall he made his way to the barrel.

Someone approached and said to him:

"I'll hold you a little."

"No... I'll make it..."

The answer was muttered, but his helper believed it at once. Akseli did not want help, for it would have obligated him to listen. Many tried in their fear of death to find support in others, and sensing the quiet strength in that sad and sullen man, they tried get near to him. But he wanted to be alone. Silent, he lay in the corner. In the dark room there was the sound of whispering and sometimes a faint weeping. From time to time the door was opened and new men came in. They always brought more noise with them and were more distressed, until misery reduced them to an apathetic silence.

All kinds of rumors which the newcomers brought with them were whispered about.

"The English say that if the shooting doesn't stop, a fleet will come and flatten Helsinki... America will never give bread if they still go on killing without investigations or sentences..."

If someone came to whisper such news to Akseli, he was plainly annoyed. He wanted to be alone, in his own desolate world, with death as his only companion. Rumors came to tear down the building which he had erected piece by piece during long and painful hours. It was a bleak and dismal-looking structure, but contemplating it he felt a flinty peace of mind.

Sometimes the others heard him breathing restlessly. He would turn over more quickly than usual, with a grunt of pain.

The others paid little attention, for the outward signs were so scant, but at such moments the outlines of the grim structure blurred, and in its place another appeared: a house on Sunday with rugs on the floor, a wedge of light shining through the window, and a white tablecloth. Elina was wearing her best dress, and the boys had on the clean shirts they had changed into in the sauna the evening before. They were not wearing coats, for their mother had made suspenders of cloth for them. Their hands were thrust into slits in the sides of their trousers, although they had no real pockets.

In the dimness of the cell, the man sitting next to the prisoner saw his jaws tighten and his eyes close.

After a severe struggle in his tormented mind, the picture vanished. Before him there appeared again a black, motionless, and mighty emptiness.

When the door opened in the evening, a clamor arose. But it subsided into absolute silence when an officer appeared with a paper in his hand: "The following will come out into the corridor..."

The names fell into a strained silence. The officer seemed to be relishing the gruff, official, soldierly tone of his voice. He also folded the paper with abrupt, jerky motions, emphasizing the military nature of the movements. Men departed. But painfully Akseli lowered his slightly raised head to the floor. A vague feeling of disappointment stirred in his mind.

Numbly he followed the farewells and the requests rising from a senseless hope:

"If you happen... to be left... could you get this coat to such and such place... they could make something for the children..."

Someone had a watch left, another a little money, and those who had been there longer had accumulated a few worthless trinkets, which the officers took away when they noticed them. There were addresses written on the wall. Those who were left in the cell promised to take care of things, then lay down again to wait for the next calling out of names and their own turn.

People kept going. Men and women, carefree daredevils, their last consolation a contemptuous pride in the face of their executioners, fathers weeping for their children, calm old men, who with a matter-of-fact sobriety, gave support to the weaker, pathological killers, who sat out their time in the cell glaring suspiciously at the others; idealists, in whose souls a black, ecstatic festival was raging, and whose voices still carried to the ears of those left in the cell over the din in the corridor:

"Kill us, but the grass on our graves will still curse you."

A silence always prevailed after the clamor, until a faint, relieved discussion began. They wouldn't come again for many hours.

A day came when no one was brought in. A tense evening went by, and no one was taken away. During the night conjecture was rife over the matter.

In the morning the door was opened and the prisoners were ordered into the corridor. Akseli struggled to his feet. Soldiers and officers stood in the corridor. There they hurried the staggering prisoners into line. Akseli did not look at them, but concentrated solely on staying upright.

He heard his name shouted. "Were you born here and here on such and such a date? Is your middle name Johannes?"

"It is."

"Over here. With them."

He went dully and indifferently.

Then they were ordered into motion. They came out into the barrack yard, and the spring sun so bedazzled the eyes of the men who had sat in the cell that for a while they could see only a blackness in which small sparks flashed. Someone asked a guard uneasily where they were being taken, but he received no answer. Another guard laughed, and the prisoner's face turned gloomy.

Gritting his teeth, Akseli shifted his feet. In the background of his painful effort, he could hear his consciousness asking: Where are they taking us, and will they shoot us all at once?

When his eyes became accustomed to the light, he saw red brick barracks, barbed wire, and, everywhere, lolling and squatting men. Many sat bare from the waist up, with their faces in their bony hands. Here and there, fires burned in pits in the ground, and men crouched around them.

A few heads turned to look at the procession, for its wretchedness surpassed even theirs.

Lauri saw them first.

"Boys, is that Aksu?"

"No."

"Well, goddamnit, he has Akseli's overcoat on anyway."

Men rushed over to the man, who had collapsed in the yard. Staring at him for some time confirmed that the ghost was Akseli.

"Give me a little water."

Elias fetched water. It was warm and stagnant.

"Where have you been?"

"Leave me alone for a while... Then I'll talk..."

But they would not leave him in peace.

"I was in three cells altogether... I don't know anything else..."

"There are many from our parish in this barrack... That's why they brought you..."

"I don't know. They're likely to come and get me yet."

"No they won't. They've been forbidden to shoot people without a lawful sentence."

"Humph... who will forbid them..."

Lauri helped by holding up his head as he drank more water.

"The Englishmen have... That if they goddamn kill one more person the country won't be recognized... That this is an Eastern country, goddamn, and a lackey of Germany, as it is, goddamn... but drink up, we can get more of this..."

"There's no basis for that rumor..."

"It's not a rumor... I've heard from reliable sources that the States' consul has issued a protest."

Akseli gazed at Valenti. The latter's emaciated face was absolutely sincere. A sparse beard sprouted on his receding chin and an all-knowing look blinked in his sunken eyes.

Akseli lay down, and Elias promised to get him a piece of bread from somewhere.

"We'll cook it into a mush with some water so it'll be easier on your stomach."

Akseli was not thinking of bread. He covered his eyes with his arm, and in that position, the boys awakened him to eat. They shook him for a long time before they realized that he was not asleep.

The summer went on. In the morning, the prisoners were allowed out. At first they got used to standing near the barrack wall, and then they sought out a place to lie down on the shady side and staggered toward it, with a look of concentrated effort on their faces. It had become a habit to calculate every movement, for raising an arm now demanded as much effort as hard work had previously.

In the barracks' yards moved staggering, exhausted men, their eyes deeply sunken, their dirty, wrinkled skin wrapped around their bones. Most of the men were lying down, but those who could move were in constant activity. Around the barracks, burning fires smoked in pits, with the greatest possible variety of cooking utensils strewn around them: metal shell casings, crumpled kettles found somewhere, or dishes bent into shape from sheet-metal roofing. And the point of that constant movement, staggering, begging, stealing, bartering, plucking, and buying was to get at least something to put into the kettles hanging over those fires.

They plucked the growing vegetation from the earth, and stripped bare the few pines growing in the area. There went a man, in his hand the tail of a sardine he had found; another had dug potato peels from the mess-kitchen garbage. Someone else had exchanged the watch he had saved for bread with a guard. From morning till night, a thousand exhausted entrepreneurs blundered about, and when the crew gathered around the concoction in their kettle that evening, it was mostly water in which swam the day's haul. Perhaps there were a few bits of vegetation in it, or the crumbs of chaff-bread left uneaten by a dying comrade.

Fearful of the guards who shooed them away, the anguished members of the prisoners' families circled the barbed-wire fence, often having come long distances, in their hands bundles they had gathered with great difficulty. Perhaps a guard could be gotten to deliver the package for a gift—but often he went and traded it for a watch, wallet, or boots.

When the prisoners looked at themselves and others after hearing of such occurrences, their faces twisted into wretched laughter:

"You wouldn't think, goddamn, they could still earn money from something like this."

If they were not bumbling around in this hopeless quest for food, they sat in the sun with their dirt-encrusted shirts in their hands and killed lice. That task, however, was just as hopeless as the food preparation.

When the rattle of shots in back of "number five" had fallen silent, a slow and silent death took its place. Many went by way of a barrack which was called the hospital, and the physicians marked as the cause of their death the diseases which attacked them just before they would otherwise have died. But many did not go to the hospital. Some withered man could no longer eat the smelly broth, and began to withdraw to solitary places during the day: alongside the barbed-wire fence, behind a garbage can, or into some corner. Mostly his hat brim sufficed as a curtain against the outside world. Behind it was waged the final silent struggle.

In the evening the burial detail came with their horses and gathered up the dead. Its leader was an old man, a grim and brutal old man, whose name few of the prisoners knew, for they called him "Graveyard."

And the deceased departed on "Graveyard's" wagon.

Akseli, Lauri, Elias, and Valenti were together on a kitchen detail. Valenti was growing weaker rapidly, and before long they had to drag him out of the barrack. Then they were forced to feed him, for he refused to eat by himself. Lauri and Akseli held up his head, and Elias stuck the broth into his mouth. With every spoonful, Akseli barked in an angry voice:

"Swallow."

And Valenti, frightened, obeyed.

They dragged him into the shade of the barrack, and when the shade moved, they changed their places, then lay down with their hats or their arms over their eyes.

Once out of the death cell at the chief Guard station, Akseli regained some of his strength. He was thirty-one years old, and had a strong will to live. The food in the barrack was no better than that in the death cell, but they got a little more of it here, and being outdoors helped him to recover. Sometimes Elias managed to wangle an extra bit of food for him. Many of the guards exchanged sandwiches for watches, money, or more valuable articles of clothing, which were still to be found among the thousands of prisoners, in spite of their having been stripped when they were taken captive. Along these and similar paths, extra food arrived in the camp, and Elias was a master in pursuit of these bits. And he divided them evenly, in spite of the fact that in procuring them he was ready to rob even corpses, as he often did.

Their cooking dish was a box shaped from sheet-metal roofing, and everything was cooked into a mush. It was not wise to eat even the bread as such, for their digestive systems were already so delicate that many died when they got extra bread and ate it at one sitting in their greed.

There was a shortage of firewood as well. A few hay barns and sheds had been left without dismantling in the barracks area, and from them they got wood. Making fires was officially forbidden, but it was winked at. Occasionally a guard, in a fit of nastiness, would kick over the dishes and scatter a fire, but the next day he might pass it by without a word.

The group had only one spoon, with which each one ate in turn. That was good in one respect: since it had been agreed that each one got a spoonful at a time, they all got the same amount. Sometimes others who had not succeeded in getting anything crouched around them.

"Give me one spoonful."

It was usually Lauri's job to refuse them, for he was able to do it without concern for another's need.

"There's not enough for visitors."

If the beggar had the strength, he took out his bitterness in cursing and railing.

Valenti would indeed have given up his spoonful, but the others would not allow it. On the basis of seeing it happen in many cases, they knew that death by starvation began when the invalid no longer wanted to eat, since he had passed the stage where he still felt hunger. And Valenti's eyes too showed that the end would come soon. Although he looked at the others, he seemed to be looking somewhere beyond them. His eyes lacked a living person's interest in the little details around him. Sometimes a person had to repeat things to him, for he did not hear what another said.

In spite of his weakness, he was constantly talking. In a faint mumble, he explained everything under the sun, and the others answered him idly. He believed the Americans would soon come to free them. He boasted of his non-existent American citizenship, and he might sometimes answer a guard's raging curses with:

"I'm going to get in touch with the United States consul. I will demand compensation."

"Shut your mouth or I'll give you compensation."

Sometimes he longed for a pen and paper.

"I've got something in mind."

Sometimes he recited Leino's poetry, using the poet's first name and speaking of him as if he were a good friend.

"I consider Eino a great man... My own style is different, of course..."

Then he brushed the dirt and debris from his clothing, which had become soiled from lying in the yard. Along the starkly protruding Adam's apple in his withered throat a large louse was crawling.

He had a piece of newspaper in his bosom, which he often read. The boys had heard what was written on it over and over, but Valenti would always ask after a day or two:

"If you'd like... this has a good style..."

Since they could think of no reason to refuse, Valenti mumbled:

To the Friends of Little Birds.

Have you ever thought of our little chirruping friends? Have you stopped to think of that sweet twittering from summer copses and groves which entertains our ears with its sound? Of those little travelers, who arrive here in our far-off North after long and dangerous voyages, from beneath the turquoise-blue skies of southern Europe or from the banks of the mighty Nile? Are your hearts not moved when you think of these little warblers' loyalty to their distant land of a thousand lakes? Shouldn't we want to ask them: 'Why do you come to us time after time from so far away?' If we understood their warbling, then surely they would say to us:

"'Who can stay away, when the bright night of the North calls, when waves ripple on the shore, when the chokecherry spreads its intoxicating scent into the soft summer night? Who would not obey the sweet summons of Finland when the arch of the sky rings out over the sparkling blue lakes?'

"Thus they warble. Have we thought of our swallows' love for their native land? Surely we have not. We accept their spontaneous songs with no

feeling of gratitude. We even see that a brutal hand may cause the death of a little warbler, a thoughtless hand, guided purely by destructive feelings. How many think, in destroying a swallow's nest, that it too is a home. Just like our own. A home, a warm nest, the refuge of joy. Oh, pass quietly by it, and whisper a soft blessing and thanks.

"A good style... a trifle... but in general, a good style..."

The prisoners lying nearby listened indifferently to Valenti's reading. Some ten meters from them sat a young boy, fifteen at the most. Huge tears ran down his sunken cheeks, but there was no sound of weeping. The weeping was obviously a reflex action, in which the mind was not fully present. He was scraping large lice from his ragged and filthy shirt and sticking them into his mouth. Watching him do it, a large-boned, mustachioed prisoner said:

"Ha, ha... What are you eating... The others will suck them back right away..."

The boy did not look at or answer him, for he was already numb to the outside world. Then the man fixed his attention on the piece of newspaper Valenti had, and crawled over to the people from Pentti's Corner.

"What paper are you reading?"

"I don't know. A bourgeois paper, in any case."

"What does it say?"

Valenti read:

"This is not the time for mercy, but for paying back evil deeds. Whence this pity and mercy some whisper about? Wouldn't it be better for the criminals themselves if immediately after their misdeeds they go repentant before God, rather than languish in prisons to harden their hearts and thus go to damnation. The dross is to be excised from our people. But we must get to the root of the evil. Are we also to have mercy on those women who have paraded in our daughters' lingerie, distributing their sweets to the raw sailors as a reward for stealing them? No. Rid society of the Red Guard women, away with the sweethearts of the Russians and the street women."

"Give me the paper... I'll roll a butt..."

"No... there's an article on the other side that has a good style..."

"Why were you reading that bourgeois style... give it to me... let me roll a butt..."

"I'd be glad to... but I'm reading the article..."

"What are you reading... I can't hear you... give it to me..."

When Valenti did not give it, the man snatched the paper without further ado, tearing it and leaving only a little piece between Valenti's fingers.

"Don't take it."

"Hah... why read that stuff..."

Akseli had been lying with his arm over his eyes, not following what happened. The last exchange of words got him to look.

"What did you take? Give it back to him."

"Why read that stuff. All bourgeois bullshit."

"Give it back."

Akseli rose carefully to his knees.

"I'm going to roll a butt."

"You won't roll any butts from that paper if he won't give it to you."

"Don't you..."

"Goddamn right I will..."

Akseli rose, trying to keep his balance, and the man did the same. He grasped the paper, and it tore it in half again. Then they came to blows, whizzing blows that might land or miss, and if they did miss, might topple the man who swung. Gritting their teeth and exerting their last ounce of energy, the men rose and struck again. Their clothes flapped around their bones as they panted and snarled:

"You'll not take a piece of it..."

"I will take it..."

Lauri crawled to Akseli's aid and squawked:

"Let him have it, Aksu, goddamn... Show him where you come from..."

And Aksu did. Whirling around, he struck a blow, but his opponent had gotten tangled in his own feet and had already fallen. The blow missed and took Akseli with it. Valenti tried to gather the torn strips of paper from the feet of the battlers. Lauri got closer to the fighters, and tried to strike, but he too fell. Both of the fighters got to their feet, and Akseli carefully prepared for the next blow.

"When he staggers that way... it will land..."

His calculation was correct. The man staggered in the direction anticipated, and the blow struck home.

"Good, Aksu, greetings from Pentti's Corner, goddamn old man..."

Conscientiously, Akseli gathered up every slip of paper, but nothing could be done with them any longer. At that point the guards arrived and the battlers were taken to the chief guardhouse. Valenti pulled his hat over his eyes, and Elias and Lauri heard him weep for the first time during his entire captivity. Having calmed down, he took his cap from his eyes.

"What will they do to him?"

"A few days without food in the incarceration cell."

"I liked it because of the style..."

For many days there was no news of Akseli from the guardhouse. On the third day after the fight, Lauri and Elias dragged, nearly carried Valenti outside. But they could no longer get him to eat the stinking broth. Instead he plucked a few straws and put them into his mouth with trembling fingers. The movement was instinctive, for many of those in the final stages of starvation lifted dully to their mouths whatever their fingers happened to come in contact with on the ground. With a distant stare in his eyes, he sat leaning into a garbage barrel. The boys sat faithfully around him and tried to talk to him. But Valenti raved in his own delirium:

"Pershing... Wilson... I'm an American citizen... Do you know 'Under the Stars and Stripes', boys? They will come and free us... Pershing will come... I've heard from authoritative quarters... *Northland's broad borders threaten, the snows of death are gleaming, the skies take on a strange blue glow, Louhi's castles are ablaze*... that's a fine stanza... but it trails away... *the sea's even surface heaves, the wolf howls and night comes on. The day's golden balance sinks, the works of frost and iron prevail*... But I have to get papers first... I will inform the United States consul..."

He spoke in a rapid mumble, and the straws fell from his mouth. He plucked at more, but his hands grasped only sand and dried bark. A couple of straws came up with them, and he died with them in his mouth, silently, so that his comrades were unaware, until his head sank slowly to his shoulder.

"Vallu's gone, boys. I mean, he was a real poet."

The boys left for the hospital to find gravediggers. They were there, loading up. Against the wall of a shed that served as a morgue were dozens of naked and half-naked bodies, brought there from the hospital. Long, thin limbs, ribs which could be tallied at a glance, non-existent bellies, and lips dried fast to grimacing gums. Others were shapelessly fat, legs and thighs puffed with edema. Lime had been thrown over the pile, and Lauri barked to Elias:

"The Reds are being whitened, goddamn."

"A buddy of ours died out there. If you would get him."

The grim old man growled angrily:

"We don't cart them one at a time. He can wait for his turn."

They returned to Valenti and waited for the load to come.

Valenti was hoisted onto the wagon on top of the others, and as the load departed, his shoes hung over the side at the end of his dirty, pipestem shins.

VI

375

Then began the ghosts' journeys to the investigating judge and to the court for crimes against the state. Those sentenced were taken to separate barracks, about which rumors circulated that it was better to avoid judgment as long as possible. Having heard of the first death sentence, Akseli began somehow to avoid his comrades. He strove for solitude and became more sullen again. They had been given permission to write home, and to receive small packages at specified times, and he had already written to Elina. Now, however, he regretted it as he lay in a corner of the barrack with his arm over his eyes.

"It would have been better... just to be apart..."

Lauri got three years, which meant freedom, but Elias got eight, which meant he had to stay.

Akseli was left alone. When the boys were absent, he stayed apart from others as well. It was more difficult in the barrack, but outside he puttered around alone. If someone came up to him and asked a question, he turned away and said: "I don't know." The stranger would move on. Finally Akseli's name was called, and he had to go for the interrogation. He was still very weak, and the interrogations were exhausting. When he was asked if he had sent along with the two Whites who had been detained a written order to kill them, he did not at first remember the incident. Then it dawned on him.

"Where did that information come from?"

"From your home parish."

He explained the matter, but there was doubt in the judge's eyes. The look in them was that of a man who already knows, a look that said: "Of course he'll deny it, like all the rest." Then Akseli was also asked about Töyry's murder.

"Will that be charged to my account too?"

"The testimony says that he was ordered to headquarters."

"That paper of mine should be among the headquarters paper... if they haven't been destroyed."

"Of course such papers have been destroyed."

Then he waited for the court session. He received a letter from Elina and a package in which there was spoiled food. With shaking hands, he opened the letter and read Elina's pretty, flowing handwriting. Sometimes his heart throbbed as the words filtered through his consciousness:

"...Father and Janne have come home, but they are so weak they can't do anything... Janne promised to do something about your case, but they would not give him any papers or information. We are all well. The boys help me with everything. Voitto has grown a lot and he is strong and is getting to look like you. We miss you so badly at home, and even if it takes years, we will think only of the time when you will come. That is all we have. We don't care about anything that happens. We get along somehow, so don't worry about us. The boys are so awfully nice that I don't know how I could bear this without them. They talk about you all the time and say that when the king gets into power he will let you go. Since they've heard from the book of fairy tales that the king always frees the innocent. There is much ado here about getting a king, there are meetings and speeches. We don't go to them, but everyone is buzzing about it. That's why the boys say that. I'll write as soon as I get an answer. God keep you. We all pray for you every evening."

At the end of the letter was Elina's name and the boys' names, which looked like strange bird tracks. Last was the little boy's name, which Elina had written. One could tell that the boy had also been holding the pen.

He put the letter away and staggered a few steps this way and that, then sat down on the ground again and grunted:

"Why did I write... Why didn't they shoot me then?"

From the spoiled food in the package he contracted another attack of dysentery, which sapped the last of his strength. He was no longer able to go out. His skin a pale yellow, in a cold sweat from head to foot, he lay on the floor, and they came to drive him from there to the court.

"I can't go."

"Get up. You have to."

He rose and managed to go a little way, then collapsed in a heap on the road.

"Get up... We're not going to start carrying you."

He got up onto his knees. The earth reeled. Finally there was only one knee on the ground, but it would not rise. He put his fingers into his mouth and bit them. There was nothing to bite but skin and bone. But blood oozed from them when he bit, and at the same moment a noise that sounded like weeping came from his throat. He struggled and rose. The guards supported him the rest of the way, for now they believed that he really was unable.

In the court he was allowed to sit in a kind of grade-school desk. He was asked his name and date and place of birth. He heard them talking about himself and his deeds, but concentrated entirely on staying in the desk. Sometimes he had a despairing thought.

"I can't give in... I have to defend myself..."

But there was little possibility of doing so, for he was asked very little, only if he had given the command to murder two captured members of the Civil Guard and had urged the murder of agriculturist Kalle Töyry.

"No."

They did not rail at him in this court as the bald-head had. The judges were almost indifferent to him. They were interested only in the papers on

377

the table, which a man read to them, demanding the death sentence on that basis.

"Finally the security-force headquarters statement on the accused."

Akseli forced himself to listen sharply. The man read quickly and fluently the questions on the official form and the answers of the security force headquarters.

...If married or widowed, how many minors and what is their means of support?"

Married. Three children. Tenant farmer in sound financial position.

...Of what character, violent or peaceable, hard worker or instigator of strikes?

Violent and a zealot. Instigator and inciter of strike riots.

...Way of life. Regular or erratic?

Regular.

...Where and with whom has he worked? What kind of statement has his employer given?

Parsonage tenant farmer. According to employer's statement hard-working but hot-tempered and rash.

...Has he belonged to a workers association and what was his position in it?

Vice-Chairman of W. L. Endeavor, a member of a strike committee, and other positions of responsibility.

...Has he belonged to the Red Guard and his position in it?

He has even been one of the leading spirits. Platoon leader and company commander. Actually a founder of the Guard.

...Where and when has he been in battle? What weapons has he carried?

On the northern front. Has carried any weapons he could get.

...Has the prisoner taken part in disarming, robbing, murdering, abusing, burning to death, torturing, and have stolen goods been found in his possession?

As a leader, he ordered the death of two unidentified members of the Civil Guard. Also believed to have ordered the murder of Kalle Töyry, for which there is, however, no confirmation.

...To the knowledge of the headquarters, has the prisoner committed any other crimes?

Generally known as an ardent revolutionary.

...Has the prisoner acted as an agitator in the Red Guard?

He has even been one of the guiding spirits.

...In the revolution?

378

He has even been one of the guiding spirits.
...In opposition to the government?
He has even been one of the guiding spirits.
...In opposition to military service?
Unknown
...Has the prisoner made threats against the lawful government?
"Blatantly."

The headquarters statement regarding the prisoner:

With reference to the above record, we consider the prisoner of no value to society and absolutely dangerous and totally incapable of ever being a member of organized society. We demand the death penalty since there is no harsher punishment. Hanging would not be too much.

E. Dahlberg	A. Yllö	A. Mellola	Hjl. Pajunen
Apothecary	Hon. Judge	Sawmill Proprietor	Agriculturist

What does the prisoner have to say to this?
Akseli drew a heavy breath.
"It's all a lie... from start to finish."
"These signatures are written under oath."
"Yeah... I don't know... Then they are false oaths."
"Are you able to sit?"
"I'll try... But I'm not able to talk... I would ask for a postponement."
"We can't give you one. Do you admit to giving the death orders mentioned in the record?"
"No... I did not give them... I can get witnesses to that."
"Why haven't you gotten them?"
Akseli looked at the chairman of the court for a while.
"How could I have gotten them?"
"You know how to write and mail goes from here."
Akseli no longer answered, but began to stare at the yellow top of the desk. A strange smile twisted his face, and he said in a near whisper:
"Kill me then... I'm not able..."
The remark occasioned a couple of "hems," a flash of eyeglasses, and someone's hand lifted the papers on the table.
"You claim that this sworn testimony is false then."
"I do... since it is wrong... I... Why didn't I shoot them myself then... or order my men to shoot them... Why would I have written it on a paper...?"
"Of course you are the only one who knows. In any case you have been

accused of aggravated treason and crimes against the state. Specifically in a position of leadership."

"I wasn't... any kind of leader... I was chosen as commander... I didn't want it myself... It wasn't any longer... it wasn't so easy..."

"Not just anyone is chosen to be a company commander... You had to be clearly active with them. And we have witnesses to that. It is clear from the testimony of other prisoners that you urged them on to the last. You are responsible for the loss of many lives."

There was a silence after these words. Finally Akseli said softly:

"I have never ordered anyone for my own sake... If it had been a question of myself alone, I would not be here... I could have gotten away... But I was given hundreds of people..."

Then they returned to the murder again. Akseli tried to follow the discussion, but his strength did not hold out. He leaned into the desk. His head buzzed and his ears rang at times. A varicolored light beat constantly in his eyes. Burning pangs rose from the bottom of his belly,and the seat of his pants was wet, for blood and mucous was leaking onto them. From time to time he mustered up his energy, took a breath, and hammered into his consciousness:

"I have to stay awake... if I want to live..."

Occasionally he was tempted to give up completely, but Elina's letter caused him to grip the top of the desk tightly with his bloody fingers.

"I do not admit it... I ask for time enough to call witnesses. There is a man here whom I sent to take them... The other was shot... he was my brother."

"What man?"

"A man who was there. Kankaanpää."

"Has he been sentenced?"

"Yes."

"What significance does the testimony of such a man have. An accomplice."

The uneven struggle continued. Questions were fired routinely at Akseli, claims and statements, which the members of the court knew to be false, but which were used to entrap him. And their opponent, a completely exhausted man, took them as gospel, and began with his last ounce of strength to correct them, stopping at times to draw a heavy breath so that he could say the next word.

Finally the session ended. Rising, Akseli staggered back into the desk, and the guards were ordered to lead him away.

At the end of ten minutes, a shout ordered him back in. He listened with total apathy to the words:

"... for participation in murder and robbery, as well as treason and crimes against the state, sentenced to be punished by death and to lose his citizenship forever."

These words were also a part of statement:

"Since the decision was the result of a vote, the sentence will be forwarded to the high court for crimes against the state for review, in addition to which you have the right to ask for mercy from said court."

CHAPTER ELEVEN

I

Elina's move from Koskela took place over a long time. Some of her furniture was left at the new place, since it did not really fit into Kivivuori. Jussi and Alma were allowed to keep one cow for its milk, and the vicar promised them enough of a hay field from the tenancy for the cow. But two of the cows had to be sold, for there was no room for them at Kivivuori. Most of the now unnecessary seed grain had to be surrendered to the rationing board, but in that instance, Jussi committed the first swindle in his life. Grunting and struggling, he carried a part of the grain to Kivivuori.

"They're not going to take everything from the children's mouths."

For a long time there was uncertainty about the cattle and the agricultural implements, for the headquarters threatened to confiscate them as compensation for the farm owners from whom grain and animals had been taken with Akseli's slips. Jussi tried to explain that Akseli's ownership of them was still questionable, but it was known at the headquarters that he had already paid his brothers for their share in them.

But the confiscation did not occur. Among the landowners and gentry, a more moderate attitude had begun to develop. No one dared openly reveal this opinion, but in confidence they went so far as to say that "wrong men" had been taken. Among the Reds, it was rumored that some landowner had been threatened when he had spoken up on behalf of Reds at the headquarters.

"A bunch of drunks put a gun to his head and told him that if he said just one more word in that vein, they would let him have it."

At Koskela, no one cared about such parish events. All concern was concentrated on Akseli once they heard that he had been spared execution. Gradually news filtered down of the fate of others who had left. Kankaanpää had died of hunger in a camp in Tampere.

Oskari wrote home about it, and told them to go to Kankaanpää's family to tell them about it.

Other news arrived in letters which the prisoners sent secretly by civilian mail, for the camp letters were censored.

Preeti brought them the news of Elma Laurila's fate:

"The girl wrote that she was taken... They said they were taking her to a German soap factory... That's all she knew... The girl herself is keeping house for a White warlord... She says she hasn't heard any more about the boy... She saw Elias in the spring and she got bread for them because she said the boy was very weak."

They spoke in whispers of what had happened to Uuno:

"They boasted when they were drunk that they tied him to a tree on the way from Lahti... And there they started shooting him from the feet up, and after each hit, they asked are you still a Red... And each time they said he answered as long as my blood is circulating... And then only after he passed out did they shoot him through the heart... In the morning they swore they had only been boasting when they were drunk and there was no truth in it... It was that Yllö's boy... Arvo didn't say anything like that... and he wasn't with that drunken bunch. They say Arvo doesn't say a word when they talk about such things, just walks away... but in the morning they denied it and said they were just talking and that a German shot him in the woods at Lahti."

The county held an auction at which all the Laurila family possessions were sold. The proceeds went to pay for Antti's care. The tenancy was abandoned, and the master of Kylä-Pentti nailed boards over its window.

Elina was already at home when Otto arrived from the camp. He and Janne were freed immediately without a sentence when the court proceedings began, although very aggravating statements regarding Janne's part in the strike riots and his hindrance of court proceedings against the strikers had been forwarded from the village. Janne was able to ward off the accusations, but was not released until a week after his father.

The boys were playing in the Kivivuori yard when Otto arrived. They looked at him doubtfully at first and then went in.

"Mother... there's some kind of man coming... clothes like Grandpa's..."

Anna and Elina did know Otto, but he was in such poor shape that they had to support him in climbing the steps. He was put directly to bed, and Anna, weeping, began to prepare food for him.

"Anna, cream, if there is any... Goddamn, I won't kill myself any more once I made it this far."

And Otto explained how many had died in the camps when they suddenly ate food sent by their families, which their parched intestines could no longer tolerate. From the foot of the bed the boys looked at their grandfather, whose bony nose stuck out from his shrunken face. But the thing that amazed them the most was when Grandpa's underwear was changed. Grandpa had extraordinarily large knees and spindly legs. And he sweated and panted heavily when he sat up, but he looked at them with a smile and said:

"What do the brothers know?"

Anna gave him cream to drink, and soon Grandpa was on his feet. He and Janne tried to secure papers which could be used in Akseli's defense during the court proceedings, but their requests were refused.

Akseli's sentence had the people at Kivivuori in suspense. They knew that it would be for a number of years, but they did not know how many. Otto sometimes feared the worst, for he had heard in Tampere about the sentences in similar cases. But he was careful not to mention them.

The grief caused by Oskari's death had abated to a degree, and it was somehow overshadowed by Akseli's case. But the family's mood was nonetheless depressed. They spoke in low tones in the summer evening twilight of the darkening room.

"Did you write to him about the eviction?"

Elina brushed away a tear.

"No... I thought I wouldn't add that to his misery."

"He'll hear about it anyway... I hear they'll add a Red clause to the law freeing the tenants — if you get a heavier sentence, you can't redeem a tenancy... So you won't even know what your redemption rights are until you hear what the sentence is... And in any case, it will hardly apply to a terminated contract... I've been thinking this way, that I would redeem the place. And then he can take it when he comes... Janne will never be a farmer anyway... It can be left to one of the boys then..."

"Yes... but to him Koskela meant..."

"You'll live here with the boys. I'll take care of this somehow when he comes."

Elina looked down at the ground. Something was troubling her.

"Well... I could stay there too... Grandma always asks me... but I feel so bad there... when I'm on their land... and now besides there's... I have the money from the cows, and Grandpa says he will give Akseli's bank money... but they have nothing else now... so I couldn't take from them..."

Otto said briefly:

"Well, you don't need to trouble yourself about that... That isn't the question now."

He was aware that his daughter was troubled by having to leave the land and return to burden her parents, although she had been given no cause to feel that way. To the contrary, they were pleased, for the presence of Elina and the children alleviated their grief over the loss of Oskari.

Victor Kivioja was already awaiting his son's return home, and said to Otto on meeting him:

"The storekeeper says his word carries no weight. I told him to speak to Arvo, that his word did... He mumbled something, but I told him if he didn't send word to have the irons taken off the boy, they would be on our legs too... Let's go together, I said... I don't know if they would arrest someone like him, but he's afraid of bad talk now when he's so law-abiding...

384

I'm telling you this, but keep your mouth shut about it... You know, god-damn, that I sold that boy's bike... what will he say when he comes... but I had nothing else on hand and all those wild boys were asking for every-thing, the ones who sell everything from eggs to human beings... They say they even sell Reds' widows and kids... If they find a buyer... it takes all kinds, goddamn... even though I shook hands with them... One winked at the other... I thought, not with Vic, boys... Yeah, he'll be coming soon. Have you heard from Akseli? The boy wrote that in the spring when he came from the death house he looked like he'd escaped from the graveyard... now goddamn, that's a real story..."

And then the boy came. He was the first to arrive from the Lahti camp, and he had plenty to tell and plenty of listeners. Lauri grew livelier as he grew stronger, and Victor sat beside him listening and occasionally pluck-ing at an auditor:

"Listen, goddamn, to what he's saying... He's quite a boy..."

The father accompanied the son even on his visits to cottages to share in the limelight as the boy laid it on: "The little boy ate the lice and the geezer with the mustache said what the hell are you eating them for, the others will suck them back right away. He was from somewhere, I don't know where, and he had a funny way of saying 'me' and used another word for 'her-ring.'"

"Listen...The boy has seen some of the facts of life... By God..."

Lauri brought the news of Valenti's death to the Leppänens. He showed his knobby kneecaps to Henna and Preeti, who wept softly at his tidings. Little Valtu looked on from the corner at the strange "uncle," who raised his pants legs and then showed his bare arms.

"Do they look good to you... I thought Lauri was getting to be the kind of skeleton they collect in those museums."

Preeti wiped his eyes on "the deceased Aleksi's coat sleeve."

"Was there, like, much suffering?"

"Hah, it wasn't any goddamned suffering... it was starvation... He starved to death like the rest of them... his body was like a dried codfish. Elku and I looked at it when it went on 'Graveyard's' cart, and his shoes were hanging over the side like this... and his legs were like flower stakes... I mean, take a look at these and you'll get some idea."

"The girl said she got some bread for him when she was a housekeeper... but she said she didn't see him any more."

"Hah... that sergeant took another girl... There were plenty of them there... and the rest were lined up and the machine gun sang. Us boys lis-tened to them and said, 'Softly, softly, the death bell tolls,' goddamn..."

He left, and they wept softly in the cottage. But the next day Preeti was already saying, when he ran into people:

"Mother and I were saying there's nothing you can do when that time comes... He should have stayed in the West... But he cared so much for Finland... He wrote poems and other things... People's dying... it's like with those forces of nature. Like that lightning... it's just its nature to strike and people don't much matter... Lauri said he was still reading a bird poem in the teeth of death..."

Preeti asked Otto to lend him enough money to get Valenti's obituary into the parish paper, and Otto gave it to him, as he did almost always when asked.

"I'll get it back to you, since I hear that the girl will get out... I don't know if they will take the announcement. They say they're not happy to take them when one has, like, died as a Red..."

Nor did they take it, but since Aune had just come home, Preeti asked to keep the money.

"Because her clothes are really so poor... And with us, with all the prices are going up... And his nephew won't raise the wages... Says he won't get into what it was like before... but he lengthened the work-day... he said last summer's agreements mean nothing... That they were got by rioting and so he won't like recognize them... And I hear that's what they've done in the church village... Otherwise he seems nice... you can sort of understand his speech better... But he doesn't know much about the work... He's not at all like Maknus, who knew about work. His old wife has to be waited on in bed altogether, they say."

Aune did indeed come home, in wretched clothing and in very bad shape. But her arrival lessened Henna's and Preeti's sorrow. Since there was not one bit of food at the Leppänens, and Aune was always hungry, like all who had come from the camps, she took to circulating among the cottages and farms, where she was often asked to eat with a family when she happened to broach her eternal subject of hunger at the right time. Aune had not visited Kivivuori after Akseli's and Elina's wedding, but now she went even there, nor did Elina remember her own bitterness. Aune came under the pretext of telling about Oskari, although Lauri had already told of his fate.

"I thought I would come and tell about him since I was one of the last to see him alive. I myself saw when they left... Oskari had a piece of bread in his hand, and he said 'to Petersburg...'"

Elina set food on the table, and Aune spoke in an ingratiating voice:

"And Akseli sat on horseback and said fill your pockets with bullets... By God, he was a handsome commander... On a black stallion... It was stolen from him then. They stole everything you let go of..."

Aune got food and sat there after eating. She wept as she spoke of Elma:

"I asked where they were taking them, and the infantryman said they were taking them to a soap factory in Germany... Elma didn't cry... she gave me some turnip peels and said goodbye. But many of them were crying and holding on to each other... It was awful... when they took young women... and the soldiers were laughing to one another..."

Aune wiped her eyes with a sleeve and sighed.

"They were singing in the cells before they took them away... And the Germans searched the women for weapons... One came and touched me there. Opened my blouse and said dagger, dagger... And squeezed..."

Aune told it in a gravely offended tone of voice, but Otto said:

"You should have slapped your tit into his mouth and said, there it is."

"Aagh... you're awful, Kivivuori... But by God, their officers were handsome... daggers on their belts and iron hats on their heads... And they weren't at all as mean as the White soldiers. They ordered water to be given the prisoners, but when you asked the White soldiers for it they said piss is what we'll give you bastards... The infantry officer slapped his leather stocking with a whip and put that kind of glass up to his eye like the German officer wore when he came from the city to look at the people... He hit it like that and said, goddamn Russian whore, you even speak poor Finnish... But there was a peppery girl there, they called her the Reds' saddle horse, and she said that a Russian at least asks, but the butchers throw you down by the road without asking and the others watch. That's what she said, but then the death bell tolled..."

And Aune sniffled again at the memory.

It was a sunny Saturday in August. Otto was warming the sauna and poking around at little chores. The boys were trailing along with him, for their mother and grandmother had ordered them to stay out of the way of their scrubbing. The door and window of the cottage were open. Elina beat the rugs that had been on the fence and brought them indoors.

She spread them out on the floor, being careful not to make noise, for Voitto was asleep in the bedroom off the entry. She was in a lighter mood than usual. The clean cottage smelled fresh. The warmth of the sunny August day was already cooling off indoors as well. From the window one could see a haze on the blue horizon. There had been a moon last night.

In the field below the well, there were sheaves of rye.

Sometimes on such occasions, Elina's grief and depression receded to the background of her mind. Waiting for news of Akseli's fate no longer weighed on her constantly, but merely dictated a basic mood of sadness. But as the clock neared five, the subject returned to her consciousness. The mail always arrived at that time. She went out to the steps.

"Vilho. Go and get the mail from the store."

The boy left, pleased with the responsibility involved in the task, which had recently been entrusted to him. Every evening Elina awaited a letter, and every evening she feared its coming. Mail time brought her father and mother indoors as well, and they kept glancing out the window as they waited for the boy.

"He may take longer. There's more mail on Saturday because the paper comes then too."

The boy returned. He was all business, pleased that a letter had come at last. Elina opened it with nervous and trembling fingers. In it were two sheets written in Akseli's small hand. Elina turned them over a couple of times before she found the beginning and began to read, but she did not read for long. Her long, sustained scream so frightened the boys, that they shrank back against the door, and Anna rushed to her daughter's side. Elina threw herself down on the bed and beat at the pillow with her fists. Having caught her breath after the scream, she shrieked madly:

"They're going to kill him... they're going to kill him..."

Father and mother took turns speaking to her, but she did not hear them. From time to time, she screamed:

"I'm going... I'm going... I won't be left alone..."

Otto had to take hold of Elina and hold her down, for she tried to get up from the bed, and her mother repeated into her ear as she screamed:

"Don't, don't... for God's sake... think of the children... you'll drive them crazy... calm down..."

The boys were crying, Eero wailing in panic and Vilho muffling his sobs, watching their mother's mad frenzy. Anna hastened into the bedroom and came back with Voitto on her arm.

"Take the child... calm down now... the children are afraid when you're like that... take him in your arms."

But Elina shoved them away:

"Take him away... I'm going to Akseli..."

When she tried to get up, Otto pressed her back onto the bed. For once he too was upset, and he nearly growled at Anna:

"Take them to Emma... you can see that they won't get better here... they'll go crazy too..."

Anna took the children to Emma Halme, calming them on the way.

"Are they going to kill Father?"

"No... don't talk like that... it was about another man... Mother just got sick... she'll get better soon."

But she was not able to reassure the boys completely. Upset, she whispered what had happened to Emma, who began to calm the children while

388

Anna hastened home. She took Elina's head into her lap and said soothingly:

"Take Mother's hand... don't scream... God will help us... think of that... ask for God's help..."

It was in vain, for Elina did not understand her words.

The seizure lasted for more than an hour, and only then did exhaustion force it to end. But in putting a cold wrap on Elina's head, Anna was frightened by her look, for it was not rational. At times she gave vent to a long, grieving outcry. Her mother fetched the children, and Elina sat up. She took the youngest into her lap, and then only did she come out of it. Anna held on to the child so that it would not fall from Elina's shaking arms. Mother and Father turned their heads away from time to time, for they could not bear the sight.

The fire in the sauna died out and the building grew cold. No one so much as went to close the damper. No food was prepared, and Anna rounded up some sort of sandwiches for the boys.

The August evening grew rosy, and then turned bluish, until a red moon lighted up the gray village and the sheaves of rye standing around it. It was truly a moonlight made for dreaming, and voices were heard in the village until quite late. But the whispers and the creeping footsteps of Otto and Anna could be heard long after the voices had fallen silent, as they kept watch in the bedroom at Kivivuori. Weeping was no longer audible there, but only a soft, moaning sound now and then.

Cautiously, listening for sounds, they lighted the lamp and read the letter, which had been crumpled in Elina's hand as she beat at the pillow.

Dear Elina and children.

I have something bad to write you now. You have to be brave now. I have been in court and got a death sentence, and my citizenship has been taken away. I am calm, and my only sorrow is that you will grieve for me. But if you can live bravely, then I can die bravely. It would have been better if we had not begun to write to each other again and had stayed apart. You have to get used to the thought now. The sentence does have to be confirmed, and I have asked for mercy, and I'm not ashamed to because I did it for your sake. I do this only out of duty to you, but I tell you not to start hoping because of it. Here too it's worse if you start imagining what can't be. I know they won't have mercy on me. They have sent papers from there saying I'm a thief and a murderer. The court didn't believe them altogether, but they said I had a part in it, and then there was the treason, because they say I tried to get Russian rule back. I tried to defend myself but I was weak and they pay no attention to what people like us say. They charge me with killing those two men in the church village, but you know that's a lie. And you know that story, the rumor they were already spreading when they heard that I had ordered them taken to the church village and wrote the paper. Of course I wrote it since we had orders to explain matters. And who was I to give orders since the church village staff was over me. They don't think at all. That fathead Mellola's name was there too, and he surely knows nothing at all about it. If he were buying logs, he would be sure to count every one before signing his name. But when a person's life is at stake, it's not worth asking and sifting, just sign your name. I don't exactly like to die because of old wives' gossip, but they must have put the murders there as window dressing because they want to shoot me for rebelling. I'm writing this just so that if there is that kind of talk, you can explain the truth to the boys. Things don't matter to me, but they will to you who are left. You yourself know me, and what I can and can't do. And I believe that there is no doubt in your mind. But they just want to shame me with the name of thief even in the grave because they hate me so much. You asked about Oskari in the letter. News must have come from here already, but I'll write a little bit here. He is buried in a village called Syrjäntaka, but I don't know any more. He died without suffering at all, so you don't have to grieve. I got to him in a minute, and he was dead already. I took his wallet and watch, but a German took them, along with mine. They say the money is worthless because it is Guard money, and Oskari's watch wasn't worth much. It ran so slow. They took my good boots too, and I've been barefoot since then. I could find something for my feet here, but since it's summer, and I don't know if I'll get to see cold weather again, I don't really need anything more. My clothes are like a ditch-diggers, and they're so torn that it doesn't pay to send them. And I don't know if they would be sent. Now things are supposed to be better, they say that a doctor even goes with you, but I don't know about sending things.

I have something else to say, since things are so bad with you. Has Father managed to do the planting? Couldn't you get some kind of hired hand and keep the place, since they say they are making a law that tenancies be freed. If Janne or your father will back a loan, in case the state doesn't give all of it, you could get the place then. And if it's hard to keep up, at least it will take care of what you must have. If you could have a few cows there, even though you couldn't do much with grain since our family has suddenly been left without any help. Greetings to Father and Mother and Otto and to Grandma too. If your father would look after things a little. Ask him for me. Try to explain things to Mother and Father and look on the good side. I'd better end this. I don't have to say anything to you because we know each other. There's no point in talking about something that words won't change. In those ten years there was a lot that was bad on my part, but I believe you know my true nature. Write if you want, but I don't know anything about the future. If this is the last, then I'll just say goodbye. It's best that you don't know the day and time in advance, but I will remember you then.

Your husband and your children's father
Akseli Koskela

The address has to say, "Sentenced to death."

II

The yard at Koskela was overgrown. The Sunday morning sunshine had caused the flies and bumblebees to buzz about the gray walls of the cottage and the flowers in the yard. It was silent and dead around the buildings. Boards had been nailed over the windows of the old place, and through their cracks could be seen the dark, dead blue of the window panes, which reflected the blackness of the interior. Shingles weighted down by a couple of bricks had been placed over the chimneys. Vegetation yellow from the lack of light grew up through the cracks of the outside steps. Long hay arched over the paths. The doors of the outbuildings were closed. The emptiness of the yard extended to the fields, over which lay the peace which had once been before the arrival of Jussi.

Half-curtains lent a little life to the windows of the new place, but the thin trickle of blue smoke rising from its chimney only accentuated the deserted, petrified stillness.

Jussi and Alma had lived alone this summer. Elina and the boys did indeed come to visit, and sometimes the boys ventured to come alone, but they did not really enjoy themselves here. Their grandmother missed them, and asked them to come often, but something the boys could not explain drove them away. The lifeless desolation of the places where they had played penetrated their consciousness in a way that was poignant and a little frightening. They wandered around, speaking almost in whispers. Their last memories of the place increased the solemnity in their eyes. Their mother's solitary weeping in the bedroom, their grandfather's heavy, grunting gruffness, and their grandmother's singing of hymns came from months ago to blend with the recent desolation.

"Your uncles are in unhallowed ground."

On one such visit, they had retreated from the threshing barn, which seemed black and threatening, toward the steps of the new place. They went inside, and Vilho said:

"We have to go. Mother said we can't stay long."

391

Otto appeared around a corner of the new place, from which a forest path led to a part of the village near Kivivuori. Both the Kivivuoris and the Koskelas had used it a good deal this summer in visiting each other, for they avoided the parsonage road.

When Otto greeted them as he entered the main room, Jussi and Alma could see that he had a reason for coming, but they did not ask what it was. Otto sat on the bench, his usual seat, leaning forward, his elbows on his knees, swinging his hat back and forth between his knees.

"A letter came from Akseli today."

"Yeah... at long last."

Otto's cap swung a little faster.

"The news in it was a little bad... He has been sentenced... and... and it was a heavy sentence."

The old couple were silent. They remained mute, and Otto went on:

"They've sentenced him to death."

The weight-driven clock with its rose decoration went on ticking slowly through a long, silent pause.

The pause was followed by a few subdued questions and answers. These two old people had already been dealt such deep and hurtful blows that the new one did not cause an uproar. Otto left, and they escorted him to the steps. At the corner he turned:

"I'll go and talk to Janne. But I'm afraid he can't do anything about it."

Jussi stood at the door and Alma on the steps. As Otto was leaving, Alma said:

"Would you tell Elina to come here before she writes... if she can... Since we write so poorly... We could get it in the same... And if she isn't able to come, then put it like this... that Father and Mother hope... that he will go... with God... when that last journey comes."

Otto mumbled acquiescence and disappeared around the corner. Jussi and Alma went inside. A brief buzzing sounded at the edge of the steps as a bumblebee moved from one white clover to another.

The hitching rail at the church was crowded with horses, and although the service was still going on, there was much movement around the church-yard. Landowners stood beside their church carriages talking quietly to each other. At times someone went to pull his horse's bunch of hay out of the reach of the next horse.

Otto turned into a small lane that climbed a small hill, into which flow-ing rainwater had worn gullies. Silander's house was behind the hill.

Janne sat barefoot in the glassed-in porch. He cast a sidelong glance of inquiry without asking what Otto's errand might be. Sanni and Allan came out, and the boy bowed courteously to his grandfather. He had just been dressed. A large bow was tied around his neck. Sanni saw to it that the boy greeted Otto properly, and urged Janne to put something on his feet, but not as emphatically as before. Her father's execution had affected her deeply.

Otto sat on the steps leading down from the porch and said:

"The news isn't great. Akseli has been sentenced to death."

The news made Sanni weep, but Janne said:

"I was almost sure of it. I could guess at it from the written statements they sent to the court. If those papers don't get a person shot, nothing will."

Otto explained why he had come, but Janne said, scratching his feet:

"I could get any number of papers and statements... But I can't get them from the kind of men whose names would mean anything."

"But they must know that he didn't order anyone killed."

"They have to know it at the headquarters. It's so childish. One of the Guards had heard someone inside say goddamn, it would be just as well to shoot them there as send them here. On that they base the claim that it was a death order. And that man is in the pit... Nor would it help if he were alive."

"But we have to try something..."

"I will try to send something to the high court... But don't start telling him anything on those grounds."

Janne fell silent, scratching himself, and then said, as if continuing the thought: "They're holding a monarchist meeting at the churchyard again... but I can't bring myself to go and listen... They're hard at work gathering coins to buy themselves a king from Germany... When will the time come when the law applies to them too..."

He rubbed his belly angrily and went on:

"And I'm always so damned hungry that sometimes I have to get up in the night and eat. It was a hell of a diet... And sometimes when we passed those trees I wished I could look up and see the soles of their shoes dangling there..."

And Janne laughed at his own words, but his father did not share his mirth, for he had to go home, and the memory of the mood there robbed him of any inclination to laughter.

Sanni squeezed Otto's hand when he was leaving.

"Give Elina my condolences... tell her... I know..."

Otto sensed in her words a slight self-aggrandizement and a pride in suffering, and he left, mumbling something vague.

The church service had ended, and there were so many people around the churchyard that they were being shooed away from blocking the road. Otto approached the group with his head thrown back, for he had pulled his hat brim over his eyes because of the sun. Watching from underneath it, his pursed lips mirroring the mockery in his mind, he stayed to follow the course of the meeting.

The powers that be were busy in the middle of the crowd, one asking questions of the other. The crowd was tightly packed at the center, but scattered at the edges, and many were seen to move farther away on occasion.

Two of the farmers and one of their wives were standing near Otto, and feeling out each other's positions in low voices.

"Well, have you thought about signing your name?"

"I don't really know... That Korri said it's not even all that legal. That they sort of decided on a republic earlier... Although you could probably overthrow it... but when you're without the parliament..."

The first lowered his voice to a whisper in speaking, now that he knew the other's stand:

"We don't have that spirit... that king spirit... We have more of that Korri spirit... They ask for coins because the Germans need them, but Mother and I said that we badly need what we have... He looked a little bit... as if he didn't like it much... But they say the Germans will even set the tolls and that the Germans will get everything if they bring that king... It's not a good idea to be so busy on the side of the Germans... the way the English are at sea... I'm not much for politics... I wouldn't have come here... but Mother was coming to church, and so I thought..."

The farmers turned to look and listen, getting support from one another in their silent indifference

Mellola and the schoolteacher from the church village were coming from somewhere on the fringe of the group. The teacher's mouth was curved into a bitter smile as he listened to Mellola's rasping voice:

"Didn't we get enough of that republic last winter... when the maid put on her mistress's dress and went dancing with them... Don't you remember when they came to the county meeting in the fall screaming that they wanted the right to vote, and set the pay for relief work by shouting... If that's what you want, then have your republic and your Ståhlberg... They say he's secretly got that Red spirit."

The schoolteacher laughed a nasty laugh.

"Who saved this country last winter? Republican farmers... but I understand this... you're longing for your old love again... your old suometar love... You lost your sweetheart Nikolai and you're trying to get a new one."

"Ha, ha... It's the Kaiser's brother-in-law we're talking about... the Kaiser of Germany, and the Germans know how to keep order... That Korri has started to whip up that Alkio spirit among the farmers... Didn't he get enough of it when they drove his yard full of horses and ordered him to give them hay... But we will bring in that king... Svinhuvud, who is a lawful man, will decide, and he favors the Kaiser's rule... and the majority of the Parliament is behind it... There will be no more rebellions... They maintain order, those Germans."

Mellola snorted at the schoolteacher from his one-hundred-and-eighty-kilo bowels and went plodding toward the powers that be.

The apothecary, who wore a Civil Guard uniform, opened the meeting. He announced that speakers would appear first, and that then a resolution would be drawn up, to be sent to the monarchist representatives of the people. They would sign it. The first speaker was the vicar. A broad stone was the dais, which the vicar mounted. He took off his hat and spoke in a gently persuasive style, at first conceding the right to form a republic, but ending with:

"...to our sorrow, we must admit that this people is not ripe for such a sweeping rule of the people. And Finland's people are monarchists of old. For our society has stood from time immemorial on four pillars. They are our national Evangelical Lutheran church, our free farmers, our educated and superlative officials, and our people's honored and beloved king."

The demonstrations of approval were quite weak and they came from the nearest quarters. The vicar noticed that, and he descended from the stone with a stiffness born of disappointment. The apothecary then promised East Karelia to the doubtful looking landowners if they chose to have a king.

During faint applause, one farmer whispered to another:

"They're all hot after those Russian pack-peddlers now... I've got nothing against it. But the English will put an army there..."

They watched and they listened, and in back of their indifferent faces, the farmer's traditional way of evaluating crop yield was active.

"Why start predicting rain when the sun is shining? It's that sort who are so wrapped up in this hubbub with the gentry."

Ellen rose to speak, and on behalf of women, voiced her objection to the way in which succession to the crown was determined.

"The women of Finland can never approve the fact that the women of ruling families have been passed over in deciding on an heir to the crown. They consider it an offense to those innumerable heroic women who have grasped the reins of their homes and farms, which were dropped by their murdered husbands."

The apothecary answered her in a playful tone, as was befitting in replying to a woman:

"The king's position as commander-in-chief of the army is unsuitable for a woman. We aren't pleased with the memory of Red Guard women with rifles on their backs, are we?"

Ellen ascended the stone, already speaking as she stepped up onto it:

"I would just like to remind the previous speaker that Katherine the Great and Maria Teresa were firm rulers. And what about Elizabeth of England? And how beloved Queen Wilhelmina is among her people."

The apothecary again responded with something kind and courteously playful, but then the public-school teacher mounted the stone. He had asked for the floor, and they had not had the audacity to deny him. Spectacles flashing, he spoke in a tone of sharp asperity:

"There's been talk here of Karl Adolf and Karl the Twelfth... but we are setting up a form of government for Finland in the year 1918. I beg you to take note of an error... People have also appealed to the fact that the Bernadottes became very much at home in Sweden and that Bulgaria's German-born rulers are very much beloved of their people... That may be true... It is not for me to take up the forms of government in Sweden or Bulgaria, for they are up to the people of Sweden and Bulgaria. But the question is, do the Finnish people want a king at this time, and I know that they do not. Let the people themselves decide the issue; otherwise the republican farmers may decide that they have had enough... Since they don't want a king, don't force one on them... They freed this country from the Red Guard without a king, and they will be able to defend it in the future without one... I speak in opposition to the current trend..."

When the schoolteacher stepped down from the stone, there was no applause, but there was animated whispering among the farmers. The master of Yllö asked the schoolteacher in an incredulous voice:

"Are you threatening a rebellion too?"

"I'm not threatening... of course the farmers won't rebel... but they want to underline the fact that they have the right to decide the issue only after there are elections... And it is questionable whose side the law is on in this case."

There was whispering and discussion for a long time afterwards. A signing was supposed to follow the speeches, but most of the crowd hurried in silence to their horses.

The farmers were concerned with finding a way clear to drive their horses out, and had no time for anything else. When someone plucked at the sleeve of a departing man, he got an evasive answer:

"Not now... when I see... maybe then..."

And the powers that be whispered bitterly in the churchyard until someone thought to say:

"They will understand when the family has had time to take root in the land."

396

The farmers felt freer when they reached the solitude of the road. The rested horse switched its tail and began a slow trot toward home. And a husband reaffirmed the result of his long period of contemplation to his wife:

"I'm of the same mind as that teacher and Korri."

Otto had been leaning against the sexton's gate, following the meeting from under the brim of his hat. He straightened up from his lax, slouching position. His face twitched and his gray mustache moved as the tip of his upper lip rubbed expressively over his lower one a couple of times. Then he left.

"Mhmm."

The same expression lingered on his face for a long time, but it vanished as he neared home. When the gray walls and brown window casings of Kivivuori came into sight, he sighed heavily from time to time.

"Where is your mother?"

"She's in the bedroom with Voitto."

Otto entered the main room and asked Anna softly:

"How has she been?"

"She's calmer with the child in her arms and she has something to hold... I read the gospel to her, and she listens sometimes... Go and see her, she's been alone for a long time."

Otto went, drawing a determined breath at the bedroom door. His daughter was sitting on the bed with the sleeping child in her lap, over which she was crouched with her elbows resting on her knees. Her hair, which she kept in a neat and attractive bun, was in disarray and hung down from her shoulders in a sloppy braid. Her dress was wrinkled, for she had not taken it off for the night.

She cast a quick, frightened glance at her father and bowed over the child again. Otto sat next to her:

"Janne promised to do all he could... let's hope now... but let's be realistic anyway."

Elina rocked her shoulders gently.

"I should have... had you ask Janne... can I go... to see him at least once... to talk..."

"I don't think so... And it would be worse for you to see him... Let's wait now... I don't want to raise any false hopes. But I'm old enough to know that you can never say in advance that something is impossible."

Otto had never really been close to his children. He always wore a front of comic raillery, but now he spoke in a grave and kindly voice. When his daughter began to cry softly, he rose and left the bedroom silently. On the steps he stopped, clawed at the nape of his neck, and grunted half-aloud:

"Goddamn... it's too much."

The boys were messing with something atop a wooden roller at Koskela. It had been left in the open air since it no longer fit in the shed. When their grandfather approached, they were ready to smile, since he always had some funny trick up his sleeve. But this time he was serious as he asked them to come along and change the horses' tethers. Eagerly they went with him, doubly glad to do so, for they enjoyed the task and it dispelled their silent fear. They had been outdoors the entire morning, for it had been heavily oppressive indoors since yesterday evening.

Grandfather had had only one horse since the rent-work had ended. Now he had Poku as a second.

They changed the tethers and spoke in a manly, down-to-earth way about horses and the sufficiency of pastures. Grandfather too lingered long about the task, and reluctantly they returned home. They heard the clinking of dishes from inside, but they stayed out on the steps to wait for the food. Grandfather sat in the middle and the boys on either side. They poked sticks into cracks between the boards or prodded an ant that had strayed onto the stone at the base of the steps.

The vegetation in the yard had already turned dark. Lambs had cropped it short at the base of the berry bushes. The gate was half open and leaned awry because the closing ring was so poor. It caught Otto's eye, but his glance slid over it without any interest.

"Was the vicar at the church?"

"He was."

"Did he deliver a sermon?"

"He did read from the Book of Kings."

"Will the king let Father out of Hennala when he comes? The way Mother read from that book that the hungry people gave us."

"We'll see."

III

The painful letter-writing was finally accomplished. Anna and Elina went to Koskela, and Elina wrote for her parents in the same letter.

Jussi was unable to add anything to the letter, and Alma mainly repeated the same thing.

"Write to him... that if ever a bad word. That he forgive... and that Mother and Father hope that he goes with God... when the last journey comes... that he goes with God."

Elina was not able to write the address but Anna wrote it:

398

Prisoner Akseli Koskela, Sentenced to Death.

The letter was sent, and then began the long days of torment.

The matter was so confused in the minds of the boys that they did not really know what was happening. It had been decided that they be told only when news of the execution arrived. But they clearly understood the expression of sorrow in their mother's eyes and her silent weeping at night.

Anna asked the villagers that they not mention Akseli in Elina's presence, or even Hennala. There was no great danger of that, for Elina avoided people. She did not go to the village, and if people came to Kivivuori, she withdrew into the bedroom.

She had taken to visiting Emma Halme often, and at home they noticed that she was calmer afterwards. Emma had been living alone. Hardly anyone visited her except for men from the Civil Guard now and then who were searching Halme's and the association's papers for material to use in charges of crimes against the state.

Anna sometimes sent her food along with Elina, for it was known that the master had left very little money. Many did try to buy Halme's good clothing, but Emma would not sell it. She did sell Halme's sewing machine and a few other tools of his. She was no longer asked into homes to arrange banquets. The cottagers sometimes brought her little jobs, paying her with a piece of meat or a little flour.

Often Elina sat with Emma in her still, dark room. Everywhere in the house there were woven and knitted pieces. The furniture was elegant according to village standards. The hall coat-tree was covered with white fabric and on it hung the master's many articles of clothing, already quite old-fashioned, for Halme had never worn out any of his clothing.

Emma had borne all her grief alone, and so was able to console Elina better than her own mother. There was nothing remarkable in what she said, but her voice rang with a deeply composed sorrow when she related softly the events of the spring. She never asked Elina to have any faith in the future, but there was profound assurance in her voice when she said softly:

"We must try to see over this black wall... We don't need to think that things will already be different tomorrow... But it's easy for me to talk... I'm old... you have to endure for thirty more years... but you have children."

The expression of grief in Elina's eyes was now calmer. She was already taking part in the daily life of the cottage, but spent most of the time with the children or alone.

Once Anna cautiously suggested that they go to church, but immediately regretted her saying so.

"I will not... no, never... I get out of the way even when I see them."

"They are said not to be urging it... it's all from the church village."

"No, they're not urging it... not them... they watch from the sidelines... why take it on themselves when there are others... If they really wanted to, they could save him... they say something and then drop it... I know... people are like that... all people..."

Anna was frightened by the encounter and no longer suggested going to church. But in its place, she often read the Bible and they sang religious songs with a lovely melody which induced one to sing along.

People tried to show their sympathy somehow. When wives walking by saw Elina walking sadly in the yard at Kivivuori, they greeted her kindly, even respectfully, even though Elina was so young. A hollow-cheeked man who had been released from the camp might appear, but he was turned away.

"The bunch of us thought that someone should come and talk to her... He was no different from the rest of us... But they got to hate him so..."

Anna thanked him, but asked that he not talk about the subject.

The days grew shorter. The aroma from the threshing barns hovered in the air over the village, and the threshing machine on the manor chugged day after day. The melancholy, drizzly days were at hand, and people spoke in half-whispers in the cottages:

"There haven't been any notifications... But I hear Latoniemi, who came from the camp, says they're taking them already... The others don't get to see them because they're isolated. He said he doesn't know if Koskela was with them... They always take them to that church wall, and then they hear the sound of guns from there... They say it's always early in the morning... And there are doctors with them, and as soon as the bullets hit them, they cut off their heads. 'Cause they send the heads to the university students in Helsinki. They say they look at them to see why the rebellion came."

Then a letter came, which Otto read first. It said that sentences had been passed, but not on Akseli. Nevertheless it made the situation worse, for Elina sensed from the brevity of the letter and its matter-of-fact tone that her husband was already compelling her to prepare herself for his death.

This silent threat governed the lives of the people at Kivivuori. They cared little for developments in the outside world. But Janne was getting more and more hopeful. He was known to be constantly active, and the headquarter often called him in for interrogations.

"Where does he really go? He's even having another man do that Haukkala barn contract."

Not even those who were closest to Janne knew why he was always on the go. But when he stopped in at home, he said to Otto:

"They'll have to back off soon... They've collected their coins for nothing... And the Reds paved the way... It will soon be the end for Germany, and it'll be a wonder if things don't change here then... I hope the bastards get a beating from their wives because they didn't get to wear their countess gowns."

But he also spoke seriously to Otto:

"I'm sure it's going to make them think differently about the shooting too. But don't talk about it yet for a while."

Every evening the mother and father waited for the mail to prevent its falling into Elina's hands first. It was October already when a letter arrived from the prison camp. Otto read it by the light of the barn lantern as the horses crunched away at their food.

Dear Elina and children.

I have something a little better to write to you. My sentence has come and it has been confirmed and the petition for clemency rejected, but that doesn't mean anything because sentences are no longer being carried out. I heard it a little while ago because one of the guards talks to me sometimes, but I didn't tell you because it was only a rumor. But now they say it is so. The death sentences are supposed to be changed to life sentences, and that means twelve years, but at least I can give some advice about living in this letter. Because the tenancies will be redeemed. They did say that those sentenced to death could not redeem them, but the things I learn here are what you hear from others in these cement coops. Write about the matter. I don't know if I dare to write it, but ask Father to redeem his too if he can. Since Oskari went that way and I know Janne doesn't care about the land, then we could get that one for us too. Your father shouldn't feel that there is anything greedy or shameful about this, but it's just because of the way things are. If he doesn't want to take it himself, what I mean is that he take the right to it, even if we try to redeem it somehow ourselves. I don't mean any kind of inheritance by this, but it's no good to let the land go if it can be had, even if the price of it has to be wrung from under a rock. Of course your father can keep it as long as he is able, but I mean then when the boys are grown up. You have to think farther ahead that way.

I even have footwear now. They gave me shoes so I'm not barefoot any more, even though these cells aren't cold. But they are moving us to another camp. They seem to think it's some kind of shame if we are taken barefoot and maybe the ground is getting cold already. This fall isn't likely to be any different from any other. I'll write more about these tenancy matters again when we find out how things stand with them. I'm sure Janne will explain to you. He knows all about it.

I would have things to write about how the sentence got left this way. It was the very devil when it was touch and go for so long. The guard told me that my sentence was ready for a long time, but that the commandant said they would not shoot one man by himself and they were waiting for the others. It was that close. When they said that, I was in a daze for a little while. Until then I tried to be like a dead man. You won't believe it, but I taught myself to stay awake standing against a wall without a single thought in my head. This cell has seen a lot of crazy things, but you don't feel much like writing about them in a letter like this. You get a little strange when you're separated from the rest of the world like this. Some of the men started to talk crazy, but I was never that far gone.

Remember to start on that redemption business and send greetings home. I'll write them a separate letter when I get a better chance. Tell the boys hello for me. They'll be big men when I see them, but we can at least talk in letters. You can tell Mother I've even thought about that God here too. She'll be happy to hear it. They've had a lot of sorrow too, when none of their own boys were left, and we'll be old people when we see each other. I'm sure you are waiting for me too, but I'm so puny now that Preeti Leppänen could toss me away. Say hello to him too. Write to me about those things then. And stay well. I won't write the things you already understand. Your last letter was the hardest to bear, but we'll talk about it sometime. And try to explain this matter to your father. That it isn't a case of lying in wait for an inheritance, but for the sake of the boys when it's there to be had.

> *Goodbye now, until I get another letter.*
> *Your husband and your children's father*
> *Akseli Koskela*

Otto went inside. Anna was draining water from the potatoes in the chimney corner and Elina was setting plates on the table. Anna spoke as she was pouring the water from the herring, which were running out:

"...when even no peddlers come around. They say the storekeeper even... well... now I spilled some on my hand."

At the last moment Anna realized what she was saying and burned her hand in her fright. Her daughter mumbled something. It often happened that they could not make out what she was saying.

Otto approached the subject in a roundabout way:

"I heard in the village there was supposed to be a little hope that the sentences would be changed. What would you say if they were changed to life?"

"I can't think about it."

"I've heard the rumor before, but I didn't want to mention it because it was uncertain. But now I hear that they're supposed to announce something like that."

After a short pause he went on:

"And I can say that it is true... And don't start screaming, but he is saved. Here is the letter."

Elina looked at the letter, but she could already see from her father's expression that it was true.

First she blubbered something confused and now too she had to resort to the bed.

Returning to life was not easy, for joy had to find its long unused paths again. At first a fit of weeping shook Elina's body, until it gradually subsided and she was calm again. Her father sat beside the bed and said:

"It is a long time... and surely they will be reduced... they can't be permanent."

"What do I... what do I care about years... if he can live..."

The others ate the cold potatoes, but Elina could not eat. She continued to lie on the bed, and when the boys had eaten, she said softly:

"Come to mother."

The boys went shyly and uneasily. Their mother drew them to her without speaking and then let them go.

Otto went to take the news to Koskela, and when the boys had been put to sleep, the two women sat in the main room. Elina held a handkerchief in her fingers as she spoke in a soft voice:

"I felt as if I could not live... even if I thought about the boys... It was so hard for me sometimes... when he was in those bad moods... But a good word was enough for me... Sometimes I even thought I shouldn't live so much as a part of another person..."

"Father says that the way the world is going, they won't be able to keep them there for very long..."

Elina wiped her nose with the handkerchief and snuffled away the last bit of her tears.

"I haven't thought about that at all... As long as there's a little bit of hope... no matter how long... knowing what it was like when there was none at all."

Gradually the tender relationship which had opened up between mother and daughter waned, and their tone of voice and discussions became more commonplace.

"You might move into the main room. Father and I could sleep in the bedroom. It will be too crowded for you with four."

"We can still manage here... Unless we go there... But it would be so hard for me on their land... It was already so awful there in the spring, after the boys were taken... I was afraid there at night. It was so quiet I felt as if death had been there..."

Anna sighed some Biblical passage. But there was in it a slight note of affectation, a sign that the days of agony were over.

Vilho and Eero were chipping at the ice in the yard at Kivivuori. There were already melted patches in it, and crevices along which little brooks ran. The debris of winter had been exposed from beneath the snow. Shreds of hay, straw strewn around, sticks of wood dropped from someone's arms during the winter, a water-soaked piece of leather from Poku's harness, and a card on which the ink from the writing was blotched.

They hacked at the ice, for Grandma had said it would melt quicker that way, and they could get the yard cleaned. Eero whispered something to his brother, and the two stood up, looked at the gate, and went inside quickly. Mother was sorting out wool beneath the window.

"The minister is coming."

The boys withdrew into the chimney corner. Elina turned dead white and her hands trembled.

"Go and get Grandma... I can't..."

But there was already the sound of steps in the entry and a knocking at the door. At Elina's invitation, the door opened, and she cast such a hurried glance at it that she saw only the vague flash of a black overcoat and a fur hat.

"Good day.."

"...day... sit..."

Elina shifted a chair. She herself sat first on a bench and then moved to the bed. Her hands were rubbing one another nervously, her heart was pounding, and her breath came quickly.

Vicar Lauri Salpakari was now a pastor and dean of the parish. People were not quite able to adapt to the title of dean for him, for their concept of the position derived its meaning from the time of Vallén: the image of a reassuringly sturdy, absent-minded, and kindly old man.

Salpakari was still slender, clean-cut, and upper-class, in a manner different from that of the other higher-ups in the community. In the minds of the villagers, he was somehow more elegant, like an apothecary or something of the sort. He had also preserved his refined manner of speaking.

In spite of his deanship, he found it difficult to sit on the chair he had been given. At first he spoke a trifle too playfully:

"What are you little icebreakers doing there? Come and say hello."

But the boys greeted him so stiffly that he too stopped smiling. His face and voice were sober when he addressed Elina:

"I just went to see Grandma and Grandpa Koskela, for I have good news now. We were able to get the eviction retracted, but old Koskela said it

404

would be better to speak to you, since it is your affair."

"Mhmm."

Elina was breathing so hard that her bosom heaved. Deep in her mind seethed all that she had suffered, and she was afraid. Not of the pastor, but of her own anger.

"I thought then that it would be good to speak of it early. You could get the planting done then and of course it would be good to get the matter settled."

"Yes... I can't now..."

The pastor shifted his hat from one side to the other, and since the atmosphere clearly indicated that he could not gloss over the hard part of the matter, he said, looking at the floor:

"I... would gladly have spoken about it... since there surely were misunderstandings... This matter has weighed heavily on me... Because you might think I wanted it this way... But I didn't... but I could do nothing about the bitterness..."

"Well... I was able to stay here... Because Mother asked permission from the manor..."

The pastor said quickly:

"You would not have been evicted from old Koskela's place... That would not have been possible..."

"No... I could have stayed there. But I didn't want to. It was so crowded."

"It was... they would not have had the right to nullify my agreement... But of course they have the authority with regard to the emoluments... I, of course, could not oppose them in any way... But Akseli himself gave them every possibility. Because he announced so publicly that he would not do the rent-work... They said I did not have the right to keep in effect a contract the terms of which the other party had so flagrantly violated... They said I had no right to grant anything from the parsonage to be enjoyed freely..."

Elina's face turned suddenly red. Her voice shook when she spoke:

"He didn't... mean... anything free... He said he is ready to pay... But he will not do rent-work... he won't..."

"I didn't really mean that... In those days we all said so many things... How many tenants could have been dismissed on those terms... Many of them quit doing their rent-work... I just meant that it gave them a valid cause... And they wanted to use it."

"Well... I didn't know anything about the agreements... I left because I was told to."

The hat shifted to the other side.

"But come back now. With Korri's help, I've gotten the matter changed now... Because the bitterness has subsided a little... I would give you all your old rights... And I think you could even redeem it. They say the Red clause will be stricken from the law... We don't even have any winter rye there, so you could have it all in your hands immediately come spring. We'll arrange for a small money rental until the time of redemption since you won't be able to do day-work. It would certainly be nice for old Koskela too..."

Elina struggled with the turmoil in her mind. How she longed to scream: "Get out of here! I don't care for your mercy..."

But she remembered Akseli's dispirited letter when she had at last revealed to him the true state of affairs, and she mumbled her assent. The pastor left shortly afterwards. The boys had darted out during the discussion and were again busy in the yard. The bright sunshine increased the pastor's good spirits. He squinted as he came out, feeling as if the dazzling light of spring were somehow fitting to his mood of the moment. As he passed the boys, he said:

"Is the stream flowing?"

The boys drew back, trying to hide behind each other. — He had the voice and clothing of the upper crust and exuded something foreign. Something uncertain and distant. They felt it and did not answer him.

The pastor's smile died away. He headed for the road, careful not to step into mud where there were spots which had thawed.

IV

Where the road ran through fields, dust already rose. In the wooded spots, there were still mud puddles, and in the gloomiest spots, there were even sheets of ice which wagon wheels crushed in passing over them.

In the birch groves there was a faint reddish tint. Waterfowl shrieked on the lake, and Wolf-Kustaa would stand glowering at the door of cabins with a bunch of handsome pike hanging on a twig. He traded them to house-wives for bread. He never said how much they should pay for them. The women waged a battle in their minds as they wrapped up the bread in the pantry.

"Should I add one more... what if he should get mad?"

Kustaa took the bundle without looking at it, growled something, and left. He even had a better coat now, for Elias, on getting out of the camp, had traded his father's coat to Kustaa for a fox hide. The fox hide Elias had traded for bootleg liquor, and he staggered pale-faced on his visiting rounds in cabins and cottages, like others who had returned to the village after having "seen the world." These people had lost a great deal. Ruin had trampled them. Many lay in the hunger pit, which had sunk so much with the melting of the snow that it was not even level with the surface of the ground, not to mention mounded. Some arrived one at a time, one from Hennala, one from Riihimäki, from Tammisaari or from Tampere, emaciated and with their digestive organs impaired forever. And many had never returned. Many a widow was still living in the changing room of a sauna with her children. Their masters having ordered them off "our land," they had gotten a place in the sauna of some acquaintance who had his or her "own lot." And they did not even dare weep openly for their dead.

But they had gained something. Many had seen the world. They had traveled on a train. They spoke knowledgeably of Lahti, Riihimäki, or Hämeenlinna, which earlier had been only distant notions. When Victor Kivioja spoke of his travels, it no longer had any effect.

"The men at the Hauho fair? Why, we went through Hauho. That's where the bridge was. Osku and Uuno crawled out along the embankment first and onto the bridge through openings in the railing... And by God, the bullets were flying, but the boys pushed on... We know them all, the Tuuloses and the Lamminkoskis. In was right in Tuulos that the battle was, where Akseli Koskela hit the German with his rifle so hard that only the barrel was left in his hand..."

They had something not everyone had. They had Fate. Fate was something larger than ordinary life. It had brought the tenant boy or day laborer from the sticks face to face with large issues. They had grown and their world had broadened.

"Let's go and look for something better. We're not going to gnaw on stinking herring minnows any longer... I mean, we've seen a thing or two."

Each had his own vicissitudes, in addition to their.shared fate. Like Elias. He went to the cabins, pale-of-face, drops of cold sweat on his forehead and a bottle of bootleg liquor in his pocket.

"I'd give you a drink, but there's so goddamned little of it."

"It might be better if you didn't drink yourself."

"That issue is settled. When I looked at the body wagon, I decided that if I ever got out of there, the first thing I'd do was to get cockeyed drunk."

He was sitting on the bench at Kivivuori. He drank from time to time, sucking in air and putting a hand to his mouth when the "good stuff" threatened to come up.

"They always took them at six in n the morning. By now it was done efficiently, not like in the spring, when one of them came crawling out of the grave in the swamp to the gate of the camp all muddy and bloody and the guard wondered because he didn't know what to do with someone who had escaped from the grave. I don't know if it's true, but there was a lot of talk about it... but it was different after they started the sentencing... I was in a place where I could watch to see if Aksu was with them... One guy had a rug on his shoulders when it was raining... They had doctors with them to see if the Reds were really dead or if they should fire another round."

His stories made Elina weep, but her grief was no longer as dangerous. At times Elias was sick to the stomach and Otto watched carefully, ready to take him outside quickly, but with great effort, Elias got the liquor to stay down.

"Boys, I'll sing you a song."

They made us go weary, our chains a clanking,
chains bound to our feet and hands,
and some they shot at the edge of the woods...

At the end of the song, his voice began to shake, and he sobbed a couple of times. Rubbing his eyes with his hands, he said:

"But goddamn, one had his chest bare when he went, a handsome young man, and he raised his hand when he saw faces watching from the barrack window and he yelled, 'Long live the revolution.' They took them to the wall of a church... About nine or ten minutes later the rattling started... And some always said to take your hats off then... if you happened to have a hat... I always had a hat that I raised. It it was lost or stolen, I stole a new one..."

Then he drank. When the women left to attend to some chore, Elias asked Otto, with a cautious glance at the door:

"Do you have any idea if Aune is at home?"

"I'm sure she is... But it would be best for you to go home now yourself."

"Don't say that... I'm going now... Look..."

When I lay my arm around your neck
hey nonino around your neck
and put my boots under your bed...

He went toward the door, staggering and singing, holding his palm up toward Otto as if rejecting his prohibition. For a while he sang, holding on to the door frame:

You fell in the fight for freedom
for the good and the rights of man.

———

408

And a poisoned chalice was poured
into the mouths of the poor.

He left, feeling his way along the fence until he dared to walk on his own. Near the store, he was forced to sit at the side of the road. After a spell of coughing and spasms, he yelled out, trying to get strength into his voice:

"Hey, big butcher..."

The time will come when the blood will be weighed,
your guts ripped out and your ass smeared with tar.

Then he drank in an obviously demonstrative way, with the bottle toward the store. A cough sent spray from his mouth and his nostrils. Having pocketed the bottle, he smacked his lips and began to sing, beating time with his hand:

The butchers' machine guns no longer rattle,
Calmness and peace prevail over all.
O my poor heart, when will you find peace?

Otto had been following Elias's progress from the window, and seeing him topple into a ditch, he went to his aid and brought him home. Elias was at death's door the entire night, vomiting a green froth.

People were watching from their cottage windows.

"The have only two cows now because they've had to get rid of them... Look at the boys — sitting there so soberly. Alma must be happy now... she missed them so much. But Jussi looks so awful... What will come of it... Otto must be helping, since they can't take care of their place... And Janne is in jail."

"They say the preacher swore the eviction wasn't his doing... I guess he can talk... The men from the congregation wouldn't have broken the contract if he had put his foot down... It's not their business... But he must secretly have wanted it himself, and so he let it happen... Because they hated Akseli so much... they were just boiling over... Now they are being so-o good, people say... They keep asking how old Koskela is doing. But Elina is so furious their sweet talk won't help... For once she got good and mad, even though she's always been a sort of shy and timid person. She's still beautiful, the way she's always been... She's not the kind to look at another man even if her own husband is away... And there would be such men.."

"There's no chance, with Jussi's eye on her... even if they felt like it."

"They'll just have to give back the tenancy... And the tenancies will be redeemed too, because they say that clause in the sentencing will be changed. They're probably a bit ashamed themselves.Anyone who was sentenced to death can't redeem a tenancy — that will be a matter for the widow and children, but when they wanted to punish them too... The way the church villagers drove the widows from their land. They scared the kids so much that one of them kept shifting from place to place for a couple of days and asking his mother: 'Can I stay here now?'"

"They say they're being more just now. Ha, ha, I guess they have to be, now that even the Germans are Socialists, and they didn't get their king. Because there had to be elections, and all they got for their killing and their voting restrictions was to reduce the seats by twelve."

The goods Elina was moving had given rise to this talk. Jussi and Otto were driving the loads, and the older boys were allowed to go along on every trip so that they could ride the wagons a lot. The load with the rocker on it was the most fun. Grandpa had fixed the chair so that they could sit on it. Grandma was carrying Voitto in her arms.

The boys no longer avoided Koskela. The boards had been removed from the windows and the shingles from the chimney. At first smoke came into the house, but it was let out through the window. And Grandma had raked the yard. — and Mother was no longer afraid. But she was sad because there was so little money. Grandpa gave her some of Uncle Aleksi's bank money for seed grain. But she was most sad because Uncle Janne was in jail.for putting up a placard. And they were getting nowhere with Father's pardon. It was Grandpa who nailed up the placard, but Janne had given it to him when there was the election. People had gone to see it and then had looked around. The storekeeper had come and torn it down and uncle had gone to jail because it said in large letters: RISE UP FROM NIGHT'S OPPRESSION YOU SLAVES TO LABOR.

Grandpa was driving Lempi with the kind of stuff that would break because Lempi walked lazily. They would have broken on Poku's wagon because Poku pranced. He has the finest gait, Uncle Kivioja says. Uncle Kivioja came twice a day to fuss at Mother about selling Poku to him when the eviction came, but Mother would not do it. And he threw his wallet down on the table in front of Mother and said take the whole goddamn thing but give me the horse.

Victor Kivioja came toward them with a small load of hay and Grandpa stopped.

"You're taking the girl's stuff... I bought a little hay because my own ran out... I got a good price from old man Paunu... He was angry about the

410

Socialist victory... It was on the tip of my tongue to say we should have killed more of them, goddamn... but I needed the hay and that wouldn't have helped... But do you know what the boy said to Haukala? He was showing off his new ditching plow, and you know it's not worth a damn to anyone who knows anything at all about machines from bicycles on up... The boy said goddamn, you had to buy a new one because you shot the old... They say he shot Artturi Rauhala, he was a top ditch digger...That's what the boy said... he takes after me with his mouth... By God, I enjoyed it..."

Victor slapped the horse with the reins and moved on. Jussi felt like smiling as he sat there at the front of the load. It was the noon hour, and Preeti Leppänen was heading for his home on the manor. Still far away, he raised a hand:

"Stop for a while... I sort of have some business with you... There was that talk about the deceased Aleksi's coat, that Mother would come and plant potatoes for you. But the way things happened... it didn't work out... I didn't... but I did remember... Tell Elina to send word so she'll know when to come."

Preeti went his way, aging and stooped. There were already patches on the dead Aleksi's coat. — "They string that barbed wire and I don't see so good anymore."

Birds slanted across the blue spring sky over the gray village. The window of the public school with its red-painted casing was open as the load drove by. In the school they were rehearsing a song for the spring festival. The children sang in clear voices, the girls devoutly, their pigtails standing out, the boys with their close-cropped heads a little stiffly, staring out from under knitted brows. One or other might be wearing a man's coat which had been made over. "Because Father left it at the poorhouse and asked Siukola to send it home." But their noses were still running as in the past. One of them glanced surreptitiously out the window when he saw the Koskelas' load going by. When the teacher's watchful eye fell on him, he joined lustily in the song:

> *Our joy is so great*
> *we can set it no bounds.*
> *Waves of the sea whisper it.*
> *Birds in copses carol it.*
> *Joyfully it rings out:*
> *Our shores are fresh and free,*
> *Free waters ring our Finland.*

V

The November evening was dank and dark. Weak gusts of wind drove a freezing drizzle and swept the smoke from the chimneys in the church village along the roofs and down into the yards. Weak gusts of wind drove a freezing drizzle and swept the smoke from the chimneys in the church village along the roofs and down into the yards. Someone emerging from an outbuilding caught the smell of smoke in the darkness. He walked quickly, his head turned against the wind, checking out of the corner of his eye for puddles of water in the yard, which gleamed in the glow of light from the windows.

Wet darkness lay over the fields, the wooded hills, and the faint glow from the windows. The outdoor lamp of the cooperative store cast a dim light onto its red walls, its yellow door, and the windows to either side of it, in which a few paper bags had been placed so as to reveal their contents of rice kernels or coffee beans.

Together with the windows of the nearby houses, the lamp lighted a patch of the main road and the stone fence of the cemetery as well, the latter only dimly.

Beyond, the road vanished into black darkness. The deserted streets of the village were silent, their only voice the soughing of the wind. Sometimes during a stronger gust there was a faint creak when the shade of the lamp outside the cooperative store swung in its bracket.

From the road's black darkness, in the direction of the railroad station, a soft shuffle of footsteps became audible. The sound grew louder as it approached the glow of light, within range of which a man's figure appeared, growing clearer as it neared the light. There was a hat on the man's head, tilted slightly against the wind, its brim badly battered. The man's head was tilted too, and remained fixed in that position. The cold had stiffened the man's cheek muscles in a clenched position. Grooves ran from the corners of his mouth to his ears, and his cheekbones stood out in high relief. His sunken eyes stared unblinkingly at the road.

On his overcoat were many clumsily sewn patches. As he passed the cooperative store, a large letter *P* in red paint could be faintly seen on its back, although efforts had apparently been made to rub or scrub it away. Under the man's arm was a bundle wrapped in a soiled newspaper. The hand of the arm around it was in a pocket and a bit of sleeve had been drawn in along with it as a shield against the icy drizzle. In the bundle were a piece of hard bread and two clumsily made wooden dippers, one larger and one smaller. The man's step was weary, but at times it seemed to take purchase more eagerly, as if will had demanded more than was suitable of

412

the body, for in a little while it slackened off, only to speed up again.

The man disappeared into the darkness in the opposite direction from which he had appeared in the perimeter of light. His figure grew dimmer and dimmer until it was completely lost to sight. The shuffling sound of his footsteps grew fainter as they receded The streets of the village were again deserted and the shade of the outdoor lamp creaked softly.

It was dark in the spruce woods. At times he had to feel for the road.

"Now which way did it turn here?"

He did not actually see the threshing barn but he smelled it. The only light came from the baking room window. Feeling his way up the steps and running his hand along the doorframe, he made his way into the entry. His hand fumbled for and found the door handle. Then he saw Elina and the boys, who had frozen into the positions they were in when they heard the first tentative footsteps on the stoop.

"Evening."

Elina set something down from her hands and started toward the door, but then stopped.She began to wipe her hands on her apron, but then checked that motion and went to a set of shelves where a towel was hanging.Having dried her hands, she moved forward, a changing play of expression on her face. Tears and smiles would not exactly make room for each other. She caught his hand, and her face flamed red, as it had on those first evenings when the excitement of meeting had still made her shy.

She mumbled an unintelligible reply to the greeting and tried to smile. The man's cheek muscles, stiff from the icy wind, tightened, and his lips stretched into a broken smile. Their hands tightened their grasp on each other and jerked up and down. That continued for a long while as they stood there in helpless confusion.

The symptoms of a smile twitched Elina's cheeks, but looking into her husband's deeply sunken eyes, she buried her face in her hands with a sob and pressed it against the front of his overcoat. There was a distant and vacant look in his eyes.

In the midst of her sobbing, she turned toward the boys and drew back abruptly from her husband's breast, made shy by the presence of the children.

"Come and say good evening to your father."

The boys came, except for the youngest, who remained sitting on the floor.

"Do you still know me?"

"Yup."

Then they withdrew to one side, still studying their father.

Suddenly Eero burst out:

"Voitto is three already."

Father smiled and Mother laughed. The boy's words revealed that they had been discussing the subject. Voitto was indeed "three" but he had seen his father only as a vague shape bending over his bassinet and could recall nothing of those days.

"He must be a little bit afraid. Maybe I'll take these rags off."

He took off his overcoat and the suitcoat under it. His bundle he left on the bench, and the boys approached it curiously. All the while Elina was busy with something. She picked up a plate and set it down.

"The boys and I have already eaten, but I'll make something for you. Vilho, go to the new place and tell them."

She picked Voitto up in her arms and took him over to his father. She glanced first at the shrinking boy and then surreptitiously at her husband, swallowing hard each time she did. His face was stiff, its emaciated and bony darkness reflecting one unchanging expression of rigid, ingrained suffering. But the worst was to look into his sunken eyes. They had an empty, dead expression in them, a hard and lifeless look. When he tried to smile at the boy, he forced a look of joy into them, but the smile on his lips was stiff and distorted.

The boy clung more tightly to his mother when the strange man said:

"Why, you're a big man already."

Elina put the boy down and asked what her husband would eat.

"It doesn't matter. Don't bother with anything special."

His father and mother arrived and were greeted with the same twisted smile and unchanging expression. Alma could not hide her emotion, but Jussi merely shook hands and twitched his stooped shoulders. Alma had to swallow a couple of times before she could say:

"How were you able to come when it's so dark?"

"Well I... I was just thinking as I came that the road sort of stuck in my mind."

His parents too sensed the despondency which Akseli exuded, but it was a little less apparent when they launched into a lively discussion. Akseli answered their questions briefly and apathetically.

"It wasn't that kind of pardon... I wouldn't have gotten out with that... It was Ståhlberg who issued this one... It was an individual pardon..."

"Did he revoke the sentence?"

"It was conditional. And I don't have citizenship... but that doesn't mean much... I've never been entrusted with any office by them... and they can't really take it away..."

He said it wearily, as if it were something he had thought over for a long time.

414

Some life appeared in the man when the talk turned to the tenancy.

"It doesn't pay to bother much about Kivivuori's being left to us... They'll make this one smaller... We'll get these fields, of course, but with some woods... It's best to say that we don't know, that Janne will most likely get it after his father... I want the last of that swamp, but I won't give up any woods for it. They can throw it in as an extra... They'll take the going price for it, but the price of the swamp won't mean much."

And old, stoop-shouldered Jussi prattled eagerly and slyly:

"Say we haven't spoken to Otto, say he has his tenancy and we have ours... what business is it of anyone's who gets what later... They might guess at something of the sort, and not give anything extra. The boys mustn't say a word about this in the village either."

Otto had promised to redeem his tenancy and give it to one of the boys when he died, and they were a little afraid in case they might not get extra hectares of land for Koskela. And Jussi had scoured the area all that autumn.

"We ought to get something from there... it has such a good bottom."

But when he got home, he sat wearily on the edge of the bed, breathing heavily and sighing:

"I think my days are numbered."

Nothing was said about the past. They knew it was not time for that yet. The parents stayed and chatted for a long time, and Elina chatted mainly with them. When she spoke to Akseli, her voice was somewhat constrained and shy. She asked if there were any of Aku's and Aleksi's underwear at the new place.

"Because I had to use yours to make underwear for the boys during the bad old time."

There were, and Vilho promised to go with Grandma and Grandpa to get them. When they left, he accompanied them and brought back Akusti's underpants and shirts. Akseli went to put them on, and afterwards he asked briefly:

"Did they take both of them at the same time?"

Elina said, with the same lack of expression:

"I'm sure they did."

They said nothing further. Little by little the boys began to approach their father. They told him stories, and that started a little competition between them.

"Poku lost a shoe when Grandpa Kivivuori was bringing wood, but Grandpa put a new shoe on him."

"And Kaiku went into the calves' pen and Mother couldn't get him out, but Grandma did."

Their father tried to smile and say a word sometimes as if to show that he was involved. Finally he opened his bundle and gave the dippers to Elina.

"Thank you. The old ones are so worn... I was just going to talk to Father about making some new ones."

The words brought a kind of smile to the man's eyes and he said:

"Just don't show them to him... We'll never hear the end about how crooked they are."

There was still a piece of bread in the bundle and the boys looked at it curiously.

"Is is prisoners' bread?"

"Yes."

The father noted the boys' interest and broke the piece in two. The bread was made of poor ingredients and was even more poorly baked, but its strange taste made it interesting. The boys ate their pieces in silence, and their father folded the paper after distributing the homecoming gifts. The paper he gave to Elina.

"You can wrap something in it."

Elina had been sleeping in the bedroom with Voitto, but now they put the boy into the main room with his brothers.

Elina undressed. Before doing so she had put out the lamp. Akseli had already undressed and settled himself in bed.

"This is where I parted from you."

Elina came to bed and Akseli whispered, with an attempt at humor:

"You won't have much joy from me now... I can barely stand up."

Elina laughed, blushing in spite of the darkness. Then she snuggled against his shoulder,and only now, under the cover of darkness, she wept for a long time. Without saying a word, Akseli held her head on his shoulder.

When her weeping had subsided to a snuffling, a whispered discussion began. It lasted until late into the night. Sometimes a gust of wind struck the window and freezing rain pattered against it.

The whispering gradually grew less frequent. A little shyly, Elina asked:

"Did you miss home?"

"What? Of course."

"Because... I was just thinking... You're so quiet and sad."

"I'm not... not really... You're just thinking of long ago, and that makes it seem so..."

The talk ceased and they fell asleep. After midnight Elina awoke. From his breathing and movement, she sensed that her husband was sitting on the edge of the bed.

"Why aren't you asleep?"

Akseli lay down again and said:

"It's just that something woke me up... I don't know..."

But before she fell asleep, Elina realized, in spite of the darkness, that her husband was lying there awake, with his eyes open.

In spite of their father's return, the happiness at Koskela was not complete, for Akseli moved about in the home circle as if he were distant and somehow a stranger. His despondency seemed to weigh on the others too, but no one said anything about it. Everything possible was shown to him, the new fence around the calf pen and so on. He looked at it and made some comment, but the others sensed that he was off somewhere else. Elina grieved at it, but she said nothing, for she was afraid of hurting the man by bringing it up. He did speak to her father and mother with more animation, as long as the conversation was about some external and commonplace matter. He told of Oskari's death in a few words:

"I did see the Germans and yelled... but it was too late... Oskari couldn't see them because he was going along on the other side of the potato field... Although I'm not really sure they were the ones... Bullets were coming from every direction. You couldn't see anything except for what the fires lighted up..."

He spoke to the villagers curtly, explaining what had happened to him in a few words.

"They moved us to Tammisaari when the sentence was changed."

People were curious about what it felt like when he was sentenced to death and was waiting to be shot.

"Well, it was nothing so remarkable... It's a little different if you're well, but we were all so weak... When you're really in pain, it doesn't seem so bad."

After a brief pause he would say:

"But it was hard when you thought about home."

His camp comrades came to see him too. Lauri was boastful.

"Greetings. You made it. If you want to see my Huqsvarna, then come outside. My goddamn old man sold my bike, but I told him to give me money for a new one."

Akseli went out and smiled faintly when Lauri, hoisting the rear wheel of the bike, pedaled until it spun dizzily and then held it out for him to see.

"Does the rim look crooked? If it does, the fault is in your eyes. Take a little look at how the brakes work."

Lauri pressed the brake pedal and the wheel stopped.

"So long. I can't stay, but I'll stop by in the evening. Then you'll be able to see, I mean, how the carbide light shines."

When Lauri was gone, Akseli sank into silence again. Once he asked Elina idly:

"What is Elias up to?"

"Nothing. Antero got the tenancy. Because the landlady said she wouldn't give it to Elias to drink away... They say he visits Aune."

"What about Aune? Is she the same as ever?"

"...Who knows... she might be a little better off... older men have been going there."

Slowly they all began to talk about past happenings, evasively at first, but then Alma told him everything. They were sitting in the main room of the new place. Her voice was calm and peaceful as she rocked in her chair and spoke to her son, who was sitting on the bench:

"The storekeeper was like the head man there. Arvo was with him, and Aaro. The overseer was with them too, but he seemed to be ashamed... he just stood in the doorway... Father and I could never have imagined anything like that... We just thought they would be kept there as prisoners as long as the war went on... But then I thought afterwards that the boys must already have known... Aku shook my hand goodbye and there was such a strange smile on his face... and he gave his jackknife to Vilho in the yard... He just said there it is and he looked at the boy and left... And Otto was told in the church village that he couldn't see them, and no one from their side was allowed to see them."

"Who brought you the news then?"

"It was a man named Jalmari Kolu. We didn't know him, but Otto did. Otto was arrested too... they said because he talked too much... so he sent Kolu."

In the midst of her sober tale, there was a ripple of laughter in her voice.

"I don't know... They probably put him there because he was on that board for a while. Father went at once and got to speak to the pastor, but he said he had done all he could."

"Did he... It doesn't pay to believe what he says."

"They say that he did speak for them. And he has said lately that the most unjust sentence was the boys'... and Pajunen said that the boys went because they couldn't catch you. He said he was against it, but couldn't do anything. Anyway, there was that lieutenant from the Russian army who was insisting on the death penalty for everyone... The one who ran away from the Russian Reds, that apothecary's relative."

"Did Halme go at the same time?"

"Yes. They say there were eight of them, and they were the first. Antto and Silander too. I don't know for sure. They say the Ylöstalo boy was there too, the one who was in command before you. They say Yllö's son and Arvo shot them. And the parsonage lieutenant was in command. There was even talk that Akusti threw his cane at them when they were shooting, but you hear so many stories. And they say Halme was so weak that he could hardly stand up. He prayed to God to forgive them for they know not what they do..."

At that point Alma's voice faltered and she covered her eyes with her hands, but that passed.

"Preeti and Otto were there when they were buried. Preeti took Aleksi's coat and asked if he could have it. I gave him Aleksi's other coat, the brown one when I thought... we would see it here... Anna took the one he had on when he was shot to a widow living near her so she could make something from it for her children... I thought I wouldn't see it then, and it would be smaller too... But there's no use avoiding such things... I no longer do... I... sometimes at night... because... without a blessing..."

Her son stared speechless at the floor until she resumed:

"Preeti said, and Otto too later, that they looked so peaceful... As if they were smiling too... I don't know about Otto... but Preeti isn't able to think up anything like that... they took Aleksi's boots, and the money I gave him wasn't in his coat pocket either... When all they had was the Red Guard money and they said right away it was worthless... I sometimes thought, when they were shouting about the wickedness of the Reds... don't your own deeds ever come to mind... Are people so hardened they never think about it... But I leave them to God.. they belong to Him... It's not up to me to levy His judgements..."

Alma rocked gently, plump and at peace, and her son stared at the floor.

Akseli did not yet take a hand in the work, but during the day he began to walk around the tenancy, accompanied by the boys. And in talking to them he began to pay attention to commonplace things. They looked at everything under the sun, and sometimes the same interest could be heard in Akseli's voice as in the boys'. One day when they had gone to see if the road needed repair, they stood looking at the huge Matti's Spruce.

"Why do they call it Matti's Spruce?"

"Someone called Beggar Matti had a stroke here... So they started to call it that..."

"We haven't gone past it alone."

"Is that so... Father couldn't either, when he was little..."

As has said it, he imagined that he really hadn't... which was absolutely untrue. In that instance, both father and sons were lying.

Then he said half in jest:

"Let's put the boundary line here then... But the spruce has to be on our side."

After that he continued, no longer speaking to the boys but to himself:

"Probably they'll take the tree for its value, but the land is good... and that's the root of the matter... the trees are soon gone... but if new ones grow... But I'll ask for it anyway..."

There was already snow on the ground. It was a twilight winter evening. Elina had called the boys to come in to eat and was preparing a plate of food for Voitto. Akseli was already sitting at the head of the table when the boys rushed in, eager and hungry.

"Go and brush the snow off your feet."

The boys went back out to the steps, from which they heard the rustle of the broom. But when they came in again, their father looked at their feet.

"Back again. That's not good enough."

The boys went out once more, and this time they made it to the table. A commotion developed over which one should get which potato. Their father looked at them, and there was a touch of sternness somewhere deep within his voice.

"Boys. What have we said about raising a ruckus at the dinner table?"

Gravely the boys stopped bickering. Elina helped Voitto with his spooning, a relieved and happy expression on her face. The only sound at the table was the clinking of spoons. Otherwise there was silence. A real Evangelical Lutheran silence.

Father had come home.